The Monkey and the Dealer

The Monkey and the Dealer

Buckland J Randall

Cheeky Kiwi

First Rule in this game: Trust no one.

Second Rule in this game: Always refer to rule number one.

Well, here I am at Page One which can be a very important page when one is writing a book.

Every book should have a Page One and rightly so. Without a Page One, you might find yourself feeling a little cheated and somewhat let down. It almost feels as if a book can't be trusted if there's no Page One.

Sure, there can be a page two and even a page five but the reader normally likes to start off with a Page One.

Page One should show a level of trust.

Now what I'm about to tell you may be considered somewhat illegal in the eyes of the law. Just remember you and I didn't make these laws.

The word trust doesn't even register in my world; only a fool would stand behind that word.

Put simply, I'm a drug dealer.

There's fuck all forgiveness in my line of work. I don't have the courts at my disposal. I can't haul someone before a judge for a non-payment. And if someone dies from taking too much of my product, I'm the one they come after. Nobody blames the idiot for taking too much; it's always going to be my fault. No matter what the outcome, I'm the big bad dealer.

So just relax. No one needs to get out of their pram with unfounded fears about drugs being bad for you. It's all bullshit, people. You've been conned. We've all been conned. Drugs can actually make you feel really good. The drugs I sell you will, that's the whole idea of drugs. They're there to make you feel good.

And if they don't, then it's high time you probably changed your supplier.

Just like anything: take the shit in moderation. I shouldn't have to put a warning label on my deals because someone doesn't understand that being a drug pig will kill you.

And of course, there's sex, lovely when you're getting plenty, which I am.

And I get plenty of sex because I've got loads of drugs, and pussy loves drugs; there's a song in that somewhere...

Now before I hear you slamming the book shut tutting because you think I'm disrespecting women, let me just add, I happen to love women. I'm just saying there are girls out there who love their drugs just as much as I do. And loving drugs can be very costly.

Maybe you want to step into my shoes and think about becoming a dealer yourself.

Then, by all means, please do read on. This book could be brilliant for you. I can teach you everything you need to know about drugs, especially the part on how not to get caught. And if you want to deal drugs, then best you don't get caught.

Whatever the risks are and whatever the rewards are there will always be little problems along the way. I like to think I have a handle on my dealing, along with life's little problems. You have to in my line of work. Everything in my life was rolling along quite nicely, until that one fateful evening. That fateful evening in question is when I met the Very Sexy Jane.

She's smart, beautiful and incredibly dangerous for my heath. She should come with a health warning or at the very least a bumper sticker reading – "Enter at Own Risk." It wasn't the smartest idea getting hooked up with Jane, but she had me over a barrel. Sometimes we have choices, and sometimes our choices become somewhat limited. She can be very persuasive, our Jane, especially as she seemed to be holding all the cards. Plus it also didn't help being sucked in by her smoking hot body. What can I say – I'm a guy.

And her arse... Oh my God, her arse, it's amazing, and that's always been my weakness really, a great arse.

Should we take a quick look at what drugs provide for me? Well, there's my luxury home; top of the range cars; a bottomless bottle of champagne; as many luxury holidays as I want and of course, all the pussy that I can troff out on. And then let's take a look at what your income provides and then tell me you're not jealous. Everyone's jealous of a drug dealer it's because we make it look easy. Let me assure you: it's not easy. You risk everything.

Right then! Let me formally introduce myself, seeing as you've all prepared to dip your frightened little toe into the waters and read on.

My names Keef, spelt Keith.

Keef Baxter, distributor of London's finest blow and MDMA. If you don't know what blow or MDMA is, look it up! It's all under W, for Wonderful. I'm born and bred in good old South London to a very average working-class family. My dad was a builder and my mum was a nurse. They both worked like dogs until cancer came and took them. They put up a good fight mind. And what was it the doctors were giving them at their end to make them feel better... drugs - go figure! Now being raised in South London didn't do me any favours except foster the need in me to get the hell out of there. It wasn't the most affluent place to grow up in. Well, not in my street it wasn't. My life then was very different to the one now. I'm not saying I'm the boy that's done well but if truth be told, I'm the boy that's done very well.

Don't get me wrong: my mum and dad were good people. It wasn't their fault I went a bit mental, they did try to keep me on the straight and narrow. But I was a product of my surroundings, wasn't I? I can't be blamed for wanting to get myself out of that life of crime and unemployment.

To be fair dad never gave up, he'd get me a job on one of his building sites. Each time I lasted a couple of weeks before I thought "Fuck this for a joke" and got myself fired. Getting up at six in the morning for shitty wages was probably the best part about the job. Then I had to carry bricks and wood about for the rest of the day. I don't think I even saw a hammer, not until some fucker threw one at me because I didn't deliver enough of his precious bloody wood fast enough. Fuck that for a game of soldiers. My hands were so blistered from carrying all that shit about I couldn't even have a wank in the evenings.

My dad thought building was his lot in life, and it was. That is until cancer became his next lot, aged fifty-nine he was. He didn't even make retirement, the poor bastard. My poor mum, bless her, she was always worrying about me. She was always banging on, "If you want to get somewhere in life Keith, you need to work hard for it." She lived by that mantra, until cancer took her at sixty-four, talk about robbed. If that's what working hard gets you, you can shove it.

You can see why it was such an easy choice to become what I became.

We lived in a small two-up two-down council house. When mum died, she had seven-grand-something in the bank to show for it all. Her funeral took five grand of that. If you think five grand gives you a posh sendoff, I can tell you now it doesn't. You get a cheap coffin along with a bunch of cheap service station flowers.

Then some repressed priest pops his nut in and starts talking about you as if he knew you.

Oh and if you're wondering why I can't pronounce my name as Keith? It's because of a stroke I had when I was younger; eighteen to be exact. Slamming a bottle of ice-cold beer down, next thing I woke up in hospital unable to speak proper. It's not too obvious, but the word I have trouble pronouncing the most is my name.

I suppose I should explain how I became a dealer… it wasn't planned, if that's what you're thinking. It wasn't like I went down to the labour and asked for a job selling drugs. It was fate really. A mate and me were visiting a friend in Kent in some small town with no importance. And on his street, as we were leaving, my mate clocked this small warehouse just begging to be turned over. So we checked it out, meaning we couldn't see anyone about. It was dark, there was no lighting on the outside of the building.

And we were both standing there debating who should try the door first and Spud (not his real name) decided to step up to the plate and be the door opener. So he goes up to the door has a quick look around and gives it a hard kick and, fuck me, the door just popped open, it did.

No alarms going off, no flashing lights, just a big old Kent welcome. The surprise on our faces! So we go in and we don't turn any lights on, and we're totally unprepared like and my phone was flat and Spud didn't have his so we had no light but our cig lighters. So we light them up and have a look around. And fuck me... it's only full of cartons of cigarettes. Remember it's dark and we only had our lighters, but we could see cartons of cigarettes everywhere. There were millions of them of every brand so we decided to skim ten cartons off the biggest stacks. We took brands that we liked – the usual stuff like Silk Cut, Marlborough Lights, BH, all the known brands. You wouldn't have known we had been in there until the next stock-take. We didn't leave any mess or damage. That's the secret of being a good burglar: don't let them know you've been.

Anyways, we found a couple of old empty sacks and stuffed them full of carton upon carton of fags. We couldn't believe our luck! No-one about, just help yourself boys: your Kent Christmas has come early. And so off we went with our Santa sacks stuffed.

Now what happened next is the fate bit. You see, when me and my mates went out on a weekend, we would normally go clubbing. We couldn't afford to drink in the clubs, well, maybe one or two beers. So with what money we had we would get some pills. When I mean pills, I mean ecstasy pills. Get off our tits for the night, have a bit of a dance and, if you were lucky, you might pull a slapper. But because I now had all these cartons of cigs, I started swapping them for pills ... lots of pills.

And I soon had this big old coffee jar full of them hidden under one of my floorboards in my bedroom. The jar could hold about thousand pills, and so I started dealing at the clubs and it went on from there really. With the money, I then bought more pills. The more you buy, the cheaper it gets, and I got better at selling. And because I had the pills I soon realised that that attracts lots of pussy and let me tell you, *that* was a fucking revelation. And from then on, I just progressed up to blow because that's where the money was and still is.

I probably sound like I'm really shallow and only in for the money and free pussy, but there's nothing wrong in that is there? Isn't it always about the money? Besides, what's wrong with money and sex?

And yes, sometimes I use a little bit myself. Well! You have to be good to yourself every now and then, don't you? But don't worry; I've got it all under control like.

The secret to staying on top in my line of work is: Never Get Complacent. If there're two things I can teach you the first being never get complacent, and the second thing is: the police never get complacent.

London is work for me. That's where I sell my wares to my deserving customers.

My customers I can discuss with you later. I think you might be a little surprised who they are though. They're a mixed bag of the decadent, the lovely, the greedy, and the sometimes very wicked. On the whole, they're good people, leaving out just one client maybe.

Every city has their hard man that gets off on being very violent.

And that London hard man just so happens to be one of my best clients. I don't like him, and I would never say that out loud.

I fear him and I make no bones about it.

I only sell to him because I'm too scared to say no to him; you'll see why later. For me it's all about keeping a low profile with my London job. I have to keep drugs in my London flat, which I really don't like to do, but there's not much choice really. Where else can I keep them? I need access to them. I store it all in a secret hole cut into my lounge celling. That way a drug dog won't smell it. I leave around nine in the mornings and I come home around 6.00PM. My style is to try and look as plain as an envelope. I play a caricature of the worker that's being played out every day of the week across England. I try and look like one of the millions of earners going about their mundane lives. Except if I have a bad day and get busted then it's going to be anything but mundane.

I try and smile, and nod when I count the client's monies. Some clients don't like it when I count out the monies. Some don't like to be reminded that they're buying drugs, and some just don't like to being reminded that they're dealing with someone like me. But no one's going to be stiffing this little black duck, thank you. It's just business and at the end of the day, someone always has to count the monies.

Time for a coffee so I pull over into a coffee shop. I like to watch who comes in, just in case someone's following me. You tend to know if someone is following you. First rule: if she looks hot, then chances are she's not following you. Likewise, why would a big old fat person be following you when you can just out walk them? In general, if someone is following you, they tend to blend in and look like your dentist.

Now, I'm not brilliant with names, so to help me to remember someone's name, I add a little title to them, such as Trust-Fund Rupert or Vampire Brad; you'll meet them later. But faces I'm quite good with. I might not remember your name, but I'll remember your face. If I see the same face twice in a day while I'm working, then that's going to set an alarm bell ringing.

I'll do my level best to be bland. Bland doesn't attract attention. If you want to blend in and not attract attention try and look like your old science teacher. How many of you can describe your old science teacher?

Business is good. I'm selling to a couple of big fashion houses in London who look after a whole bunch of models who have the odd little habit going on. I say 'little'. There's nothing little about a habit, but it's much cheaper for the fashion heads to keep their girls on my powders than it is in a fifteen-thousand-a-week rehab unit which then returns the model all bloated and too sedated to work.

I clock a couple of the models as I make my rounds, stick thin they are with bad skin and straw hair. They're so depleted. That's what happens when you start living on coke. I don't sell directly to the girls, not because they're models, it's because they only want to get more fucked up on my blow to keep slim, and when they start falling apart and the jobs stop coming in, then of course it's all my fault, because I'm the big bad dealer. So it's their agents I deal with, the agents don't give a shit about them anyways, just as long as they can dribble their skinny arse frames down a runway without falling off then we're all good to go.

Now if you want to score off me, and let's be honest you probably do, my simple rule is you have to be introduced to me. And when I mean introduced, I don't mean: "Hey Keith, this is my new friend Dave, he's cool." That shit I don't want to hear. The reason I've been around this long is because I don't get greedy and I don't deal to just anyone. I'm extra careful around new clients. If they're cops, I would know.

I've got way better at spotting cops. It takes time that, you just get better at it. I can see a copper from a mile away and if I did ever miss one, they're still easy to spot as soon as they open up their mouths. They're always so fucking eager to do a deal, trying just a bit too hard to be your mate. Because they know if they get caught, they won't be going to prison so they don't show any fear. It's a dead giveaway, whereas your regular Joe is a bit nervous because they know they can go down if they get caught. So you just have to be on your guard... If you're not, they will sneak up on you with the rest of the humans.

Right then, I'm off to my next drop.

You're going to love these two guys. Proper regulars they are.

Chapter 2

I've known these guys for a few years now, and they're good guys. There are a gay couple called Darren and Barry. They've been together for twenty-something years now, both in their late forties. They built their own online gay dating company, and it became really huge. They got bought out for millions and now they lead a very debauched and decadent life. The downside is they're both well overweight and are probably facing imminent heart attacks. The plus side is they party a shitload and buy regularly. They fly first-class all over the world partying and they do it with no expense spared. Their London townhouse is WOW. It's one of the coolest houses I've ever been into. It has its own indoor pool which they never swim in because that would require some form of exercise. It's also got an outside pool but again never used because of the exercise thing. The house has its own lift, which they both use all the time because the stairs would probably kill them.

They're both larger than life and not just in size! They're fun to be around. I've seen them at their parties. They really go for it. Sometimes I'll do a late drop off, as I said, I know these guys fairly well. Their parties are basically rooms full of bare-chested leather clad men getting their rocks off, with Darren and Barry joining in wherever there's a gap.

Their parties are invite-only and their guests spend a lot of money on themselves to get there. And every gay man and his fag hag wants an invite to one of Darren and Barry's debauched events.

They had this huge party a few months ago that I made a late delivery to and they had four huge gold cages suspended from the ceiling in their ballroom, and each cage had a naked dude dancing in it. But their form of dancing included the use of large dildos of varying sizes. If it's pure obscene decadence you're after, then Darren and Barry's ballroom is for you.

My next drop off is to Georgina Tara Blackman in Richmond. She's known to all simply as GT Blackman. Manager to two of the world's biggest rock bands. GT is the queen of entertainment. No one fucks with GT. She gets my best coke and I never bullshit her. She has a computer-like brain and she can pick a scam a mile away.

She was born in Greece to a father who came to the UK in the late-sixties searching for a better life with nothing but a small suitcase and his newborn daughter. He then starts a business booking puppet shows for children's birthday parties. Then he sees the future in this new fad called rock music. He then progressed to booking all the up and coming bands in the early 1970s, becoming the UK's biggest promoter through the 1980s.

GT started working for her dad at fourteen; by age twenty she was booking the bands with her dad. She and her dad were the only business who knew how to fill a stadium. She once told me it was like printing your own money. Then as the tax systems caught up with music, she moved into managing bands – two in particular. The Negative Zero, who, under GT's wing, have sold over fifty million albums and the Two Four Sixty who have sold probably double that.

GT dresses sharp; straight out of Samantha from Bewitched. GT doesn't come to you: everyone comes to her. Music producers, clothes designers, drug dealers, agents, managers... everybody goes to GT's office in Richmond, London if they want a wafer-thin slice of the music business.

She owns a massive house perched up on the top of Richmond Hill, where she and her staff work out of. The outside of the house looks like any other beautiful house on the hill. It's not until you go inside that you see where her money's being spent.

The hallway to her office is long and wide and tastefully covered in framed photos of her shaking hands with the famous and the mega-famous. In the middle of the hallway behind a huge glass cabinet is this iconic jumpsuit that Elvis Presley wore on stage in some 1974 show, along with his huge rhinestone belt. Her house/office has cool stuff everywhere. Her office alone takes up most of the second floor.

I think of her as probably the smartest person I know. She looks up from her desk and invites me into her domain.

"Hello Keith, love. What you brought me this time then?"

I tell her: "I bring you treasures from a far off, forbidden land."

She yells for Tony, he's her money man. I've known him as long as I've known GT. It was through him I met GT.

"Alright Keith?" he says as he walks in.

"Yeah, you Tony?" I said. He takes my blow and then he's gone for about thirty minutes. He's always gone for about thirty minutes. I'm never sure what he's doing for that long. Is he checking it over in his lab? Does he even have a lab? Who the fuck has their own lab? I'm a full-time drug dealer and I don't have lab.

Is he just slow at counting out the monies? It's always thirty minutes. What the fuck is he doing?

I can't ask GT what Tony's doing. What happens if she says, what do you think he's doing? I can't give the biggest rock manger in the world my lab theory. She might not know about Tony's secret lab under the stairs.

Then Tony comes back into the room with thirty grand for me. Thirty grand always looks smaller than thirty grand should look, but it's a lovely feeling carrying thirty grand on you. I love buying a posh dinner with a big wad of cash, don't know why, just makes me feel good.

GT tells me she's got a big party coming up. Lots of big show-off names will be there. GT doesn't do drugs. But she understands the drug culture and the appeal of it all. Her people will hand my blow out to the appropriate peoples that require it and it's all done very discreetly, without any fuss, while I stand in the wings completely unknown, providing the chemicals to make her clients feel totally known.

I leave GT's place with my pockets filled with fifty-pound notes. Have I mentioned how much I love cash? Now, one more drop and then I'm done for the day. If London wasn't such a big place, I would be home by 1.00pm. It's sitting in traffic all day that steals my time.

Next stop Barons Court, and the client I'm meeting is Mr. Arthur (Rings) Butterfield. Arthur Butterfield is a local London hard man. When I mean hard, I mean evil. Butterfield has a foot in almost every pub in London. By that, I mean he owns all the door staff and security that work them. He's one of those people who could kill you over a spilt drink. He's the man that looks after pubs and clubs that no one else can. Piss him off and he's fucking frightening. If I'm being honest here, I find him frightening all the time. And one thing I've never done is piss him off – not unless I want my balls liberated from my body.

He's known as Rings Butterfield because of all the gold and diamond knuckle dusters he wears on his fingers. His hands are the size of shovels. Whenever I shake his hand, I feel like I'm about five years old. He's six-foot-six, and about four feet wide and wears his silver hair short and swept back in a seventies style with big silver mutton chops on his sides. He wears large black-rimmed glasses which makes his large head look even larger than it already is, and his voice is deep and kind of slow. He's got that sort of voice you don't have to ask to repeat itself.

From fifty yards away, he might look like a gentle giant but there's nothing remotely gentle about Rings Butterfield, or his firm that keeps London's gangs under control. He's sixty-two times around the sun, he's got two stunning-looking daughters in their early twenties who I stay well the fuck away from. And his wife is a lovely blonde bombshell called Tracy. When I mean lovely – I wouldn't do anything to piss her off. Tracy is about five-two in her early fifties. Looks younger than her age, with fake tits and she's always well turned out. She's your typical orange gym bunny and when she's not doing that, she's shopping. She wears lots of expensive bling on her petite little fingers, and on each of her ears sits a large round diamond.

When she talks, she sounds a little like David Beckham with a cold, and yet she's every bit as hard as her nutter husband. I suppose there's one good thing with Rings Butterfield: there's no bullshit. Be straight with him, and he'll be straight with you. That's why I don't deal with gangs. Nothing is straightforward with a gang. They will pull a gun on you take your drugs and cash, and just walk away. But not before they've given you a very unnecessary kicking. That's the reason Rings Butterfield has been put on this planet: to keep the London gangs in line.

I hand over the forty grands worth of blow to Arthur's righthand henchman who goes by the name of Terry Royce. Terry Royce is born and bred in my native South London. He's in his late thirties and scares me shitless. He's been working for Arthur since he was eighteen and because he also has a love of all things evil he's slowly risen up the ranks to become Butterfield's evil shadow.

Most criminals in London know of the very dangerous Terry Royce. His face shows little emotion as he looks at me. I'm not even sure if he has teeth, I've never seen him smile. He's tall, built like a mechanical bull with a shaved head and his nose is bent to one side. He's not what you would call a handsome man, even though he's always well turned out. He's just got one of those faces that looks like he's chewing a wasp.

So Doctor Frankenstein, if you're still out there and you would like your mental monster back, I know where you can find him. He's not using his old name anymore; he's now going by the handle of Royce. But he often talks about you and your old castle and how he misses his old bedroom in the bell tower.

Royce gained his reputation for taking out some well-known Liverpool hard man called Hammer who threatened him with – you guessed it – a claw hammer. The name "Hammer" says it all really. Who the fuck is dumb enough to front up to a fight against someone called Hammer? You must know something's about to go seriously wrong. So anyways, Royce didn't give a shit and he got the better of him and took the fucker's hammer off him, and then went to town on the dumb fuck's knees with it. And then, for good measure, he gouged one of the guy's eyes out with the claw of the hammer. And if that wasn't sick enough Royce then made the guy eat his own eye by stuffing it down his throat.

Arthur and Tracy never take the blow from me or deal monies with me: that's always done by Royce. And always in the front room which is a lovely room tastefully decorated by crazy Tracy. Royce always sits in the same large cream leather chair, with me in front of him on a smaller cream chair. We always sit in the same place. There's a lovely Indian carved coffee table that we do our business on; when I mean business, I don't mean having a poo.

Royce never has to taste my blow. He knows and I know that if it's shit, I'm fucked. So therefore: it's never shit.

Royce always counts out the monies in front of me. He does it really quickly, like a seasoned bank teller. There's a lot of cash counting done in Rings Butterfield's world. Royce always puts the monies in a crisp white envelope and always asks me to put it in my inside pocket out of harm's way. In other words, he doesn't want it out on show.

Arthur and Tracy have never told me how to behave in their house: that's Royce's job. If he says, "You leave your coat at the door when you enter their house," then that's exactly what you do. If there's a complaint about my blow or the monies – and thank Christ there's never been one – then Royce would take care of the complaint. He's always been fine with me, touch wood, and doesn't look down his nose at me because I deal, not like some of them do.

"Mr Butterfield would like to thank you, Keith." He says as he stands up and shows me to the door. He always shakes my hand with his huge spade like hand, and as always, he says: "Be lucky son," and then I leave. I'm always on my best behaviour at the Butterfield house. I know how wrong it could get if I wasn't. And I never ever want to upset their pet gorilla Terry Royce.

There are very few people I think of as real evil, but those two would come to the top of my list. Royce especially, as I think Butterfield might have one or two limits to his evil, meaning he might stop stamping on your face with his big shoe if he was interrupted by his phone, whereas Royce would let it go to straight to message.

I know, of course, where all the blow will be going. Rings has a blowout with his firm once a month. He has it at one of the pubs he looks after: a pub that he's cleaned up and got rid of all the dealing.

A boozer in Hammersmith called, of all things, "The Honest Dealer." Used to be a shithole; now it's a trendy shithole.

Arthur takes it over once a month on a Sunday evening for his goons and their gold-digging girlfriends to get pissed up and act leery in. The wives are all at home, of course, looking after their kids. Well, maybe not all the wives. Tracy Butterfield doesn't; she goes and hangs out somewhere posh and has her hair and nails done.

One thing about hanging with hard men: you have to be just as hard to hang with them. Sooner or later – and in my experience, it's always sooner – it's going to kick off, and fuck that when it does. I like my teeth in my mouth, they really help me with the chewing process. And my nose I would like to keep in the middle of my face, thank you very much. I have nothing to prove to no one; you're only as tough as your last fight. Especially when your last fight was with a guy built like an angry tank with a shaved turret. Being a hard man gets you noticed and I don't want to be noticed. But that's London for you; that's what all big cities are like.

But now out in the deep countryside of Sussex I'm known as Keith Fillmore Baxter. I feel the name gives me a slight air of grace and it helps me hob nob. I reinvented myself out here so I can spend up, and because there's loads of rich people about, I don't stand out as some flash South London git. East Sussex is in the southeast of England and the village I live in has no less than four churches: just enough for me to confess all of my wicked sins to. There's a small park in the centre of town for the village children. I hope to Christ that none of them turn out to be mine. And a stunning old community centre built in the late seventeen hundreds which occupies centre stage as you enter the village. And then we have the usual array of hairdressers, fruit and veg shops, and not one, but three bakeries.

This is where I spend my weekends when I'm not working in London. No one out here knows about my London life. This is where I've became the quintessential country gent.

And then there's my home, which is a long way from what I grew up in.

My home I bought (I say 'bought') seven years ago. It's all mine – lock, stock and barrel.

Grangemore Manor is a nine-bedroom, late sixteenth-century manor house built by Lord Grangemore. He was the Mr. Rich of the town and lord of all its lands. The property itself sits tucked away from prying eyes on a stunning hill overlooking a lake. I have fifteen hectares of land with seven stables and a country cottage which I rent out. There's a grand entrance to the property which is inviting and yet at the same time somewhat forbidding. The driveway down to the house takes a good five minutes to walk – fifteen, if you're proper pissed. It's lined with beautiful giant oak trees which lead you down to the house creating a spectacular entrance. At night they're all floodlit to create this wonderland feel.

Next door to the house is a large garage with six large doors which houses my classic car collection – more about them later. And as you pull up to the front of the house a large fountain greets you, which was installed sometime in the early eighteenth century. It costs me fuck all to run because I have my own spring. The fountain is of six large horses with King Neptune standing in the middle of them, holding their reins. It has two hundred and nighty-seven jets of water that shoot up, and it's been featured on numerous magazine covers. It's makes a right statement – it was said to have cost fifty-thousand pounds when installed. In today's money, that's about a half a million.

As you enter the house through the large oak front doors, it takes you into a large wood panelled hall with lovely old beams supporting the roof. This room was where the servants would ask 'one' to wait before you were led into meet the Lord of the Manor. It's quite imposing when you first walk in. It smacks of pomp and power. It was totally restored by the last owner Rupert and his wife, which cost them a fortune and Rupert's third marriage. As you enter into the main house, you're then met by the most stunning wooden staircase made from a tree that was felled here over four hundred years ago to make way for the house. I'm told they only selected the very best of the tree. This very staircase is where I will be standing in less than two weeks from now, fighting desperately for my life dressed as a big game hunter while two naked bodies lie just feet away from me drenched in each other's blood and brain matter. You've heard the old saying, "If these walls could talk…" well, if they could, they would be screaming, "Run for your life!"

So how did I come to acquire such a masterpiece of a house? Well, that's an interesting story as it goes.

And again this story stays on the page: I don't need any tax people sniffing about. I used to supply a really well-to-do London lawyer called Rupert Stonily; you may have heard of him. Doesn't matter if you haven't: he's not around anymore. He's not dead… at least I don't think he is. He was in his early forties when I knew him and he had done really well for himself, considering he had already paid out two gold-digging wives. Rupert loved the good life, and he loved his blow. He could afford to. He made some serious money.

His London firm he was a partner in was old and respected and had a lot wealthy clients on board. His offices were situated a stone's throw from the Old Bailey, where he did most of his work out of. I liked Rupert. He was nice guy, spent most of his time around high-profile cases and was known as a man who could win a lost case. Always dressed smart and had an air about him, yet he made you feel at ease when around him. Tall, with wavy blonde hair which sat above his horsey face and his hands looked like they had never seen a day's work outside ever. They were so white, they were almost transparent.

And his horse face conveyed the story of a man who could talk his way out of anything – legal or illegal.

He was well read and I spent many an hour drinking his very expensive fine wines with him that he had collected from around the world. The only times that I came to Sussex (before I lived here of course) were to deliver to Rupert. He was one of my constant regulars when I first started selling. He did a shitload of blow, and he liked his hookers – especially ones with limbs missing. That was Rupert's thing: limbless hookers. He used to fly them in when his wife was out of town.

One time he had run out of blow and asked for emergency delivery and when I arrived at Grangemore he had this hooker tied up in her wheelchair (he didn't make it easy on himself) blindfolded, gagged and dressed up in this tiny PVC Wonder Woman outfit. She had her legs spread open with a bunch of red plastic tulips sticking out of her. And he had written shit all over her in red pen but it wasn't in English, so God knows what it said.

I remember him introducing us to each other. She couldn't move or speak, let alone see me, so she just sat there and nodded. He poured me a large glass of wine while I sat down beside her and counted my monies out. And just when you think Rupert can't get any stranger than strange, a cab pulls up with another hooker.

Except this one has all her limbs and she could walk and talk. When I mean walk, I mean in a fashion. She had this thing with one of her legs that it wouldn't stop growing. It was huge. It looked really weird, she was this beautiful looking girl with this one really massive leg following her about. I got talking to her because I couldn't talk to wheelchair wonder girl because she was all gagged up and blindfolded.

She ended up being really cool, this chick with the leg. We hooked up in London and had a dinner a couple of weeks later. She told me Rupert's thing was he liked to rub his shaved balls over her big leg while she brushed her hair.

Remember now; there's nothing as queer as folk.

Anyways, that's public school boys for you. And, after all, he is a lawyer remember. You can imagine how perverted and twisted they must be by the time they make judge.

Rupert travelled first-class everywhere, which used to impress me, and he never got messy on booze or blow. He taught me a lot about the law, and what to do and what not to do if you ever went up against it. I had visited Grangemore quite a few times doing drop offs, always when his wife was away or out of town.

So one day I'm at Grangemore doing a drop off – and remember, back then Rupert was probably my biggest client at the time. I never met him at his offices. It was normal for us to meet at Grangemore. So it was to be a very normal drop off. I hand over the twenty grands worth – which is a lot back then – he hands me a large brown envelope full of cash. Then I have a couple of glasses of his expensive red wine over a nice chat. Then I call a cab and head back to the station with monies in my hand.

Only this time, Rupert didn't have the cash on him. He said he had got caught up in some big court case, but would sort me out next drop. I wasn't happy about it, but he had never let me down before. And twenty grand to someone like Rupert, I knew he was good for it.

So three weeks later, I'm back at Grangemore with another twenty grands worth of blow and when it's time to leave, he again gives me some old bullshit about not getting to the bank on time and he will fix me up tomorrow. Now remember, I really liked Rupert but he's in hock to me for forty grand now. There's nothing I could do.

I had to wait until tomorrow so out I go on the Friday to Grangemore at the agreed time and he's not there. I knew his wife must be away if he told me to come here. I felt like he was making a right fucking fool of me.

Remember the old saying? Nick forty grand off someone and he'll crack your skull open with a baseball bat.

Well this is where Rupert started playing the clever condescending smart-arse lawyer with me. And I was playing it cool because I wanted my forty grand back, but he started treating me like I was an idiot. One thing folks: Rupert might be a clever-university fuck but I'm a street-smart fuck.

So now I'm starting to get really worried and fucking angry, so instead of going back to the station I decide to wait it out at Grangemore. It was getting dark, so I jimmied the door to one of his garages and sat in this old Rolls Royce to keep warm. Hours went by and I was fucking livid. I knew he was stitching me up, and there was no way I was leaving without my monies.

Then, about two in the morning, I hear this car pull up to the house. I climb out of his old Rolla to see who it is. And sure enough it's Rupert alone and carrying his briefcase. He heads straight for the front door. So I follow him. He couldn't hear me walk up behind him for the noise of the fountain.

Just as he puts the key in the door and opens it I say:

"Evening Rupert."

He fucking shat himself, he did. The last person he expected to see was me. He started saying he was sorry that he missed me and that he had got caught up at the courts with a big case.

I said "It's okay Rupert. As long as you have my monies, then you and I are still on the best of terms."

And then he said "Yeah, about that. I just haven't had time, Keith; I've been so busy with a big case you understand?"

And I'm thinking 'Oh yeah, I understand alright. You're trying to rip me off, you stupid posh fuck.'

Now I'm not prone to violence, but I like to think with drug selling it's all part and parcel. It's not like I can go to the police and tell them some fuck won't pay his debt. If I get ripped off, I don't have any union backing me up, and there's no small claims court for unpaid drug debts that I can drag his sorry arse into. And even if there was, he would manage to weasel his way out of it. He's a fucking lawyer – after all, that's what we hire them for, isn't it?

I followed him inside, listening to his bullshit and as he turned around, I nailed him with my fist hard to the side of his stupid arrogant head. As I said, I don't like hitting anyone, but forty grand is a lot of money. I was still building my client base back then. So anyways, Rupert went down like the sack of shit that he is and then he started screaming.

"Don't hit me Keith, don't hit me, I'm sorry!"

What a fucking pussy he was. I only smacked the guy once.

I said "Rupert I'm not only going to hit you, I'm going to fuck you up. Now where is my fucking money, you prick?!"

He tried getting to his knees, giving me some old shit about, "I'll have it for you tomorrow – Keith, I promise!"

I spotted an old iron rod by the fireplace. I was really pissed by now, because I knew he wasn't going to give me my money. I walked over to it and picked it up. It's light to hold but felt really bone-cracking strong.

I lifted it up above him and said, "Rupert, it's money time, or your fucking kneecaps are coming out, ya fucker!"

"Alright, alright!" he yelled, "Please, we can work something out Keith, can't we?!"

"I've heard that sad line before, Rupert, and the answer is always the same. No we fucking can't. Now give me my fucking money. Have you got my fucking money Rupert, or do you want to lose your fucking kneecap?! If you want, I'll let you choose which kneecap you would like me to take first."

Then he started crying "Don't do that – please, I will get your money, it's just going to take me some time."

"Fucking time is something you don't have Rupert," I said pointing to his left knee with the iron rod.

"Please Keith, I will get you your money, I promise, just give me a few days..."

"NO!" I said, "FUCKING NOW!"

So anyways, after a bit more yelling from me and a bit more crying and screaming from Rupert and a good solid whack to the back of his head with my new friend the iron bar, he started suddenly seeing sense. I let him get back up and we go into his main sitting room. He's crying like a baby still and starts telling me how it's gone horribly wrong and of course I'm thinking "Boo fucking hoo Rupert, just give me my fucking money."

Turns out our Rupert not only has a love for blow but a love of gambling too. Fucking gambling is the pot of shit you never want to get caught up in: you lose everything gambling. You only ever hear about the big wins. And even if the gambling stops and you get yourself all better you still owe monies to everyone. And the thing with gamblers is you have to wait forever to get your monies back: that is, if they ever pay it back. And I wasn't prepared to wait forever, not for forty fucking grand.

So Rupert starts spilling the beans on what he's been up to and how much he's in the shitter for. He's been sneaking off to the casino after work and playing blackjack and losing everything. And remember this fucking dumb muppet makes hundreds of thousands a year? So the more he spends, the more he loses until he can't cover his losses. It's the same old sob story.

And now he's getting desperate for money, so what does the old (not-so-sly) fox do? He starts borrowing from his firms' wealthy clients, without them knowing. Yes reader, I'm starting to get the feeling my forty grand is well gone. The more he loses, the more he steals (and I use the word steals, whereas Rupert likes to use the word borrow) and now the senior partners at his firm has noticed monies missing.

I know! It just keeps getting better, doesn't it? The more he tells me, the further away my forty grand gets.

"How much money have you nicked?" I ask.

"Around two hundred thousand," he says, "and I haven't nicked it. I borrowed it."

I thought 'For fucks sake. I'm never getting my forty grand back, not if he's in that sort of debt." Two-hundred thousand is lot of money in anyone's book, especially when it's not your money in the first place. Now his firm doesn't need that sort of information getting round that one of the partners is a thief. And not only is he a thief but he's thieving from their trusting and well-paying clients.

One thing his firm doesn't want is that sort of info out in the public domain. It's not good for business that. And one thing they definitely don't want is a bent lawyer. If he's done it once, he could do it again so he can never be trusted now. He tells me the wife has drained the savings accounts as she's already abandoned the good ship SS Rupert for calmer seas.

And there's more. He's maxed out his credit cards to the tune of a hundred grand and that's not the worst of it. And I'm thinking 'There's still worse to come? What can possibly make this worse?' Rupert The Clever now owes a hundred grand to a money shark and the deadline is Monday morning. And because he's a month late with that payment he now owes another twenty grand in interest.

Owing me forty grand is one thing. Owing a London mobster a hundred and twenty grand is fucking serious.

Those animals will cut pieces of his body off, and they won't stop until it's fully paid, and paid with interest. And I know I'm way down in the pecking order when it comes to getting my forty grand back. By the time it's my turn, there will be nothing left to cut off him. So as Rupert spilled the beans with even more grim news, I'm now finding out the cars are all leased. His house in London is rented, he's got no savings and the only thing he owns is Grangemore.

And even that's done through some offshore company, through some weird company deal that I don't understand. So, as he talks, I calm down and start thinking how am I going to get my forty grand back? Rupert's sitting on the sofa in front of me with his sorry-arse head nestled in his sorry-arse transparent hands.

He tells me if he resigns and gives up law, his firm won't press charges. I tell him, "That's wonderful news but it won't get me my forty grand back will it? And his firm will also find the two-hundred thousand to repay the clients? I'm crying with joy Rupert, so why do they want you to give up law?"

"So they don't have to go to the trouble of having me barred from practicing law," he says, "not good for business that."

"Well, I suppose it's better than jail," I said.

"Is it?" replied Rupert, "At least in jail I would be safe from this loan shark who wants his hundred and twenty grand back."

"You're not safe from them anywhere," I said, "Not least in jail: they won't stop until they get every last cent. And each week there's even more interest topped on."

"I've got until Monday morning to pay up," said Rupert, "Where am I going to find a hundred and twenty grand?"

I suggested, "Maybe you should make a will, Rupert."

"What's the point?" he said, "I haven't got anything to leave."

"You've got this amazing house. It's got to be worth millions," I said, "Just sell it, get the money and then we are all happy, especially fucking me?"

He explains that, due to some strange tax deal he's done offshore, he can only sell it for a hundred thousand.

"As soon as the price goes over a hundred thousand, the IRS gets notified. Then I'm fucked because I have to pay tax at the highest corporate tax rate. Tax I don't have. And I could be in quite a lot of trouble if the taxman were to take an interest in me. Setting up shelf companies in tax havens is a way of not paying any tax in the UK. And sending the payments through a bank in the Bahamas is a simple way of avoiding tax. So even though Grangemore is not in my name, I still own it. The deal was that I was going to sell it to the firm after ten years through a set of shelf companies I've set up in the Bahamas. I would make a profit of a couple of million and still not have to pay any tax. But now that my firm hates me that deal's fucked, isn't it? No matter which way I look, I'm fucked," he said, while downing another glass of his expensive red wine.

"*You're* fucked!" I said, "What about my forty fucking grand? I'm never getting that back, am I? At least Rupert, you've got some imaginary bank somewhere in the Bahamas paying you out in your imaginary money."

"No! You don't understand, Keith. The imaginary bank just has my house. I can't get cash from it."

"I don't understand imaginary banks, and I don't understand how I've let you scam forty fucking grand out of me."

"I'm really sorry, Keith," he said, "I never meant to stiff you. You've always been good to me."

"You can fucking save the sermon, Rupert; I've heard that old reading before and with a lot more conviction than you're giving it."

We both sit in Rupert's sitting room in silence contemplating our losses while drinking more of his expensive red wine. I was gutted that I let it get to forty grand, so much for fucking street-smarts. Then I had this thought. It was almost as if someone saddled up to me and whispered it inside my head. Was it the ghost of Grangemore? Who knows? But suddenly I had a plan – and not just a plan, it was the fucking master plan. This is one thing: I do well when the chips are down, especially when the chips happen to be mine. That's when I can come up with the great idea to save my arse.

"Right Rupert, listen up. You've got no way out of this; that is except prison or being a body parts donor. Personally, I think you better decide which body parts you're willing to let go of first because that's what's coming first. Your firm has said they will bail you out of the two hundred thousand, as long as you go away. That bit's kind of sorted for you. Your wife's left, so she's out of the frame; you just have to come up with hundred and twenty thousand in cash."

"Which I haven't got, and I have no way of getting," said Rupert.

"No you haven't Rupert, you're right there because you spent it all. But I might be able to save your life, Rupert. I might be the person that just might be able to keep your miserable body intact before they rip bits off you. So here's the deal: you owe me forty grand and you owe your shark a hundred and twenty grand."

"Making a grand total of one hundred and sixty thousand pounds. So what's your plan to save my life?" said Rupert

"Simple Rupert. I will pay your debts off. I will pay your shark the one hundred and twenty thousand by Monday. And the forty thousand you owe me, I will wipe the slate clean. On one condition."

"And that condition is?" asks Rupert.

"You sign over Grangemore to me, lock, stock and barrel, and then you fuck off never to be seen again."

"Bloody hell Keith! This house is worth millions!"

"Then sell it," I said.

"I fucking would if I could, but I can't can I?"

"No you can't, but sign it over to me and at least you get to live. And living with all your body parts is a lot easier than living without them. Ever tried signing your name without your thumbs? I'm told it's the thumbs you really miss, especially if you want to hold a large glass of red wine."

He considered.

"It's up to you, Rupert," I said.

"Keith, this place is worth millions; I can't give it away for a hundred and sixty thousand."

"Well Rupert, the offer is on the table until 9.00 AM tomorrow morning. That's when I'm leaving. And since you've made me miss my train, I'm going to have to crash here for the night. Now which room can I have?"

"Take any room you want," said Rupert, "I won't be sleeping."

So I went upstairs and selected a room, which wasn't hard because there's loads to choose from.

When I woke it was about 8.00AM. I slept like a log; I was quite surprised I slept so well considering. I showered and dressed and went downstairs. Rupert was still on the couch in the sitting room.

"Christ Rupert," I said, "You look a bit shit, mate."

He didn't say anything, just sat there staring straight ahead, his normally perfectly combed hair looking quite messy.

"I need a coffee, Rupert, where do you keep your coffee and pot?" I said.

"I'll take it," Rupert said, looking straight ahead.

"Take what?" I said.

"Your offer. You get Grangemore, I get the cash," he said.

Now that stopped me in my tracks. 'Fuck me,' I thought.

"Alright then, let's have a coffee and discuss the details."

"You sure you can get that sort of cash, Keith?" he asked.

"Yeah. I'm sure," I said.

I had it stashed in my flat under my floorboards a hundred and fifty-five thousand from all my drug sales. Who said crime doesn't pay? I was going to pay off the flat I was living in over the next few months with that, but this could be a sweet deal for me. The thirty grand left I would need to fund more buying of blow, but otherwise I think I could pull it off.

As me and Rupert sat in his kitchen discussing the details, I couldn't believe that it was going to happen. 'Fuck me! I'm going to own Grange-more!' Rupert had all these contracts for me to sign. It meant that I had the same deal as Rupert. The house was in my name but it wouldn't be registered in my name: it would be a company that owned it. A company which would be in the Bahamas, which I kind of thought might be a good idea for someone gainfully employed as a full-time drug dealer.

Now I don't understand contracts especially ones in the Bahamas with their imaginary banks. But one thing I did understand was I didn't trust bloody Rupert, especially with my hundred twenty grand.

So I gathered up the contracts and said, "I'll be back by the end of the day. I need to have these checked out."

"What... you don't trust me?" Rupert said.

"What do you think Rupert?" I said.

I made a call to Ed Pellow. He was a lawyer I sold to and he did some sort of contract law stuff in property. It was Saturday morning and Ed was on his way out with his kid to some football match when I rung. But he agreed to see me at 12.30PM at his place in Chiswick, London. I was so grateful – I had no one else to turn to. Ed met me at his door at 12:30PM on the dot.

"Hello Keith, this is a bit unexpected. Are you in spot of trouble?"

"No, nothing like that. I just need you to look over some contracts for me."

"What sort of contracts?"

"Property ones," I said.

"Well, as it's my field of expertise," he said, "I suppose there's no harm in me taking a look."

So I explained the situation to Ed and he told me to pop back about 5.00PM and he will see what he can find out. I thanked him and headed back to my flat to start sorting shit out. While I was at my flat, I started lifting floorboards to make sure I had the monies, which I did! And then I waited about, drinking coffee until 4.30PM.

Ed met me at his front door at 5.00PM and took me into his office. "Have a seat," he said.

"The contracts are good; well written out, and no one is going to find the owner in a hurry, if indeed at all. It's not easy sifting through companies based in the Bahamas. They don't like authorities sniffing around. So they make it quite hard and in this case the way the contracts are written makes it pretty much impossible."

"Can I be sure the house is mine?" I asked.

"Oh yeah, it's yours," said Ed, "Once they're signed, it's yours, no dispute about that. It's all lawful in a roundabout way."

I thanked Ed, gathered up the contracts and before I left I gave Ed five hundred worth of blow for his help.

"That's very kind of you, Keith," he said as he shook my hand.

"Good luck with your new home then."

'Fuck me,' I thought as I'm standing in Ed's driveway, 'I'm going to own Grangemore Manor in Sussex.'

I got back to Rupert's about 7.00PM that evening. He was looking in slightly better shape as to when I had left him earlier.

"How did it all go?" he asked, "Is your solicitor happy with the contracts?"

"Yeah, all sorted Rupert. We're good to go."

"So did you bring me my money?" he asked while looking out his lounge window.

"Yeah of course I did Rupert. So then I could come with you to the casino and watch you gamble it away trying to double it. Let's just set up a meeting with your shark and then you can hand him over the cash so my new house is safe."

Then Rupert asks: "Please Keith, you do it for me."

"Do what?" I asked.

"Hand over the money to him. I can't face him Keith."

"This isn't part of the deal," I said, "It's your fucking mess Rupert. You clean it up."

But like the good lawyer Rupert is, he managed to sweet talk me into it and we set up a meeting at my place in London for tomorrow morning. My place was the best place to meet. It meant I didn't have to carry the monies about London with me. So on Monday morning me and Rupert The Brave headed to my flat to hand over the monies.

We had the meeting set up for 11.00AM and we were both shitting ourselves – for good reason.

The two men coming were a Mr. Butterfield and his associate Mr. Royce. Now this is before I had met Arthur Butterfield or Terry Royce, but even then I had heard of them. They knew who Rupert was but had no idea who I was so this was to be the first of many meetings between myself and them.

When 11.00AM finally arrived, the knock came at my front door. Rupert, of course, panicked, freaked out and started crying.

"I can't face these guys Keith, you do the talking!" and he went off and hid in my bedroom. Great, thanks for the big strong arm of support there Rupert. You big girly coward.

I went out into my hallway to let them in. I could see Butterfield and Royce standing outside the door. I could see their shadows through the glass panels. The pair of them looked so big standing there. And when I opened the door they looked even bigger – they seemed to be blocking out the sun. We exchanged names and I asked them in.

Remember this was my first meeting with Arthur and Royce and they looked so intimating and big!

Even when they entered my lounge, they filled it. I felt so small, they could crack me like a nut. And if I'm being honest, I thought maybe that's what they would do once they had all my money.

Arthur did all the talking and Terry Royce, true to form, didn't say anything – not a fucking word. He just stared at me showing no emotion. That to me is even more scary when someone as big and scary as Terry Royce just stares at you. But meeting Arthur in his true business form wasn't as bad as I thought. He was very pleasant.

Pleasant because I told him I have his monies.

I remember when they sat down in my large Chesterfield chairs. I can sit in one with my legs curled up in it. Arthur had to squeeze into his. As did Royce in the other Chesterfield with his face still like stone. I gave Arthur the monies which were in my brown leather money bag and he in turn handed it to Royce, who then started counting it out on my coffee table like a pro.

This took Royce about 15 minutes. So, reader, if you were ever wondering how long it takes to count out a hundred and twenty thousand, there you go. You can now tick that one off your list.

Meanwhile Rupert is hiding his terrified arse in my bedroom. Then Arthur asked me what I did for a living and I said "My usual line? I'm in sales."

"Sales, you say? What sort of sales would that be then, Keith?" asked Arthur.

And – for some unknown reason, and I've never done this before and I've never done this since – I said "Drugs."

Even when the word popped out of my mouth I couldn't believe I had said it. Arthur just gave a little smile while Royce sat there in silence counting my money.

"It's refreshing to see someone being so honest about their chosen profession," said Arthur, "I hope you're not this honest with everyone."

"No, I'm not," I said, still reeling from the shock.

I think Arthur could sense I was intimidated by them and could hopefully see this wasn't me at my norm.

"Well then Keith," he said, "Maybe you and I could do a little bit of business then." He explained to me his last supplier had let him down and they had had to sadly part ways. I caught Royce out the side of my eye giving a little smile when Arthur said that. I knew what parting ways meant with someone like Arthur Butterfield and the evil Doctor Royce.

But to be fair to Butterfield, we have had a good working relationship since that first meeting and it's been good because I know if I screw anything up with him, I'm dead. I remember them leaving. Arthur went out the door first, shaking my hand with his big shovel-like hand. Why a man needs a hand that large is a mystery to me. I bet you he can't pick his nose with those huge fingers. Terry Royce then stopped behind him, turned around, looked at me dead in the eye and said:

"Be lucky son."

And then he followed Arthur out.

I remember having to change my shirt after that meeting as it was soaked through with sweat. I was also feeling really hungry after that but I couldn't eat because of all the adrenalin pumping round my body. I put my body on the line for Rupert that day. If it had gone wrong, I would have been fucked.

After that day I had one more meeting with Rupert at Grangemore. He told me I could keep all the furniture. He didn't want or need any of it and he didn't want his bitch ex-wife having any of it. He said: "Whatever you don't want, burn it."

The only thing he took was a case of wine from the cellar and the classic old Rolls Royce from the garage.

He left a bunch of keys sitting on a table in the hallway with a note saying.

All the best Keith.

Rupert .

Lying under the note was a beautiful old bound book detailing the history of Grangemore. And beside that was a beautiful old sixteenth century sword that once belonged to Lord Grangemore himself. Rupert was a good soul – just made the mistake of picking the wrong addiction. If his addiction had been booze, he could have gone all the way. If it had been a drug addiction, he could probably have just carried on as normal, especially working in the courts. When it comes to gambling though, the dealer takes it all.

And Rupert?

I heard a rumour somewhere he went to live in the backwaters of Greece where he had a brother. I like to think he got himself sorted and got back on his feet and lived the elegant life once more. Life's full of little lessons. Some cost you nothing... some cost you everything.

Chapter 3

It's Friday evening. It's been a good week and I'm getting ready to head into my local village pub where most of the townsfolk seem to meet up. First things first though: if you're going to get ready, pour yourself a drink and rack up a couple of lines. I know I'm going to be drinking so I'm taking my brand-new white Jaguar two-door sports car with the black wheels: it's lethally fast, and makes you feel special when you drive it. And when I've done a couple of lines it really connects my internal sensors to the car. It gives me such a buzz. I don't drive my classics pissed. You end up dead in one of them. New cars are safer for everyone involved and they don't attract as much police attention, and by now most of my cars know their way home from the pub.

I'm being hooked up with some girl who's a friend of a friend. I don't mind blind dates. I find them quite interesting really. Even if I don't fancy them, I still find them interesting. The ugly ones – and that's not a term I use lightly – are never really that interested in me or my cash. They seem to have a bit more depth to them. Then there's the girl next door type; they normally like their blow. I've had plenty of them but after a few months of me, they get burned out and end up going back home to mum and dad to clean up. And then there's the really good-looking ones with the flesh out. They're always happy to let me pay for everything and that always make me feel like I'm being played, and yet that seems to be the type of girl I go for. Plastic tits, short skirts, too much makeup and cock-sucking lips packed with filler.

What does that say about me?

I park up outside the pub and do a couple of lines to straighten up before I go in. I love that rush you get when both nostrils are jam packed with mother blow ready to explode in your head. I meet up with the usual gang of country ladies and gents and start my way to a good night with a double vodka & tonic with an extra slice of lime, just in case I get a bout of scurvy.

Then, at about 9.30PM my friend Zoe walks in with an absolute stunner who just happens to be my blind date.

Fuck me I thought. Yum bloody yum!

Am I glad I had those two lines of blow! She hasn't got chance the poor darling. That's the wonderful thing about being in a haze of cocaine; you have all the bottle you need to punch well above your weight.

"This is Keith. Keith this is Jane," says a smiling Zoe. Even she can see I'm like a bantamweight going up against a heavyweight.

I secretly sneak a quick look at Jane's tits, (even though they're not hers – still great tits). Her surgeon should get a knighthood for those. Or at the very least a statue of himself erected outside a shopping centre somewhere. I wonder if he rebuilds cocks? Right, stop looking at her rack before I blow it – and that would be such a shame, especially before she got to blow me. Her skin... it's a beautiful dark olive, flawless skin, and in that sexy white cocktail dress it really shows off her features. Her voice is different too; it's got a sweetness and huskiness all rolled into it. And that is one fine arse, as she bends over to put her bag down.

She works in import/export, whatever that means, and Christ can she put away the booze. It's always interesting watching your date get pissed and then slowly lose their shit – and knickers, but not in this case. I may have found myself struggling a little bit to keep up here. I was probably just tired.

She was drinking double gin & tonics all night and didn't miss a beat, and then she did a couple lines of blow with me and Zoe which seemed to have little to no effect on her. I did the blow and the doubles and I can't even remember getting home, or who parked my Jag in a bush by the front door. And to cap a good night off some pissed arsehole smeared pizza all over the bonnet, why would someone do that? Did someone drive me home? I have no idea. And my coat for some reason was wrapped around my fountain's King Neptune... maybe I was trying to keep him warm.

I could have looked on the CCTV but who wants to look at themselves pissed on film? And especially when you notice sick on your pants. That means someone must have thrown up on me. God, I hope it wasn't me. I suspect the reason Jane didn't come back to my house was because she was the one who threw up. I bet that's what's happened? I better ring Zoe and check that she got home okay.

Zoe didn't sound as hungover as I did, she starts off telling me that I was having a joint outside the pub, and I was staggering by that stage. And then I took a big old drag from my joint looked at Jane and said: "Sure you can handle this?" Then I turned this weird green colour, and then threw up in my mouth.

"You tried holding it in," she said, "But your cheeks weren't big enough to contain that much sick so you just kinda sprayed it around like a popped bottle of champagne."

"Please tell me I didn't get it on anyone," I said.

"No, you missed us thank God, but somebody's lovely white jaguar wore most of it. You tried cleaning it off with your jacket. But that just smeared it about and made it worse and then you seemed all right after that. Maybe it was something you ate."

"Yeah, it sounds food related," I said, thinking 'what am I like?!' Now I know why Neptune, was wearing my lovely expensive jacket in the morning! How sad do I sound, throwing up on a joint! I can't believe I fucked up so bad. I never throw up (I say 'never'). I sound like I'm about fifteen years old again.

"What I *can* remember is that me and your friend Jane were discussing her fabulous breasts and she told me I could touch them."

"No darling," said Zoe, "You were telling Jane how much you admired her rack and then you tripped and fell forward and landed face first in them."

Zoe also reminds me we're supposed to hook up again tonight and Jane's also coming.

"Try and get some sleep," she said before hanging up, "I bet you look like shit."

I feel too embarrassed to go, I thought, and I'm worried what she will think of me and my vomiting party trick. I make a pact with myself that

I'm going to start cutting down on all the booze and drugs; it's about time I got cleaned up.

But by late afternoon and a couple of double vodkas in me, along with eight valium, I've decided it's important I go out and enjoy myself. And after a fry up at a local cafe I'm starting to feel a lot more together. This time I'm not getting pissed or stoned – okay, maybe a little pissed – but no more hurling custards on cars. Especially on cars that I own.

We meet at a different pub this time, which feels slightly easier when it comes to seeing Jane. And this time we're not walking in the front door with Keith's sick all over our heels. Jane's dressed a bit more casual but still with her fabulous tits on show. Lovely tight white jeans with cool ankle boots; she wears it all so well. I apologised to her for sticking my face in her tits and explained it must have been something I ate.

Me and Jane ended up getting on really well that evening. We did some more blow together and ended up back at Grangemore, where this time I didn't throw up. However, I did lay Jane and her fabulous rack which was nice. I could see Jane was impressed with Grangemore but not that impressed for her to start redecorating the entire place. This was starting to feel right. Finally, maybe I've found someone who's cool. She's quite open about herself which is refreshing. She tells me she grew up in all girls' boarding school eventually becoming head girl. I respond by telling her I was expelled from my school at fourteen and sat at home getting stoned listing to dance music. She then went onto Cambridge University and earned herself a degree in politics while I went out in South London robbing people's houses. She's really clued up and interested in world events, while I'm interested in porn and progressive dance music. We seem made for each other.

We hang out for the weekend and I decide to take Monday morning off. My only client that I really need to hook up with is Belle. She must have run low for her to call me this early in the week. Belle is an old hand at the blow game. She never runs out, and she always keeps her stash topped up just in case for a rainy day. But she's getting old, close to 80, so she probably just dropped her stash. You would be surprised how many calls I get from clients who have just dropped their stash down the toilet.

Monday afternoon, two o'clock is my only appointment I have to keep. Every two months. My contact comes to London with the goods. As soon as it lands in the UK, it's all cut and sold, and in a matter of hours it's probably gone through several buyers and sellers.

This is the most risky time: buying. You've got more chance at getting busted at the trade than any other time. Customs officers and police can be stalking a drug mule for months before they make their move.

My man is Russian and he's called Joe. The reason he uses a Western name is he thinks that it attracts less attention. Joe is an old hand. He used to work for the KGB, so he tells me. He's sharp and he's always watching.

We trade in a hotel lobby as most businessmen do. It takes one hour and there's no weighing or counting out. We do that later. We're not going to rip each other off; we've got a good thing going here. So why wait around for one hour? That's how long it takes to make sure we're not being followed.

People who use hotel lobbies are in and out within twenty minutes. If people sit on their own in there for an hour then they're either watching – or been stood up.

Joe and I both take our time getting to the lobby. We both have our own ways of checking things out. Remembering rego plates and faces, all the basics. Sounds paranoid, but it's much easier to do that than do ten years in a cell. If you're aware of your surroundings you're normally pretty safe. But if I do get nicked there's no way I can explain to a cop why I'm carrying hundred and fifty grand on me.

You just hope it doesn't happen; you just have to make sure you did things right.

We have a code me and Joe, if we think there's a tail on one of us, then we send the text "I might be a bit late," and then we abort. Thank God I've never received or sent that text.

Joe's in his forties and dresses like a straight businessman. He has a short-cropped beard and is balding. He looks very nondescript; he could blend in anywhere, especially in a hotel lobby. He's average height, with not too strong an accent, he wears brown shoes and sports glasses and is quiet in manner. Perfect for a drop off man. We don't talk about drugs or the business in case there's a bug. It's strictly light and social. You don't know whose listening and the rule is: wherever there's internet, people can listen in. We've done this many times so we know how it works and we both know what's at stake. And when it's your freedom – and if, like me, you like your freedom – then you become very aware.

With the drop off and pick up done, I head back to my London flat taking extra care not to attract attention. Carrying eighty grand's worth of blow is always risky, so I'm watching for anything out of the ordinary. The problem with eighty grand's worth of blow is if you do get pulled, then the police will always say it has a street value of double that. It's something the police and customs always do. It simply means they can get the courts to impose a tougher and longer sentence. If you're carry-ing a thousand pounds worth of blow, the police will then say it's worth two thousand pounds. It makes for a more serious court case; the more street value it has, the better chance of a conviction with more time. And even when there's little to no evidence, it's really all about the street value.

Back at my London flat I divide up my bootie and get ready to head round to Belle's place. I'm feeling good today. Sun is out, business is going well, and I really like this Jane girl. So now let's go make some money.

Chapter 4

I like Belle.

She feels solid. One thing, though, and this is very important: at Belle's apartment you need to be on your guard. The reason you need to be on your guard is Jeffery Bojangles, known simply as Jeff. And Jeff's not a person: he's a monkey. That's right, a monkey, a bloody great chimpanzee, to be precise. He's been living with Belle for the past twenty years, since she rescued him from some Hollywood animal trainer.

Belle doesn't warn anyone about Jeff. I remember my first time meeting Belle, I was a little nervous seeing all this wealth and stuff about. I was met by her butler, Brad, who explained to me how it all works with the blow and monies. And I was kinda listening but I kept dropping in and out, as I was just a little weirded out that he was a real butler. I've only ever seen them on TV before. He may have mentioned Jeff; if he did, I was probably looking out for a human.

Brad looks about hundred and ten, he's as deaf as post, and his eyes look dead. My first time there he made me a really strong pot of coffee. I like my coffee me, and I didn't want to come across as some sort of a wimp, so I drunk it even though it tasted a bit shit.

Within ten minutes of drinking Brad's coffee, I felt the sudden urge to take a dump. I was shown to the toilet by Brad, who walks at breakneck turtle speed. By this time I'm cupping both my bum cheeks so I don't shit myself. Then Brad finally shows me to the toilet which was just in the nick of time. I just got my pants down, sat down and then – fuck me – I blew like I had struck oil. Christ knows what was in that coffee, if indeed it was coffee. The noise my arse made. It came out with such a roar and I'm thinking, 'What the fuck has this old butler gone and given me? Has he stitched me up here?'

Turns out Belle drinks her coffee strong. No wonder she's all skin and bone; she's probably shat her insides out.

Anyway, there I was. I'm holding onto the toilet seat, it was that intense. If you think about it, when was the last time you held onto the toilet seat? And the noise that continued out of my arse, it sounded like machine gun stopping and starting. I'm thinking I hope no one hears all this. Looking back, if you were in the hallway, you would have heard everything. And yet it still kept coming. Now my poor arse sounded like someone was pouring a pot of thick chunky vegetable soup out of it.

Then, without any warning, I'm sitting there with the toilet pan full of shit and then the toilet door suddenly flies open, slamming violently into the wall. In walks a fully-grown chimpanzee in a suit.

The only time I've seen a monkey for real is at the zoo and it wasn't dressed up in a suit. Plus it was safely locked away in its cage.

The phrase 'I shat myself' couldn't have be more poignant, except I had no more shit to give. So I did the next best thing. I screamed, like a big girl, and then fainted on the toilet.

But unlike Elvis, I woke up on the toilet floor with my pants around my ankles in complete bewilderment. I could see one of my shoes sitting out in the hallway. How did it out there? Then as I looked up behind me standing on the toilet was a fully-grown chimp in a three-piece pin-striped suit. I started screaming out: "There's a monkey in the toilet! There's a monkey in the toilet!" It was fucking terror, I tell you. I've got my underpants around my ankles and my pants have become all twisted up around my feet so I couldn't stand up.

Then the monkey panicked because I was screaming so it starts jumping up and down on the toilet. So the both of us are having a scream off with each other; I don't know why I was screaming, I've never seen a full grown monkey kick off in a toilet before and it's not as much fun as you might think. I'm kinda laying sideways with one leg trapped against the wall and the other one caught behind the toilet. Then the monkey starts slapping me about the head with its big monkey hands. I'm still screaming out: "Help, there's a monkey, there's a fucking monkey in the toilet!" I'm trying to cover my head from the raging monkey blows which are raining down on me.

Take it from me, monkeys can slap *well* fucking hard. Don't ever let the three-piece suit fool you. I kinda felt that I wasn't fully in my body now, things started slowing down from that point. I think I stopped screaming and passed out again. My mouth may have been open but I don't think any noise was coming out of me. It kinda felt like I had stumbled into a horror movie. I'm desperately trying to untangle my tangled pants and underwear while still being belted about the head by the screaming Jeffery.

I've had little to no training with animals – especially monkeys. I once had a rabbit called Cliff when I was a kid. But I don't remember it sitting on the toilet smacking me about the head with its fluffy padded paws.

And then all of a sudden, I see Belle at the door yelling: "Jeff, come here you naughty boy!" and with that the monkey stopped hitting me. It then jumped off the toilet seat and landed right on my nuts with both its big hairy feet. The pain was like lightning hitting me. I then jetted upwards in searing pain and knocked myself out on the toilet pan. I have no idea how long I was out for. When I came to, my pants were still wrapped around my ankles and the toilet stank real bad. There's no Belle or monkey about, they've gone. There's just Brad the Butler standing over me holding a pair of pants.

"Would you like to slip into these, sir?" he said. Then he placed them beside me and walked out. I look down at my pants and there's shit in them. What! the fuck just happened? Why have I got shit in my pants? I haven't done that since I was sixteen. And I had this memory of a monkey standing on the toilet hitting me? I then cleaned myself up, which wasn't pleasant, threw my shit covered pants out and was then formally introduced to the mental monkey Jeffery as if this was a normal everyday occurrence. Oh - and another thing about Jeff. He likes to grab men's balls and squeeze them really tight for some perverted reason. And when I mean men's balls, I mean mainly mine. Anyways you've been well warned, if you visit Belle, cup your balls and keep an eye out for the evil Jeffery.

Anyways I do the drop off at Bellle's without a problem – meaning I didn't run into Jeff. And it was on the journey back to Grangemore, I started thinking about sexy Jane and what different positions I will try out on her tonight as she seems to be up for anything. Then I thought as she's new and I really like her, maybe I should hold back on some of my kinky stuff. There's plenty of time for that, and in the past I have scared off one or two ladies with one or two of my uninhibited requests – or as I like to refer to them, 'open-minded suggestions.'

So perhaps it won't hurt if I leave the leather swing and ropes in the closet just for a few more days. I should think of these first tentative days with Jane as my Lent; and maybe it wouldn't hurt me to do some normal mainstream regular sex stuff for a change.

I get back to Grangemore at around 7.00PM. It's quite nice coming home to someone. The house is all lit up. Jane is looking most ravenous dressed in very tight jeans, and a slightly revealing see-through top, with her wonderful rack beautifully displayed. I'm telling you that surgeon should have a star on the Hollywood Walk of Fame for building those melons.

She's got this way about her that I haven't seen in a woman before. I've got the feeling she could chase a bank robber down in high heels without breaking a sweat. And what bank robber wouldn't want that? And she's cooked us a fabulous roast lamb dinner with all the trimmings. My day just keeps getting better.

Turns out Jane had got bored going through my drawers and stuff and decided to do some shopping for a lamb roast instead. I've never attempted something as grand as a roast before, so fair play to her. That's quite impressive to see your new lady friend cook a roast for you. I wouldn't attempt to cook a roast. Doesn't cooking a roast take like a whole morning or something? I remember mum's roasts did. Jane had lit some candles for the dining room table and laid it all out; there was even soft dinner music playing. I'd never seen the dining room table look so festive. The only thing I had ever managed to lay on this table is a couple of half-pissed barmaids from my local.

Fuck me, I'm really liking this and there's even a bottle of white wine opened sitting in a lovely silver ice bucket which I didn't know I had.

"You sit here," she said, as she places me at the head of the table and pours me out a large glass of white. "It's not often I get to cook," she tells me, "And you do have kinda of a wow factor kitchen to do it in."

Then she went and brought out the roast lamb on a lovely big silver tray that I didn't know I had and placed it centre stage on the table.

"Wow!" I said, "This looks amazing!"

"Yeah, I used to love helping my mum out in the kitchen. I quite enjoy cooking," she said as she starts carving up the succulent roast lamb.

I'm smiling at her, she's smiling at me... is this living the dream or what? Sitting in my luxury manor with a woman who is sporting the most fantastic rack ever. And now she's serving me a home-cooked roast dinner after a hard day at the office selling drugs.

But as she started slicing the joint of meat, something didn't look right. I could see the roast was still a bit raw in the middle and I could see small shards of ice sticking out of it. It looked kinda brown on the outside, yet blue on the inside and there was blood coming out of it.

And I'm thinking 'Have I been eating my lamb all wrong until now? Is this how you eat roast lamb? Blue?'

I hope she's not on one of those crazy raw diets you hear about, mind you! Whatever she's doing, it's certainly working for her. But I don't want to have to sit down to a plate of organic merino cooked raw. The happy smiles had left our faces now. I was now sporting my, 'Christ, this looks fucking awful!' face, while Jane was wearing her, 'Shit! this doesn't look right!' face.

And fuck knows how bad her mother's cooking must have been if she taught her these roadkill methods. As she was slicing the meat (I'll call it slicing for now – it was more of a sawing really.) The silver tray was filling up with blood and ice.

Then there were these black things hanging around the raw meat that looked like they used to be potatoes. And there was these limp green things on another silver dish that were once beans. But like the true English troopers we are, we both carried on saying nothing, as if everything was perfectly lovely.

I poured her a glass of wine, at least she had managed to open a bottle of wine with some normality, so not all was lost. I complimented her on her choice of table wine. That was until I tasted it; she had hand-picked a sweet dessert wine. I was slowly realising: not only can't she cook, but she can't pick out wines either. And yet, as this gastronomic disaster unfolded, I could see she had worked really hard at reversing the cooking process so I didn't want to say anything that might upset her.

And then she poured the gravy from a lovely silver gravy boat that I had no idea I owned.

"I didn't even know I had a gravy boat," I said.

"Yes, you have five of them," said Jane smiling, "And you have nine different glass jelly moulds."

"Well I never," I said. "The kitchen for me is all about toast and coffee and not always in that order. I eat out mostly."

"To be honest, so do I," said Jane.

Watching her stir the gravy I thought, 'I wished to fuck we were eating out now.'

The gravy boat looked like Jane may have had thrown up in. Gravy comes from a jar and it's brown. You just add hot water and stir, whereas this was more beige in colour and it looked really lumpy. It didn't so much pour from the dish. Rather, it seemed to tumble out.

Jane had added cold water thinking it was hot, and to thicken it she added cream.

And still, I didn't say a word.

Meanwhile Jane hacked more of the yummy frozen lamb onto my plate. Thank Christ she goes off in the bedroom, as there would be no point in chaining her to the stove: she'd burn the fucking house down.

"Looks great," I said as she placed the plate of burnt shit in front of me. I started off by sawing through my frozen meat so I could attempt to eat it. It was like chewing on a cold hard piece of leather, which, incidentally in a couple of hours is what Jane could be chewing on if she lets me bring my leather swing out.

I took a sip of my dessert wine which as I suspected didn't compliment frozen lamb. I'm trying hard to swallow my tasty meat but my teeth are designed for grinding; what's really needed here are ripping teeth, and since we've all learnt how to make fire, (apart from Jane that is) we don't really have a need for canine teeth anymore. All that's needed now is for one of the lit candles to fall out of its silver holder and set the curtains on fire and burn my house down.

"How is it?" Jane asks.

"Hmmm nice," I said, while my teeth worked even harder at trying to rip the raw meat apart.

Jane is still serving herself when I try one of the black roast potatoes which taste like a piece of warmed coal. And the gravy hasn't softened any of the food on my plate; rather, it seems to have offered it protection like a rubber bathmat would.

"How was your work today?" she asks.

"Good," I replied, "Good; good day."

It's not like I can say, 'Great! I bought a hundred and fifty grands worth of blow from a Russian ex-KGB agent. And your day, dear?'

I watch Jane as she sits with her plate of uneatable food in front of her. "Try the wine," I said.

"I will in a second," she answered.

Then I watch her put a fork full of her roast lamb (I'm still calling it a roast) into her mouth. Then I watch her as the chewing begins. I can see from the expression on her face that something was wrong; either that or she's wearing dentures.

You can see the determination in the way she's chewing as the food is shuffled from side to side in her mouth. I'm thinking, 'If she can get this down her, then she must have a throat like a snake.' Then she grabs her napkin, puts it to her mouth and spits her roadkill into it.

"Oh Christ! This is bloody awful," she said, holding her mouth as if she's just been punched, "It's not cooked."

The fucking relief on my face must have said it all as I spat my food (I say food) into my napkin.

"At least try the wine," I said, which she did.

"Christ!" she says, "Is this wine off? It tastes like shit!"

"I think it's a dessert wine," I said, "More suited maybe to a creamy custardy pudding than a roast lamb."

Jane smiles and said, "Sorry babe I saw the kitchen and thought I could pull it off; I really fucked it up."

"It's okay," I said, "Let's order an Indian takeaway and maybe let me choose the wine this time." We start clearing Jane's roadkill off the table and back into the kitchen, and that's when I saw the kitchen mess.

Fuck me; there were burnt pots and pans everywhere there was even a 60l stock pot out with stuff in it.

"Are all these my pots?" I ask, "Or did you bring extra with you?"

"Sorry," she says, "I'll clean it up."

"Maybe with the help of a JCB you might. You make a start and I'll order the food in, but first let me open a bottle of wine."

Forty minutes later we have a clean kitchen and were sitting down to edible cooked food, even if it was a takeaway.

"Why do you have so many sauce boats?" asked Jane. "Do you collect them?"

"I wouldn't call myself a collector," I replied, "I'd like to think I have one for each room though."

The meal may have been a disaster but the sex that evening was anything but.

Finally, I've found a girl that just might be more disgusting and perverted than me. I didn't need to bring out the leather swing as Jane had kindly offered up her ass on a silver platter. How refreshing it is to hear a beautiful girl say: 'Hope you're not afraid to push the boundaries a little bit?' I can only hope she wasn't referring to her cooking.

And what a difference it makes when your sexual requests are answered with: 'If you want to?' instead of 'Isn't that illegal?' The only annoying part was I couldn't say no to Jane's requests, not when she said yes to mine. I remember her standing over me saying, 'Just relax babe, it won't hurt, I let you do it to me, didn't I?'

One or two of Jane's requests took me into new and somewhat untested territory. Requests such as face sitting. That one should come with a bloody heath warning, or at the very least, some basic helpful instructions. I almost passed out doing that one. I hope my bug eyes and crow sounds didn't frighten her. If I'm being totally honest, I didn't know I could make those sort of high-pitched sounds while gasping for air.

There are sexual things men will tell each other over a few beers. And then there are sexual things men don't talk about with other men over a few beers. The things Jane did to me last night I probably wouldn't talk about with other men, especially if I was in prison drinking homebrew.

And I would also hope that she wouldn't tell her any of girlfriends that I screamed out, 'How many fingers is *that* in me?' That kinda shit the girlfriends don't need to know.

I like to think of myself as a strong and adventurous male when it comes to having sex with the ladies. But I've now discovered I'm not. I may have one or two rational fears in the sexual limitations department, especially when it's to do with my arse.

Thanks to Jane, I now know what a prostate rub is and why it's so important to relax and not tense up, and that Jane is wasted in import and exports; she really should've gone into medicine as a proctologist. I'm sure she would have risen up the ranks.

There were one or two little things (I say little) that she did to me that I feel a little ashamed of, and I'm probably going to use alcohol and drugs to block those bits out. I've been walking around telling myself this morning that deep down I'm a good person really and that's why my bum hurts so much.

Being stomach punched that was a new one on me. I may need to do a few extra sit-ups before I can feel the benefits of that strange practice. Actually, that one I could probably leave out if I'm being honest. She could have ruptured my bloody spleen doing that to me, and there's never any warning when its coming. As soon as I relax *POW* from out of nowhere a punch comes slamming into my stomach.

And as for my leather sex swing – the one that has all the ropes and attachments – well, that can stay safely tucked away in the back of my closet for now. I've decided that I might not be quite ready for that yet, as Jane's requests seem plenty to keep me occupied with. And as I said: I may have blacked out when she was sitting on my face. That's not normal, is it? One minute I'm eating her out, thinking to myself 'Keith lad, you're doing a grand job here.' And then the next thing I know she's standing over me looking down at me smiling. I've never passed out while having sex before, at least not until I've cum.

And why in God's name would I like to try anal stretching? What can of scary shit have I opened there?

Chapter 5

Tuesday morning arrives. Jane is already up and sitting downstairs in the kitchen. Christ, I hope she's not trying to cook breakfast; my stomach feels a bit punched in at the moment. I don't think I could go through the motions again pretending that her food's edible. So I shower, dress and hope for the best. I find she's in the kitchen with a pot of coffee she's just made.

"Alright love?" I said.

"Yeah, good babe," she replies, "Cup of coffee?"

"Yeah, that would be nice. Have you made coffee before?" I asked.

Jane smiles, "Yes, I've made coffee before. Have a seat," she says, "I want to discuss something with you."

Of course I'm thinking, please not a fucking discussion at this time of the morning. That can't be good.

"Look Jane I said if this is about my high-pitched screams last night. It's just I wasn't expecting you to do that. A warning might help and maybe use a lubricant."

"No, it's not about your screaming babe."

"Is it about my nose bleed? Again, I just need you to give me some sort of warning that you're going to do that…"

"It's not about that either, and no I'm not giving you any warnings, that would take the fun out of it. Look, just sit down. We need to talk."

"Go on then. What's on your mind?" I said while I pulled up a chair and gently eased my sore arsehole into it.

"Have you hurt your back?" she said, as I slowly sit on my tender arse.

"No, no; my back's fine. It's all good," I said.

Jane sits on a stool in front of me stirring her coffee.

"You remember when you asked me what I did for a living," she said.

"Yeah, you work in import & exports. See, I told you I'm a good listener."

"Yeah about that, I left a little bit out," she said, staring into her cup of coffee.

"Jane," I asked, "Are you a part-time stripper? Because that's ok if you are."

"No, I'm not a fucking stripper! Why would you think that?"

I tell her, "I'm okay with you stripping Jane, it's your body."

"Keith! I'm not a part-time stripper. Just be quiet and listen for a minute. I do work in imports and exports. But I didn't tell you the company I work for and what my role is."

"It's okay Jane," I said, "It's nothing to be ashamed about, working in imports & exports. Lots of people do it."

"Keith! I work for UK Customs, and when I say import and export, I mean import and export that is illegal. My job is to identify and track the illegal traffic of drugs and drug monies entering and leaving the UK."

I could suddenly feel my mouth getting very dry. I wanted to pick my coffee cup up and take a sip. But it was just too tense a moment to do it.

Of course, I'm now thinking, 'How long have they been watching me and who else have they nicked?'

This is the moment I've always dreaded.

I could feel my throat getting really dry now.

"Are you a cop?" I ask.

"Kind of; I can't arrest people," she said, "But I have what they call a full access intelligence pass. Meaning I have access to any privileged information regarding illegal drugs or money laundering that our intelligence agencies like MI6 or Interpol have."

I'm now thinking any minute armed police are going to smash their way through the doors of my kitchen with their ray guns set to stun while screaming: "You're nicked Mr Baxter!" And I've just had those doors painted...

"Okay," I said, "What's that got to do with me?" I was trying to play it cool and a little aloof. After all, I haven't told her anything. Maybe she has no idea of what I do; I'm probably freaking out over nothing here.

Besides, I've been too careful to make mistakes. She wouldn't have anything on me. She's probably bluffing.

Fuck it! I could lose everything here. Someone must have dobbed me in. I bet that bloody chopper that flies over Grangemore every Saturday morning is a police chopper, probably filming me.

I ask, "Have you guys bugged my house?"

"No," she said.

"Have you been following me in your choppers?"

"Choppers?" she said, "What the hell are you talking about, choppers?"

"The one that flies over Grangemore every Saturday morning, has that been filming me?"

"No, no one's following you and no one is filming you from a chopper. This isn't a movie."

Jane thought: 'Why would he think we're flying choppers above him? How much blow is this guy shifting to think he warrants a state chopper buzzing over him with a film crew?! And I still can't believe he thought I was part-time stripping...'

"So, what it is you want with me Jane?" I ask knowing that any minute now there's going to be smoke bombs and police swinging into my kitchen hanging off Tarzan ropes.

"Well," she said, "I know what you do in London."

"Oh yeah? What do I do in London then?"

"I know who your Russian contact is and that his real name is Bas, not Joe."

"I don't know what the fuck you are talking about darling," I tell her, "I don't think I've even met a Russian."

Now as soon as I said that last statement, I thought that was stupid arse thing to say. 'Never met a Russian?' What's wrong with Russians? They're good people, just a little hard to understand, that's all.

"Keith, I'm not here to bust you."

"Good," I tell her, "Nothing to bust me for, I haven't done anything wrong."

"If I wanted to bust you Keith, I could put you away for the best part of ten years: I'm not here for that."

"Good," I said again, "because I don't know any Russians." Christ I've just gone and said it again; what the fuck's wrong with me?! "Actually," I said, "let's go talk outside."

"Keith, for the last time your house is NOT bugged. Do you think I would be having sex with you in your house if it was bugged?"

'Fucking hell,' thought Jane, 'Why is it every time you tell someone you're with customs they just assume you're there to bust them? And a stripper? Is that how people see us in customs and excise, dancing around chromed poles getting five-pound notes stuffed down our underpants? I know we're underfunded; but stripping? How the bloody hell has he managed to stay under the radar with theories like that?!'

We go into my lounge and I open a bottle of vodka. It's only gone 9.30AM and I'm pouring out double vodkas.

"Go on then," I said as I pass her a drink, "Actually, before we go on, is Jane your real name?"

"Yes Keith, it's my real name. Just let me explain, will you? We got a tip off about you a couple of years ago from some girl you pissed off."

"What girl?" I asked, knowing it could be any number of girls that I've pissed off over the last two years.

"It doesn't matter Keith. My boss shut the case down because he thought you were straight, but I kept an eye on you and found out some stuff."

"What sort of stuff?" I said laughing it off while still secretly shitting myself.

"Well, your Russian friend Joe has been making some stupid mistakes."

"I don't know any Russians called Joe," I said, "Especially ones called Joe"

"Well, by Friday evening you won't," said Jane. "Your Russian friend will be shot and killed this Friday at 6.40PM and his body will just disappear. He's going to be killed by a Greek thug called Stavros Markress who's with the Greek mafia. And then they're going to be the new players in town. Your soon-to-be-dead Russian friend has chosen money over loyalty, and that poorly made choice is going to cost him his life on Friday."

"So why not stop it from happening then?" I ask, "Isn't murder still against the law?"

"Because I'm the only one who knows it's going to happen. I intercepted the email about the hit. It was in code, but I worked it out," as she hands me her empty glass for a refill.

"I still have no idea what you're talking about," I said as I poured her another double.

"It's rather simple," explains Jane, "Your man Joe – real name Bas – has swapped sides and he's made a deal worth twenty million pounds in cold hard used cash. And you and I, Keith, are going to help ourselves to that twenty million in cash and then go off and have a nice life."

"Jane, what the fuck are you talking about? What twenty million pounds and what comic book have you just stepped out of?"

"Your Russian friend Joe is delivering twenty million pounds to the Greeks on Friday evening by way of a white van. And he's going to pick up twenty million worth of coke from them. Except they won't have the coke with them. Because they're setting your Russian friend up. They want the money and the coke. Except you're going to steal the twenty million just before their meeting."

Now I know I'm fucked, she knows Joe. I knew her tits were too good to be true; only someone working undercover would have great tits like that. Why didn't I see that one coming; everything I've stolen and worked for I could lose all because of Joe, the stupid muppet. "Don't worry my friend," he would tell me, "I'm ex-KGB officer, nothing to worry about." Fucking KGB officer my arse. What the bloody hell's he doing business with the Greek mafia for?! You never do business with the mafia; everyone knows that, they always end up shooting you in the back of the head, they can't help themselves. If Joe walked in now I'd happily shoot the dumb bastard in the head myself.

"So, who are these Greeks?" I ask.

"They're the latest crime wave to invite themselves into London wanting an extra-large slice of the pie, and another thing; they won't be needing you Keith. They have their own people they use, and they will stop anyone muscling in on their game. All you will be left with is the scraps. But think what we could do with twenty million...!"

"Are you fucking mental?" I said, "I'm just going to walk in and steal twenty million in cash off some drug cartel?"

"Keith," she said, "I've got a plan that's simple and brilliant. It's fool-proof."

"And if I say no?! Which, I might add, is looking very promising at the moment."

"Listen Keith, I want what you have. I've worked fucking long and hard to get what I've got, and when I look around I'm thinking: is this fucking it? And at the end of it all, I still won't have an eighth of what you have. So either you come in with me, or I offload all the info I have on you to my boss: and there's a lot of info. You'd be looking at a good ten years even on a good day with a sleeping judge. Or... We can both get very rich to the tune of ten million each for practically no risk."

"Very little risk for you maybe, but it seems like I'm the one who's taking all the risks here. What are you going to be doing in all this fool-proof plan of yours while I'm liberating twenty million in cash? Actually, to be fair, Jane, do you even know what twenty million pounds looks like in cash?"

"No," she said, "Do you?"

"Well, no I don't," I said, "Which makes a very valid point as to why I shouldn't be the one stealing it."

"It will be in a white van; your friend Joe will drive the van into the basement of their building; you won't have to lift one bank note. It's not like you're going to stash it in a briefcase and walk out with it. You just get in the van, turn the key and drive it away."

"And where do I drive this van of twenty million to?" I said.

Jane takes a swig of her vodka, looks at me, smiles and says:

"That's where I come in. You take it to the bank, of course. Where else would you take twenty million pounds?"

"Oh the bank!?" I said, "I feel such a fool for even asking, that was such a first-time robber question. Do I just drive up to the teller and say: Hey! could I make a deposit and get a receipt with a balance please?'"

"Listen, you will be taking it to a Swiss bank not far from the building where you're collecting the van; everything will be set up waiting for your arrival. It's not like a regular bank, it's where large amounts of money, gold and silver are shipped to and then out to reserves around the world. You would be surprised to see how easy it is to deposit large amounts of cash in England. The bigger the amount, the less paperwork; the less paperwork, the less chance of a paper trail. Twenty million buys you an invisible paper trail. Banks need cash because it shores them up against collapse. Swiss banks are no different. They still like their shiny gold but they love their cash and the one thing about Swiss banks is they restrict prying eyes. And that part I will have all sorted," as she finishes her second vodka of the morning. I'm starting to think I preferred Jane more when she was part-time stripping.

"This is all part of my job," she said. "I deal with banks every day. I know how they work and what details they require and who will be doing what."

"Why are you dealing with Swiss banks?" I ask.

"Because that's where illegal money ends up after the drugs get through the ports. Customs can only track money so far once it's in the banks; especially a Swiss bank. It's impossible to gain access. Swiss banks don't open their books to anyone, let alone a customs department in the UK. Why do you think the Nazis loved banking with them instead of their own banks? Our twenty million will be safely tucked away without any messy paper trail. We can both give up work and just drink, eat and fuck."

"Yeah, speaking of fucking have you been fucking me over from the very start?" I ask.

"No! God no," she said, "When Zoe introduced us, that was just a fluke, and I thought why not? You seemed okay. It wasn't until afterwards I remembered who you were. I actually really like you. I wouldn't be letting you do your freaky shit on me if I didn't like you."

"It might come as a bit of a shock," I said, "but in some cultures, my freaky shit is considered liberating and very caring."

"Oh really?" said Jane, "Name one culture that practices what I did to you with that bunch of grapes?"

We both just looked at each her for a few seconds.

Now I'm thinking, '*My* freaky shit? What about *her* freaky shit?' Then I started looking at her tits and thought about some more freaky shit.

So, I ask, "If your lot and MI6 know about Joe; then they must know about me. Not that I've done anything wrong mind, because I haven't."

"I only know about you. They know about Joe. You're just a little fish compared to Joe. Customs want the big fish and Joe and the Greeks are swimming in the same pool as them. We're after the ones dealing in the hundreds of millions. But believe me, your Russian friend Joe would sell you out just like that. He values his drugs far more than he does people. To Joe, people just get in the way of his drugs. Do you know he could retire fifty times over if he wanted to. But he can't, because he's too greedy. Back in Russia, the streets are littered with the wreckage that's been left behind from your man Joe. Because of his greed, he's about to set off a drug war that will change the face of London. Sadly for him he won't live to see the pain and damage he's going to cause."

"Why will it change London?" I ask.

"Because the Greeks use guns and knives to solve everything. Not themselves, of course. They mainly enrol young kids from street gangs. They arm them with guns and knives and then send them out to sell their drugs to anyone buying. And when they don't pay up or there's a problem with a buyer, then these kids will just stab or shoot them. Then the police think its gang related and then all the attention gets turned on to the London street gangs. Meanwhile, the mafia sits at the top and stays hidden well out of sight, slowly becoming untouchable because there's just not enough police and money to reach them."

"And then the news becomes all about young street gangs and their knives. And that's who going to shut down your business Keith. Not me, not the police, but a bunch of fifteen-year-old street kids riding push bikes. Because they're kids they don't even get life for murder. Five years and they're back out on the streets."

"All this is about to happen, and it's going to be a whole different playing field. The government won't have the money to stop it. There will be some new laws but that won't change anything. It's all a con, Keith, and I don't want to be a part of it anymore, so that twenty million is my way out. I've watched people get richer and richer while I stay poor. Stuff that: I'm joining the ranks. Whoever said crime doesn't pay was talking through a hole in their arse. Crime does pay and it pays big time."

"Only if you don't get caught," I said. "And are you prepared to spend a long time banged up if we get caught?"

"We won't get caught," said Jane finishing her third vodka. "Not if we follow my plan. Customs and police have been tracking this deal for months now. They're not going to bust Joe because they need to catch the players at the top. But there's one place that we can't track."

"Go on," I said.

"Basements. We can't track in a basement and in the building where the exchange is happening, there is a very deep basement so we can't see or hear them."

"I know when Joe will arrive, there will be white vans coming and going all day long. The police can't stop anyone that goes in and out because we don't want them to know that we know. So, all you do is swap number plates on the van and you're good to go."

"Hang on Jane. How do we know Joe won't be sitting in the van? He's not going to leave twenty million sitting in it, is he?"

"Yes he will. It's all part of the drop off plan made by Joe himself. Your man Joe will be killed somewhere in the building and his body will be taken out – most likely in the back of a white van. But I know Joe will leave the keys with the caretaker's office in the basement of the building. He will give the caretaker a code and the caretaker will hand the keys over to the person with that code. And I know what that code's going to be."

"Once you give him the code, you're handed the keys and then all you have to do is just drive it out. You will have ten minutes to get the keys and change the number plates and then drive out of the building; it's that simple."

"Why ten minutes?" I ask.

"Because that's how long it will take the Greeks to deal with Joe and then get themselves down to the basement to get the code."

"But won't the police have the number plate as soon as I drive it out? Then I'm fucked."

"No! You will put the fake number plates on the van which I will give you. They just stick onto the old ones. There will be at least twenty white vans in the basement that time of day; there's a lot of deliveries coming and going."

"So where are you getting these fake plates from?" I asked.

"Our customs warehouse has loads of them and the ones you will be using will be totally untraceable. The plates you will be using are registered to a catering company that doesn't exist; we use them when our guys are doing undercover work. If the police check the plates it will show up as a catering company based in North London. And if the police ever do go looking for the catering company, there's no company to find."

"But won't your people know where the number plates have come from?" I ask.

"No, because there's no paperwork trail. I've made sure of that. The only data I'll put on the computers is where the company is based. I won't be using our work computers. I'll use a police computer to do all the import on. I've booked myself in for a meeting at London's busiest police station. They're going to be looking for a bent copper, not a bent customs agent," she said while gesturing for a refill.

I pass her glass back with another double. It's only just gone 10.30 AM.

"But won't they know it's you that's logged in?"

"No. I'm using an old code and it's registered to a bent police officer that they haven't removed from their database yet. There are at least five thousand people in and out of that building on any given day. Maybe even more. They won't check out the number plate: no one's going to know anything's wrong. When you drive out of that basement, you're just another white van, and it's not like the Greeks can go to the police and say: 'We've had our van nicked with twenty million in it.' By the time the police even figure out that there's something amiss, it would be way too late by then. Anyways, if the police did find out, they would think that some other player nicked it and Customs will think the same. And the Greeks would think Joe was setting them up, so killing him was fair justice."

"I feel sorry for Joe or whatever his name is. He's been alright to me."

"Trust me," says Jane, "Your mate Joe is a complete evil bastard, times ten."

"This all sounds a bit too easy," I tell her.

"All brilliant plans are simple," Jane said, smiling with pride. "No one will be expecting this to go down, especially not the Greeks and the Russians don't have any clue."

"And what happens to the van afterwards? It's going to have all my DNA over it."

"Simple. After it's been emptied, drive it somewhere quiet and set it on fire. And remember to take your clothes and shoes you're wearing off and throw them into the burning wreck also. And remember to remove any clothing labels and have nothing in your pockets. Don't forget to take spare clothes with you, otherwise you'll be hailing a cab in your underpants, and wear gloves – rubber ones, not leather."

"Why not leather?" I ask.

"Leather leaves DNA."

"I've never set a car or a van on fire," I tell her.

"It's easy," Jane says, "Just stick a rag in the petrol cap, light it up and then run. That's the important bit: don't forget to run."

"What?! You've set vans on fire before?"

"No, but I've seen loads that have been. Once they've been torched, the fire brigade turns up and sprays gallons of water all over it. There's no DNA or clues left. The fire services are very good at washing away any important clues. Oh, and one more very important thing babe. On the day wear shoes that are one size too big."

"Are they to go with my red nose and big cully wig?" I ask.

"No genius, just in case there is a footprint left behind. The police will be looking for a shoe size bigger than yours. You would be surprised how many people we catch because of a simple footprint; in fact, it won't hurt to wear two sizes too big. It's the little details that get you caught and it's the little details were going to get right."

We talked through the morning and by 11.00AM, I was proper pissed. Jane suggested we go out for breakfast to straighten up. I said I couldn't drive in my condition. So Jane, who had consumed more than me, took it upon herself to drive. It was sunny outside so Jane picked my classic Series Two SWB Land Rover to drive. And at the time being half-pissed I thought that it was an excellent idea, so I let pissed Jane, who had never driven a farm wagon before, drive us out on a public road.

Chapter 6

"Look," I slurred, "These old vehicles take a bit of getting used to. This is old technology you're driving here; in fact, the word technology hadn't even been invented when these were being put together."

Jane assured me that she knew how to drive one and that it would be most wise of me to buckle up. I reminded her that trucks of this age didn't come with seatbelts to buckle up with, and with that; we were off. Now as I've said I have a long driveway and there's no traffic on it. Yet Jane still managed to somehow drive my Land Rover (some would say crash it) into a ditch. Luckily, these old Land Rovers are bulletproof and can drive themselves out of most bother, including Jane bother.

Of course, our Jane didn't blame it on her pissed driving. It was the Land Rover's fault. She even managed to convince herself that it was most likely a design fault that caused it, and I should get it checked out next time I take it in for a service. I reminded her that these old trucks are full of design faults and that since I've owned it, it's never had a service.

Within a short time, we found my local cafe and after parking half on the footpath and half on the road we went in.

We had a lovely breakfast – lovely because Jane had nothing to do with its cooking.

"I have to go to work tomorrow," Jane said. "Everything has to look normal. You have to go about your business and me about mine. Also, I still have a few things I need to put into place. I'll go back to London this afternoon and I can call you tonight. I won't see you again until next Monday. My shift pattern has me working the weekend shift. I'll know if anything unusual has been picked up on the wire."

"So how do I get a hold of these fake number plates then?"

"I'll post them out to you," she said.

"I'd better give you my London address then."

"It's alright," said Jane, "I already have it."

"What! So, you've been following me?"

"Only once," she said, "But your nosey upstairs neighbour kept looking out the window so we left."

'Nice one Religious Brian,' I thought, 'At least someone's looking out for me.'

"Is my London flat bugged?" I ask.

"NO! For the final time Keith, your house is not bugged. However, last night in bed I did stick a small microphone up your ass, so try not to cough too loud."

"I don't know about small," I said.

Jane smiles. "By the way – that large hook hanging from your bedroom ceiling. What's that for?"

"Don't know," I said, feeling a little embarrassed that she's spotted my leather swing hook. "It was there when I bought the house, want another coffee?"

"No thanks," she said, "I thought it might be for hanging your leather sex swing on."

"Ahh," I said, "So you found that did you?"

"Yeah, I was just opening doors and there it was. That kinda thing could give a girl quite a nasty scare... I had no idea they came with so many attachments and ropes. Is it the executive model you bought then?"

"Yeah, about that; I didn't want to come across all pervert-like so that's why I kept it hidden in the wardrobe."

"Babe when you start hiding sex swings in your wardrobes that might be considered just a bit perverted. Also that swing is the least of your perversions. Listen babe, I've got a train to catch, you can tell me all about your big sexy swing on the way to the station if you like."

We get to the station in one piece, thanks to my driving, and we go over Jane's master plan once again.

One thing I have learnt today is if your ass is a bit tender; don't go out driving in an old Series Two Land Rover. They still have wagonwheel suspension and the seats feel like they've been made by the same company that made the suspension. Every pothole or any tiny pebble I drove over felt like someone was pushing a carrot up my arse.

Of course, I didn't tell Jane that; I didn't want to give her any new ideas, especially when it comes to using root vegetables.

I drop Jane at the station. We French kiss and say our goodbyes. Then I watch her and her fantastic tight ass walk away and board her London train.

As I sat in my truck, and the quietness settled in, I start to I realise how huge a task I have in front of me. In four day's time, I will be ripping off one of the most dangerous drug cartels in Britain. If I get caught, those animals won't bother with the police. They will just execute me slowly and painfully.

I awake the following morning to the sound of my mobile ringing. My bedroom is dark with the heavy curtains blocking out the light. My throat is dry but apart from that I feel quite good. I pick my phone up and there's a message from Jane telling me all's good.

I go down to my kitchen, grab a glass of water and drink it down trying to rid myself of my throat dryness. It's 5.00AM. I haven't gotten up this early since I tried working for a living. Everything seems so quiet. I look out my kitchen window. Why the fuck people feel the need to get up at this hour is beyond me.

"What if this all goes wrong, this nicking twenty million?"

I don't even have a will. I don't have anyone close that I could leave anything to apart from my brother and he's banged up doing time for three armed robberies. I wonder how long it takes before anyone notices I'm missing. Christ, listen to me! Nothing's even happened yet.

I wonder if anyone comes to my funeral. Then again... who is stupid enough to go to their drug dealer's funeral?

I should be planning my funeral with Jane; after all, she's going to play a big part in watching me get killed. Why aren't I more pissed off at her? I should be planning her fucking funeral, not mine. Why aren't I more pissed? Is this what love is? You start forgiving people who accidentally get you killed?

I know what my tombstone will say:

Here lies Keith Baxter's broken bullet ridden body.

A good soul at heart, he was.

But he let his guard down, didn't he, all for a piece of arse.

If I'm going to do this, I have to formulate some sort of a plan of how to get in – and just as importantly, how to get out. My entire plan so far consists of me walking into a building asking for a key and then stealing a van with twenty million in it.

It sounds just a bit too simple.

Now I know Jane said, 'Don't go near the building because there's cameras all over the street.' But I have to. I know I can't take my car, and I can't walk it. I can't take a cab because the driver of the cab could be interviewed, but there might be a way. Maybe I could ride past the building on a push bike. I could cover my face with one of those smog masks that you see couriers using in the city. Then there's no car number plate you can trace, I'm just another courier on his bike wearing a smog mask. I can buy a bike and then dump it where it will get nicked; so that means anywhere in London.

Then I can ride past the building nice and slowly and take a closer look at what I'm walking into. I can dress up like a bike courier. I know they wear lots of Lycra. Can't be that hard.

Now I haven't ridden a bike since I was ten and I have no idea if I still can. Only one way to find out.

There's a bike shop in Acton which I've driven past before. I can pick up what I need there.

Now I can feel a plan coming together.

I'm going to take on the Greek mafia unarmed, dressed in Lycra, riding a push bike.

Fucking genius that is.

I go to the cycle shop and buy myself some supersonic featherlight bike that's called 'The Whisper' from some salesmen kid called Andy. Andy loves his job and didn't let me leave until I was fully kitted out in bright yellow and green Lycra, along with a pair of studded shoes which felt more suited to a football field. I ring Jane. She's worried that I'm falling apart. If anything, I tell her, I'm becoming stronger. I don't tell her I'm about to do a reconnaissance on an eight-hundred-pound Whisper, dressed as a banana. But if I'm going to pull this off, I'm doing it my way. It's not as if I'm doing a fly-by on a hang glider, it's just a push bike! The street where the building's located is called Kokota Street. There's a well-known newspaper company on the street, hence all the extra security cameras. That's why the Greeks love working out there; they know who is coming and who is going. I did some searching for the street on my computer. I can see the building but the large basement doors to the building are on a steep slope.

I might as well get on with it. I change into my Lycra suit and get myself ready for my journey. I put on a small backpack to add to my costume. My bike shoes clatter like football boots on my lounge floorboards. Once kitted out, I check myself over in the mirror. Yep. I look a fucking dick. I look like one of those runners in a marathon – the ones that you see dressed up as a gorilla, or in my case, a genetically modified banana.

I take the train to the nearest exit near Kokota Street and activate my camera with is attached to my bright yellow cycle helmet and prepare for takeoff. Luckily for me Kokoda Street is much less busy than the street coming out of the station. And even better it's a short street, so thankfully I don't need to play the part of a London courier for too long. So off I go but I'm really struggling to get the bike moving as it's stuck in top gear and I'm wobbling all over the road. I'm forcing the gear lever down with all my strength then finally the lever changes down, but this time it hits the lowest gear setting. Now the Whisper went from whispery quiet to an old banger with chains and clogs clanking away as I peddled out. With the bike now stuck in its lowest gear I must have looked like I was peddling for the English cycling team. My legs and peddles were now going at break-neck speed, there may have been smoke coming off them as I was giving it my all, and yet I hardly seemed to be moving. If I didn't gain speed soon, I was in danger of tipping over. Then one of my feet came out of the pedal strap.

I could see the building on my left getting closer, but I still couldn't see into the carpark. But worse now; my one good foot that was still clamped in its stirrup was getting a right cramp on from doing all the peddling. Now I'm feeling dizzy due to my lack of oxygen but like a trooper, I keep on going. I couldn't stop; there's cameras everywhere. Then as I get to the building entrance, I turn my head so my helmet's camera can catch some of the footage of the basement. If you hadn't seen me go by, you would have certainly heard me as I was wheezing like an old traction engine. My lungs couldn't take much more, my legs were cramping up in severe pain. And now I could feel the dreaded bike wobble coming on.

I just couldn't get enough air through my smog mask. I hadn't realised that I had the breathing vent shut off. As soon as I turned the corner the dreaded bike wobble became the dreaded bike tumble, and so over I go. Flying over the handlebars I went. Wing Commander Baxter dressed as a banana slamming headfirst onto the busy road.

I crawled to a parking meter perched on the footpath and hoisted myself up, ripping my smog mask off as I went. The injured Whisper lay on the road and I secretly wanted to leave it there so a bus would run over it. But being the true pro I am, I ventured back out and dragged its sorry scratched up carcass back to the pavement. My breathable Lycra was now soaked through with sweat. I stood there for a couple of minutes, leaning on my Whisper, waiting for the burning feeling to leave my lungs. Then finally, some well-dressed city guy walks up to me and asks,

"Are you all right?"

Finally, someone in this cold, unforgiving, bleak city who actually gives a fuck about his fellow man steps up. My nose is banged up and bleeding, my Whisper is scratched and my banana suit is ripped, but someone in London finally gives a shit.

"I'm okay," I said, feeling a little more reassured in my faith in humanity.

"GOOD!" he said, "Because your bike is blocking the fucking foot-path, you dickhead, this is for the people who are walking."

And then he stormed off in a huff. I should have said something back, but I was too out of breath.

I'm going to have to make some health changes here, not only am I cutting down the tobacco in my joint, I'm also going green, from now on I'm only rolling my joints with organic papers.

So, in my fully soaked breathable Lycra, I headed for the nearest train station relieved the ordeal was finally over.

Who nicked my abandoned Whisper after I left it? Fuck knows. Whoever it was, good luck to them. That's one bike that had way too many design flaws for my liking, and don't get me started on the seat.

Why would anyone design a stupid slice of a seat that rides up your arse? It feels like it's been designed in a German fetish club. Looking round, I'm seeing arses getting bigger not smaller.

I told you not to get me started.

Once back at my flat, I showered and threw my Banana Man costume into the rubbish along with the stupid shoes. I downloaded the footage onto my laptop and surprisingly, it wasn't too bad for a first-time courier. I had managed to get a somewhat decent view of the car park and entrance before I crashed. Which tells me straight away that this courier thing is not as much fun as I thought it would be.

There was some footage of me peddling when I was looking down, that looked a bit mad, you could see my legs going for it. Realising too that I now had the incriminating footage on my laptop I would have to dump that as well, this is turning out to be an expensive day. But I can't afford to leave any incriminating evidence.

Over the day, I watched the footage over and over hoping I would see something that gave me the edge.

There wasn't much to get the edge with; I could see the booth where the car park attendant would be. And I could see where the transit might be parked, and right next to the booth were two goods lifts. There was a large concrete column facing the booth apart from that there was nowhere I could hide. And there was a camera over the booth so I will need some sort of disguise. Apart from that it looks all clear.

I've also found a small car park on the next street over, so I can park my car there out of site from Kokota Street. I can see there's a small alleyway just a few yards up from the car park entrance. I should be able to slip down there unnoticed. That little gem didn't show up on my computer search, so my cycle trip might be starting to pay off now. There doesn't appear to be any cameras over the alleyway so that looks like my way in. This heist might be looking easier than I first thought. Listen to me... 'Heist.'

Then I hear a knock at my door, I can see it's a motorbike courier through the glass panels as I open the door into the hallway.

"Package for Baxter," he yells.

"That's me," I answer taking the package from the courier. "Yeah, I used to do a bit of courier riding myself." I start telling him. "Yeah. Done my fair share of road miles."

"Yeah! Whatever mate," he said, "Just sign here, will you?"

So much for the courier brotherhood, I thought, as my courier turned and walked silently back to his bike.

I opened the package It's the number plates from Jane. They look real enough, so that's one part of Jane's master plan sorted. She's also given me the address of the bank and the name of the person who will take the monies off me. His name is a Mr. Robert Banknote.

Banknote!!? Is this woman having a fucking laugh? Mr. Banknote who works at the bank. Am I really asking for a Mr. Banknote? Are there some red flags I'm missing here? Who would even have the bottle to front up to a job interview at a bank with a name like Banknote? It would be like having 'Warden' for a last name and then applying to the prison service to be a guard.

Turns out the bank is about twenty minutes from Kokota Street where this Bob the Banknote works.

I still can't help feeling that I'm being set up here, with some CID copper in the police interview saying to me,

"Really... You didn't spot the joke with the name, Bob Banknote? How fucking gullible are you?"

I look at the bank's address. if it says 'Dollar Road' then I'm out of here. It doesn't, it says Zia Street. But there is a street close by called Coin Road. I need to rest and get some sleep and calm down. My chest is still hurting from my bike work out. I decide for the good of my health I should take a couple of pills to come down with. I take some really strong painkillers that were prescribed for a friend and after an hour, it's just what the doctor ordered. But then I decided I should have another two so I can be fully relaxed. Once a drug pig, always a drug pig.

I sit back and feel the slow thick stone of the pills coming on and all the worries of the world taking a back seat. It's not enough to knock me out, might be for a horse called Blossom, but not this little drug lush. I just need to shut myself down for a few hours.

I think it's important for everyone to shut down every once in a while.

This is why I love drugs.

Let me tell you something for free folks. There's no fucking war on drugs! The war on drugs ended sixty years ago when the pharmaceutical companies stepped up and declared victory. Now anyone can get drugs, all you need is a GP and you can get ripped for free. There's no drug war darlings, that ship sailed long ago. Dealers like me turn over hundreds of thousands a year, while the big drug companies turn over hundreds of millions, and they get a pat on the back for doing so.

After my well-earned rest and my little rant, I wake up and check my phone. I've got a couple of deliveries to make and while I'm out there I can pick up a disguise. I'm also very aware that tomorrow could be my last day working as a free man. Either I'm going to be ten million pounds richer or dead. I don't see a third choice. So, I might want to make my disguise a decent one.

Now where do you pick up a disguise from? Just saying it sounds fucking mad. Am I going to have to go to a joke shop and buy one? Do I just walk in and ask the person at the counter, "Where's your 'bank rob-bery' disguises?"

I can't just walk into the building with a stocking over my head and say 'Hello!! I'm the Key Man don't be alarmed, I'm here with the code.' I need to get something really convincing.

I search the internet and find a costume joke shop near Notting Hill, so not too far out of my way. Then I have a drop to do at Darren and Barry's. It must be a big party; they've asked for decent amount. I shower, get my orders together and hit the road with my two drops to do. Darren and Barry's is later in the evening so I can catch up on some sleep before then. I'm feeling a little bit paranoid if I'm being honest. I mean if Jane can sniff me out there might be others. This is what the thought of jail does to you, it makes you all jumpy and nervous.

I need to calm down and level out. It's all about balance, so I take one more of Lee's pills.

Who's Lee? Lee's a proper bona fide Rockstar, he was in the book, but my editor Liam thought he should be taken out so he's in the next book. What is it with you editors?

They're great pills these, they're designed to calm down manic mental patients who are kicking off. They're kind of like taking 30 ml of valium with half an E, along with a nice relaxing joint. So, when I take three, it's like taking 90 ml of valium, two Es and three joints. Taking four I'm flying like a spaceman. That's the deal with good drugs. You usually want more, but at the same time you gotta make sure you don't tip over.

I'm never trying to catch that first-time buzz as some people are. Me, I want a bigger and stronger hit than my last buzz, I want to see how far it will take me. Saying that, I don't want to shut down completely. I still want to be conscious so I can enjoy it. Nothing worse than coming round and you've got dribble all down you.

I make my way through Notting Hill in bumper-to-bumper traffic to the costume shop for my disguise. The shop is small and smells of rented costumes and the staff don't seem the least bit interested in helping me. There was your usual array of sexy police girl outfits and celebrity dress ups. So, I rummaged around looking for something that looked vaguely real, but there didn't seem to be anything. It was mainly all plastic and rubber masks. In the end I went with the best of a bad bunch, a fake Jesus beard and an Elvis wig. When I tried them on, I looked like Elvis in his Jesus years. I paid the uninterested staff member and left with my cheap looking disguise in an even cheaper plastic bag.

The disguise looked ridiculous, but where else am I going to find a disguise at this point of time? What I need is my own special effects person. I'm just hoping that in the dark underground basement it might not stand out too much. I also called into some random shoe shop as Jane suggested and bought a pair of shoes two sizes too big. They were a pair of brogues in light brown, not the sort of thing I would normally buy, but they were only going to be worn for an hour. But annoyingly, when I picked up the pair I wanted, I didn't bother to check the size properly. I thought the pair I handed to the shop girl was a size 10, but in fact they were a size 12. I can't believe I did a dumb thing like that. So, when I asked the girl for the shoes to be a further two sizes bigger, the girl looked at the shoe size which of course said size 12 and so she goes and gets me a size 14.

I didn't bother checking again because I was too busy checking out the sexy girl in the short skirt, who was sitting next to me trying on some long, black boots. She was far more interesting to look at than a pair of brown brogues. I could see right down her top and it looked like she might be wearing a nipple ring. She had some serious tattoos on her arms, but I couldn't make out what they were. And she had a really big tattoo wrapped around one of her legs, but I couldn't make that out either. She looked so fucking sexy trying on her boots, while I stood at the counter being anything but sexy buying my sensible brown brogues.

"Cash or card?" the girl at the counter asked, but I wasn't paying any attention to her, so I said:

"Yea, in a bag will be fine thanks love," as I carried on perving.

"I'm sorry?" the girl at the counter said, "Do you want to pay, by cash or card?"

"Oh sorry," I said, not realising she was watching me play the part of a committed pervert. And at the same time the girl trying on the boots looked up and realised I was being a perv too.

"Cash," I said, feeling right embarrassed at being caught out.

Now I didn't know where to look. Fuck it all, I was really quite enjoying her. I paid cash to the girl and left the shop feeling somewhat like a dirty old man. As I left, I clocked the sexy girl now standing in front of the shop mirror admiring the boots.

Fuck she looked hot, her hair was blowing in the breeze and yet I couldn't feel any breeze in the shop. I slowed down my walk so I could drink the last of her in for my memory shot, her short-pleated skirt really showed off her amazing legs and arse. As I walked past her, for a brief second, her eyes met mine and she didn't look away or even look annoyed, she just looked. I tell you what, just having her make eye contact with me has made my day, pervert or no pervert. Standing outside the shop I thought do I wait here for her? Or do I walk? So of course, I walked off, didn't I.

Unwittingly, I had just brought a pair of light brown brogues that were now four sizes too big for me. I didn't even look at the box; I just threw them in the boot of the car, got in and drove off. In hindsight I probably shouldn't have taken that pill before buying my disguise and shoes. But I was thinking this could be my last day of freedom. If I get caught, I won't get any pills, not for stealing twenty million. I headed back home. I need to shower, straighten up and take my final delivery of the day – or in this case, the evening – to Darren and Barry's.

If it's a cool enough party I might be tempted to stay back for a while, depends on how dark the party gets. If this is to be my last night of freedom, the last thing I want is a night of heavy dark, gay fetish shit being performed all around me. I'll see plenty of that in prison. I weigh up a decent deal's worth of forty grand for their big party. It's a lot of monies worth, so I take extra care when packing it in the car making sure that everything is just right. My pill has worn off, but I have another three on me just in case the party is worth staying for. I'm not taking any coke tonight as I don't want to be strung out tomorrow, not on my first big day of van robbing. I miss Grangemore. I wish I was tucked up in bed with Jane and all this shit got swept away by the rain.

Chapter 7

I cruise through London's night life to Darren and Barry's place. We have a code that I text them when I'm arriving so they're out looking for me, not me looking for them. Especially as I'm walking around with forty grand's worth of blow on me. I arrive at about 11.00PM and the place is awash with people dressed in sexy and revealing fetish wear. But this time there's lots of scantily dressed girls about. Turns out Darren and Barry are having some big anniversary party and they're pulling out all the stops. Some guy dressed as what looks like a dandy greets me at the door.

"Are you Keith? he asks.

"That's right," I tell him.

"Darren's up on the fourth floor. I'll buzz you up in the elevator. Follow me darling," he said in slightly Kenneth Williams voice.

I walk through the house clocking all the interesting people about.

Way more people than usual, and I can see there's plenty of lovely expensive champagne about, which I might have to partake in a glass or two of later... actually, I may have to take full advantage of tonight's champagne. That's the problem with me, one glass of champagne is never going to be enough.

We squeeze through the throng of people with my dandy shouting, "Coming through darlings, coming through."

This is definitely the most ladies I've ever seen at a Darren and Barry party before, normally it's wall to wall men eyeing each other up with maybe the odd, stoned, fag hag hanging off her bear's arm. But this party has a different vibe; I can even hear cheesy Italian house music being played.

This is so rainbow for Darren and Barry. I think I might see how tonight pans out.

Only Darren and Barry and a very select few get to use the elevator during their parties, for obvious reasons. The rest of the guests use the

THE MONKEY AND THE DEALER

long winding staircase. As I'm the one carrying the party by way of a big bag of blow, I'm considered as one of the select few. There's this huge black guy in charge of operating the lift, who has a small VIP list with him. He smiles at us with two rows of large, perfectly formed whiter than white teeth. His teeth look like they could devour a whole boiled rooster in two bites, bones and all. He can't hear what my dandy's saying over the music so my dandy has to yell in his ear.

"This is Keith."

The huge man looks at me,

"Darren's Friend! Keith B!" yells my dandy, "He's expected."

The large giant looks at his list of names and spies the name Keith B.

"Step inside, young man," he said, while still wearing his big, beautiful smile.

"Darren's up in the office waiting for you," says my dandy, and he walks off to join the rest of the party.

The lift is quite small, so it can only carry four regular people and that's at a squeeze, or two people if you're Darren and Barry, and that really is at a squeeze. Very cool to have a lift in your house though. The lift doors have a little window in them and I can see the people partying on each floor as I pass on up. The fourth floor contains Darren and Barry's home office along with some storage rooms. The only way you can access them is by the lift. I've been up here a few times making deliveries. The lift opens up directly into their office, and like the rest of their house, the office is beautifully decorated with tasteful pieces. As the doors open there's Darren with a couple of friends chatting and laughing about shit.

"Come in, darling," Darren yells to me as the doors open, "You're just in time for a glass of very rare champagne that's come my way."

Darren explains that he just bought six bottles of the stuff at a snip, only two thousand pounds a bottle. What a great guy to do business with our Darren is, I'm thinking as he pours me a large flute of the bubbly nectar. If I ever turn gay, I hope I find someone like Darren or Barry to be with. Pure fucking class.

"Darlings," he says to his two friends, "I just have a little business to conduct with my dear friend Keith here. I'll see you down in the ballroom."

And with that he sends them down in the lift.

"How's the champagne darling?" he asks.

"It's the best I've had, Darren," I reply, and I wasn't pissing in his pocket. It was the best champagne I had tasted.

"What is it?" I ask.

"I can't pronounce it," says Darren, "It's all French to me, but I've been to where they grow it and just fell in love with the stuff darling."

"Now then," he said, "Let's get the business out of the way and then on with the pleasure."

I put the bag of blow on the desk and as it's a special event, I've put a pink bow on it.

"Oh, I love that, darling," says Darren, "You're so creative."

"Thank you," I said, "Nothing like pushing the boat out when it comes to presentation."

"Well, of course darling," he said as he puts forty grand in wonderful clean crisp bank notes in front of me. Just then the lift doors open and out steps Barry, dressed in full drag, from top to toe in pink ruffles and sequins. And yet he never thinks to shave his beard off.

He's got this big beehive wig on that has little bumble bees stuck on pipe cleaners buzzing around it and then it gets knocked sideways as he tries exiting the lift, right fucking funny that was.

"I told you it was too bloody big, darling," Darren says, in his big deep drag queen voice.

"Rubbish, darling!" said Barry in his even bigger drag queen voice, "We just need a bigger lift."

"Hello Keith, darling. Don't I look stunning?" as he straightens up his crooked beehive. "One can't have big enough hair darling," he explains to me while hitching up his cleavage.

"I agree," I said.

"And while you're at it, Keith darling, can you explain to old mutton chops here that my wig's fine, it's the poky little lift that needs enlarging."

Then Barry spots my pink bow, "Oh darling" he says, "That's my favourite colour, how did you know?"

"I'm a good listener," I said.

"Should we have a toot first, darlings?" said Darren.

"I should say so," said Barry.

"I might just stick to the champagne," I tell them, "I've got a big day tomorrow."

"Nothing could be as big as tonight, Keith darling," said Barry, "You wait and see what we have planned for later."

"Oh, go on then, just a quick toot," I said; I don't want to come across all rude, do I?

"And don't forget," said Darren, "You must stick around for the entertainment, it's going to be full on."

"Yes, darling, full on," said Barry, as he chops himself, Darren and me out six large lines of blow.

I'm looking down at the lines thinking, 'Fuck, that's a lot of blow. These guys are taking they're partying hard tonight as the three of us snort away.' And the speed he cut it out with, very chop chop.

"Right, darlings," said Barry as he tops up our flutes with more expensive champagne, "Shall we join the party?"

"Yes, lets," said Darren.

We all try and get in the lift, but we can't all fit in, Barry's bees are getting in everywhere and the lift doors are refusing to accept all three of us.

"Well, that's clearly not going to work, darlings." said Barry, knocking his beehive wig sideways again, "I'll go down first. I'll send the lift back up and you two can follow me."

"Follow that, darling? That's not going to be easy," said Darren smiling.

We wait by the lift drinking more expensive champagne, and then we both squeeze into it when it arrives.

"Make sure you're in the ballroom at 1.00AM, for the show," Darren said as we exit the lift. Then he points to the pool. "The bar's that way darling. Enjoy yourself." And he walks off to greet his guests.

I discreetly swallow a couple of my 'be-good-to-yourself' pills and head for the free bar.

"What can I get you?" says the young barman, whose totally naked but for tennis shoes and socks and a sun visor. Not batting an eyelid, I put my empty flute on the bar and ask for a refill.

A champagne bottle appears, not two-thousand-pound bottle, but Moet which I can still happily drink. I hang at the bar drinking the best part of a bottle. The champagne and I are getting along fabulously when I could feel the first stage of the pills kicking in. The first stage is always wonderful with drugs because you know there are more wonderful stages to come at you. Yummy champagne and wonderful pills along with some choice house music, can it get any better?

Oh yes, it fucking can! Right then this beautiful girl rocks up to the bar, all dressed up like a princess warrior, which just so happens to be one of my most favourite princesses. She's dressed in a black and red leather tiny PVC mini skirt. And her cleavage is just about hanging in there. She has long black hair tied back and her beautiful blue eyes were set to stun. Her boots alone look like they've been sewn onto her perfect, long, tanned legs. She's got this tribal tattoo running down one of her arms. She's got this amazing energy about her, she looks in her mid-twenties and she's calling herself Princess Ladybird Sam. She may have been a real princess for all I know. I would like to think I'm in that league of pulling royals, especially when I'm off my chops.

Speaking of firm tits, I took a quick peek, she didn't catch me though. We talk for a while at the bar and I order her a glass of champagne. I can't take my eyes off this stunning woman. I can see the outline of her nipple ring, I do love nipple rings me. This girl could be a gift from royal heaven on what could be my very last night of freedom, so as she talks, I slip my last pill in my mouth and swallow it with a swig of champagne. Then some guy walks past and catches her skirt (I say skirt... more like a belt really) on his coat and it rises up above her ass. Fucking NO knickers on! This just may be the best night ever. I've not only climbed to the top of the mountain, but I stayed on and watched the sun set. Keith Baxter: ladybird climber and sunset seeker. I can feel my pills kicking in and the rush coming on as this beautiful creature seduces me. I say seduces me... she's not wearing pants and that's all that's needed to seduce this little stoned duck. If all goes well, my third pill should kick in just about the time she starts kissing me. The music is pumping. I'm feeling unstoppable as we drink more free champagne.

Princess Ladybird was doing most of the talking while I just looked at her nodding my head. To be honest I was probably quite out of it by now, even though I felt I was perfectly fine. I started to fantasise what she's going to be like in bed. Then I notice the handcuffs on her wrist. Fuck me, I'm thinking, this girl is going to destroy me! How much better can it get? I ask her, "What's with the handcuffs?" and then she says,

"Do you really want to find out?"

"Yes, I fucking would, ladybird lady." I'm now rushing from my pills and the bottle of champagne that I've knocked back has set the pace for the evening. When I refer to setting the pace, all that means is I'll remember fuck all in the morning. Soon I'm about to have amazing sex with this stunning honey and claim my rightful crown. This is what being a god must feel like. She leans in and whispers,

"Do you think you can handle them?"

And I'm playing it real cool – after all I'm being seduced by a royal no less, so I said, "Yeah, I can handle them." At the same time, I'm thinking how fucking cool I am. So I lean in and I can feel her warm breath as our lips are almost touching each other's, then I quickly realise I'm getting a hard on, so I lean back so she can't feel it. The bar is really busy now with the naked barmen serving up drinks, and yet no one clocks the heavy petting session going down at the end of the bar with the princess about to kiss her very stoned frog. I don't want her to feel or see my hard on yet, so I lean back a bit more so it's not digging into her.

Luckily there's people sandwiched in around us and that gives me the cover to compose myself.

Then she produces a small key from a chain around her wrist. God she looks so fucking sexy in her outfit. She then slowly lifts up her cuffed wrist and undoes the handcuff with this wicked little smile on her face.

I'm playing it as cool as a cucumber because I'm about to get laid by a princess without knickers.

As I said, the mountain peak is just a short reach away. I'm actually standing on the summit now waiting for the chopper to take me there as we speak.

She then snaps it on my wrist and gently kisses me on the lips. I can feel the tightness of her lipstick as she pulls away.

"They feel alright, these do," I whisper to her in my best sexy-off-my-face voice.

"Good," she whispers, "I'll be back for them later." And then she turns around and walks away through the crowd, lifting her tiny, short leather skirt from the back to reveal her fantastic arse.

Then I got bit confused for a second or two, because as I lost sight of my gorgeous princess walking through the crowd I couldn't work out why I wasn't being dragged along with her, especially now that I'm chained to her. So I pulled on the cuff and then this massive, naked, fat guy with the biggest cock ring I've ever seen turned around and just stared at me. He was butt naked, apart from his big leather boots and a Zorro mask.

I know! A Zorro mask? What the fuck's that going to hide? So I pulled on my handcuffs again and this big fat fucker stood right in my face and then barked at me like a dog.

Now I'm thinking I've just lost my princess, I'm flying off my tits and I'm confused as to why this big naked dude with a cock ring is barking in my face. Time to move on, Keith, I told myself. I try to step away, but I can feel my cuffed wrist pulling. I look down at my wrist and realise in stoned horror that I've been handcuffed to this big fat naked guy. What the fuck's going on here? Where's my fucking sexy Ladybird Princess buggered off to?

So I say to him "I'm Keith, you are?" and then this big naked guy gets right in my face and starts barking at me like a dog. And he doesn't bark quietly, he barks fucking loudly.

"It's all right mate," I said, "Calm down; what's going on then?" and again he just stands there barking in my face, "Have you got the key?" I ask.

Again, lots of loud barking and people are starting to look over our way and I can hear lots of giggling while this massive, hairy, naked man that has a cock ring the size of a dinner plate hanging off his wang just keeps barking at me, and I'm fucking chained up to it. I look down at his wang. Fuck it must have to hurt to have a hole that big driven through the bell. I can see people looking over at it and they all kind of wince a little when they realise how big it is. I don't know anyone here apart from the hosts and now I've been handcuffed to this fat, naked hairy guy.

"Where's the fucking key?" I keep asking him, and all he does is just stands there barking in my face. I'm saying to him, "Will you fucking calm down mate and stop with the loud barking, you're making a right scene. Just give me the fucking key, will you?!"

But all that does is rev him up even more. If he pushed me down and sat on me, it would take a tractor to pull him off me, the guy is enormous. There's roll after roll hanging off him and people at the bar are now starting to give us a bit of a wide birth due to his commotion and his intimidating size. He looks like he hasn't shaved in about a month, with this big, chromed Prince Albert hanging off his stretched dick. I can't believe this, and now I'm really off my chops. Then I notice the tattoos on his arms, one of his tats is of a guy on his knees with a woman digging her boot heel into his back. Then there's another one above that with a man's face covered in a mask with a whip draped over it. Then I click that this big fat naked guy I'm chained to is my Princess Ladybird's slave. And she's fucked off on a walkabout and left me chained to her big man. I soon worked out that he's only allowed to bark and not talk. Big fucking help that is, and he's on my arm and I don't know how unsteady he is mentally.

Christ! I don't even know what breed he's supposed to be.

"Right Keith," I tell myself, "All you've got to do is walk around the party, find your princess and she will produce the key and set you free."

"Okay let's go find your mistress," I say to him, "Where's your trainer at then?"

So off we go naked man and me. We went from room to room squeezing through the throngs of party people, with Princess nowhere to be found. And as I'm leading him about I could sense that people were looking at me as if I'm the naked guys' dominating boyfriend. And I could see they were all looking at his big cock ring: you couldn't miss it flapping about. And I bet they all assumed that I'm into big fat naked men with massive cock rings. And still, every time I tried speaking to him, he just kept on barking and woofing at me. He looked like he was in his mid-forties and hadn't done any physical exercise since his last sports day at preschool. And on top of all that all my pills have kicked in. So much for having great warrior sex with my pant-less ladybird.

I really want to have a dance now as they're playing some really good house music in the ballroom, but now that I'm chained up I can't. We keep on searching the house. There are a lot of people here now. In every room it's pretty much packed and even outside it's becoming rammed. I catch a reflection of myself and Rin Tin Tin in a large mirror. We looked fucking serious chained to each other. He looked so hardcore and I looked like his Barbie bitch wife. We were getting lots of smiles and nods from the hardcore guys known as "The Bears". Bears are normally big men with lots of facial hair and enough body hair you could stuff a mattress with. My naked man was covered in wet body hair, it looked like a mat. And he had his cock and balls shaved, which of course really helped show off his chrome table piece.

Now looking back at it, the other guests probably assumed that we were walking about looking for other like-minded couples. As if there was another likeminded couple there that looked like us.

In the end we headed up into the packed ballroom looking for her. The room was done up like a forest, it was really trippy. The ballroom had been decked out as a forest for the bears to play in, and here I am, handcuffed to the biggest bear of them all. The music was brilliant and I tried dancing as I walked through the dance floor searching for my ladybird, while people kept bumping into naked man. And the room was getting really hot and he was sweating away because he's so big. And as I'm slowly moving through the dance floor searching for my lost princess, I notice that the people dancing were suddenly opening up around us giving us plenty of space. So I start dancing trying my best to look like I fit in while my big hairy naked bear stood there with his big wang out on show panting like a dog. It's only then when I looked back at him, I noticed that naked man was jerking off.

"OH FUCK THIS!!" I said, "Get these fucking cuffs off me now, this has gone way too far you big dirty bear."

Now that was probably my first big mistake of the evening.

Because all that did was make him bark really loud at me, as if little Timmy had just fallen down a well. Loads of people were looking at us. Now it looks like we're having a right old domestic on dance floor. All this horror because I won't let my bow wow have a wank. So I tried walking off but Lassie wasn't having any of it, he was staying put. I'm pilled off my face and the only thing I could do was either stand there and look as if it's my thing to hold his other hand while he wanks or carry on dancing. So I decided to dance, while pretending to myself this is all normal. I occasionally looked up, and I could see lots of people looking at me, as he was really starting to get into himself, and people must have been thinking 'Dude, why don't you and your husband just go get a room?'

And then suddenly the music stops and Naked Bear is standing there with this massive hard on just looking at me. Then the DJ starts making some announcement "Ladies and gentlemen will you please give it up for... the greatest band in the world... THE VILLAGE PEOPLE!"

Then the ballroom crowd went nuts. Darren and Barry had gone and hired a Village People tribute act to do a couple of numbers. My big hairy bear just froze at the sight of The Village People, turns out he's their biggest fan. And here comes his idols (even if they are tribute ones) to perform right in front of him and for some reason he wouldn't move from the centre of the dance floor. And that's where The Village People tribute act were planning on doing their big song and dance routine.

Everyone else had moved away so they could do their show but Naked Bear stood rooted to the spot with his big hard on. He just wouldn't fucking move and now there's these big bright spotlights trained on us.

And then it fucking hit me who Princess Sam was, she was the girl trying on the sexy boots in the shoe shop. I thought she looked familiar!

Then the music starts up and it's a bloody disco track of some kind. And like a deer caught in the headlights I just panicked. I didn't know what to do, so I start dancing as if I'm really into disco while chained to my naked hairy bear who just stood rooted to the spot like a startled moose. And then the song kicks in and of all the songs that they had to do "YMCA." Then the Village People start dancing towards us getting closer and closer while we stood rooted in the middle of the dance floor. I could see The Village People's policemen and the construction worker looking at me really crossly. They were thinking why is this naked man and his wife just standing there? Move out of the fucking way you morons. But we didn't move an inch, naked man just stood firm with me dancing madly away beside him. I could feel all the eyes in the ballroom on us. I didn't want to look up. The Village People were clearly now taking a back seat to our little couples show.

I caught a glimpse of Darren in the crowd looking at us. He must have been thinking 'WOW! Keith loves his Village People along with his obese hairy men with large chromed appendages.'

Then for the band's big finale they sung "In The Navy." I hate that fucking song at the best of times. I can't dance to it it's such a weird song so all I could do was march on the spot like a toy solider. I looked fucking ridiculous. Then the policemen from The Village People danced up to me and put his policemen hat on me and started marching with me. It looked like he had suddenly just realised that I might have special needs so now he's trying to incorporate me into their dance routine as he's clearly unsure how damaged I am.

Everyone's got their phones out and filming us, with me wearing the policeman's leather cap holding hands with my special bear providing all the live entertainment needed for a good fetish party. Then the song ended and the crowd went wild, but not at us – we just stood there like a couple of planks while the band took their bows. They were standing in a circle around us accepting all this long applause while my big naked bear and me stood their looking vacant and bewildered.

Then the policemen came up to me and took back his hat, and then he patted me on the head. Can you fucking believe it? The bastard patted me on the head as if I was his big special boy.

With the band now gone naked bear unfroze himself from the floor and we exited the ballroom. My head was going into shut down mode with all the pills and booze I had ingested. We went into one of the living rooms and sat on a long white couch. Neither bear man or myself spoke or barked a word. For the next few minutes I just remember feeling confused and thinking what the fuck just happened? Meanwhile, Naked Man probably thought 'Well that was fun, I love The Village People, and my new best friend got a pat on the head from the policemen.'

Naked Man was all sweaty. His carpet of black body hair was all soaked and matted; the amount of sweat he can produce! He looked like a gorilla who's just climbed out of a steam room. We looked so hardcore sitting there together no one dared sit on the couch next to us. Most, if not all, of the partygoers had seen us out on the dance floor. It really looked like we were an item now and we probably do this sort of thing to keep our marital relationship fresh.

I have to get out and get some fresh air and as we're walking down a small flight of stairs I trip and bump into some flash git who's coming back up.

He stops looks at me with quite an aggressive tone and says, "Watch where you're fucking walking."

Before I had time to say anything naked guy lent in and growled at him in a really deep voice. The flash git nearly shit himself: you could see proper fear on his face. Last thing you want to be doing is wrestling with a fat naked man with a huge cock ring on a staircase. That's strictly for horror films that is. So, at last maybe my bear has a use. Or maybe he just wants to rape me, the night is young. I've really got to find my warrior princess and get these fucking cuffs off me before Naked Man gets horny again.

I stand at the bar with my bear and order myself a double vodka. It's about two in the morning now. The party is packed and then from nowhere Warrior Princess Ladybird Sam suddenly appears.

"Hello," she said, "Have you been looking after my little pet? I hope he hasn't been any trouble." And then she grabs his left nipple and twists it really hard. I can feel myself wince just watching it. Then she tells him he will be a very sorry slave if he's been naughty. Of course, I could have told Princess Warrior that her pet dog was being disgusting out on the dance floor. And that he wouldn't stop when asked too, and he may have also pissed on my leg in the toilet. But I had had enough: I just wanted this drenched hairy man off me.

"Yes," I said, "he's a bit of a handful," as I hold up my cuffed arm desperate to be released. "If you wouldn't mind Princess, the key please. I thinks it's your turn to take Barkie here out for his walkies." And with that, my wicked sexy warrior princess produced the magic key from her wrist and just like that I was freed. The fucking relief I felt to have him off my arm I can't tell you. He didn't seem too bothered either way.

Looking back, he didn't really seem that bothered that Princess Warrior had even showed up to unlock us.

I think he just liked me and probably thought we shared a love of Village People music. Me and Ladybird chatted a little more, but I was on the double vodkas by this time and as I'm proper pilled, I could sense I was way out of my royal princess warriors league. Shame really as she had no knickers on! She could have any guy she wanted here but I suspect it was a lady's honey pot she wanted and I couldn't compete with that.

Now if Princess had said to me, "You know Keith I'm sick of dry humping beautiful girls all day long, day in, day out. Would you do me the absolute pleasure: bend me over and do me like a little bitch." In my stoned head that's what I wanted my beautiful half naked princess to say. I also heard her say "Please don't make me beg for it Keith, you big old horn dog you. I want you to fuck me like a sex robot on crack, and don't stop telling me all your disgusting sexual requests, I want to hear every last one of them before you cum. Then when you've finished, I'm going to make you the best breakfast you've ever had; remind me again how you take your coffee." Sadly, this script was only happening in my head, as my dream Princess Ladybird walked off taking her gorgeous body with her.

And Naked Bear man?

Well he left with my warrior princess to have his balls kicked and stamped on and maybe have his cock ring rung before he heads back home to the wife and five cats.

Chapter 8

Meanwhile in Munich, a bald white male in his late-forties, slim and well-dressed, boards a plane for the UK. He stows his used but well-packed overnight bag above him, takes up his business class seat and looks straight ahead preferring not to make contact with the person sitting next to him.

He's not a nervous flyer. He's worked out the odds, they seem to be in his favour. Four hours ago, he slit a man's throat from ear to ear. He did it slowly, and with the victim's own carving knife.

He orders an orange juice from one of the cabin crew, he smiles and politely thanks her when she returns with his beverage.

And after he cut his victims throat, he then stood over him calmly watching the life force slowly drain out of him. The victim was a man in his late-thirties called Churro. He has two young children a thirteen-year-old boy and a ten-year-old girl. Breakfast will be the last time they saw their father alive.

He grassed someone important up. And that important someone is sitting in an Italian prison very pissed.

This isn't just any kill. It's been sent out as a warning to all: Don't Grass a Made Man Up. (A made man being someone of high-ranking importance in the mafia.) So, the hit was put out and the man they chose is now sitting quietly sipping his orange juice and browsing through the inflight magazine while eating a bag of salted crisps.

He's known to his employers as Mr. Deacon. His real name is never used because no one knows it. When he cut Churro's throat, he slit long and deep while holding his victim's head back. The panic he would have seen in his victims' eyes would haunt any person.

But Mr. Deacon sleeps well at night. This is not his first murder; there's been many. Mr. Deacon is a hitman and one soon to be on a crash course with Keith Baxter. Not only did he cut Churro's throat wide open he also sliced off his lips to send out the message: Don't Blab.

He then fed them to Churro's cat.

It's a whopping 32 degrees in Munich today as the victim's sticky blood hardens on the warm kitchen floor. Mr. Deacon's been very careful not to step in it. The one thing he always does well is check everything over to make sure there's no trace of him ever being there, and of course to make sure his victim is properly dead.

He doesn't mind watching someone die. It's the peace at the end he finds rewarding. He's the sort of chap who can look at a fresh body and totally disconnect himself from the brutality he's just doled out. As he looks over to the cat sitting by its food bowl, he watches it chew and finish the remains of Churro's bottom lip.

Meanwhile, back in London, the party's in full swing at Darren and Barry's and even without naked bear on my arm no one's game enough to come near me, not after seeing us out on the dance floor giving it our all.

I have to get home and get some sleep. I've got twenty million to liberate in a few hours and I'm coming down fast. As I'm leaving, I catch a glimpse of Darren snogging some young guys face off, but I decided to keep my stoned head down and just slink away. I can see my big smiling lift operator. He's been dismissed from his lift duties and had now been promoted to acting door bitch. He flashes me his huge smile and asked me where my big naked man was. I told him he's having a little nap in the back of my car.

"I'm just going to go and check on him now; make sure he hasn't tangled himself up on his cock ring."

He just smiles as he opens the door for me.

I awake in my London flat with the curtains pulled to preserve the dark even though I knew the sun is up and waiting outside.

It's 11.00AM. I make a coffee with my new espresso machine that I've only just brought and make myself some toast; my coffee tastes a bit shit, stupid machine. Then I check my phone. I know there're messages waiting for me and I know there's going to be one from Jane which there is. It just says, 'Call me,' and there's also one from Belle. It's the same message as always. I'll deliver to her last thing. And there's one from a regular fashion client called Ali, wanting a large drop for a fashion party she's hosting. This has been a very good month. My clients seem to be buying lots more and lots more often.

And there's one message from Darren and Barry which reads:

Hello Keith darling.

Someone looked like they were having a good time last night!

Aren't you the cheeky pony?!

Glad to see you like your men big, strong and hairy.

Was that big chrome cock ring an engagement ring?

Darren & Barry x

PS – There's a group of us going to a club called Fist on the 21st for Maximum Fingers Night.

You and your husband are very welcome to join us darling x

Fucking hell! Why do I have to be the wife? And there's also a photo included. I open it up and it's fucking horridness. It's me and Naked Bear on the dance floor and he's got a hard on. Can it get any fucking worse?

Yes it can! It gets way worse... There's also a second photo of us. This time I'm with Naked Bear dancing with The Village People. And you can see in the photo that me and Naked Bear are the only people on the dance floor. It looks like it could be our wedding photo from our big fat naked bear wedding. You can imagine the confusion taking place when the priest asks for the ring! And then the look of horror on my side of the family when they see where I place it.

I zoom in on Naked Bear's cock ring. Fuck it's big. What's this bear done to himself to get something so serious rammed through his knob?! And he's so fat there's hardly any cock showing because his massive tummy's burying it. There's just this big purple knob poking through with this huge, chromed ring glistening away. That should help make life easy for me in prison if this photo should ever surface. My arse would be spread-eagled on my first trip to the showers. "Now gentlemen," the Warden would say, "Please form an orderly rape queue. Mr.

Baxter's arse will be making its way round your cells soon enough," as the photo of me and Naked Bear gets passed from cell to cell.

I finish my awful coffee and delete the two photos. I bet every bear in London has those photos by now, compliments of Darren & Barry's photo streaming service. They're probably sharing photos of us at this very minute, specially the ones of me dancing while he wanks himself off. They're probably on some specialist site in Iran as we speak, showing the wicked and evil ways of the west. I still can't believe he had a wank and right in the middle of the dance floor while everyone watched us, how fucking hardcore is he? And where was he intending to cum?

And my sexy princess where did she go for all that time? What happens if the party got raided? What happens when the police say: "We have to handcuff you now sir, and in this case it's mostly for our safety."

What am I going to say? "It's okay officer. We've actually brought our own cuffs to save time."

I've done some crazy shit in my life but last night might just take the cake. Can't wait to grow old and tell that story to the grandkids. Most grandpas talk about growing up in the war or how far they had to walk to school with only one shoe on. Or that time they came home really pissed from the social club and took a wee on Grandma while she slept. My stories are going to have the whole family sitting round the fire with their mouths open in utter disbelief. I can see the kids pleading with their mums to please let them stay up so they can listen to Grandpa's old Naked Bear story. The one where he's handcuffed to the big fat cock ringed bear who howled like a wolf. A good time to trot that story out would be just after the Queen's Speech on Christmas Day. Everyone's relaxed and full of dried out turkey. Or in my case, full of champagne, and expensive Japanese single malt. Just as the coffee and mints are being handed round with the cheese board would be the perfect time for me to say, "Hey kids! Did I ever tell you the story about the cock ringed bear?"

I ring Jane.

"Hello. Are you feeling okay?" she asks.

"Yeah I'm fine. Just wanting to see it all go through without any hitches."

"Nothing's going to go wrong," she said, "You're going to do everything right. Joe will arrive at 6.00PM on the dot."

"I fucking hope so," I said, "What's the code I give to the guy in the basement booth then?"

"You just say you're here for the van keys for a Mr. John Galitis. Then you get in the van and go. You should have enough time."

"What do you mean 'I *should* have enough time?'"

"Listen, I incepted an informant's email today at work. As soon as our Russian steps out of the lift on their floor, he's dead. They won't waste a minute talking to him. They know the more time they waste, the more time our Russian has to think. Remember he's ex-KGB. The Greeks will then go and check out the van and it will take about four minutes for the lift to get down to the van. That's how long you have, but remember the van's only going to be a few seconds' walk from the booth."

"Christ, that sounds like I'm really cutting it fine, and all I say is 'I'm here for some keys for John Galitis?'"

"That's it babe, he probably won't even look up."

I fucking love it when she calls me babe.

"So then, what do you feel like for dinner tonight?" I said, trying to sound like I've got my shit together.

"You on top of me on your dining room table," said Jane.

"Well then, I better get a move on then, don't want to get caught in the rush hour traffic, do I? Especially as you're going to all that trouble of laying my dining room table just the way I like it. See you in the evening sometime." And I blow her a kiss and we hang up.

Right then things to do. I write the name John Galitis on a small piece of paper and put in my coat pocket.

I've got three drop offs: one's in a hotel, another is in a trendy cafe, and I'll leave Belle's to last. The best places to do drop offs is in a cafe or hotel lobby. No one expects a guy in a suit to be dealing packets of blow out in the open over coffee first thing in the morning. It's a little weird to think I could be ten million richer in a few hours – and if me and Jane stick together, I will be twenty million richer. That's if I can trust her.

I do my first two drop offs. The first to a city banker called Simon, then the next one which is a ten grand deal to a girl called Rebecca who's a trader. She's about thirty and sounds like she's pretty successful. She tells me she's put some big deal together that's paid off so now she's treating her friends. I like her. She's cool, she's got a really sexy body and yet her face is all ugly like. I know I sound shallow. It's the one part of me that I really dislike about myself. I say the one part. But a fantastic body looks really strange with an ugly head stuck on it. Even her hair looks nice, it's just the face. It's really confusing when you clock her from behind because when she turns around, you're just so disappointed. If she just had her face warts removed it would make a big difference. And maybe if she wore a patch over her wonky eye, I could probably work with that.

Just imagine if she hadn't made it as a successful trader but instead had become a top plastic surgeon.

That would be so weird trusting your surgeon with a face like hers.

I've known her for a good couple of years now. She's what I would call a semi-regular. I only really hear from her when it's a big pay day which is fine by me. We have a cup of coffee and a quick chat. She's rented some big manor house down in Devon for all her friends to party in. Sounds like a good weekend. Hope she doesn't get handcuffed to any big fat naked bears wearing a cock ring. If she does, I'm sure she would handle it. She comes across as a somewhat innovative kind of girl. I'm sure she could pick the lock with her thumbnail or bite through it with her stumpy little teeth.

Then it's off to Fashion Ali for her usual. I had a joint before I left the house to calm me down a bit. And I brought ten pills which I've hidden with my deals of blow all stashed in my car seat. I'm not going back to the flat after tonight just in case it gets turned over by the Old Bill. If they do give my drum a spin, they won't find anything.

Chapter 9

With Ali's drop done, I'm now heading over to Belle's apartment.

I also get a text from Jane which reads: *It's green. 6.00PM*

Fuck, it's really on then! That gives me about an hour and forty. Now my nerves have set in again. It's really going down. In less than two hours I'm either ten million pound richer or I'm dead. I've just got to keep my cool. I'm starting to worry about every little thing now; I know fuck all about Jane. Yes, she has a great body and yes her mind's like a bear trap and just maybe she's the best lay I've ever had. How do I know who she really says she is?! I'm spinning out here. Keep your fucking nerve, Keith, it's going to be a long night. I've got to calm down, I'm starting to act right fucking strange. It's all going to be good; just relax you can fucking do this, it's in the bag.

As I swing into Belle's road, I thank the parking angels as there's a car space right outside her building. I check my surroundings and then check myself into Keith mode and head up to Belle's Apartment. Her butler Vampire Brad greets me at the door.

"Good afternoon, sir," he says.

"Good afternoon Brad," I reply, "How is everything?"

"Everything, sir?" he said. I'm not sure why Brad has to make out everything I say sound like a bloody riddle.

I follow him in as we walk through to the kitchen. Ugggh! There's a sharp pain suddenly shooting through me. As Jeff the bastard monkey shoots out a hand from nowhere and grabs my balls and then gives them a good hard squeeze. The pain in my balls makes both my legs buckle.

Brad the Evil keeps on walking; he doesn't even look back as Jeff calmly walks back to his chair and continues watching TV. I really want to punch that fucking monkey in the mouth, but if I did, he would probably rip my nut sack clean off me.

Imagine telling that wee gem of a story to the grandkids, about the time Granddad had his nuts ripped off him by a monkey for punching it in the face.

Everyone would feel sorry for Jeff of course. Doesn't matter about the poor old drug dealer who suddenly has an unusually high voice. My nuts feel like they're on fire and I know that monkey's laughing at me as I limp behind Brad into the kitchen.

Brad informs me: "Mrs. Belle has gone to the airport, sir, to pick up her guests that have flown in for the weekend. Your envelope, sir."

In turn, I hand him Belle's bag of blow also in envelope. "We should have been posties you and me Brad." There's zero response from Brad. He just looks at me with his dead black eyes.

"Right then," I said as we both stand there in awkward silence looking at each other blankly. I've never really had to look into Brad's eyes before, they're all watery and red looking. I'm wondering if he's sizing me up to snap my neck shove his fangs in and then drink my blood. I'm a little creeped out by Brad if I'm being honest, this is the first time it's just been me and him and it feels a little weird. And what's with him dressing like he's going to a black-tie dinner in the 1950's about? I've never seen him dressed in anything different. He would look way better if he was fitted in a pair of nice sky-blue slacks and a black turtleneck. He looks at least a good two hundred years old. Tall and skinny with long manicured fingernails that would make quick work peeling a boiled egg.

"Mrs. Belle has informed me to ask if you would you like a coffee, sir."

"No thanks Brad. That's very kind of you to offer but I best be on my way, lots to do people to see, you know how it is."

"I wouldn't know, sir. If you will kindly follow me, his bag is all packed."

"Excellent," I said as I put my envelope in my inside pocket and proceed to follow the walking dead. "WOAH! Just a minute. Back up there Bradly. Whose bag is all packed?"

"Why Master Jeffrey's bag, sir."

"And why are you telling me this?" I ask slightly confused. I'm thinking why I would give a fuck if that evil nut crunching monkey has his bag packed? As far as I'm concerned: fucking good. I hope the evil bastard is being sent on a one-way pilgrimage back to Hollywood. Let's see him try and squash Tarzan's nuts on their first day back on set; see where that gets him.

"Why Master Jeffery is going to stay with you sir."

"I'm sorry Brad, have you stopped taking your pills? What are you talking about?"

"Master Jeffery sir, he's packed and ready to accompany you."

"Accompany me where Brad?"

"To wherever it is you're going, sir."

"Alright I'm sorry Brad but you've lost me on this one."

"You promised Mrs. Belle, sir, on your last visit that you would look after Master Jeffery while she has her house guests; Mrs. Belle is relying on your kindness sir."

Then the conversation that me and Belle had comes back to me and I'm like, I thought she was joking.

"Hey Brad, I'm really sorry but I can't look after Jeff tonight. This is really not a good time. I've got some very important stuff I need to take care of tonight; any other time, sure, but no-can-do tonight."

"There's a manual in his suitcase, sir, it has all the instructions on what to, and what not to do for Master Jeffery."

"Yeah about that Brad, as I said, I'm really sorry big dude but that's a no can-do on the monkey front."

"It's important you follow the manual sir," as he walks me to the door, "Master Jeffery responds well to his daily routine."

"Yeah Brad, again I'm really sorry but it's not going to happen. As I said, I've got some very important business to take care of tonight, and by business I don't mean monkey business."

Then Brad opens the front door and then suddenly as if by magic, I'm standing outside Belle's apartment.

With the door shut.

I look down and there's Jeff with his suitcase; what the fuck just happened? How did I get out here and where the fuck did Jeff come from? I start knocking on the door. What the fuck did Brad just do to me? How did I get out here with Jeff? I don't remember walking through the door. I'm just suddenly here and why the fuck won't Brad answer the door? How did Jeff's suitcase get out here?

I look down at Jeff and he looks up at me and smiles or is he just baring his teeth at me?

"No fucking way Jeff are you coming home with me," I tell him, "And especially not on heist night."

I start knocking on the door. "Brad," I yell, "I know you're in there buddy, open up"

If Brad can hear me which I'm sure he can he's making a bloody good job of pretending not to.

"Come on Brad," I yell, "Open the door please! I can't do this tonight." I look down and as I'm knocking so is Jeff.

"Please Brad open the door," my voice now raised, "I'm not leaving Brad until you open this fucking door. You're not getting rid of me Brad," as I knock loudly with my fist, "I know you can hear me in there."

Just as me and Jeff are knocking, the next-door neighbour opens her door with the chain still on its latch. "They're not at home young man," says some little old lady with blue rinsed hair.

"No no! It's okay," I reassure her, "Belle's butler Brad is in there, he can't hear me. He's a bit deaf."

"I don't know who Brad is but you need to leave and come back another time when they're home."

"Listen lady, I'm not leaving until he opens the door."

"If you don't leave now," she says, "I'm phoning for the police."

"You don't need to do that," I tell her, "He's just a bit deaf."

"I'm phoning for the police," she said and shuts her door and locks it.

Fucking nosy old cow. That makes two species I'd like to punch in the face now. Shit. Shit. Shit.

I quickly weigh up my options. I've got wads of cash on me and a shitload of blow stashed in my car seat and to top it off, I've got a monkey in a pinstriped suit carrying a brown leather suitcase. I'm never going to be able to explain that one, so I take my leave with Jeff, and his brown suitcase in hand. Thank Christ my car's parked right outside, I can't start walking around the streets in broad daylight with a monkey on my arm.

For that matter I can't take him home either, I won't make it to the building where the van is by 6.00PM. He's just going to have to stay in the car until I can come back for him, there's nothing else I can do. It should all be over in an hour then he can come back with me to Grangemore.

I get to the car park behind Kokota Street with just under twenty minutes to game time. So, to keep calm I start reading Jeff's manual. I can't remember the last time I even bothered to read a manual but something tells me I should read Jeff's.

It's really weird having Jeff sitting beside me in my car. I'm not sure if he's calm or just really confused. I let him have a look around the back seat and investigate things so he's kept busy. The manual consists of two pages in a red folder with one page being an A4 photo of him sitting in his favourite armchair. And then on page two is Jeff's dietary requirements.

Jeff likes most fresh fruits but not bananas.

You have to be fucking kidding me, a chimp that doesn't like bananas? I thought all monkeys liked bananas.

Isn't that why we have bananas? I'm sure Noah's ark would have had a stash of bananas on board for the 250 species of monkey Noah claimed to have taken.

Don't let him eat strawberries; they give him a runny bottom.

Christ! That sounds like a delightful experience, Jeff with a runny bottom.

Jeff can't drink milk; it bloats him.

I get that one, it bloats me to.

Jeff shouldn't eat nuts; they can make him become very windy.

I tell you what this manual really knows how to sell Jeff.

Jeff has three types of vitamins to take in the morning. Just give one of each to him. He thinks they're sweets.

Before bed, Jeff has a pint of beer to help him relax. Stronger the beer the better, shouldn't need more than one though.

Fuck me, our Jeff doesn't like bananas, yet he loves his beer; what's next? A game of darts?

The bottom of the page says that Jeff will tell me when his nappy is full.

Nappy! No one mentioned any nappies. For Christ sakes, I've got to change his nappies now, I didn't know monkeys wore nappies. The manual says he's got a bag of nappies in his suitcase along with his tooth-brush. What! I didn't know monkeys brushed their teeth. What do they use for a toothbrush in the jungle?

In the mornings Jeff likes Radio 4 and some TV as long as it's not golf. Jeff doesn't like golf.

Jeff doesn't like fucking golf? I feel like I've just stepped into the Planet Of The Apes here. What's wrong with golf? The manual also says that Jeff likes a fresh suit each day and there's three pressed suits in his suitcase. Christ! The bastard's living better than me, and he gets to shit in his pants.

Ten minutes to go until I'm on.

Jeff climbs back into the front seat, he's got all this foam over his big lips and he's dribbling everywhere. I haven't seen him do that before. I didn't know monkeys dribbled like that, it looks very unpleasant when primates start dribbling. I'm pleased that phase of our human evolution bred itself out. It would put you right off if someone's speaking to you and then they start dribbling all over themselves like that.

"You okay Jeff?" I ask. His eyes look really big and saucer-like. "What's with all the foam? You look like you just ate a bar of soap. You'll never get a girlfriend doing that," I tell him. He just keeps looking at me with this weird look on his face. I've never really noticed how big Jeff's eyes are. No wonder it's us that made it as the dominant species.

Eight minutes to go to heist time.

"Well Jeff," I said, "You wait here. I'll be right back for you soon, and you're not to touch anything, especially the radio. I've got it programmed to the stations I like. And if you're a good monkey I'll buy you beer and a banana, or whatever it is you like to eat." I reach down and grab my pills not leaving these little beauties behind, and then I notice something's wrong. I've got my pills, but I can't find my bag of blow. I know I put it in its normal hiding place. I don't need it. I just want to make sure it's safe and well-hidden. I don't want anything to go wrong now.

Then I look over at Jeff who's still looking at me with those huge bulbous eyes of his.

No fucking way. I've just clicked why Jeff is looking at me with those eyes as big as saucers. That's not foam on his lips, that's my fucking blow.

"You bastard monkey!" I yell, "You've eaten all my blow." I look over on the back seat and there sure as fuck is my bag of blow emptied. He's even licked all the crumbs out of it the greedy bastard.

"Jeff you evil monkey, you've just eaten all my blow. There was five hundred pounds worth in that bag; no wonder your eyes look like saucers! You're off your monkey chops!" That explains the dribbling! He's flying. His mouth has so much coke in it that it's stopped working, all it can do now is just try and stay on his face.

Christ what if he ODs? What the fuck do I tell Belle? "Yeah sorry about that Belle! I gave your monkey five hundred quid's worth of blow to play with... which may have, and I stress the words *may have*, caused him to have a stroke which was quickly followed by a massive heart attack. Was it the blow? I guess we'll never know. But don't worry Belle, I made sure he took the whole lot at once, I didn't want him to suffer. You did want me to kill Jeff with a drug overdose didn't you? Or have I misread our little arrangement?"

This could kill Belle, she's an old lady; but to be fair to me, who gives their monkey to their dealer to look after? Still, I don't want to upset Belle. I like her – she's cool. I must have fed her the line somewhere that I was good with animals. I must stop doing that.

I have no idea what to do with a flying monkey – not unless it's a plastic one hanging off the side of my cocktail glass. Keep the patient hydrated, I remember something about that being important. I give him a drink from my water bottle, but it just runs straight back out of his big stoned mouth; fuck Jeff's a right mess.

To be honest though, I've been worse, and he should be safe in the car, he can't really go anywhere, not in his state. If you were to walk past the car and see Jeff, he would just look like some old hairy dude who just happens to foam at the mouth a lot.

There's nothing I can do for him. He's just going have to let it wear off.

"Sorry Jeff, I have to go and steal twenty million now, wish me luck. If I don't go now, I've missed my window. You wait here and enjoy your ride." And with that I jump out of the car, shut the door and go to the boot. I open the boot to get my disguise out and no sooner had I stuck my poor unprotected head in the boot, fucking Jeff leans on the car horn. Of course, I shit myself because I wasn't ready for that and my poor head goes slamming into the inside of my boot and it bloody hurts like hell. I'm trying to rub the sharp pain away with my hand which kinda helps. I swear to God I will slap that fucking monkey as soon as this is over.

I then quickly run around to the car door and move Jeff back into the passenger's seat.

"Jeff, leave the bloody horn alone, will you?! Now just sit down and don't fucking touch anything. I'm about to do a very important robbery. And that sort of shit you just pulled doesn't help." I then shut the car door and go back to put my Elvis wig and Jesus beard on. Just as I put my Elvis wig on the bloody horn goes off again. I look through the back window and sure as eggs, bloody Jeff's leaning on it again. And again I rush around to Jeff and move the stoned fucker back into the passenger seat. I'm starting to get myself into a slight flap now.

"Right, listen up Jeffery boy, you're starting to really piss me off and not only that, you're embarrassing yourself, fucking stop with the bloody horn and stay in your goddam seat, will you!"

And again I shut my car door (I don't slam it I'm trying to stay in control here) and I go around to the boot and again Jeff starts with the bloody horn.

I rush around to the front of the car. "Now listen you stoned fucker, leave the fucking horn alone!"

This time I say it in my very stern voice. Now at the time I didn't know anything about chimps, basically all I knew was what was in Jeff's manual, *How to be a Monkey.* Up until this point he had been quite manageable, but give him a shit load of blow and he just seems to fall apart. Of course, I'd watched David Attenborough and his animal documentaries. But not the episode on chimps taking blow. Apparently, a full-grown chimp can rip a man's face off in one brutal smack. I didn't know this at the time. If I had known that and, bearing in mind Jeff is also fully charged up on blow, I probably would have shut him in the boot rather than taking the chance of him battering me senseless.

As soon as I shut the car door Jeff leans in on the bloody horn again. I don't know how to disable a horn otherwise I would have. And I can't leave him in the car while he plays musical horns, I've got no fucking choice but to take the stoned fucker with me. I open the door, and grab Jeff (and then I turn my head lights off) which fucking Jeff had just turned on.

"Right! You're coming with me matey. Looks like I can't leave you in here, can I? Especially as you have no musical rhythm whatsoever when it comes to playing the car horn."

And with that his hand shoots out and pinches my nuts. OOCH! Fucking Christ! I drop to my knees in pain... That's much, *much* harder than normal. My eyes are filling up with water, my nuts are on fire and now I want to throw up. I slowly get up off my knees, straightening my wig that has slipped down over my face which isn't helping with my vision.

I tell Jeff, in my now suddenly-high voice, "I haven't got fucking time for your shit." And with that I stagger with him around to the boot of the car. "I'm not going to get busted for your stupid shit Jeff, so you better hold onto your shit son. You're about to go on your first major robbery." I straighten my Elvis wig and look down at Jeff. He's so ripped. Jeff can't stop dribbling so there's only one thing for it. He's going to have to wear the Jesus beard. I'm taking a stoned monkey wearing a suit and a fake Jesus beard on my first heist. And all I had in the boot to cover his dumb-arse head was a builder's hard hat so that's what Jeff's going to have to wear.

Then he wants his brown suitcase, so I give into him, anything to shut him up.

Then I put the shoes on. What the fuck's this? They're bloody enormous. This is not going well *and* my nuts still hurt.

Jeff's starting to behave *really* weird now... it must be down to all my coke he's eaten. I grab the fake number plates and slip them down the inside of my jacket. I shut the boot and grab Jeff's hand and make for the basement where the van will be. The big shoes I brought are impossible to walk in. I have to take big strides like a skier or I'll trip myself up in them. Now I look like a circus clown on his day off, out shopping with his monkey.

One thing I quickly notice though is our Jeff suddenly has a spring in his step. The coke has really revitalised him. Just what I needed on my first van robbery is a revitalised monkey. One thing these big shoes have managed to do is take away any spring I might have had. I'm walking with a really long gait and Jeff is having to walk quite quickly to keep up. We arrive at the end of the alley I look both ways and remarkably there's no one on the street.

"Right. Let's do this Jeff." We turn left and make a steady pace for the entrance to the basement.

Suddenly a couple of businessmen walk out of a doorway onto the street but they head the opposite way.

And they don't notice Elvis and his flying monkey.

I'm sweating and my heart is pounding as we walk quickly along the sidewalk. Thank Christ it's only a short walk. I can see the basement entrance coming up and, just as I'm about to turn into it, a white van starts driving out.

I quickly turn around and face me and Jeff towards the wall of the building. The driver doesn't seem to notice us. As the van pulls out and drives away, I edge myself and Jeff up to the basement entrance.

"Righto big boy, this is it," I say, as I ready myself and Jeff for the descent into the last open space I may ever see.

It's just gone 6.00PM as we walk down into the dark. I see the booth with some old guy sitting in it.

There're two white vans parked by the entrance. One facing inwards and one facing outwards. I spot the elevator on the far wall. It's about ten car spaces away from the two vans. I head for the booth which is facing the entrance. The guy in the booth is busy writing something and doesn't bother to look up when I approach him. And because he's quite high up in the booth he can't see Jeff, who's only waist height standing beside me.

"I'm here to pick up the keys for John Galitis," I tell him. I can feel my heart going for it. Without even looking up he swings around on his chair and turns to a large board filled with keys hanging off it. He tells me, "It's the one facing inwards over there on your right." He then hands me a set of keys with a brown cardboard tag with a number plate written on it and on the back of the brown tag are the initials 'J.G.' written in bold red pen. I notice the clock above him reads 6.06PM. I'm running behind time and glance towards the lifts. The doors haven't opened but I'm shitting myself that they soon will. Me and Jeff make a straight line for the van parked near the entrance. I quickly check the number plate on the ticket and it's a match. I then walk to the front of the van and open the passenger door.

"In you go Jeff," I said quietly. I then place the suitcase on the floor under Jeff's feet and shut his door. I'm now really aware that time is ticking on. I grab the fake number plates out and quickly stick one over the front number plate with a hard press of my hands, then I quickly walk around the back of the van and press the other fake plate firmly over the back number plate. My adrenalin is now flooding through my body. It's not excitement I'm feeling, it's sheer terror. I climb inside the van with my big clown shoes which isn't easy and put the keys in the ignition.

I can hardly feel the pedals in these stupid big shoes. I straighten my Elvis wig and remind myself to next time buy a medium sized wig. My head is way too small for a large. I look over my shoulder onto the floor of the van. There's a large pallet on the floor with a green canvas over it. I want to look under it but I haven't got time. I need to get out of here now. Just as I'm about to turn the van key over, out the side of my vision I see the goods lift door open and a large figure suddenly appear.

I turn the key and start the van. Then I hear this bloodcurdling yell coming from the lift, yelling at me.

"HEY YOU!!"

I slam the gears into what I think is reverse, but having not driven a transit before, I've actually slammed it into first, and I ram the bloody thing straight into the concrete wall. It's the big clown shoes I'm wearing. I can't seem to make the clutch work with the gears. I can hear the yelling getting closer so again panicking, I try the gears again and this time manage to find reverse. I skid out of the park and then slam on the brakes. Just as I'm about to slam the gearstick back into first, because I know where that gear is now, the passenger door comes flying open and this mountain of a man starts climbing into the cab. And who is it that's climbing into the cab, raging like an out-of-control bull? It's none other than Terry Royce, Butterfield's righthand butcher fucking attacking me.

It then all goes in slow motion. Royce suddenly realises that there's a large monkey in a suit sitting in the passenger seat. And just for a second Jeff and him just stare at each other in total silence. Royce looks shocked and disabled but only for a couple of seconds; I don't think he even looks at me.

And then Jeff, who is off his face, panics and grabs Royce tightly by the balls just as I plant my foot onto the accelerator.

But then, to steady himself as the van launches forwards, Royce grabs a hold of the glovebox handle which in turn freaks Jeff out and he then doesn't just squeeze them, he gives them a good old fashioned monkey vice grip. Then as the back wheels start squealing in first gear there is this loud high-pitched cry which comes from Royce and his face goes all contorted in searing pain and his eyes open up as big as saucers.

Then as I take off in first gear Royce's big hand is stuck in the glovebox handle. So now he's running beside the van with the door open screaming in pain. With his bloodcurdling scream filling the cab, and with his hand firmly trapped, he couldn't let go. Now Jeff's having a freak out of his own. He's monkey screaming at the top of his lungs while still squeezing Royce's nuts with his bionic full force coke grip.

I've got my mouth wide open and I'm screaming, but there doesn't seem to be any noise coming out of me; you may have heard me if you were a bat or a dog walking by. By this stage it's just fear and panic that take over, so I just put my foot down and as the wheels squeal, Royce lets out this really high-pitched scream and then just as suddenly as the scream started it stopped as if something in him had just gone pop. And just for a split-second Royce looked up completely cross-eyed with his mouth wide open. And that was when I noticed his teeth for the first time. No wonder he never smiles – too many sweets as a kid. He then seemed to lose all power and released his hand from the van's glovebox handle. Lucky for Jeff, at that precise point in time, he also let go of his vice-like grip on Royce's nut sack.

And then just as that all happens, the van door that Royce is holding onto slams into a huge concrete pillar.

Royce's huge body slams into the giant pillar with such force his head goes straight through the door window causing his face to take the full savage impact from the pillar, then the giant of a man falls backwards, collapsing onto the ground in a heap. But as he lands, his massive body gets caught under one of the back wheels of the van. So then, as I'm reversing the van, it jumps over his trunk of a body as if he was a speed hump. Still in a panic, I then slam the gearstick back into first and again drive over his huge body for a second time. The back of these vans have little-to-no suspension so it was kinda bouncing on him.

I'm still trying to work the clutch, but these big clown shoes I'm wearing keep slipping off the bloody pedals. The dinged-up passenger door that's still open then somehow manages to slam itself shut as I plant my big clown shoe down on the accelerator. I then turn the steering wheel straight and launch the van at the ramp with the van's front guard digging into the cement base as I ram it up the steep grade. The van bounces out onto the road with the engine screaming still in first gear. Then I see two men in my side mirror dressed in dark suits running after the van. I straighten the van up and crunch the gearbox into several gears finally finding third gear and with clown shoe down I tear off.

I'm driving for all I'm worth now, Jeff's is holding on to the dashboard for all he's worth and still screaming.

Now London streets are busy at the best of times, so all I'm doing is looking for some empty road. The van and I have no idea where we're going and I'm truly terrified because this wasn't in the plan. The two men are still running behind me as I turn off Kokota Street and barrel down the wrong way down a one-way street.

There's a turning on my left and I screech into it not knowing if it's a dead end or a way out. My Elvis wig has slipped down over my face and it's covering my left eye. Jeff's hard hat is on such a slant he looks drunk. Thankfully the small narrow street that I've turned into isn't a dead end. But in my blind panic I turn left and it takes me back into Kokota Street. And as I tear down the road again the two suits that were chasing me can't believe their luck that I'm now coming back towards them. I clock them with my one good eye and plant my foot down but they're not getting out of my way. I've managed to find fourth gear as the van picks up speed hurtling towards them. They're both standing on Jeff's side when I scream past them knocking one of them with the side mirror. But I could see their faces looked somewhat confused as they watched a monkey in a suit wearing a false beard and sporting a hard hat being driven by Elvis in a white van.

I turn into the little side street again but again my big shoes misread how much power I needed on the pedal and the transit loses its grip and goes into a slide, slamming into a post box on the footpath. The two suits are running down the road after me as I crunch the gears back into first. Now there's a black Mercedes car screaming to a halt beside the two suits as they both jump in and then the black car and the suits takes off in hot pursuit of me. I scream the van around the corner into the same tight narrow street for a second time. Jeff is still screaming and now he's slapping the dashboard with his big monkey hands, which, to a panicked driver being chased down by a bunch of crazy mafia hoods, can be very off-putting.

This time I take the right turn, and this takes me into another narrow street with cars parked up on either side. I race the van down the street, the black Mercedes close behind. Of all the times I've fantasised about being in a car chase, not once in my wildest dreams was I ever driving a shitty old white transit van.

The van is just as horrible and boring on the inside as it is on the outside. It has little-to-no handling ability. Going around a sharp bend at fifty is the same as going round a sharp bend at twenty. And Jeff is sliding all over the seat due to my excellent but highly dangerous driving. The brakes are brutal. It pulls up as you would expect a horse to pull up. Then I take the next right turn. Every time I change gear the van does this launching sequence. Thank Christ for safety belts, which me and Jeff aren't wearing. The black car is sticking with me like glue. I can't seem to shake it. I'm now just driving. There's no destination anymore, no game plan. I can't pull up to the bank with this lot in tow. Of all the fucking things to go wrong, what the fuck was Terry Royce doing there? He must have clocked me even in my Elvis wig, he would have known who I was. What the fuck am I going to do now? I've just driven over mad Terry Royce – twice.

Butterfield is going to hunt me down and slowly take me apart for hurting his favourite gorilla.

I've been driving now for about ten minutes. They can't get past me so I can now set the pace. Only drawback is I can't stop. If I do, they can just climb in the back of the van or walk up along the side of me. The black car is weaving all over the road trying to see a way round me. I know I'm really fucked and I can't outpace them. This is London: it's all slow. They can't phone for backup because the streets are changing all the time depending on which one I turn into.

Then I see a large delivery truck up ahead slowly backing out over the road. It's one of those trucks with a long shipping container on its deck, he's going to take ages shifting that thing around. I've got no choice so I put my clown foot down and floor it. Then it all just suddenly went into slow motion again, everything just slowed down to a real proper slow. And I can see the back of the lorry getting closer and I could even make out the detailing and the artwork on its cream paint work.

And everything went all silent but it was such a beautiful silence. I felt like I was looking down at myself. Strangely, Jeff looked like he was having a good time. And I even had time to question myself as to why I put that hard hat on Jeff. And then all of a sudden I'm back in the room and everything was going breakneck speed again. And then the van flew past the back of the lorry just missing it by a couple of inches just before it blocked the road off. The driver didn't brake – he didn't even see me go around him. I had no idea what was on the other side of him. Thank fuck for me there was nothing coming the other way. It would have been all over if there had been.

Luckily for me the black car was never going to be quick enough to get around the truck. So it had to haul up quick with the truck now blocking the small London back street. I glanced in Jeff's broken side mirror and the driver of the truck wasn't a he, it was a she and she just saved my life. The petrol gage tells me I've got 1/4 of a tank. I hope to fuck it's not faulty. I have no idea where I am as London all looks the same, especially when you're in a panic. I've been driving now for about twenty minutes and I need to get this money offloaded – if indeed there is any money.

I keep driving for about another ten minutes hoping I'm far enough away from the black Mercedes as possible. One saving grace is there's about million white vans in London so I should be able to blend in. Of course, my white van is the only one with a smashed-up passenger door and a stoned monkey sitting in it wearing a hard hat. I pull off into an underground car park and find a park and shut the motor down. Jeff and I sit in the van in a bewildered silence. If this is Jeff's first time on blow then wow... what a wild ride he's having.

Jeff's still got his hard hat on, it's on a slant almost covering one eye but it's still on. I look behind me. There's the pallet on the van floor with the canvas cover tied over it. I have to take a look; I may have been set up here, I have to know.

I wriggle my clown shoes free from the footwell and drag all of me into the back of the van. I regain my composure, undo the canvas cover and under that is a large layer of plastic cling film sealing whatever it is up. There're layers of the shit... I can't make out what's under it which is slightly worrying. I don't carry a knife so I look around for something to cut with. All there is an empty Coca Cola tin. So I bend the can into a basic cutting tool and rather than saw, I have to hack at it. Whoever wrapped this did a good job.

I finally break through the dense layer of what feels like roll upon roll of plastic and I manage to rip a section of it up. And then I couldn't see anything because it was too dark in the van as there's no windows. I open the side door from the inside. The large door slides open about halfway and lets enough fluorescent light from the basement roof to flood in. It looks like money. I pull a wad out and check through it. It looks like fifty-pound notes. I pull another wad out and look through it. This is real money – if it's not someone has gone to a lot of trouble to make it look real. I've never seen so much money, there's so much of it, I sit back for a second just taking it all in.

Then I see a car coming down the basement ramp, so I quickly reach over and slide the door shut.

Right let's get out of here. I climb back over the front seats.

And as I'm doing so I accidentally (and I promise you reader it was an accident) before the animal rights people chime in with, "You mean bastard!" I was trying to get back to my seat when I accidentally kicked Jeff in the side of his head with one of my big shoes. Anyways, he went off and started yelling at the top of his monkey voice, and if I'm being honest, I thought he was being a little over dramatic with it all. And then he starts jumping up and down in his seat, bearing in mind he's still ripped off his tits on blow. And there's no side window in the van and we're in a basement so his screaming is traveling.

Of course, I'm thinking, I can't have a screaming Jeff in the van. Not at this stage of the game. I'm stuck bent halfway over my seat and I'm saying things like "Jeff, I'm sorry it was an accident! Fucking calm down, will you?!"

And then he starts shaking his face the way monkeys do and he's doing this 'HOO HOO HOO' sound at me, whatever the fuck that's supposed to mean. Of course, at the time I didn't know that 'HOO HOO HOO' was monkey talk for, "Kick me again and I'll rip your stupid human face off your stupid head." So I just lie still and wait until Jeff finally stops with the noise but the face shaking continues so I have to wait that out until it finally stops and then he looked quite relaxed after that, but still very stoned.

"Right Daphne," I said, "Now that you've calmed down some, can we please move on and get past this. We've both been through a lot today; I'm just asking that you hold onto your shit just until we get home." I start the van up and slowly drive to the entrance. I've got the bank details on my phone. But I can't get a signal, so I drive to the entrance and back into a park and wait until I get a signal. When I do get a signal, I find I'm about forty minutes away and that was mainly going through back streets. And it's getting dark so it's probably going to be a little bit safer driving now. But then just as I go to drive off, I get this strong waft of shit. It smells really gross. Even with Jeff's window missing it stinks.

Then I click, don't I. Fucking Jeff here has shat himself. That's what the horrible smell is: it's Jeff's fucking bum.

I quickly reverse back into the car space. This can't be happening. I get the manual from Jeff's case.

Where's the page on monkeys shitting themselves? Turns out all the face shaking is Jeff's way of saying take me for a shit now! No wonder he looks so relaxed. He's just done a big old coke shit.

Monkey bottoms feel quite strange to wipe. They're not like a human bottom. I hope all this ass wiping will come in handy for my next pub quiz. If they do a section of questions on monkey butts, then my team might be in with an unfair advantage. I think Jeff's diet could do with a specialist looking at it too, as his shit stinks. I put a new pull up nappy back on him. This is my first venture into the nappy world and for some reason, I just always figured I would learn on a human. I get Jeff dressed again. His eyes are pinned but he's emptied out big time so one less job to do I suppose.

We have to leave and get this twenty million to the bank. It's a bit strange really having twenty million in cash. It sounds amazing when you say it but when you see it stacked up on a cheap wooden pallet in the back of a battered old transit van, it somehow loses some of its shine. I get Jeff back into his seat and I feel a little calmer now knowing that no matter what crap comes my way in life, nothing will be as bad as changing Jeff's filthy nappy.

Me and Jeff make a pact that we will never speak of this unholy nappy changing event ever again. And if he promises to keep it quiet from Belle, then I won't tell her he's a big fat drug pig.

I start the van up, reach down and pick up Jeff's hard hat and put it back on him. He really stands out without it. And I reprogram the sat-nav on my phone again to make double sure I'm going the right way. I'm also worried the Greek mafia are out there looking for me in this shitty van. Then we move off and as I begin to pull the van up to the basement exit, I have a slight panic attack that the black Mercedes will be waiting outside. But if they knew I was in here then they have killed me by now. Then I notice some guy walking with his bags of shopping towards one of the cars and snap myself out of it.

I'm about forty minutes away and I stink of monkey shit. I'm sure I can taste it. It's kinda got a nutty taste to it. The satnav weaves me through London while I scan for any black Mercedes or police cars. I'm back to driving carefully. I'm avoiding the main roads as I'm very aware the passenger's seat window is missing. And even with the hard hat on Jeff's getting looks. It's fucking cold with the window missing so I put the heater on full.

My driving has improved somewhat over the evening. I'm not making the van kangaroo-hop anymore. We continue through the back streets and I'm making good time considering it's a Friday evening. As we're driving, we come up to another white van that's unloading what looks like some band gear. The driver sees me and waves to me that he will only be a minute. They've blocked the road so I politely wait for him to move himself and his speaker cabinets. But as I'm sitting there waiting, Jeff reaches over and starts blasting the vans horn at him. I grab

Jeff's big monkey hand of the horn, "Fucking stop that will you! What the fuck are you doing you dumb arse?!"

It's getting dark so the guy humping the gear out of his van can't really see me, but he's put the cabinet down. And he's just staring at me, then fucking Jeff leans in and does it again.

"Leave it, you fucking bastard!" I yell.

By now, the guy unloading the van (who just happens to be rather big) thinks I'm yelling at him and then he starts walking up to the van looking all angry and full of muscles. And now a car has pulled up behind me so I can't reverse my way out. I'm fucking stuck now. Then Jeff undoes his seatbelt and calmly sits on the passenger's floor well. "Good. Fucking stay down there ya wee prick while I apologise to the man."

After that little scene gets sorted out, no thanks to Jeff, I keep driving in the direction of the bank. I'm tired, thirsty and in fear of my life and at the same time thinking tonight has become a really bad parody of a certain Clint Eastwood movie. Except my Tormenter is called Jeff not Clive or whatever his bloody name was. My phone tells me I'm getting closer as we plot our way through a busy London with people none the wiser that they're being followed by twenty million pound in cash and a drug-fucked monkey in a suit.

Meanwhile across town Jane sits at her desk checking on any police activity in or around Kokota Street.

She knows if Keith goes down, then she will probably be going down right behind him.

'I hope he doesn't fuck this up,' thought Jane. 'I've put in so much to this job and what have I got to show for it? A car that's on HP, a one-bedroom flat that I'm renting because I couldn't afford to buy it and one cheap holiday a year. And then you got Keith, living the high life in his mansion, tax-free. And he's supposed to be one of the bad guys? It's such bullshit that crime doesn't pay. They have the best lawyers, while we have the ones who only just passed the bar. Even if I stayed here another twenty years, I probably wouldn't make a senior promotion. It was only supposed to be a temporary job for a year, then off to Australia for a tan and a glass of white

until they got sick of me and threw me out. If it wasn't for the free gym membership and parking space, I think I would have left and done something with an end in sight eight years ago.'

'And Keith? Well, he's alright. It was just fluke we met. I had no idea that Zoe knew him. It was about three years ago his name was given to us at Customs. It was me and my then partner Rod who checked him out, and to be fair he came back clean. Even his tax records were clean. It was much later on I was looking at a photo of a Russian dealer we had some dealings with and in one of the photos Keith was in the background so I was quietly checking him out when my boss moved me onto another case and no one followed it up. And then I intercepted the message at work about the money being in the van. And then I happened to meet Keith the next day at a pub, so it was all fate really.'

'Do I fancy him? Yeah, he's alright, not sure about the sex swing in his wardrobe. I've had one or two boyfriends who had odd sexual requests, but none of them had a leather swing in them. And you should have seen the box of attachments it came with. I'm telling you one thing; if he thinks he's using them on me, then I hope he can take as good as he can give, and then some.'

Chapter 11

The traffic is really heavy. If that black Mercedes comes up behind me or alongside me, I'm finished.

It's bumper to bumper. I'm at a crawl now and Jeff is getting some funny looks as other drivers slowly crawl past.

My phone tells me the depot is coming up on my left and I'm starting to have a bit of a moment, that this bank thing might all be a set up. I'm thinking, 'Am I going to get busted at the depot? Why would I get busted at the depot?' I'm spinning out a little bit here. I'm overthinking shit.

The corner comes up and I turn in. I'm looking for number 317, but these are all houses on both sides. There's no banks around here. I check the satnav and it's saying I'm here but it's all big houses with gates. I see 313 then 315. I'm hoping like mad that I'm going to see a sign with the word "Bank" on it somewhere.

That doesn't look like it's going to happen around here, I must be in the wrong street, now I'm lost. I'm lost with twenty million sitting in the back of me van. I slowly drive down the street, I see 317 but there's no bank there, just a big house with even bigger gates. I swing in to have a closer look. I'm really starting to get worried here.

And just at that moment as I'm checking my phone, the gates start opening. Now the house owner's nanny is probably on her way out to shoo me away, or worse, call the police. How the hell did I get myself in this situation? But no! It's some guy in a suit who comes out and he's motioning me to drive in and follow him. It looks safer in there than out here, so I drive in and I'm taken down past the side of the house by way of a steep driveway which leads into these large green truck bays numbering from one to four.

The suit walks up to me and says, "We were getting slightly concerned that you weren't coming."

"Is this a bank?" I ask.

"Certainly is," the suit answers, "Just back it into bay three, will you? Right up to the door."

I park the van up and jump out. The suit radios to someone and then suddenly the large bay door behind me raises up and two guys in suits walk up to the back of the van with a large forklift trolley. They open the back doors of my van and slide the trolley into the back. At this point I'm close to crapping myself as this has all suddenly gone very James scary Bond on me. Next thing the pallet comes rolling out of my van with all the money and in through the big green bay door it goes, while one of the suits slams the van's back door shut then turns and follows the pallet. Then the large bay door slowly shuts and all my money is gone. I turned to the suit and asked, "How do you know who I am?"

"Your van registration. We were expecting you some time ago sir."

"Are you Mr. Banknote?" I ask, waiting for him to say, 'You trying to be funny sir?' But no, he is Mr. Banknote and he's anything but funny.

"I won't keep you, sir."

And with that he walks off back to the front gates, so I get back in my van. Jeff's sitting on the van floor which is fine by me as no one's clocked him. Then I drive back up the steep driveway and up to the dude in the suit who's opening the gates and then he motions me through. I didn't know what was going on. It all seemed to take no more than about four minutes from start to finish.

And I'm now twenty million quid lighter and not really sure what's even happened. So, as I'm driving through the gates I stop by the suit and ask, "Do I get a receipt with that?"

The suit just smiles at me and says, "Receipt? Yes, very droll sir, very droll."

And then he walks back into the property as the gates shut behind me and we're done? There was no counting of monies, no stamping of bank books. No one asked me, 'Would I like an account balance?' I thought at the very least I would be sat down with a free coffee and given a free pen. It was all done so quickly. They had my registration so it must be the way things are done. They certainly weren't the chattiest bunch of people I've ever met. Bank tellers are normally quiet, smiley and chatty, and sometimes you do get a free pen. For twenty million you would think at least a free calendar, or a free money box, would have found its way into the back of the van.

As I'm driving, I'm in a bit of shock really and at the same time bloody relieved. All I want to do now is dump this chuck wagon and set it on fire. This van must have so much monkey hair and DNA in it the police labs would just assume a primate nicked it. They're going to be looking for an ape who wears a size thirteen shoe. Which basically means CID will be out looking for Bigfoot.

Right, I need to ditch this van, as it's time for Mr. Transit here to meet his fatal ending. There's a small open carpark up ahead. I can pull in there and then light this shitheap up. I pull in and there's plenty of spaces due to loads of clamping signs over each vacant parking space. If they want to clamp this soon-to-be-torched luxury carriage they're most welcome to it. The car park doesn't have any direct lighting so I can get on with my work undisturbed. I've never set a car or van on fire and I'm a bit worried I'll get caught in the blast. Is there a blast? There's always a blast in the movies. I wish I could talk Jeff into lighting it up.

I don't want to end up as a burn victim, whereas Jeff's old. It's not the same for him. I figure if I stuff my tie down the petrol tank, light the end of it and then run like fuck it should work.

Here I am sitting in a shitty car park with monkey in a suit about to blow up a stolen transit van.

I've got a lovely manor in the country I could be sitting in scoffing red wine and necking some fantastic pills. But no... I've elected to go down the coked-up-monkey-with-the-stolen-van route. I get out of the van and go searching for the petrol cap. There's a petrol cap looking key on the van keys so there must be a petrol cap somewhere on this hay wagon. I find it, now I'm thinking how far do I need to stuff my tie down the tank before I light it? Then in the silence the van horn starts sounding. Fucking Jeff! I run round to the cab, "Fucking stop that!" I yell under my breath. "What the fuck is wrong with you? It's Friday night; people are about getting their fish & chips and you're doing your bloody horn thing again." I reach over and pull him out. "We're going to get caught, you stupid arse monkey." Then I give him quick talking to as to why his species aren't running the planet, mainly because of doing dumb shit like that.

Now remember I did say I don't know a lot about blowing up vans. And for that very reason I can be forgiven for using my lighter as a torch. And it's important to remember here, I was probably a little stressed out at the time. And I'm quite sure there must be others who have made the same mistake before, and I don't mean just the suicide ones. But to have a proper look, the lighter flame may have been a tiny bit too close to the petrol spout. Now I know basic science would probably advise against doing that. I know naked flames and fuel don't really gel. But I never really bothered with all that science stuff at school, the only thing I was interested in was girls and of course, cigarettes, alcohol and drugs. And it didn't need to be in any particular order. Science class to me just meant I could look at more girls than I could in my woodwork class. And playing with the Bunsen burners was far more entertaining than listening to a teacher's insane ramblings. And as I was being so easily distracted in class through no fault of my own, how would I have known about the petrol vapour flame thing? You would think car manufactures would have built some kind of a safety valve into a highly flammable petrol tank by now. If I wasn't so busy being me, I would probably start a campaign to have that safety law introduced.

So there I am in the dark with my tie sticking out of the spout. I didn't know that it had soaked up some of the petrol. And I also don't know that the petrol gauge in the van was broken. So the van may have had more petrol than I really needed for the job.

I figured I would have least a few seconds to get away from the bonfire.

But it was so quick – the flames just engulfed the whole van, and then the whole back end just lifted up off the ground with an almighty explosion and I went flying. I was suddenly looking up at the night sky as I went sailing through the car park in midair. Plus I was also still holding onto Jeff's hand and Jeff in turn was holding onto his suitcase. So they both came sailing along with me.

I must have travelled a good twenty feet when I landed on my arse on the hard asphalt carpark. Take it from me, there's not a lot of give or bounce in hard asphalt. So, as I landed, I'm still holding onto Jeff, and he lands right on top of me. Now I don't wish to sound unkind here, but Jeff really needs to shift a bit of weight. He's a lot heavier than he looks. Less pasta and maybe some salad might help his fat little self. And he landed feet first on top of my stomach. Then as I launched upright from being winded, his leather suitcase came slamming down right into my face.

Jeff was fine of course. I managed to break his fall with my nice soft tummy. And his brown suitcase wasn't scratched or damaged as my face took the full impact of that. Wouldn't want his precious suitcase to land on the unforgiving asphalt, would we? Not when my face can be used as Jeffery's personal catcher's mitt.

By now the van is fully engulfed in brightly coloured flames and thick black smoke. Jeff's still sitting on me and I try to tell him to get the fuck off me but there's not enough air in me to be able to speak yet. Jeff seems happy though, he didn't get hurt. Not even a singed hair and now there's a pretty bonfire for him to look at.

He must be thinking to himself, 'Coke is so much fun.' I push him off me and try to get up. I need to get us out of here before fire engines and police start arriving.

The noise of the explosion alone must have woken people to the fact. I grab Jeff by the hand and put his suitcase in my other hand and start limping away. My suit pants are ripped down one leg, my jacket is all muddy and wet from the carpark landing, and my Elvis wig took most of the fireball and went up like a candle. It's now smouldering by the burning wreck. It certainly doesn't resemble anything Elvis-like now, it's looks more like a hamster that's burst into flames. I've got cuts all over my face, my lip is fat and bleeding along with a great big graze down my leg, and I have no eyebrows. Do you know how weird people look without eyebrows? My hair which is normally combed neatly now looks like I've just gotten out of bed after a heavy night out and to top things off, our Jeff wants to stay and enjoy the bonfire so now I'm having to drag him away like a naughty monkey child.

I look back as I cross the road there's black smoke bellowing out of the burning beast and now there's curious homeowners coming out of their houses to see what all the commotion is. I want to run but I'm in too much pain and then I spot Jeff's hard hat sitting out in the middle of the road. We quickly run into the road and retrieve it. Last thing I need is to leave a crime piece sitting out there for the Old Bill to find. Then we head quickly (I say quickly) along the footpath in the opposite direction of the carpark trying to get us as much distance between me and the burning van. Now it's common knowledge when a chimp walks it kinda looks like it has a limp, well now I've got one too. So now we look like a double act as we waddle along.

I've never had so many hits to my body in one day. I'm really hurting. Meanwhile, our Jeff's still flying from his coke feast.

By all accounts, Jeff lives a quiet life with Belle and Brad and he never leaves the apartment. Belle has a large balcony that wraps its way around her apartment, so he gets plenty of fresh air. But after today he'll either never want to leave the apartment again, or he'll start chasing Belle around the kitchen table trying to nick her blow.

Thank God it's dark now. I can hear the sirens getting closer, but by this time we had limped a safe distance.

I could see a pub on the corner so I know I can't hide in there, not with bloody Jeff in tow. Can you imagine people the next day talking about the geezer in their local with a monkey in a suit? There would be photos and videos of us being streamed over the internet in a matter of minutes. Then coming down the road I spot a black cab. He stops and pulls over to let a punter out at the pub. "Please no one get in," I said to myself. "Come on now don't hang about, start driving towards me." The driver waits for another minute hoping for a fare then he heads down to where I'm standing. I step out from the dark to flag him down. And thankfully he's seen me and starts slowing down Jeff's standing behind me so the driver can't see him yet.

"Hello mate," The driver says but then he sees my battered face and the blood and ripped clothes. But just before he decides to drive off, I stop him.

"Please! Wait! I've been attacked. This is my first time in London. I can pay." Plus I've got Jeff's suitcase in my hand so I probably did look like an unlucky tourist. Luckily the driver feels sorry for me. And tells me to get in. You have no idea the relief when he said the words, "Get in." He reaches behind himself and opens the cab door and as I step in to my getaway car, I hoist Jeff up onto the seat.

"What the fuck's that?" the driver yells, looking back over at Jeff.

"Yea! He's a rescue monkey. It's a tragic story; he's just been rescued from a science lab."

"What, in a fucking suit?" the driver said.

"The suit was the rescue people's idea."

"So why it is wearing a hard hat?" asks the driver.

"So he can blend in," I said.

"Blend in to what?" asks the driver, "A fucking road crew?"

"Just society in general," I said.

I know you're thinking, 'The drivers' not going to believe that shit story.' I don't know if I would either.

But think about it – some geezer with a monkey gets into your cab, why wouldn't it be a liberated lab monkey? Sounds way better than me saying, 'This is Jeff the ball-crusher and the reason he's dribbling is because he's just eaten all my coke.'

"Do you do this for a living then this monkey liberating?" asked the cabbie, "Cause I don't want any trouble with the law."

"It's more of a hobby," I reply, "And no, you're safe; the Old Bill ain't that bothered about liberated monkeys."

"So, where we going then?"

I give him the address of where my car is parked and we head off.

I'm aware there's bound to be police around the area where my car is parked, especially with what's happened to Royce, they will be everywhere. Every animal in London will know what went down. He must have clocked me. He knows my face even with my big Elvis wig on. The cab driver pulls in to let a fire engine past as it races to go put out my burning van. Our driver has his radio on playing old time jazz standards as he takes us through the London streets as me and Jeff sit in stony silence.

I look like shit. I'm filthy dirty. My body feels like I've been hit by a truck; well close enough, I've just been blown up by one. And I've got no eyebrows. And the reality is most of my injures have been caused by a stoned overweight monkey.

And why is Jeff's suit so clean? There's not a mark on it. Jeff's like bloody Teflon; even his face is clean. His little monkey eyes are still pinned though. I wished to fuck mine were. If you were to shine a torch into one of Jeff's eyes, it would be like looking down a railway track going through a long tunnel.

I spot the car park where my car is. "Just up here on the left," I said. As the driver swings in, I pay him off, quickly get Jeff into my car and drive out of the car park.

It's a one-way I'm driving on and it takes me straight through the street where the police will be. They won't be stopping cars if the street is sealed off. But as I start to cross over the road, there's no barrier over the street with a diverted traffic sign flashing. There's no police, no nothing. Everything looks completely normal. There should be some sort of commotion going on. I reversed over a man for Christ' sakes, and then I drove over him again. There was car chase with a monkey dressed as Jesus wearing a hard hat. There should be police and detectives everywhere combing the street looking for clues.

I head for Grangemore. I can't take Jeff to my flat and Butterfield knows where I live so I'm fucked there. He will have his people waiting outside for me and it's only a matter of time before they find me.

Jeff's face just stares ahead as my car headlights find their way through the darkness. He looks so human sitting beside me. I bet he's feeling way better than I'm feeling. As soon as I get to Grangemore, I'll ditch my clothes and burn them in the morning.

I take a look at myself in my rear-view mirror. I look stupid without eyebrows. Jeff still looks like he just stepped out of the salon. There's way less traffic on the country roads and so I lob my clown shoes out the window. One shoe every few miles just in case. I don't know why I waited every few miles. I'm probably spinning out a bit. And Royce isn't going to be looking for my shoes, not when he can have the whole me. What I need is a long line and a stiff drink, followed closely by one more of each. Just let me shut down for a bit and switch off. I need a recharge.

At last I turn onto my road. It's such a good feeling to be coming home to Grangemore. The gates have their welcome lights on for me as I pull in the driveway. I drive down seeing the house in the distance welcoming me home. But this time I continue around to the back of the house where I have a disused garage. With my London car locked safely in the garage, I walk with Jeff and his suitcase to the back door of the property. When I say walk, I'm still limping as my body still feels bruised and broken from my escapades. The house looks so inviting at night. I've installed loads of security lighting, so it looks like someone's at home, and someone is at home... Jane.

Keys in hand, I enter and soak up the warmth of the central heating. I walk Jeff and his suitcase through the kitchen down the long hallway to my favourite room in the house: the lounge. Favourite room, because it has the bar in it. As I open the door there's Jane sitting on the couch nursing a drink.

"It's about time babe. I've been worried sick, and is that what I think it is?"

"Yes Jane, it's a suitcase. But don't worry – I've got more in the loft if you really want one."

"Christ Keith, is that a bloody monkey?"

"Well Jane, you did say you were up for a challenge in the bedroom," while I struggle to lift Jeff onto a bar stool. "Here, this ones on me," I tell him, as I pass a can of lager over to him.

"And what's happened to your suit babe, are you okay? I heard on the wire there was some trouble."

"Well if your wire is connected to the mafia's telephone, then yes we did have some slight trouble," I mutter while pouring myself a scotch.

I reach under the bar and take some cubes of ice from the freezer and drop them in my single malt.

"So, Jane, enough about me how was your day dear?"

"Keith, where did you get the fucking monkey from?! And why is it wearing a suit?"

"The monkey belongs to a good client of mine. It's just for the week-end."

"It's drinking beer Keith? Is that good for it to be doing that?"

"Jane, you're looking at the party-hard monster of all monkeys here. Booze, drugs, ball crunching; all in a day's works for this chubby bad boy. Here! Have a read... It's all in his file," handing it to Jane. She quickly flicks through it.

"Looks more like a manual than a file," she said.

"Manual/file... same thing," I tell her.

"No – they're two very different things Keith. A manual tells you how to work something, where a file is a collection of information on someone or something."

"Yes! That's exactly my point," I said.

"The bank depot was asking where you were Keith! What happened?"

Then an almighty loud beer burp comes out of Jeff as he puts his empty can on the bar.

"Your monkey manual here says he should be put to bed after his beer," said Jane. "I didn't know monkeys drank beer?"

"I don't think he's quite ready to sleep yet," I tell her between sips of my single malt. "Not after all that blow he's had."

"Christ babe, you've been out doing blow with your monkey? What the fuck is wrong with you?"

"He's not my monkey Jane, I'm just looking after him. I didn't know he was going to do five hundred quid's worth of blow in one hit, did I?"

"Why would you want to give a monkey so much blow?" she asks. "Please tell me he's not a client of yours. How does that even work? What are you getting paid in? Bananas?"

"No, Jeff doesn't like bananas, it's all in his file," I tell her.

"It's a manual sweetie," said Jane.

"Listen he's not a client, he just happened to have stolen all my blow that I had in my car."

"He stole your blow," said Jane. "Please tell me you didn't take Bubbles here on the robbery with you."

I don't dare answer that one, so I just said, "His name is Jeffery Bojangles, not Bubbles."

"Oh my God," said Jane, "You actually took that monkey with you, didn't you?"

"I didn't really have any choice in the matter. He kept playing with my horn."

"I don't even want to know what that means Keith. Just tell me what happened when you picked up the van, and who else did you take along with you?"

I could tell Jane was getting well wound up at what had happened and I didn't have the energy to argue back. What I wanted to do was pack my nose full of blow, have a shower and then listen to some music. I got the money to the bank, I got rid of the van... surely I deserve a medal for that at the very least. And yes, there's a monkey sitting at the bar? Jane just hasn't adjusted yet. I'm sure she'll come round.

"Keith, are you listening to me?" she said.

"Of course I'm listening to you. Look there may have been one or two others involved," I said, looking over my glass of scotch. "I only really had a spot of trouble with one person really. The other guys lost me in the car chase."

"You were in a car chase?" asks Jane looking quite worried now.

"Well, more of van chase really, they were the ones that were in the car."

"Who the fuck are they?" asks Jane in an even more bewildered look. "You were just supposed to pick up the van and drive it to the depot and then come home. I thought we had a plan, Keith."

"I know we had a plan Jane, and I, for one, was very committed to our plan. It's just not everyone I ran into was willing to see our plan through the way we intended to. The Greeks clocked me as we were leaving and there were two of them, so they may have seen my face as I was trying to get away. And there was a slight scuffle with one other gentleman who may have been accidentally hurt."

"Would this gentleman that may have got accidentally hurt, have a last name that would fit nicely with Mr. Rolls?"

"The very one," I said.

"Keith! What the fuck did you do to Terry Royce? He's in a coma in hospital."

"I may have accidentally reversed over him in the van," I said while opening Jeff his second can of beer.

"You drove over Terry Royce," said Jane looking really freaked out now.

I just couldn't believe what Keith was telling me. Why would anyone get into a car chase with a monkey? Is he setting me up for some big lads' joke here, and how did he manage to get a monkey into the country?

He must have slipped it in under the radar. And why would you go and run over a London gangster? We never discussed that as part of the plan. All he was supposed do was pick up the keys and drive the money out and deposit it in the bank. Was I supposed to say to him, don't take any monkeys with you? Do I really need to be that specific? Why would anyone with twenty million in the back of their car go out looking to run over one of London's biggest gangsters?

"Twice!" I told her, while putting Jeff's empty can in the bin.

"What..." said Jane in a high voice.

"Twice," I said, "I accidentally drove over him again after the reversing accident."

Jane just looked at me blankly.

"It's all over the police wire that Terry Royce got dumped outside a hospital near dead. Now the latest is he's slipped into a coma and that he's had both of his balls crushed. Why did you do that babe? Of all people... Terry Royce... he's a well know London gangster."

"I know who he is love, his boss and wife score off me."

"Fuck Keith, this is not good. These guys are well dangerous and why his balls? Were you trying to kill him by crushing his balls?"

"No! It wasn't me that did that. The ball crushing was all down to Jeff. All I did was the driving."

"Who the fuck is Jeff?" asks Jane looking more and more bewildered and yet still staying surprisingly together.

"The monkey in the suit drinking my beer."

"You call it Jeff?" asks Jane.

"Well, that's his name Jane. Why? What were you wanting to call him?"

"I'm wanting to call him a fucking cab back to the zoo babe, what are you going to do with him?"

"It's only for the weekend and hey! I did put the monies in the bank, didn't I?" I say as I try to steer the conversation back to some of the good stuff that I did.

"I know you did babe and that's all fine, well done, you're worth ten million but we are not out of the woods yet."

Then I just looked at her for a few moments. I mean her mouth was moving and everything, I think I just stopped listening for a minute. I've had a rough day, I'm fucking sore all over and I need a line and another drink. And I don't want to be the one bragging here, but it was me that just made us twenty million richer. A line of blow, a belt of scotch, and a blowjob, that song's pretty much written itself really. When I tuned back in, she was still off on one. Talk about bloody stamina.

"This Royce thug you drove over is probably going to wake up soon. And once he realises his balls are gone and he now sounds like a ten-year-old boy, he's going to be wondering why you and your stoned monkey here had to leave the party so early. His first meal when he wakes up will be you. Terry Royce is a mental case Keith, he won't stop until he finds you. He's been known to the police since he was seven. We know he's killed people – there's just never been enough evidence to put him away."

"I fucking know Jane. It all went a bit wrong and slightly out of control. And yes, now we're all a bit fucked."

"I'm sorry – I had no idea Royce would be there. Would this Royce or Butterfield know where to find you?" asks Jane.

"Of course they would; they've been to my London address."

"They've been to your house! Christ, how deep are you in with these guys?"

"No, it's not like that. I've had some business dealings with them a long time ago and they score blow off me from time to time... other than that I have nothing to do with them or their empire of shit."

"So this Terry Royce – did he recognise you?"

"I don't know... I had my Elvis wig on and Jeff here was wearing his fake beard."

"You were wearing an Elvis wig? Are you taking the piss? And why would you put a fake beard on a monkey when his face already has a beard?"

Oh my God! I've teamed up with a fucking idiot. Why would anyone put a fake beard over a real beard? And an Elvis wig? Does he think he's Elvis? Christ, how many red flags have I missed here... I'm normally really good at separating the idiots from the regular folk, how the hell have I missed the clues? He's got himself a monkey that he dresses up as Tattoo from Fantasy Island, and then he dresses himself up as Elvis. If he starts humming Hound Dog, I'll bloody swing for him. Did Elvis have a pet monkey? Is that what it's about? I know he had a lot of bodyguards... was one of them a monkey?

I said, "It's all they had in the joke shop, otherwise he was going to have go as a favourite TV character or in a saucy nurse's outfit. But to be fair he did have a hardhat on."

As soon as I mentioned the hardhat I could see by her face, I probably should have left that detail out. I better not mention the changing of his nappy, that could set her off. She's not ready for that yet.

"Listen babe, I don't know what you're talking about. Just tell me: would Royce remember you if he wakes up?"

"I don't know! Maybe. I'm thinking he would remember Jeff."

"Yes babe, if he wakes, he's going to remember Jeff alright, but I'm also thinking his local dealer who was dressed up as Elvis Presley might jog his memory too."

We sit in silence for a moment.

"Look there might be a way out," said Jane, "And it's looking at this point in time as our only option here."

"And what's that option?" I ask, "Go away and live on a remote fully-staffed desert island?"

"Not quite babe. You have to make sure Royce never wakes up."

"What! – You mean kill Royce?"

"Keith, the only thing standing between us and our twenty million is the person who knows you nicked it. And that, my dear, is your man Royce."

"I can't kill anyone," I said, "Especially a mountain of evil like Royce."

"Remember babe, your mountain is in a deep coma so he's not going to be fighting back much is he?"

"I don't remember you using the term 'deep' in your last sentence when you were describing him in a coma."

"Well that's all a coma is babe isn't it? It's just a deep sleep."

"Yeah, I know that," I said, even though I clearly didn't. Then I started zoning out again. It's just been one of those days.

She's got such a great rack our Jane, I've said it before and I'll say it again, her surgeon should get a knighthood for that. I wonder what they look like when she runs in slow motion. I should try and get her to run towards me topless in slow motion. I would have made a great breast surgeon me. Do what you love, as my Nan would say. It's such a shame I didn't follow that path, I wouldn't be one of those doctors who wasn't afraid of making them too big. My motto would have been as long as the patient can still tie her own shoelaces, then she's good to go.

"Keith, are you listening? We've come this far and now Royce is standing in our way. Sooner or later he's going to wake up or die. We can't sit around hoping it's the latter. We have limited choices here."

"The 'we' bit sounds more like me all alone again," I said as I pour myself a belt of vodka.

"Listen babe, I can find out if he's being watched and who's visiting him and whereabouts in the hospital he is. And I know how I can get you in and out without being detected. Just leave all that to me and you will be fine."

"And what about Butterfield?" I asked.

"Don't worry about Butterfield, he won't be going near the hospital. He doesn't want any heat coming down on him. Remember he won't know it's you that ran over Royce or stole the van but he certainly will when Royce wakes up from his slumber."

"And how do I kill him without getting caught?"

"It's easy," says Jane, "You put tape over his mouth and you hold his nose shut. It's very quick and painless. No one will know as long as you don't forget to remove the tape when you leave."

"Really!? It sounds a little bit too easy... what if he wakes up?"

"He's hardly likely to wake up babe you've run over him twice and crushed his balls."

"Why can't I just pull out some plugs and let him die naturally? Then I won't need to suffocate him."

"You have to do it this way, babe, and besides, the staff would suspect something's amiss if there's a big plug from his breathing machine laying on the floor next to him. They're not stupid. If the staff suspect a thing, they would have a guard posted on his door and then we're really screwed."

"Do you think you can you rebuild a man's balls?" I ask.

"Well, you can ask Royce if he wakes up, babe, or better still you could offer him yours in way of compensation. That's if he doesn't rip them from you first and then stick them in a jam-jar as a trophy for his desk."

"Yes, thank you Jane. If we can we move away from the ball ripping and jam jar trophies? This really isn't helping with my confidence here."

"Sorry babe, it's just that we have to move fast; we don't have time on our side. As long as you're dressed in some doctors' scrubs, you should be able to move about the hospital freely."

"Doctors' scrubs? Okay, even if I was to go through with this crazy idea of yours, where would I get doctors' scrubs from?"

"The hospital laundry of course," said Jane, "It's the same for all hospital staff."

"Wouldn't they want some proof of who I am, or can just anyone walk in and ask for scrubs?"

"Listen, I can get your name down on the doctor's roster. I'll take care of all the paperwork and finer details, all you need to do is front up for your scrubs and then that should get you in and out unnoticed. You will be some doctor from some medical agency; they have about fifty doctors turn up for every shift, no questions asked. The only question they may ask you is what size scrubs you want."

"And what's with your monkey, why is it shaking his face at me like that?" asks Jane, "Is he about to kick off?"

"Not quite," I said, "I think he wants the toilet, come on Jeff, there's one through here."

I help Jeff down with his pants and he puts himself on the toilet for a piss. He looks tired, poor monkey.

"So Jeff, when Belle asks you 'How was your weekend with Keith?' You just tell her we watched some old Tarzan movies and ate some buttered popcorn. Don't tell her the bit about eating all my coke and then crushing a man's nuts into soup. She might think I'm a bad influence on you. What a fucking mess this is Jeff: first I'm impersonating a bike courier, then it's a van robber dressed as Elvis, now I'm a playing doctor who's about to murder a patient."

I fix Jeff up and take him back into the lounge where Jane is working on her laptop.

"No news on Royce," she said, "The hospital is still saying he's out for the count. However, our people are saying there's lots happening at the Butterfield residence, lots of comings and goings. The police are treating Royce's hit as a gang retaliation, so they're expecting something to go down in the Butterfield camp. But Butterfield isn't going to make his move yet; he's well aware he's being watched but everyone in his camp will be asking questions. He's going to be thinking it's the Greeks who did this. No one's sure what Butterfield's part in this is yet. Maybe Royce had ambitions above his station and decided to partner up with the Greeks, who knows? Either way it looks like no one's onto us yet, so we still have time, but the clock is ticking."

"Right – better have a shower and clean up I suppose. And that means you're going to have look after Jeff."

"Fuck that," said Jane, "I'm not good with monkeys, and furthermore they stink."

"Not our Jeff," I tell her, "He's been spruced by Brad."

"Who's Brad?" asks Jane.

"Just a vampire I happen to know."

Just then Jeff's head hits the bar surface with a solid thud.

"Christ, has he had a heart attack? It must have been all that coke that's shut him down." I try patting his little bloated monkey face. It's all dry – he really needs a moisturiser. "Jeff! Are you there, little buddy?" I'm starting to panic a little bit now. "Jane do you know mouth to mouth? I think he might need it!"

"Yeah, right Keith, I'm going to start snogging your monkey for your perverted entertainment."

"Jane! He could fucking die! This isn't my monkey. Please Jeffery Bojangles wake up!" I said, as I shake his chubby little face.

Then Jane said, "I think I know why your Mr. Sleepy Head is out for the count." She points to my empty Scotch bottle clamped in Jeff's slumped hand.

"He hasn't drunk my scotch?"

"I'm afraid so," said Jane, "And he's out for the count."

"You fucking bastard monkey! First my coke, now my best bloody scotch!"

I lift him off the stool, lay him on the couch and take off his little jacket and bow tie and undo his belt.

"Do all monkeys snore like that?" asks Jane.

"Only when they take large amounts of my blow and then wash it down with half bottle of my scotch. Fuck this. I'm going to go jump in the shower so I can become a doctor. Care to join me Nurse Jane?"

"If I say yes, your monkey stays down here, right? I'm up for most things but the animal thing I'm drawing the line at."

"On this occasion Jane, I think our Jeff's way too out of it to perform in the bedroom department."

"Good!" she says as she empties her glass of vodka. I slink into my bathroom, undress and get into the shower. I do that so I can watch Jane get undressed, and also I stink so I need to wash my bits before Jane gets in. Must be at least a pint of stale sweat on me. I can see her through the shower doors as the water runs down the glass. She looks so fucking hot as she peels her clothes off. Then as she gets in she notices all my cuts and grazes.

"Christ you have been in the wars babe? Let's see if we can make that all better..." as she goes down on her knees.

"Oh yeah, that's the spot," I tell her. "Right there, I think that's going to make me feel a lot better."

Nothing like a hot shower as your dick gets smoked like a cigar.

Chapter 12

Shower over, and with a satisfied cock, I start getting dressed so I can go and commit a cold-blooded murder in a hospital. Then Jane walks back into the bedroom and suddenly smacks my arse with a belt, and it fucking hurt. There was even a big red mark across my arse from it.

"Christ girl!" I said, "That fucking hurt!"

"What? You can't take a little pat across your arse?" she said.

"Oh, I can fucking take it. Don't you worry about that!" I told her (if I'm being honest reader, I can't) and with that she slapped me right across the arse again but this time the leather belt tip catches me right on the balls. Talk about white lightning? I drop to my knees in searing pain and Jane takes this as me wanting to do some subservient role-play.

"My turn now," she said, and then she just walks up to me and shoves her pussy right in my mouth. Now! If you're thinking, 'Wow!! This is starting to get a little erotic.' Let me assure you, for me, it was anything but erotic. My ball bag felt as it had just been waxed with duct tape and then flicked with a wet towel by someone who's done a masters in wet towel flicking.

I wanted to scream out in pain but her pussy was firmly wedged in my mouth and I'm really trying to play the cool lover here, which isn't easy when your balls are on fire. Then she smacks me across the arse with her fucking belt again, and again it bloody hurts. I bravely didn't say anything I kept on munching but inside I was screaming like a little bitch.

"Will you promise to come and visit me in prison if I get caught?" I ask Jane in-between eating.

"No," she said, and then told me to shut up and keep eating as she's about to cum. Now I do like a lady who can be a bit adventurous but fuck me I think she's working off some anger issues here. WHACK! she hits my sore arse again with the belt, and yes that one really found it's mark. I am now silently screaming in Jane's pussy. What I wouldn't do for a cuddle… I figured the more of Jane's pussy that was stuffed in my mouth, the more muffled my screams would be. Then she comes at my arse with the belt but more in a rat-a-tat-tat style of slapping. Our sex ended with Jane cumming (thank Christ), with my mouth drenched and my balls still busy wiping away their tears. Jane then calmly walks off into the bathroom as I sit on my bed feeling as if I've just been in an erotic bar fight with Motley Crew's Vince Neil. There's scratches and welts all over my back and arse. This isn't me, is it?

I think at one stage she punched me. Christ, she cums big time. She can't really expect me to keep this painful shit up every time she wants to cum. And when I was troffing her out, she slapped me on the back of the head. What the fuck's that about? Who likes being slapped on the back of the head? I'm lucky I don't wear dentures – they would have shot straight up her. I'm going to have to say something when she comes back out of the bathroom. I've never really minded the kinky shit but not this nosebleed kinda shit. I think I'd rather watch than partic-ipate. Then Jane comes back into the bedroom in a sexy skimpy little pair of white knickers that really show off her toned arse. Her body is so toned… there's so much definition in her. Right now she looks like she could run up a mountain. Could she be air brushing herself?

"Everything alright babe?" she said.

"Yeah, all good," I reply, eyes fixed firmly on the pleasure.

"I enjoyed fucking you tonight," she said.

"Yeah, me too. It was excellent," I reply in a nodding-dog kinda way. God, I hate myself at times.

Now reader! Before you go off on one about me being a blow-arse for not saying anything, I don't want her to think I'm some kind of a wimp. And another thing – the more I think about it, the more I'm con-vinced she punched me on my ear. Maybe she's working through some anger issues. I still think I should send her breast surgeon a thank you card and a box of chocolates.

My balls are really tender. I still haven't cum (well, not twice) and my arsc hurts from all her whacking. Then she bends over in front of me to pick up her jeans. WOW! Now ask yourself this reader: how many times will a ten walk into your life? A proper ten mind, not an eight or a nine, I'm talking a proper fully-fledged, out and proud ten. I dull out two lines of blow for myself while Jane gets herself ready.

I'm sure if I take some painkillers, I can probably work with this pain shit she's into. I'm sure over time I can teach my bruised body to build up some sort of tolerance to it all. And who knows... I might enjoy some of it. I say 'might enjoy.' I hope she doesn't start on my face though. I've just had all this dental work done and I don't want to have anything disturbed there.

"Keith, what are you going to do about your drunken monkey?" asks Jane.

"I think you're being a bit harsh on me there dear. I did have a rather stressful day at work. It's nothing a handful of little blue pills can't fix."

"Seriously Keith, what are you going to do with him?"

"Listen," I said, "You stay here in case he wakes up or has a stroke; whichever comes first. But the rule is Jeff can't die from suffocation, especially if it's at your hands. It has to come from Jeff. I'm just nipping into London to commit a murder on a sleeping giant with some gaffer tape while dressed as a doctor. Then when I get back from murdering, I will put Jeffery the pissed to bed. Until then I will put a blanket over him and tuck him in, so he doesn't roll off the couch and crack his evil head open on the coffee table."

"Keith, please be fucking careful."

"Relax Jane, I'm only going to tuck him in."

"I'm serious Keith, you need to be really careful tonight, you can't leave any clues about when it comes to Royce."

"Relax darling. I've got it all covered. I'll be fine; I'm not scared of Royce – he's a fucking clown."

Of course, the reality is I'm shitting myself. Royce is a sleeping generator just waiting to fire back into life. If he wakes up, I'm dead. But for Jane's sake, I'm trying to play it cool and look like I'm in some sort of control.

If only she knew.

Randall the writer thought Jane might have a different take on that one.

You're so right there RandalI. I most certainly do have a different take to what Keith has; he was pacing about, he couldn't sit still. We went over the plan a couple of times and then he did a couple of lines of coke which oddly seemed to calm him down. Most – if not all – people when they take coke, get high, yet when Keith takes it he seems to relax. And the size of each line, I mean Christ, I like my coke just as much as the next girl. But he's got a nose like a bloody trumpet. He chopped out lines without even looking down. Then he rolls this massive spliff and smokes that up in between lines. So, you can see why I'm not exactly relaxed.

He's going off to murder someone whilst off his chops and I've put my pension on the line for this. Out of all the people I had to team up with, I had to pick the only rockstar in town without a band. I wished I just did the job myself now.

One thing's for sure. I wouldn't have taken a bloody monkey in a suit with me. My God, my poor Dad if he found out I'd planned a robbery with a drug dealer and a monkey, it would kill him. He worked so hard as a chartered accountant and now he's having to live with the loss of Mum and then I go and get mixed up with Keith and his monkey. I don't think Dad would believe any of this. Not his little girl who was once head girl at the very best girls' school, where I seemed to do little wrong. Truth is, of course, I did plenty wrong. I just made sure I didn't get caught. Being head girl gave me lots of freedom to leave the school grounds so I could meet boys. When I say boys, they were more men in their late twenties, early thirties. But they had money, cars and decent drugs which for me was free. Sure, I had to fuck them. I never fucked anyone I didn't fancy and besides all the guys my age were either drunk or totally inexperienced, and in my case all three of them were both. At least with the older guys I could get into clubs and not have to pay. I wasn't gold digging; I just didn't have any money. One of the guys I dated for a few months was married and was earning £360,000 a year. And I'd just turned fifteen and he took me to all these weird sex parties where everyone was fucking everyone and no one batted an eyelid. And there's my poor Mum worrying about me while she's slaving away at our local supermarket as a clerk, having no idea her precious daughter was out having foursomes most Saturday nights with guys twice her age. My only worries back then was sneaking back into school at six in the morning without waking any of the nuns. And now look at me. I've teamed a with a dealer whose sidekick is a monkey. And why did he crush a gangster's nuts? And then run over him twice! And still the monster lives...

"Seriously Keith, before you go, what are you going to do about your stoned monkey?" asks a slightly worried Jane.

"As I said, I'll take a blue pill; it normally does the trick. Don't worry darling – I can still perform."

"Keith the monkey has to go. It's too much attention. Next time you go robbing, maybe take along a hamster or an old golden retriever – something a little less obvious than a primate."

"Jane, he's going back to his owner soon. It's not like he's a mate that I go out on the rob with," as I rolled a nice fat joint.

We head upstairs, both of us tired and drained from coming up with mad theories and even madder plans. I brush my teeth and notice how pale I look in the mirror. It's gone well past four in the morning and my joint has taken some of the edge off, but I still look drained of colour. Jane is already in bed asleep when I walk into the bedroom.

As I peek through the curtains out into the dark, I can't see a house light anywhere in the distance. Everyone's tucked up in their beds sound asleep except me. I fall into bed engulfed in the fresh white sheets and large king-sized feathered duvet and then fall into the Land of Nod while cuddling Jane.

Chapter 13

"Wake up Keith! Someone's downstairs; wake up!"

"Go see who it is then," I grumble as I'm woken out of my deep sleep.

"Keith, I can hear someone downstairs."

My bedside clock says 8.14AM. Christ, is that the time already? But she's right; I can hear noises downstairs, so I put on my dressing gown on and head for the door.

"You wait here," I tell her, as she lays all tucked up in the warm bed.

"It's that fucking monkey of yours, isn't it?" she says through muffled sheets.

Fucking Jeff. I'd forgotten about him. I head downstairs to the lounge and walk into Jeff hanging from one of the roof beams by one arm, watching TV. The volume is screaming from the telly as I stumble over to the remote and turn it down. Jeff's got some old channel on that plays old reruns from the fifty and sixties. He's watching some old black and white TV show called 'Mr. Ed, the Talking Horse.'

"It's a bit loud Jeff," I yell, "Can you come down off the fucking roof? It's a bit early for all of this. Come on," I tell him, "Let's take you to the toilet before you shit yourself again."

And straight away he climbs down, just like that. Yet ask him not to press on the car horn and he pretends he doesn't understand. Jeff and I both squeeze into the downstairs toilet and I help him down with his pants. Wish someone would help me with my pants first thing in the mornings. I'm going to have to wait until I'm in the nursing home before I get that sort of preferential treatment. Fat lot of good that's going to be at ninety.

I go to my fridge hoping that all of those fresh vegetables and forest berries that Jeff eats are washed and sitting there all ready for me to dish up to him.

But surprise surprise, as our Cilla would say, there's not! My fridge hasn't seen a vegetable or a berry in it since the day I moved in. It's seen bottles of champagne and vodka and maybe the odd left-over curry but no fruit and veg. There was once a packet of blue vein cheese I discovered on one of the shelves. But that turned out to be an old block of butter. There are some condiments in the door shelf which I once brought for a BBQ a couple of years ago. But none of them have been moved or opened since then.

"So, it's chocolate Pop-Tarts for you this morning my fine furry hungover friend. Hope you also like your coffee black."

I go and get Jeff's suitcase and dress him in a clean suit and shirt. His suits are better than mine. This one he's sporting today is purple with thick black stripes down it. I must ask Belle where he gets his suits made. Imagine when I tell people I have my expensive suits made by my monkey's tailor. Me and Jeff end up sitting in my kitchen together listening to breakfast radio like some old married couple. He must be well hungry as he hoovers up Pop-Tart after Pop-Tart along with his pot of warm coffee. I hear Jane coming down the stairs into the kitchen just as I'm cooking more Pop-Tarts for Jeff. I've only eaten two and I've still managed to get chocolate Pop-Tart on my nice fluffy white dressing gown. Fucking Jeff over there has had about ten Pop-Tarts and he's as clean as a whistle. How does he do that?

"Hello you," I yell out, "I've just given Jeff here a really good hard fuck, and you're up next if you play your cards right, so you might want to lube up."

"Um... No thank you! I am good."

I swing round in fright to find it's not Jane standing there but bloody Hearst the gardener. I didn't hear him come in.

"Umm it's okay. I better get back to the garden now. Wolf will be needing my help. Um I just wanted to say that the fountain will be turned off for a couple of hours so we can clean the leaves and stuff out of it."

And before I could say anything he swung round quickly and bolted for the safety of the kitchen door and as far from the monkey fucker as possible.

Just at that moment Jane walked into the kitchen. "Who was that you were talking to?" she asks.

"Hearst, my gardener! He not only thinks I'm having sex with Jeff, but he also thinks I want to fuck him as well now."

"Why would he think that babe?"

"I told him to lube up and be on standby, I thought it was you."

"Wow. You're out there with your invites aren't you! Is that part of his job description?" asks Jane, "What sort of sites do you advertise on to find these sorts of gardeners?"

Christ! It's only gone 9.00AM thought Jane. It's not enough that takes breakfast with his monkey, now he wants to fuck the gardener.

And answer me this, who the fuck makes suits for monkeys?

I've met a lot of interesting people along the way and never once have I met anyone who makes suits for monkeys. And then asking his gardener to lube up? Can't wait for the shit to hit the fan when his gardener finds out that there're employment tribunals he can speak to. And since when do monkeys drink black coffee? I'm looking at them sitting there and I'm not really sure who's in charge. And please tell me that's not poo on his white dressing gown. And if it is, then whose is it?

"Keith, it's none of my business but you need to set yourself some boundaries with your staff," she said while pouring out a coffee for herself, "I'm thinking they probably find you quite scary."

"Of course, they find me scary; they think I'm having sex with a monkey! Would you want to work for someone who's having sexy times with a primate before breakfast?"

"Look," said Jane, "Let's you and me go out for breakfast and leave the primate to his coffee and space food. I'm really hungry babe."

"Jane I can't leave Jeff alone in my house. He would wreck it. And what happens if someone comes to the door and Jeffery answers it? Anyways, he'll be gone by tonight."

I grab my phone and ring my London neighbour, Religious Brian. I need to know if I've had anybody call.

"All right Brian? Just thought I'd give you a ring and ask if it's possible you could sign for a package for me if you're around."

"A package, what are you expecting? Do you want me to open it to make sure it's not damaged?"

I knew then there hadn't been anyone looking for me. He would have said something straightaway.

Brian would find it impossible not to say something so juicy as someone had called for me.

"No, if you could just sign for it, Brian, that would be great."

"Would you like me to ring you when it arrives?"

"No, just hang onto it for me. That would be great, Brian." Of course, there's no package coming but it's a good way to speak to Religious Brian without arousing suspicion. Last thing I need is Brian getting all spooked.

"Actually, while I've got you Keith, I was wondering would you like to come to a church meeting with me next week? There's going to be a fascinating discussion on what do you really believe. We have a wonderful speaker coming in to talk about why Jesus is so important and why the second coming is imminent. There will be tea and biscuits after. What do say Keith?"

I say, "I'm now driving through a tunnel, Brian, and you're breaking up," then I hang up.

"Any news from your people Jane?" I ask.

"No, they still think it's all gang related, so we're okay there. As long as our Mr. Royce doesn't wake up, then everyone gets to live. And when you go to the hospital tonight you need to sign in under the name of Dr. Wright and if asked, you're working under a Dr. Parks. But don't worry; he's a consultant so he won't even be there."

I go and open the French doors onto the patio. It's a lovely day outside – blue sky, rare for England. It really makes you appreciate the garden stepping out of the house. But then I remember Jeff's in the room.

Last thing I need is him escaping onto the grounds of Grangemore. Oddly enough he doesn't show much interest in the outside world. I think maybe he's seen enough yesterday to put him off that show forever.

The day goes by quickly really. I do a couple of lines when Jane's upstairs, and a couple more when she's in the toilet. And probably a couple more when I was in the toilet.

I fuck Jane later in the day. Twice if I want to brag! The second round was a bit painful if I'm being totally honest.

It really feels like she likes to get out all that pent-up anger during sex. You know what she did to me?

She bit down on my nut sack. How much frustration are you holding in to do that? Now there's a big bite mark across my sack like it's got a zipper. It really fucking hurt – I went cross-eyed. What's wrong with licking and sucking? I've now got bite marks on me. Why would she think I like that? I don't think I've sent out any signals that I like being hurt, have I? I'm going to have to say something before I end up in A&E. Maybe she's confused about my leather swing. Are people with swings supposed to be into pain? I bloody hope not. I find my swing quite relaxing really, especially after sex. Sometimes I have a little sleep in it.

I watch Jeff knock back a couple of beers. He's funny when he drinks beer out of a bottle. He looks so human and he burps way better than I do. So, respect to the monkey for that. I know one thing; he won't shit for a couple of days, not from all my Pop-Tarts he's hoovered up. But when he does blow, his arse is going to go BOOM! He's living pretty much on chocolate Pop-Tarts along with bags of salted peanuts and crisps. And of course, beer. I didn't want him to get all dehydrated. To be honest, if I was being treated like Jeff here, it would be the perfect day out for me; and he doesn't have to shave.

As the evening gets darker, I can feel myself building up for the evening's crescendo. I leave a goodbye kiss on Jane as we pretend this is all normal. Then there's the drive into London that seemed to just happen really. My body was there, but I wasn't. Probably for the best.

I drive to Belle's place first to drop Jeff off. I say thank you to Jeff for saving my life, and for gratitude I stick an E in his mouth as a parting gift which he chews up like a sweetie. In about thirty minutes he's going to be feeling one very chilled out monkey. Brad answered the door looking a little surprised to see me and Jeff standing there. Jeff walks straight in past Brad no hellos or anything, and then suddenly he stops. He then turns around and slowly walks up to me, reaching out to shake my hand. I look at Brad and even he's looking a little shocked.

I slowly extend my hand out in the name of friendship – where's the wildlife camera team when you need one? This may be the most honest communication man has ever had with a monkey. I smile at Jeff knowing finally that we have bridged the friendship and united ourselves as two species. I catch Brad out the corner of my eye, how would he understand what Jeff and I have been through? Brad wasn't there when Jeff and Royce were...

"AGGGGHHHHH!!"

That fucking bastard monkey just squeezed my nuts! The fucking evil bastard he is.

As the pain shoots through my body, I feel like I'm going to throw up, and as I looked at the little prick, I swear to God he winked at me.

Chapter 14

I leave Belle's place in pain and head to the hospital for the shift change. I park the car and I get changed into a pair of fresh scrubs which were given to me by someone in the laundry and uniforms department with no questions asked. I then head for the floor that Jane said Royce should be on. I'm getting the feeling that no one's really in charge as I walk around but they all seem to know what they're supposed to be doing. So that's what I'm doing now. I'm looking like I'm on a medical mission. I look around for anything that will help me to find Royce's room at the nurse's station. Above the desk is a list of patients with their room numbers and there's my man Royce: Room 311.

Finally, I get to put that evil bastard Terry Royce out of his misery for the good of mankind. I figure if I think that I'm doing the world a great favour it might be easier to kill him. It's a massive maze here. No wonder patients die on trollies and never get found for days. My scrubs hat is pulled as low as it will go, hiding my hair. I don't know why I was so paranoid. No one seems even slightly interested in me. I open door after door. Everything looks the same. The next door I open, there's a group of people in their scrubs standing around a bed having some kind of meeting.

"Can I help you?!" says a rather stern voice.

"Ahh I'm looking for room 311," I said.

"Which department?" the stern voice asks in a 'take-charge' kinda way.

"Surgical ward," I said, in my finest of doctor voices.

"This is the surgical ward," said the man belonging to the take-charge voice. Now I'm thinking, 'Who's this wee arsehole?' He's about 5"3, overweight with a red face and a comb over, looking like he could have a heart attack at any moment.

"Your name," he asks.

"Dr Wright," I said, "I'm sorry I must have the wrong room."

"No, you haven't. You're late Dr. Wright." The stern voice said as he looks down at some paperwork on a clipboard. "You should have been here over twenty minutes ago!"

"Ahh yes! Sorry about that," I replied, still wondering how this little prick knows my fake name.

"Well, come in man," he barks, "I haven't got all day."

He then hands some paperwork to a nurse and tells her to take it to the prep department. The nurse says, "Yes Dr. Parks."

Did she just say Parks?

"I think you better walk with me Dr.Wright," said the stern annoyed voice of Dr. Parks. "I'm going to have you assist me this evening."

And I'm thinking... 'Am I in a fucking dream here... assist me? What the fuck does that mean?' Now being a brilliant fake surgeon is one thing. But teaming up to assist a real surgeon is a totally different thing altogether. Maybe assisting him means making him cups of tea or picking up his dry cleaning.

"And let's just hope for the patient's sake you don't mess things up because you chose not to be here on time, Dr. Wright."

"Yes, Dr. Parks," I replied.

We walk into a room and thankfully there's no patient: so far so good, then. We all stand around a long table waiting on the great Dr. Parks to teach with his words of wisdom. Then the great man says, "Bring the patient in."

Christ this is not what I was expecting. I've got to get myself out of here. I start looking around for a way out. Then, I suddenly click where I am.

"Masks on!" says Dr. Parks.

I'm in an operating theatre.

Oh my God. I'm in an operating theatre pretending to be a surgeon, and I haven't even got my first aid certificate. Christ, do we get a patient each? There's only one door out of here.

I can't just walk out, can I? That's going to attract the wrong sort of attention and Parks sounds mad enough to chase me down. I've never even seen an operation or had one, let alone 'assisted' in one. I once clipped a dag off a dog's arse once, but that's as far as my surgical training extends.

Then a nurse came over to me and starts putting rubber gloves on me and my new friend Dr. Parks. I'm shitting myself now. I wonder how much jail time I'll get for impersonating a surgeon in a hospital operating theatre.

This was supposed to be really straightforward. I walk in, find Room 311, commit a murder and leave. I'm now going the full hog and becoming a serial killer and a fake surgeon. Now I'm going to murder someone innocent on the operating table. I'm never going to see day light again. I've gone from a van-driving killer to a murder-surgeon in less than two days.

I'm standing by the table where the patient is going to be placed and while I wait Madman Parks rambles on. I'm rubbing my nervous hands all over the bar of the bottom of the table, not realising that my gloves are meant to stay sterile.

Then four nurses wheel in the patient on a trolley and lift him onto the operating table. The patient's a big old lump. No wonder the NHS is going broke shifting big old lumps like this about. Then Parks starts making announcements about what he's going to do and what's best for the patient. I'm not really listening because I'm looking for an excuse to get myself out of here. What a bloody shit fight this is. I can't believe that I'm even in here. I'm noticing the other doctors are all giving me a wide berth now. They don't want to stand next to Dr. Parks' naughty dog.

Then as I look down at the patient's face, I clock who it is... It's fucking Terry Royce.

Mother of mercy. I am so fucked.

Dr. Parks starts showing the group of doctors (and the one fake doctor) Royce's extensive injuries.

"The police are treating this as an attempted murder due to the many injuries the patient has incurred," says Parks. "His head has suffered serious blunt force trauma, resulting in a comatose state and the impact this has caused to his chest and ribcage will take several surgeries to rectify." Parks then removes the sheet covering Royce's legs. I nearly threw up at that point. What a mess his legs were in. They have these huge tyre marks up his legs and thighs. It looked like I've been trying to do a burnout on his legs when I ran over him. There's no flesh on them. It's all been ripped away. What the fuck have I done?

Then Parks removes a small sheet covering Royce's manhood. Fuck me! Even old man Parks is taken back by the state of that injury. What the fuck did Jeffery do down there? Parks explains all Royce's injuries but my eyes are firmly fixed on Royce's big purple nut sack. It's the size of a coconut. "Now of course whoever did this to him," said Parks while lifting up Royce's purple ballbag, "Is clearly deranged."

I need to get myself out of here. Just then Parks turns to me and says, "Ready then Dr. Wright?"

"What? I mean, yes Dr. Parks," I replied, "I'm ready."

"Okay Dr. Wright," said Parks, "Let's take a closer look here at the patient's scrotum. This is what we will be working on this evening before any infection sets in. There's been some serious trauma on the patient's scrotum. Now what could have been used to inflict such damage is anyone's guess," said Dr. Parks. Of course, I'm thinking, 'I could hazard a good guess.'

Parks is holding Royce's ball bag in his hands while he prods it with some medical instrument.

"Now Dr. Wright, if you can start massaging it so we can reduce the swelling and then I'll make the incision." I'm thinking 'WHAT! Jesus fucking Christ, I'm being asked to massage Royce's big purple coin purse. This has gone way too far now. First, I'm impersonating a surgeon. Now I'm being asked to impersonate a bloody rent boy.' I pick up his black bruised ballbag in my hands. I want to cry out in shame but I know I can't.

I can feel all this liquid sloshing around in it as I move my fingers from top to bottom. I can't believe I'm massaging Royce's nut sack. I want to throw up and faint all at the same time. I can feel all eyes are on my hands as I move the liquid around his bloated sack.

"Don't be afraid to use a little force on it," says Parks, "He's not going to wake up and bite you." I want to say, 'If he wakes up, he's going to do a lot more damage than that.' Then Parks squirts some liquid all over his sack.

"This oil should make it easier to massage, Dr. Wright, make sure you massage all over it now."

Oh, mother of Mary? I've got some explaining to do when I get to heaven. As I slowly massage the oil into his sack. Parks is waffling on about some medical shit as I rub away in shame. I can feel my eyes welling up. I just want to sit down in the corner and have a bloody good cry. The feeling is so disgusting. I can feel all this liquid splashing around in it.

"Can't feel his balls can you doctor?" says Parks while looking at some monitor for a read out.

"No Dr. Parks," I said while swallowing a mouthful of sick.

"Yes, they appear to have been crushed," said Parks. "Give it a good old squeeze Dr. Wright. Don't hold back now. You want to make sure all that liquid is moving about freely and it's important to massage all the lumps out."

"Yes, Dr. Parks," I said. To think my life has down come to this. I've now invented a new form of dogging. No car park needed; just a large room with men dressed up in scrubs.

I keep looking up at Royce as if he's to suddenly wake up and say, 'I'm nearly there Keith, lad. Don't stop.'

"That's it, Dr. Wright," said Parks, "Make sure you get the oil right up to the base and hold his John Thomas out of the way Doctor. You'd think you had never held one before? I'm presuming you were privately educated."

"Yes, Dr. Parks," I reply, as I hold Royce's limp cock in one hand.

"Now hold the man's John Thomas out of harm's way," said Dr. Parks. "Don't what to cut that now do we?" Parks then takes Royce's ballbag in hand and then slices it open over a kidney shaped dish. There's a rush of blood and crushed balls that comes oozing out.

"Okay Dr. Wright," Parks says, "I want you to insert your index finger deep into his sack and then rub your finger all the way round the inside and scrape it all out."

I pick up Royce's ballbag. Deep down I really, really don't want to do this. Everyone's watching me. Bunch of fucking perverts they are. "Well, get a shuffle on Dr. Wright," said Parks, "I have somewhere to be this evening. Get both your fingers in there and have a good old scrape out." "Yes, Dr. Parks," I start to slide my fingers into it and it feels so disgusting. The liquid feels thick like a lukewarm school custard. If Parks asks me to lean over and suck the poison out, I'm giving up medicine.

"That's what's left of this patient's balls," Parks tells the group as holds up the kidney dish full of goo, "Make sure you get it all out now Dr. Wright."

I now have both fingers right in Royce's nut sack having a good old dig around while holding his cock in my other hand. I'm only just holding it together here. Thank God there's a surgical mask hiding my terrified facial expressions. I can feel all the remnants of his crushed balls mincing through my fingers. I scoop out Royce's crushed nuts along with all sorts of other shit.

"Well done Dr. Wright," said Parks, "Make sure we get it all now. Run your fingers all around the rim. Don't want any infection setting in, do we?"

"No Dr. Parks," I replied.

I'm thinking that fucking bastard monkey Jeffery should be the one in here cleaning this horrendous mess up. A nurse hands me another small dish to scrape the last of the offending goo into. My rubber glove is covered in Royce's minced balls and then as if it can't possibly get any worse, his cock which I'm still holding starts getting stiff.

"Don't worry about that," scoffs Parks, "Nothing unusual in that." Christ al-fucking mighty. I've not only cleaned his blackened nut sack out; now I've managed to get the bastard hard.

"Well, that's all we can do for this chap tonight," said Parks, "Tomorrow evening he's due in for more surgery, so let's keep him sedated. Dr. Bassar if you would be good enough to sew the patient's scrotum up. The rest of you may step out and take a break."

We all follow Parks out of the operating theatre. No one's speaking. I think we are all in a bit of shock really. I know I'm questioning myself if I want to continue with medicine. My gloves are covered in Royce's exploded balls as I sit down and take in what just happened. Parks and the other doctors have already stripped out of their nice clean scrubs and left the room. Clean because they didn't do any ball scooping. As I take off my gloves, a piece of Royce's balls flicks off my glove and hits me in the side of my mouth. Great!! Now I'm not only cleaning his balls, I'm now eating the bastard's too. I want to curl up in the corner and die.

I sit in the pre-op room and slowly come to terms with what just happened. I need to get out of here. I'm not ready, or in the mood to go on house rounds with Dr. bloody Parks. I can't kill Royce tonight; not now.

I finally get up and leave. As I travel down the hallway looking for the exit, I see another face walking towards me that I recognise. Must be one of Parks' group looking for me but then I suddenly click who it is. Fuck me! He's not one of my colleagues – it's one of the Greeks that I sped off from on our car chase. I panic but only for a second. Then just as I'm about to turn round and walk quickly away, he stops. And then as we just look at each other, it suddenly dawns on him as well that he knows me.

Within two seconds you can see on his face the look of surprise when he clocks who I am.

"Hey you!" he yells down the corridor, "Wait up." He's not 100 percent sure yet who I am. So, then I turn and walk the other way as fast as I can. I'm fucking shitting myself as I walk quickly down the hallway without looking like I'm running. "Wait up!" he yells again, and as I look around, he's starting to run after me, so with that I too start to run. I can hear him chasing me. He's not yelling anymore.

Now I'm running through a maze of busy corridors and doorways looking for a way to escape. I can hear him getting closer as his footsteps get louder. Now I break into a full sprint. It's my only chance to get away. There are people shouting at him as he knocks over a trolley that someone's pushing. I see no way out except outrunning him, which with my THC filled lungs, isn't going to be easy.

Then I burst through a door which leads onto some stairs which I take three at a time.

I can hear his feet hitting the stairs as we both race to get to the bottom. He yells at me to stop as we spill out onto another corridor. I'm gripped with fear as he's gaining on me as we rush down the long busy hallway. I can hear people yelling at him to stop because he's not doing any weaving, he's just knocking people out of his way like bowling pins. Then I have a stroke of luck as an orderly wheels an empty bed out of a room into the middle of the corridor.

I manage to just get squeeze around it. However, the Greek is less lucky and slams straight into the bed, sending the orderly and the bed sailing into the corridor wall. I can see the Greek is winded as I dart through a door that luckily takes me outside into a garden. But even though I'm ahead of him, I don't know how to get out of the garden. I spy a wall and quickly scale the fence panels which drop me out onto a carpark. As I land on the hard asphalt, I look up and there's the Greek looking down at me from the floor above.

We both freeze for a moment looking at each other then he starts running again, so I do the same. I run across the carpark not knowing where I'm going and I've still got all my hospital gowns on which are flapping in the wind as I run. If anyone's watching it must look like I'm a doctor who's just killed one of his patients (which I tried to) and who is now on the run (which I am) from the authorities, which I always am.

Chapter 15

It's dark as I run down a street leading to God-knows-where. As I look behind me, I can see the Greek climbing over the garden fence and landing in the carpark. I've got some distance on him by now but he's still chasing me and he looks faster and fitter than me. I run down a street with huge office buildings that lay side by side not knowing where it will take me. It's dark; I have no idea what street I've come out onto, so I have no idea where the carpark is with my car. There are no taxis about so I keep running as fast as I can. As I'm running, my phone decides to liberate itself from my top pocket and slams onto the road. There's broken phone everywhere I scramble about on the road trying to retrieve the bits. I pick the bit up that I hope is carrying my SIM card and then keep on running with no way out in sight.

My lungs are bursting with pain due to the mountain of cigarettes and joints that I've consumed over the years.

I haven't run like this since I was at school and even then, I never really mastered it. I see a couple of homeless people in doorway wrapped up in cardboard and blankets, sleeping rough. It's my only chance. I have to hide. I can't outrun him. I dive into the doorway and scurry under a disused blanket with my chest beating like a drum. I'm not so much panting as I'm now gasping for air. My whole chest is burning and my heart feels like it could explode at any given moment.

I really need to join a gym. The only exercise I ever take is walking to the pub and that's from the carpark. If it wasn't for my semi-regular sex sessions, I would probably be in a care home by now.

The other two homeless guys haven't bothered to even look up as I lie there trying desperately to be quiet.

Just at that moment I hear the Greek running towards me, his footsteps getting closer and louder.

But luckily he sprints straight past me at a breakneck speed. He didn't even notice me or my two flat mates in our dirty damp cardboard house. I lie as still as I possibly can, praying and hoping he doesn't return.

I think about running back to the hospital but my chest couldn't handle another fun run.

It starts raining so I pull my dirty old cardboard sheet up over me in case I'm spotted. My body is shaking from all the adrenalin speeding round my body and I'm drenched in sweat. If the Greek returns, I'm dead. I can't outrun him and I probably can't out fight him, not in my buggered condition.

So, I sit there trying to calm my chest down and just put myself in the lap of the Gods for the next hour.

I'm frightened to move from my hiding place they're bound to be out there looking for me. How long do you have when the mafia is looking for you? I lie there with a beating chest and wait for my recovery to happen so I can sneak away.

I must have been there for most of the night when suddenly some lady is trying to wake my two flatmates up.

"Hello," she says. "You okay? Would you like a cup of tea in the van? It's much drier in there."

Confused, I follow the nice lady to her large white van. I also notice the van has some church slogan painted across the side. I'm thinking they must be some religious group out helping the needy. And today is their lucky day: I'm Mr Needy.

In the van is some basic seating and a man serving teas and coffees in cheap horrible white styrofoam cups with a plastic spoon that bear no resemblance to a real spoon.

"Hello mate," the tea maker says, "Step in and get warm." He then hands me a cup of tea – at least I think it's tea. It looks brown and it has a teabag floating in it. "Just checked yourself out have you mate?" the guy serving the tea asks.

"I'm sorry?" I said, not understanding any of it.

"The hospital. You checked yourself out, did you mate?"

Not really understanding what the hell he's on about I then realised I'm still in my hospital clothes.

"Yeah," I tell him, "Just checked myself out I did."

"What's your name mate?" he asks.

"Keith," I said, at the same time suddenly releasing that probably wasn't a good idea telling him my real name.

He then said, "I'm Alex, I'm with the Cider Mission. I haven't seen you round here before Keith."

"No," I tell him, "I'm new around here."

"So how long have you been rough sleeping Keith?" he asks with a caring voice that only the wounded use.

Of course, I'm thinking he's one of those fucking do-gooders that goes around helping the homeless. It's a shame he doesn't practice the art of making a decent cup of tea; that might help the homeless. I would have thought being homeless would be difficult enough lifestyle choice without some do-gooder making you a shitty cup of tea with a plastic straw for a spoon.

"So, where you from Keith?"

I know he's fishing so I just say, "All over London really."

"Have you been rough sleeping long?" he says with his kind, helping, fishing voice.

"About five years," I tell him; I've got Alex clocked. There's no mystery. He a nice guy, he's just a soft touch, you come across them every now and then. They just seem a little bit brittle; they get taken advantage of and get bullied by bullies who can spot a victim playing the victim a mile away. But since I'm in a bit of a crisis here, I'm going have to rely on Alex to show me his full potential here in getting me what I want.

"Would you like to come back to the Cider Mission with us Keith? It's much warmer there and you can just hang out if you like; no pressure."

The Cider Mission, whatever that means, sounds like my safe passage out of here.

"Yeah, Alex that might be a good idea. It does get a bit cold and damp out here," at the same time pretending to be warmed by his milky white shitty tea.

"Well that's settled then, you can come back to the mission and have a warm bed for the night."

BED? Did he just say bed?! Fuck me! I'm not staying in some flea-infested hostel for homeless people. I only want to use this twat to get me somewhere safe.

When we finally arrive at Alex's Cider Mission, I'm feeling slightly wrecked from pulling a heavy shift on the wards. We walk into the building which looks about six floors high. I'm noticing there are a lot of homeless people at Alex's Mission – so many in fact, it looks like a homeless town. We walk into a dining room where there's about a two hundred homeless people having dinner at various tables. Me and Alex get served by somebody who I'll never see again.

"How's your dinner?" says Alex looking up from another table. "I can book you in after breakfast if you like?"

I'm looking around me and I'm thinking fuck! I'm being booked in? Jesus fucking Christ! Do I want to hide out this much? Then some old boy sits at my table. He has no teeth and a bottle of cider hidden in the inside of his old canvas coat. He might be wearing a hat but then again it might be his hair, I'm not really sure.

"All right," he grunts as he starts to hoover up his dinner. I'm amazed how quickly they can eat here. From what I've seen so far I don't think any of them have any teeth. It's like sitting down to a meal with a bunch of snapping turtles. And they all seem to be able to drink entire mugs of boiling hot tea in two to three gulps.

"Yea I'm good," I said, "And you?"

"They've cut some of me sick payments," he starts telling me, "The fuckers. I'm only getting hundred nighty seven a week now."

"What were you getting before?" I asked, trying to be polite.

"Two hundred and forty-seven pounds," he said while eating a whole fried egg in one go. He didn't even chew it; he just ate it like bird. He then starts pouring beans down his throat with his spoon. Again: there's no chewing. His beard looks like a Heinz advert. How many times a day does someone choke out in here? Now he's just eaten a half sausage in one go. The man would be lethal swallowing a sword.

I'm now thinking maybe I could lead my double life from in here, no police would suspect a homeless guy dealing sacks of blow. My street-smart qualities have all kicked in now. I could hide out here, I've got enough cash, so no problems there. I already like the food and I'm right up for taking full advantage of smiley fragile Alex. One of the staff is walking round with a basket of apples offering them about. He comes to the table we're at and offers one to my new friend who's just swallowed another sausage whole.

"Would you like an apple?" the staff member asks.

"No I fucking wouldn't. You can shove your shitty apple up your arse. Now piss off!" he says in-between large gulps of his boiling hot tea.

The staff member unfazed turns to me and asks, "Would you like an apple?" I look at his little face. I can't help myself.

"I would love an apple," I tell him, "I'll save it for later." Then I place the apple in front of me on the table.

If I intend to fit in here, then it looks like the unwashed feral look seems to be what everyone's going for this season. If I'm to stay, I'm going to need an unkempt beard to keep beans and scrambled eggs in and a Burt & Ernie Sesame Street hair do.

When was the last time any of these guys saw a bar of soap? No one seems to talk they just have a series of grunt noises they make at each other. Have I got to learn a whole new language in grunts? Christ, I feel I've only just mastered bloody English. It's like they're a lost tribe and the Cider Mission is the only place they seemed to have flourished in. I finish my meal and thank the chef who looks up surprised that someone can speak without grunting.

"That's alright," he said, to a madman standing in front of him, still wearing his ripped hospital gowns.

After dinner, Alex takes me through to a barren looking office to book me in, whatever 'booking in' means. He has a series of questions for me, and I answer each one with a completely made-up story. He then offers me a doctor that can help me reduce my dependence with my made-up drug and alcohol problem.

Hell yes! I'm thinking the more I listen to Alex the more sense he's making. Maybe I *should* see a doctor for some free drugs. I know exactly what to ask the doctor for. And it sounds like I don't have to bother trying to convince him either. Free food, free drugs, full beards of beans this place is starting to grow on me. I'm then shown around the rest of the building which looks fucking huge.

"There's over three hundred men living here at the Cider Mission," Alex tells me, "You can come and go whenever you please. Would you like an apple Keith?" he says as he offers me one from a bowl on the desk. "That's very kind of you, Alex. I'll save that for later," and I put it my pocket next to my other apple.

"All we ask is that you attend a key working session once a month,"

"Yeah, fine by me," I say, "I don't mind a bit of metal work." I'm thinking cool, metalwork's the one subject I didn't fall asleep in.

I'm next introduced to Helen who is to be my key worker. Again, I'm still not sure why I'm going to be needing all this help with my keys. It's certainly sounds like I'm going to have a lot a trouble locking and unlocking things. The way Mission Alex is explaining it sounds like I get my own staff member as long as I'm living here. Why do homeless people need their own PA? It doesn't look like any of them work. Why will I need a PA? Helen informs me in quiet and caring voice that she's going to finish booking me in.

I follow Helen down a hallway to an office that's looks like it can't decide if it's a waiting room or an office.

"Would you like an apple, Keith?"

"Yes, I would, thank you Helen," I replied, "That's very kind of you."

Everywhere I look there's an apple logo. The Cider Mission and their devotees must eat one a day because somewhere in the Bible it mentions apples with Adam and Eve. And the inventor of this strange cider religion believes God is sending him messages through the apple. Helen starts telling me I can spend up to two years here until I feel I'm ready to live semi-independent again. I want to say: "Imagine, me living semi-independent; gosh! Do you think little old me can do it Helen? Really?"

But instead, I tell Helen that my goal is to one day get myself a little one-bedroom flat somewhere in West London. Helen liked hearing me say that. I could tell she could see a wee glimmer of hope in poor me. Helen and me sit in front of a small desk with an elderly computer that is taking up way too much space.

And then she starts telling me what her role will be while I enjoy my stay here at the Cider Mission.

"Is there anyone we can contact in case of an emergency Keith?" fragile Helen asks.

"There's just me," I said, then I pause. "I'm all that's left. I was adopted and both my adopted folks were killed in a car accident on Christmas day when I was fourteen. Because of that, I started running away and getting into trouble with the police. I didn't have anyone I could turn to for support. That's why I turned to drugs and alcohol to numb the pain. Do you think the doctor could help me with cutting down on my drug and alcohol use Helen? I really want to stop."

"I'm sure he can Keith, he's very good. Have you ever been prescribed methadone before Keith?"

Methadone? I'm thinking they're going to give me Methadone? Fuck me; I know how strong that shit is. Me and a mate nicked some of that shit off a smackhead once and necked it. We couldn't get up off the floor.

And now my lovely Helen's going to get me some prescribed, all legal like. I'm not even thinking about the Greeks now; I'm going to get proper off my face on prescription drugs.

"And maybe something to help me sleep would be good Helen. Do you think that's something the doctor could help me with?"

"I'm sure he can," said Helen, "If you have trouble explaining yourself Keith, I can come with you and then I can fast track your prescriptions if you like."

"Yes, that would be really helpful if you could do that. I can get a bit tongue-tied when I get nervous."

"There's nothing to be nervous about Keith, I'll sort it out for you."

I tell her the story of when I was stolen at sixteen off the streets and sold into a family of travellers as a slave.

I was in all the papers when they found me. It had taken me almost two years to escape from my evil captives. Even now whenever I see a white van, I have this compulsion to smoke a foil. I still have the scars where I was whipped with an electrical cord just for singing happy birthday to myself. She tells me how terrible it must have been as she makes a doctor's appointment for me that evening.

"Wow that's quick," I tell her. "You can get me into a doctor that quick?"

"Well here at the Cider Mission we can get clients fast tracked," then she smiles her big helpful smile at me.

The doctor's surgery is only a few doors down with the off-license placed conveniently next door. We quickly make our way into the waiting room and that's my first insight to how fucked the NHS is. Since being a dealer, I've always been able to afford to go private so this comes as a bit of a shock seeing this. There must be at least a hundred people in the waiting room which is the size of a small carpark.

There's every poor person from every conceivable background sitting here all waiting to see a doctor.

Helen goes up to the receptionist and then after a minute comes back and sits beside me.

"Won't be long," she said.

"Won't be long?" I said looking round, "There's at least a hundred people in here; this is going to take all night."

"No, it won't," she said smiling.

And she was right. Within five minutes, my name was called.

"How did you pull that off?" I asked my Helen. She explained to me that when they bring over a client, they tend to walk out in a huff if they have to wait for anything like the general public is expected to. So, they fast-track us. I'm thinking maybe I should get myself on the waiting list for a disabled parking permit especially now that I'm classed as a pissed stoned fucker.

And within fifteen minutes, we've seen the doc and picked up my prescription. Helen then takes me back to the hostel and to my room. Then she hands me my bag of drugs so she can go through them with me.

We empty the bag on my bed in my small room. Fuck me, the amount of drugs I was given is staggering.

I've never been given so many pills... well I have, but not all for me. And Helen knows her drugs as she takes me through my party bag. She knew what all the pills did and how often I need to take them and how often I needed to come to reception for more; (*more* - how hard am I expected to party here?!)

My first outing with my drug bag I was given thirteen pills in a series of small plastic pill cups which I necked with a fresh can of beer that I picked up from the offy on our way back from the doctors. Helen then tells me my next medication will be before breakfast and then another lot after breakfast. And then she offers me an apple.

"It's a wee bit early for me," I tell her, "I'll save it for later," and I put it with the others. Then I'm told I get my methadone.

I know, methadone, I can't believe it. I'm really going to light up when that happens.

It was now late evening and it felt like I had started to get the hang of this partying hard thing as I necked my third can. I could feel the stone from my new pills as well as my refreshing beers. By 12.00PM I was on my way to being well bladdered. The pills mixed with my beers were a lot stronger than I had anticipated and by 1 o'clock I was shouting at the weatherman on the telly. Why has no one ever mentioned the Cider Mission to me before? Why the fuck aren't England's most wanted hanging out in here? It's all free.

It's very weird walking around in here. From the outside it looks like an ordinary old office building.

Yet inside there are hundreds of people living here, it's kinda looks like an old World War One military hospital. Everyone I pass in the busy hallways looks like they have been affected by some form of shell shock. I haven't seen much drugs around yet, it's all booze. I know that they are about. I saw one or two who use in the dining room earlier on. And they're not here now so they must be out nicking to feed their habits. I'll keep well clear of them lot. Remember you can't trust a junkie, especially if I'm in this wasted condition. But first things first, let's have some of that lovely methadone. I take five capfuls which I figured must be enough to start the process off, and it was.

Wow... This is fucking lovely. I relax in my chair dribbling and having a lovely time going in and out of the Land of Nod. It only takes a few minutes for the methadone to settle in properly. I decide to take a little stoned walk around and see who else is about to party with. I'm now floating about the random hallways hammered out of my head.

There is a lot of noise in a place like this, mainly people shouting, and everyone in here appears to be not only half-pissed but partially deaf. I saddle up in one of the TV rooms which is just a room full of pissed men and a TV. I relax into my wing backed chair while sucking back a beer. Every now and then someone starts yelling at the TV for whatever reason and then one of the staff members comes running in to see who's kicking off. Sometimes my Helen comes in to calm things down, bless her. Each time she does I study her for any weakness. Helen's the type of girl who needs to keep busy. Otherwise, I bet she gets lots of voices in her head bothering her. Then those voices might go from a whispering to a screaming. So best she keeps busy I suppose.

Jane must be wondering what the fuck's happened to me. I must ring her later and tell her the good news that I've started a new chapter in my life. As from now on, I'm a homeless person. Yes! My descent from a promising young surgeon to a homeless drug addict in less than a day is quite remarkable really, even for me.

I'll give Jane a ring tomorrow after I've had breakfast. It's now 4.00PM, I stretch out pissed and stoned and fall asleep. And fuck me, did I sleep! Right up until 8.30AM.

And that's because I woke to the sound of a rubbish truck picking up bins from outside my window. I'm going to have to let my Helen know about this, I'm a sensitive soul. I can't have that sort of noise going on outside my window not at this ungodly hour.

Then there's a knock at the door and it's some staff member offering me an apple.

I take it, as it's just way too early, and I say thank you and then put it on a shelf with the others. I feel quite good this morning. My head still feels a little bit fuzzy but I'm looking forward to breakfast and some fine conversation.

Across the hall is a shower which smells just like the prison my brother is in. I'm quite hungry as I head down for breakfast. But as I'm walking through reception a staff member collars me reminding me to come with him to the meds office. I'm told to go and line up with the other crazy-eyed people for a fresh batch of pills. There's are about ten people waiting outside the meds office as I join the queue. They have their very own meds office? I want a meds office at Grangemore.

The staff already have the pills lined up in these little paper cups for all the party-hard crew. I get talking to some guy in the queue who is wearing a crash helmet. He looks pretty wasted and he's called Dutch. I've never met anyone called Dutch before. And what's with the fucking helmet? He looks like he's about to go out for a drive in Herbie. As it turns out, Dutch finds alcohol very moorish and when he drinks he falls over and cracks his head open. Fuck me... What does that say about your level of drinking when you're having to wear a bloody crash helmet?! But luckily for Dutch he can stop anytime he wants, so he tells me.

"I'm sure you can," I tell him.

Now I wasn't intending to take all my pills this morning as I'm still feeling quite pissed from my first hit that I had. And coupled with the fact that I have no idea what the pills are that I'm taking and I've still got loads more methadone to knock back yet. I should take it easy.

But the pills are good, don't get me wrong, it might just be a good idea to slow it down a little bit. But the staff member is checking that we're all taking our pills (just like the doctor ordered) so I have to neck the bloody lot don't I. So, from there, I follow the herd of beards that are coming out of their rooms for their morning migration down to the dining hall, so I happily tag along and migrate with them. It's the same counter as for dinner except it's full of breakfast dishes now. I watch bearded men hoover up their food like bearded birds which is probably a look into the future. And by the time I'm heading back up the stairs I can feel my pills kicking in.

I head back up through reception with a full tummy; did I mention how lovely my breakfast was? I haven't had breakfast like that since I was a kid. As I'm wandering through, one of the staff stops me and introduces herself as Amalie. She looks about twenty-five, rather cute but sadly I don't think she's a Helen.

"Hello Keith, I've got your meds here for you to take."

"Why Amalie you darling girl you! For me? You shouldn't have. I must say I'm very impressed with the way staff here dish out the pills."

You also see bowls of green apples dotted about the Cider Mission, except they're not real apples, they're made out of foam. They look real but I'm told by Dutch they're not. When the clients get pissed up and angry which is often, they tend to throw the apples at the staff. You can imagine when some pissed up fucker gets angry, bats off a foam apple at a staff member's face, not knowing it's fake. And then seeing the staff member not even flinch as it bounces off their head? I retire to my room feeling full of pills and breakfast.

Now if you haven't had methadone before, it can come across as well fucking strong. If you're an addict, 70ml wouldn't hold you; it wouldn't even touch the sides. But I'm not an addict so I decide to stick to my five capfuls. But because I'm really quite stoned I accidentally picked up the bottle and drink another 5 capfuls.

As soon as I realised I had drunk it all, I knew I had to just stay calm and hold on to the floor.

Within seconds I could feel this lovely warm cloak of loveliness crawl over me.

Within two minutes I'm fucked. I can't seem to get out of my chair. My legs have walked off and left me. I wouldn't mind a sip of my cider but I can't get my hand to raise the can to my mouth. Even if I could get it to my mouth that isn't working either. I'm dribbling like a two-year-old. Every now and then I wake up; but I have no idea how long I've been out for. I wouldn't mind going for a piss but that's clearly not going to happen in my mashed-up state. I end up sitting in my chair for over an hour. Fucking lovely it was. I thought I had only been sitting there for about ten minutes. I don't think I've even moved my head.

I can hear radios being played next door and sometimes I can hear voices but I'm not sure if they're the ones in my head or if they're ones that are just passing down the hallway. My body feels like I've just been wrapped up in a massive fluffy sponge cake and each hit my head gets I see sparkly stars. I still can't get out of my chair, but the good news is I've managed to work my hands and I can now have a sip of my now flat cider. Except I can't really tell it's flat because I haven't landed yet.

Then there's a knock at my door. "Keith!!" the voice on the other side says, "It's me Alex. Can I come in?"

"Hello Alex," I said, "Please come in. Can you get me a TV for my room Alex? I really need a TV on to help drown out the noises to help me sleep."

"Yeah, I'm pretty sure I can get you one Keith. Can it wait until to-morrow, as I don't want to miss my bus home? It's my girlfriend's birth-day today so I really have to get away on time as I'm meeting her for a late breakfast."

"Yeah, I could really do with it today Alex, it would really help me settle down to sleep, you know."

Then Mission Alex pulses for a second looks down at his feet and I'm thinking wow... Have I misjudged this guy?

"Okay Keith," he said, "I suppose I can get a later bus home. I'll go see if I can find you one from the storeroom."

"Thank you, Alex," I tell him as I watch him trot off down the hallway without his mobile phone which I just lifted. Then I swallow some more pills. The great thing about loading up here is the staff here are basically employed to do one of two things, break up the fights and ring for the ambulance.

I open another can of cider to help take the edge off the first one and take a couple of big gulps. I take Alex's SIM card out of his phone and slip mine into it. Everything drug and alcohol wise is kicking in now but I feel perfectly in control as long as I stay sitting down. My door is halfway open and the hallway is starting to get busy with fellow drinkers knocking about. I think what happens is you get ripped during the morning (which I think I've managed quite well) and then you go and have a good kip for two hours before lunch, which I still have to do. Then you have your meal, maybe finish with a cup of tea and a chocolate digestive biscuit which hopefully should put you in the mood for the evening party phase.

I'm going to have to pace myself if I'm going to keep up with this bunch of piss artists. Some of these old boys here are proper pros.

I better ring Jane before I'm given my next lot of pills – don't want them kicking in as I'm talking to her. I don't realise of course that I'm probably more fucked up than I think. It's those cans of cider. If I stayed off them, I'd be alright like. The booze is always a giveaway. I'm normally very good on the drugs.

"Hello," Jane answers.

"It's all good," I said, "I'm doing real good."

"Where are you Keith?" she said, "Are you okay?"

"I'm in a safe place where the Greeks won't find me," I said trying my best not to slur my words.

"Why would the Greeks find you babe?" she said with a slightly worried voice.

"Because we ran into each other at the hospital when I was doing my rounds."

"Keith sweetheart, you don't do hospital rounds. You're not a real doctor remember? Now what's happening about the Greeks?"

"They were at the hospital. I don't know if they were waiting for me or if they were just visiting their mum."

"Visiting their mum?" said Jane, "I think we can safely say they were there for Royce."

"Either ways, one spotted me and chased me around London for a while until I managed to get away and become a homeless person in a hostel."

Now you can't blame the poor girl for being slightly worried, can you? But I had it all under control. The problem with our Jane is she's a bit of a worrier. Luckily for this partnership, I'm the calm one.

"I'm in a homeless place; I had a full cooked breakfast, it was so lovely."

"Keith are you off your face?" she asks, sounding angry.

"Nooo," I said trying to sound completely sober, "All I've had is toast jam and bacon and eggs."

Of course, she knows full well that I'm ripped.

"Don't worry about me," I tell her, "It's all good. What did you have for your breakfast?"

"Jesus Christ Keith, what the fuck are you doing? What about Royce? What's happened to him?"

Fucking hell, thought Jane, it's not even lunch time and he's half fucked. The biggest event to happen in my life, and I have to team up with South London's version of Keith Richards. I can't believe this. All he was supposed to do is hold a fluffy pillow over a mobster's face who's in bed asleep, now he's hiding out in a hostel for the homeless. This was such a sim-

ple plan. I should have asked his pet monkey Dave or whatever its stupid name is to drive in and do it. If he's got another animal with him, I'm going to lose my shit. He's done the monkey, so what's next? A llama? Maybe a dragon? Why is it each job he takes on the simpler it is, the more bonkers it becomes? He needs a TV crew following him about. He's proper TV gold. What the hell has he done about Royce? We have twenty million at stake and he's off his face in a homeless hostel.

"It's all good," I said, "I cleaned the big man's sack out. Me and what's his name old man Parks. We did our best for him Jane, we're doctors goddamn it, not magicians Jim, I mean Jane. They're sending in the priest as we speak so it's all good, the job is done."

"Keith... we have a lot at stake here. What's going on?"

"Listen, I can't talk now I'm waiting for Mission Alex to bring me my TV. It's his girlfriend's birthday today. He's going to be late home. He really needs to start thinking of other people's feelings."

"What the hell have you taken Keith?" said a proper worried Jane.

"A fellow doctor gave me some meds. It's all good; I'm in safe hands at the mission."

"Of course you are," said Jane. "How many Greeks were chasing you around London yesterday?"

"Just the one; he remembered me, which was nice."

She's a smashing girl our Jane, but fuck me she doesn't half worry. I mean I'm the streetwise one here. These are my people I'm living with. Well saying that, maybe not the geezer in the crash helmet. But I've got a good feeling about one or two of them here, especially the one that looks like Jesus.

"Where are you are Keith?" asks Jane.

"The Cider Mansion," I answer, "You would have loved the breakfast this morning."

Then there was a knock at my door.

"I have to go," I said in my best trying to be sober voice, "I'll call you later."

I hang up and hide Mission Alex's phone behind my pillow.

"Who is it?" I yell.

"It's me," says Mission Alex.

"Can I come in Keith?"

I manage to get out of my chair and open my door and there stands Mission Alex holding a rather big old heavy TV.

"Come in," I said, "That TV looks heavy. You want to watch your back lugging that about. I've got to take a piss; won't be a minute." I stagger into the toilet across the hall to change the SIM card back over in Alex's phone.

Then I walk (I want to say walk) it's more of a stagger really, back into my room and place Alex's phone quietly beside my sink while he tunes in my TV.

Of course, I could have kept Alex's phone but it's too early in the game to start nicking off the staff. I'm not interested in cheap phones; what I want is the key to the meds room.

"That's the best I can do Keith for now," said Alex, "But I've got you the basic channels so at least you're up and running."

"Thank you Alex. You're a proper geezer for doing that."

Mission Alex is growing on me. But it looks like he's going to be a bit late home and that's not a great way to start his girlfriend's birthday, is it? Some men just can't seem to keep it together when it comes to relationships. I think being on time is so important especially on a girl's birthday. I'm feeling pretty good about things now, things being my drugs that is. I know I'm going to have to go back home. I can't stay in here forever.

And I'm going to have go back and get my car from the hospital.

The Greeks know I'm about and they want their money back, it's only a matter of time before they find me. And what about Royce? Well, when I opened up the man's monkey-throttled ballbag I unknowingly filled it back up with finger-licking germs. But I didn't know any of this yet.

I take a well-earned morning nap and dream of Greeks, broken balls and homeless cider drinkers.

I awake some hours later. My bedroom window looks out onto a busy main street and I can hear the noise of London still going about its day. I've got some blurred photos in my head of who I spoke with last night. All my blurred photos seemed to be of men sporting beards with beans in them. I lie in my bed listening to all the unusual noises going on around me. There are lots of doors opening and closing and people shouting up and down the hallways, and then there's a knock on my door.

"It's meds time," says a happy chap called Dan. Dan tells me he does the evening meds and he's one of those people with loads of energy. Not the sort of loud happy chap you want at 5.00PM but he has a fresh cup of pills for me and I could do with having the edge taken off. He watches me take the pills and then he takes the empty cup and throws it on his trolley. He thanks me and wishes me a happy day and asks if I would like an apple.

Pills and an apple? "Yes please," I said, and I take the apple from him and place it with the others.

Then he wheels himself and his trolley of R&R off to the next lucky punter.

I can hear my next-door-neighbour, who I must pop around and introduce myself to, throwing up in his sink.

Or at least I hope it's his sink. He sounds in bad way. The walls here are cardboard, you hear everything. He just keeps hurling. I sit on the end of my bed for a few minutes getting up the courage to take a shower. There's a shower only across the hallway, I don't have a change of clothes or a towel though. The sun's coming through my window and my room looks smaller in the daytime. It kinda reminds me of a hospital room as the vinyl floor rises up the wall by about six inches. The curtains are stained and thick with cigarette discolouration. Then there's another knock at my door, fuck me there seems to be a lot of people checking in on me. How bad was I last night?

I open the door and there's my lovely obedient Helen standing there.

"Afternoon Keith," she says with big smile on. "I've brought you some clean clothes and some soaps and shavers from the stores and a lovely apple."

"Well, that's a very nice Helen," I said as I take it from her and carefully place the apple next to the others.

"Also Keith if you're interested, in the dining room at 8.30PM they're holding a really interesting talk about the father and founder of the Cider Mission, Dr Samuel D Cider. A true pioneer who travelled the world preaching the truth."

Oh fuck it! Now my Helen's preaching shit at me. I've been round the block a few times. I know when someone's on a religious rant. Well, she's off on one now – you can't stop them once they're rolling. I don't want to hear about some tosspot who went around preaching to the broken. If I've learnt one thing about religion and their devotees, it's *never challenge their belief system*. If you do, they won't trust you. No point making enemies. If they can be brainwashed to serve Jesus, then there's a good chance they can be brainwashed to serve Keith.

I let Helen bang about on about her cider king for what seems like forever, and then I see a gap as she draws breath and I quickly jump in and ask Helen if I could have a word with her later on.

"Of course Keith, how about after dinner? Which is just starting now if you would like to go down."

"Well yes I would," I replied, "I might have a quick shower first."

I shower, then head down for dinner feeling much better for my shower and also my pills have kicked in again. There are about a hundred faces when I walk into the dining room all eating like pelicans.

Ten minutes to scoff a dinner down seems about normal here and then they're gone and then a new beard sits down and takes up the spoon. My Helen walks into the dining room just as I'm finishing my coffee and invites me to a key working session. Again with the keys! Why am I going to have so much trouble with my keys? I then follow Helen from the dining room to an empty office on the ground floor to begin my transformation.

So far she's dressed me, fed me and now my Helen is to bring the new Keith out from his damaged self.

Helen starts off by saying these sessions are about you and what you want to get out of it; she also hands me my cup of after-dinner meds, and then she offers me an apple.

"Thank you very much," I said, "I'll hang onto my apple for later."

The office we're sitting in has four basic chairs, and on one side under a window is a long wooden bench.

She has lots of paperwork to take me through, but she says not to worry; she will fill most of it out herself.

I'm thinking what sort of fucking PA are you? You can fill the whole bloody lot out yourself! Seems I have a bit of training to do with my Helen here.

Helen's make up looks nice and I complement her on her choice of dress and boots. And I can tell my Helen likes her compliments – she even goes a little red in the face. And if we're making keys, shouldn't there be a lathe lying about?

"Keith," she said, "I was hoping to make an action plan with you, I think we could make a really good team together," as she removes her cardigan. She tells me once we start stripping away the layers we can be fully open and exposed.

Well I wasn't expecting that! Am I going get laid? She seems to be very up for it. Is that what an action plan is? I don't mind having sex with Helen, but is it necessary to call it an action plan? I'm probably not as fit and supple as I was in my teens, but still, do we really need a plan of action for sex? I'm looking forward to the stripping bit though. She's probably got a right nice body under that frumpy mum made dress. I have to know so I ask Helen, when will the action start, and who's meant to start it.

"I can start it off Keith, if you like, I've had a bit of training on how to remove the layers," says an excited Helen.

Fuck me! She's really into the whole stripping thing isn't she.

"Should I lock the door Helen just in case someone walks in on us?"

"No no," said Helen, "That's ok, we don't lock doors here. Sometimes another staff member might walk in and just want to observe. They will only join in with your permission Keith."

"Wow!! That's very liberal of you Helen, I'm very impressed. Should we at least shut the blinds?"

"If it helps with you letting go Keith, I don't mind."

As Helen fills in some paperwork, I start to prepare myself by getting aroused. I don't want to let my Helen down and look a fool.

"We don't have to do much today Keith," says Helen, "What we can do, if you like, is I can take you through a few of the exercises so we can slowly build you up."

Christ! I'm not sure what my Helens means by exercises. I know the basic positions like the 69, and the doggy style and the reverse cowgirl position; what the fuck does she want to build me up to? I hope she doesn't mind the taste of a man's tongue coated in a rich layer of hops and yeast, plus I've had a coffee. Maybe I should go and brush my teeth. Maybe she has some mints in her bag? That probably looks a bit rude if I ask her for mints. She might think I meant for her. I don't want to offend my Helen.

"Okay!" I tell her, "I think I'm good to go. You have the floor my dear."

I can feel my dick getting hard just thinking about what Helen's going to do with me, the cheeky little minx she is.

"So Keith, here's your copy of our action plan," said Helen as she sits back down. And then she passes me a stapled pack of about five A4 pages. Christ, I'm thinking, there must be a lot of different sex positions that I'm expected to do here. She really likes everything done in order, the nasty little drill sergeant she is.

It's always the bloody quiet ones. I had no idea there were this many positions that I'm expected to work my way through. Then as I read through my action plan, I start to realise there's no sex involved on page one or two – or for that matter, on any of the pages. It appears I've misunderstood what an action plan is, and by page five it's very clear that there's no sex involved at all. Rather glad I caught that one before I stuck my hand up Helen's dress. What a stupid name for a plan 'Action.' Fat chance of finding any action with a plan like this.

However, I find Helen really lovely to talk to. She just seems like she wants to listen. I started off by telling Helen all about my friend Jane and how demanding and irrational she can be.

"Jane drinks," I told her, "And she can be a bit too clever for her own good at times, and she's not always the best of listeners. And her cooking can be a bit hit and miss with more miss than hits. Of course, Helen I would never say anything to her. I wouldn't want to hurt her feelings. All I really want is for Jane to be happy, so that she doesn't have to sell her body."

Yes I was probably embellishing the odd fact here and there, but Helen seemed so happy to smile and listen.

"And you say Jane drinks?" asked Helen.

"Like an angry fish," I told her, "I've heard her friends call her Major Blackout. It frightens me the amount she can put away." I thinking I'm starting to get the hang of this offloading thing.

We spend a good hour discussing Major Blackout's problems and why she does what she does.

"You're so right Helen," I told her, "It really sounds like Jane has a lot of issues." I'm blown away by Helen. She's really good at pointing out Jane's problems.

"How did you meet her?" asks Helen.

Well by now reader, my pills have kicked in, and as my Helen was having such a good time, I decided to give her the full show, you should have seen her little face.

"I met her through my local church. I used to help out there whenever I could, I still do. I think she had been in prison – I'm not a hundred percent sure for what. But I once heard Father O'Malley say she used to work the docks selling her body for companionship."

Then I thought, do we still have docks in London? Docks with hookers wandering about looking for horny seamen? Calm down Keith lad, I told myself.

"I guess Helen, I just want to see Jane get well, and in the process, I guess I forgot to take care of me. I feel such a fool."

"You're not a fool Keith," said Helen with her best compassionate face on.

My Helen was lapping all this up, you should have seen me. I deserved a bloody Oscar for my performance. I should have been an actor me, one that made a lot of money and didn't need to work very much.

I tell Helen how much I've enjoyed our little chat and how much insight I've gained about Jane.

My Helen is in fucking heaven listening to me. "I just want to get my life back on track," I tell her. I can see the earnest oozing out of her, it's fucking beautiful. Someone somewhere in Helen's strange little world has told her, if you can make a difference with just one person, then you can make a difference in the world.

My Helen can't see my sticky web of deceit. It was only going to be a matter of time before she walked into it. And now is as good a time as any.

"Well Helen," I said, "This has been amazing. Do you like apples Helen?"

"I certainly do," she replied, so I give her one of the apples she gave me.

"Could I just ask of you Helen one very small little thing?"

"Of course, Keith, what is it?" she said, thinking she may have just had major breakthrough with the good ship SS Keith.

"I have to pick up my car and I can't drive because of my medication. I'm hoping you would do it for me?"

I said it in my best hurt puppy voice. I think Helen was also a little shocked at this homeless man who now owns a car. Thank Christ I didn't drive one of my classics from Grangemore – how would I explain that I live on the streets yet drive an Aston Martin?

"That car is all I've got left. It's like my home," I told her.

Helen tells me that I can park it in the staff carpark under the building but I would have to pick up the car myself. The staff can't drive a client's car for insurance reasons. And then there was some more talking but I wasn't really paying attention to her by then. I was too busy thinking of an excuse to get Helen to pick up my car.

And then I came up with, "I'm so afraid they will tow my home away. I don't know what else to do."

This time I give it my all, there was emotion, there was drama, and of course there has to be a tear, just a bit of welling up in the eyes normally does it. But with our Helen, I gave her the full matinée performance.

And after my heart-rending performance she finally surrendered. And why wouldn't she? It was a brilliant performance.

"But you must promise not to tell anyone Keith, as I could get into a lot of trouble for doing this."

"Of course, I won't tell anyone," I told her, "This is strictly between you and me Helen."

Thank Christ for my Helen, I can't go and pick up the car. And the longer it sits there the more chance it's got at being checked out. The Greeks will be watching every corner of the hospital now.

They know I left on foot because I was being chased so my car must be close by, unless they think London's favourite hitman takes the bus.

Speaking of favourite hitmen...

Mr. Deacon is in his greenhouse attending to his plants, plants he takes a great deal of pride in. He prefers plants to people. Plants don't bore him with words; they just sit quietly and be. The greenhouse is what one would describe as medium sized, Victorian brick-build. It's a well-ordered greenhouse with a well-swept floor. Mr. Deacon takes pride in almost everything he does. His house is spotless. His car is cleaned within an inch of its life. The lawns around his well-kept home are kept perfect. Mr. Deacon believes firmly in attention to detail, a belief he takes with him when he does his murdering. You don't leave clues when you're paying attention.

His home is placed in the middle of nowhere in the countryside of Cork in Ireland. Mr. Deacon is a content man as he's soon to retire. You only have a short life span as a hitman before you leave just one clue. Mr. Deacon has enough money to retire on, not bad for a man of 40 years. Just one more job should do it. Then he simply throws his phone away and the world keeps spinning with one less hitman. Mr. Deacon isn't your typical hitman, if there is such a thing. He uses any vice of any description to kill his victims, just as long as its quick. If it's a knife, there's no stabbing. It's too messy and it takes too long. The only time he uses a knife is across the throat, and the only time he kills with gun is when he makes his own. They're crudely made, but untraceable. He likes to do things quietly and quickly. Which in a way, if you were to be one of his unlucky victims that's the way to go, quickly and quietly.

His mobile phone rings. It's a man called Michael Cassim. He's been promoted recently to second-in-charge of the Greek mafia. He's keen to make a name for himself. Mr. Deacon takes the call and accepts the job of finding their wanted man. Mr. Deacon has complete confidence in his own abilities to find him. He's told there was a robbery of a white van containing a lot of money, leaving one man seriously hurt. And they think whoever did it is a real pro. Mr. Deacon quietly thinks to himself, if the robbery left one man injured then there should be some clues left behind. Mr. Deacon wouldn't leave a man behind still alive.

"I really appreciate you getting my car for me Helen. It means everything to me that car. It's all I have left."

As we leave the office there's a pissed fight going on in a hallway that's being broken up by two staff members. We quietly step around it.

And it's nice to see Helen's working for me now. Sooner or later my car would attract unwanted attention and it's in my name. It would only be a matter of time before the Greeks have a name and face to match it. I've given Helen the keys and thirty quid. "This is all I have," I told her. I explain where it is and where to pay. I also remind her it should only incur a small fee if she goes first thing in the morning. I knew having my own Helen would be a good thing. I'm all tired out now from ranting at my Helen so I swallow some more pills and hit the hay.

Chapter 16

The mission is quiet as I wake at 7.45AM. The morning is alive outside but in here most people still seem to be in their rooms sleeping. There's a knock at my door and there's some staff member wanting to give me a new bottle of methadone. Christ, the people living in this hostel are expected to party hard. I thank the Party Master for my new bottle and then he offers me an apple. "Thank you very much," I tell him, and I place it on a shelf alongside the others. At this rate, I should be able to open my own fruit stall.

I have breakfast and then walk over the road and grab a bottle of brandy and head back to enjoy it. The great thing about living in a hostel is no one batters an eyelid at someone with a bottle of brandy midmorning. On the way back, I see Mission Alex entering the building to start his shift.

"Hello Keith, you alright?" he said as he holds the front door open with his big apple pie smile on. They seem to love their big smiles here at the mission. As we go into the building, a couple of smackheads are on their way out the door. I'm not sure if it was the pills but as they passed me, I could see they were proper on the gear. Their teeth were rotten and both their faces looked like skeletons with their dark sunken eyes. That's smack for you: what it gives, it takes double.

I follow Mission Alex up the stairs to the first floor. He's talking to me about some shit but I'm not listening.

Mission Alex has this problem of sounding really boring. I know he means well but so did the Titanic. I settle into one of the wet rooms and start watching some morning TV show sitting next to this guy called Eddie who's sucking back on a plastic three litre bottle of extra strong cider.

If there's a price to pay then Eddie looks like he's been paying through the nose. His face has more grooves than James Brown. I like a drink me, but I couldn't drink that horse piss. His cheap nasty bottle of cider hasn't seen an apple in its life, which is a little ironic as it's now surrounded by them.

Then I must have fallen asleep, probably due to me upping my methadone intake.

"Hello Keith," whispers Helen, "Your car is downstairs." And she hands me my keys and the combination to get in and out of the carpark. "It's a lovely car Keith."

"Helen, thank you so much for doing this for me. You've really helped me out here. Did you have any trouble collecting it? No one tried to stop you?"

"No it was fine," said Helen, "The parking machine wasn't even working and the barrier was up. So looks like it didn't cost you any-thing," she says as she hands me my thirty pounds.

"Well, that's a bonus, thank you Helen. What's the time?" I ask.

"It's about two-thirty," she said.

I'm thinking fucking hell Keith Lad, you've just napped for three something hours in the middle of the day.

"I need to replace my phone, Helen. Is there anywhere around here that I can do that?"

"Yes, there's a shop on the main road that does most brands. Would you like me to come with you?"

"No that's very kind of you Helen, but it's important I do these things for myself if I'm to live independently."

I'm thinking that if I have to listen to any more of my self-help throwaways, I'm going to throw up.

But my Helen loves them and that's the main thing, and let's remem-ber the old saying: A happy Helen is a useful Helen.

I walk down to the basement to where my car is and retrieve the money and drugs from the hidden compartment in the front seat. There's enough cash to keep me going in here for about a year.

A year here in the Cider Mission, I would have a complete break-down from all the drugs and piss I seem to be consuming.

I head down to the shop and pick myself up a new phone.

Once up and running I see there's one or two messages from some clients that pop up, but they can wait. Otherwise, I'm back up and running. I stop off and buy two £120.00 bottles of red for my cocktail party for one, which starts in an hour. I'm flush with cash I've got a few pills with me, so a good night is not only to be expected, it would be rude not to accept.

I get back into my room for about 4.30PM which just so happens to be my cocktail hour. I don't have a corkscrew so I gently push the cork into the bottle with only very minor spillage. And it's a nice wine, very pleasant. I also have three or five pills to help take the edge off. I forgot of course that I have a cup full of meds coming at 5.00PM which is in seven minutes time. And sure enough, at five past five, there's a staff member knocking on my door with a cup of drugs.

"Hello Keith, I have your pre-dinner pills and would you like an apple with them?" the staff member asked.

"I would love an apple," I say, which I take and place along with the others. I'm then handed a cup containing about seven pills which I neck with my fine wine.

I must give Jane a ring before I get too wankered.

I think it's all the excitement that's happened in the last forty-eight hours. I don't normally get this fucked up by 6.00PM. This place feels pretty safe to get fucked up in considering it's full of so many fucked up people. I pour myself a glass of red to help take the edge off my pills and sit on my bed watching some forgettable TV program. Then I find a Rave Channel and think 'I should have a wee dance to this.' I played a couple of banging tunes. Then by 7.00PM I thought that I might give the methadone a miss tonight and see what the rest of the sailors on the good ship Cider Mission are up to. I should give Jane a ring too and get an update. But as the evening is marching along, the little methadone bottle sitting by my bed keeps teasing me. Saying things like, 'Go on Keith – just have a half. You bloody well deserve it, you do. Especially after a day like you've just had.' And after a brief word with myself, I thought 'Fuck it.' So, I reward myself with a hit and take my seat for the flight.

When I come round, I thought, 'Wow that was nice. The pills really gave that little flight a bit of sparkle.' I take out my new phone and decide to ring Jane. She must be getting worried about me. I don't want her to mess things up just as I've lined it all up.

"Hello," she answers.

"It's me Keith. You alright?"

"Yeah I'm okay. Where are you? Are you still hiding out in your homeless camp?"

"Here at the Mission, Jane, we don't like to use the term 'homeless.' We prefer the term 'hopeless.' Any news on Royce?" I ask.

"Well," said Jane, "He's on life support, which sounds promising, and they want to switch him off. But they need a family member to say farewell and pull the plug."

"I'll be his family member, might as well. I've already been his family doctor. Has he got a family?" I ask.

"He's got his mother but she's having a major breakdown about losing her baby boy, so they're trying to find the brother who lives up North somewhere. However, Keith you need to keep your head down babe, the Greeks are all over town looking for you."

"What do mean by that? Who are they looking for? There's only two of them that know what I look like."

"I don't know," said Jane, "Maybe they found themselves an unemployed sketch artist and he somehow managed to draw with his favourite red crayon a pissed bloke taking too many drugs?! And speaking of pissed blokes that take too many drugs, where's your car?"

"It's here at the Cider Mission, and don't worry it's in their underground carpark so it's safe and no one saw me drive it in here."

"Right, I'll get the train into London and meet you at your house of horrors for 9.00AM. Hopefully I will know something by then. Just keep your head down until we can figure things out, and you need to be straight when I pick you up."

"I will be," I said. "When you arrive, come to the first-floor reception and ask for me. I'll be about."

"This place has a reception?" Jane asks.

"Yes, it has a reception," I tell her, "I don't just stay anywhere me. Oh – one more thing. The male staff may want to pat you down. It's really more of a hobby for them than a legal requirement."

"No, it all sounds lovely babe," said Jane, "You must introduce me to your travel agent. See you for 9.00AM. Remember Keith – be straight."

I open my second bottle of wine. This one tastes even better than the first. Fuck, methadone's strong when you're not used to it. I think I'm nodding off, I'm not sure. I sometimes lift my head up and I've been dribbling. I don't normally dribble when I'm listening to dance music, let alone pass out.

I wake up about 8.30AM with the sun streaming through a crack in my old worn-out curtains. I feel a bit groggy this morning but no hangover. That's the lovely thing about pills: no hangovers, just regret and depression.

Better get myself down for my last breakfast, I shower and shave and head down to the dining room.

Jane said she will be here at 9.00AM, so with bad traffic that gives me about forty minutes to relax.

"Morning Chef, I'll have the full English this morning with my eggs fried and a pot of tea with extra toast – brown, if you have it, please? And could I have my bacon well-cooked?"

I find a table by myself where I don't need to grunt or watch some grunter dribble beans down his beard.

Just as I'm finishing my breakfast, I see my Helen walk in with Jane. Janes in a short tight bright yellow dress accompanied by a sexy black belt with a small Bat Girl buckle. She's wearing black and yellow ankle boots and she has her white framed sunglasses sitting upon her head. She looks fucking amazing. Everyone's looking at her. And standing next to Jane is my Helen (sadly my Helen doesn't look as amazing). She just looks like a regular Helen. They both walk up to my table with Jane leading the way. She has such a take charge kinda way about her. She looks so *wow*.

"Hello Keith. You alright?" she said in what I could only describe as a badly hidden sarcastic tone.

"Yeah I'm all right. I slipped off the wagon again," I said as I play the part of a confirmed alcoholic, "I see you met Helen then."

"Yes Keith. Me and Jane have just had a lovely chat," said Helen looking at me slightly different to the way she looked at me before.

"Oh, that's nice," I said, when really I'm thinking 'That's not good. That's most definitely not good.'

"Yes Keith, we better get going. Helen's given me all your meds and your prescription for methadone."

To be honest, I probably wasn't going to mention the methadone to Jane. Methadone never sounds very classy does it? When was the last time anyone said to you, fancy a good dribble? I've got some lovely methadone in the bathroom cabinet. I would've rather my Helen had left the methadone bit out of her discussion about me with Jane.

"I better get you back to the care home before you're reported missing again," said Jane, playing the part of London's best dressed social worker. "We don't want the police out looking for you again, do we?"

"No, we don't want that," I told her. Of course, I know what Jane's doing. She and Helen have been talking.

Then Jane said, "Have you been giving blowjobs to strange men for drugs again? You know how that makes you all sick and then you have to take all those antibiotics again." She turns to Helen and says, "He doesn't charge them any money. In fact, Keith's told us he prefers the older gentleman. We better get you all checked out again once we get you back to the home. You don't want all those nasty awful STD's back in you again, not like last time. Remember the scratching/ Keith? You scratched yourself raw, didn't you? Poor love. Helen, I hope Keith hasn't been too inappropriate with any of the older male staff here. He just needs it to be made clear to him that *no means no.* Female staff are fine; he's not remotely interested in them. Are you Keith?"

I stand up, defeated, and follow Jane and Helen out of the dining room, knowing I've been stitched right up.

I thought, you evil Nazi cow Helen, so much for your confidential policies and procedures. I couldn't believe it. She's just gone and told Jane everything! I thought that was supposed to be between us, it's the last time I offload to the big blabbermouth Helen. You Nazi mental case, you've made me look a right prize bellend. Thank you very much Helen! Well done. You can shove your action plan right up your arse.

I can see in Helen's eyes she's afraid of me now she thinks I'm a pervert who likes sucking off old pissed men in hostels.

I hope when Helen goes home tonight, she has a bloody good think about what she's done today.

"Everything all right Keith?" Helen asks.

"Yeah it's all good," I said, "Just happy to be going home." Really what I wanted to say is, "NO Helen! I'm not all right! You just went and blabbed all my shit to Jane, you evil cow." But I don't say anything do I, why would I? There's no point. No one believes anything a man full of old-man STDs says.

We leave the Mission and walk down to the basement to where my car is parked. Jane doesn't say anything but she does have a little smirk of satisfaction beaming from her face. She knows full well that she just sewed me up like a kipper along with Mrs. Helen the Deceitful.

"Any news on our man Royce yet?"

"Yes, they've managed to track down his brother. He lives somewhere up in Manchester. From what our people can gather he's on his way down to London as we speak."

"So, the brother has the power to switch him off then?" I ask.

"Basically," said Jane hopping into the passenger seat.

"Do the brothers get on?"

"Don't know," said Jane, "We didn't even know he had brother. It's up to the doctors to convince him to shut him down, otherwise it will be left up to the courts and that could take ages."

"And the Greeks?" I ask, "Any news on that one?"

"Well, that's got interesting," said Jane, "We've had some developments on that one. Our friend Butterfield is also on the warpath, according to our underground sources."

"You have your own underground sources?" I ask. "Since when did Customs have their own underground sources?"

"Since the government made drugs illegal," said Jane, "Sorry to bust your balloon, babe, but people would rather spy on people for the government than go to prison. We don't have enough room in our oversubscribed prisons for everyone, so we have to make deals."

"Deals! What sort of deals?"

"Well, if you're looking at a ten year stretch or more for drugs, we give you the offer of either working for us for free or doing ten years in a shitty cell. Which one would you go for?"

"So they give us information and for that they can do whatever they want just as long as they keep the information coming our way. If we didn't have these informers, we wouldn't be able to bust anyone. How do you think we hear about drug deals? We don't have the manpower or the budgets to set that up. The police can't do it because they don't have enough manpower either. It's the same all over the world babe. No informers means no drug busts. And no drug busts isn't good for our customs business. Sixty per cent of customs work is drug related, so if the government were to legalise drugs, we would probably cease to exist, except at the airports maybe."

"Then why do it?" I ask.

"Same reason you do it?"

Money. And she was right.

I don't sell drugs because it's a good business model. I do it because of the money. I can't sell my business. I can't even declare it. And Jane doesn't give a fuck who sells what to who; her business is in catching people and as long as there's people like me, there will always be people like her. What a lovely world we've created all because the government doesn't want to put a tax on drugs!

I drive through London looking for an artery to take us out of this shit hole. What a strange experience that was living at the Cider Mission! It's put me right off apples it has.

"What do you want to do with your money?" I ask Jane.

"Not have to work, go on holiday forever," she said. "Also, that guy that chased you from the hospital, what did he look like?"

"What did he look like? He looked big and fucking angry, that's what I remember."

"Yeah, I need a bit more than that to work with babe, we know about these guys. They're on our database. If I can figure out who he is, we might be able to even up the score."

"Score! What score?" I ask, "I don't want to settle any old scores. I want to stay well away from those nutcases. You want a description? He had horns and fangs and he could jump entire buildings while firing lasers from his eyes."

"Babe they're going to find you. That's what they do. You took twenty million off them."

"WE Jane," I remind her, "WE took twenty million off them."

"Babe if they find you, they will torture you. We had one of our informers worked on for three days by one of their sadists who liked working on teeth. Except this sadist didn't go all the way through dental school, and he wasn't interested in learning about pain relief. When the police found our informer's body, every tooth bar three had all been drilled out with a power drill. He held out for some time though; there's a lot of teeth in persons' mouth. We know it was a power drill because he snapped bits of the drill off in the guy's jaw. For three long days they did that to him. They're animals babe, I saw the photos, I saw what they did to him. These mobsters are always trying to outdo each other with their sick torture methods. They don't care; you're just another piece of meat to them. They won't stop until they've got everything."

I digest this for a moment.

"You must remember some details about him," said Jane "You've got to give me something to work with."

"The guy that chased me from the hospital was definitely the same guy that chased me in the van. He had black swept back hair and looked like he was in his early forties, he had a fat face with a big forehead. And one of his front teeth looked like it was gold."

"Which tooth?" Jane asks.

"Don't know, that's all I remember. Oh and he was wearing a dark suit. And he had no socks on."

"How do you know that?" asks Jane.

"I remember when he was chasing me we had to climb over a fence and I noticed then he didn't have any socks on. People normally wear socks, don't they?"

"Is that him?" asks Jane, who has been scrolling through her phone whilst I've been nattering heroically away.

"Is that who?" I ask, wondering what's she's on about. Then she shows me a photo of the very Greek that's been chasing me about all over London.

"How the fucking hell did you do that?" I ask, "That's the bastard who's been chasing me. How the fuck did you do find him so quick?"

"I told you we had our own database on these guys," said a gloating Jane.

"His name is Marcus Cassi. He's thirty-four and has a serious record for hurting people and extorting monies."

"Excellent. He sounds delightful. Just the sort of chap I want coming after me."

"He's not that high up in the food chain," said Jane. "He just seems to like hurting things that are alive."

"Well, me and him aren't going to get along very well now are we? I hate being hurt."

"It says here that he's also known as Chopper."

"Chopper! Christ, how did he get that bloody handle?" I ask.

"You don't want to know! Luckily, we have the upper hand on him, we now know who he is, and that might buy us some time."

"Time for what?" I ask. "Are you asking me to kill a member of the mafia? Are you fucking mental Jane? First off, you said 'Let's do a robbery,' which, due to very bad timing, required a coked-up monkey to be my wingman. Then I had to blow up a van which didn't want to be blown up and I nearly got myself killed in the process. Then I have to pretend to be a doctor and kill one of London's most evil hard-men. Now you're telling me it's time to take out more nut cases in a very long chain of organised crime."

"Two things Keith," said Jane, "First off I never expected you to take Bubbles the Chimp with you to do a robbery. And secondly, who the fuck takes a chimpanzee in a suit with them anywhere, Keith? Planning a robbery can be very simple. You take a stocking for your head and a sawn-off shotgun. That's the entire check list in two. Never have I heard the words: stocking, check, shotgun, check, chimpanzee in a suit, check."

"It wasn't planned that way," I said, "And I remember quite clearly asking 'Could I have a gun?"

"Well, I didn't stop you," said Jane.

"You did stop me! You said 'You won't need one.' You said that at least three times."

"Well, from now on Keith, can we leave all your circus buddies at home while I try and sort this mess out?"

"I can't go around London killing people. I'm a dealer, not a murder man."

"Look babe, you've killed one asshole already – well kinda in a fashion of sorts. Once the brother gets into London, he'll take care of Royce. And a couple more festering assholes won't be missed."

"Jane, they kill people for a living. I'm not a murder kinda of guy. I sell bags of white powder in the city to old ladies with monkeys and portly gay men who I'm told like rough bum sex. Killing people I don't do."

"Babe it's only a matter of time before they ID you. Listen – don't worry. I'll come up with a solution," she said as she slides her phone into her bag.

"I had a nice little chat with your special friend, Helen," said Jane. "She seemed nice, sounded very committed to her job."

"Yeah, she's not my special friend for a start, and I wouldn't listen to her. She makes things up, she does."

"Oh, I thought she was really interesting," said Jane, "But you're saying she makes things up?"

Yes reader, I know what Jane's doing. I just think it's a little bit sad that she gets so much pleasure from rubbing it in. If it were me, I wouldn't have said anything, well, maybe one or two small points. Now she knows everything thanks to my unruly PA Helen.

Chapter 17

We finally pull into Grangemore and it feels good to be home. The smell of the warm country air hits my nose, probably because there was no coke up it. As I open the car door and step out, Jane walks ahead just so she can show off her fantastic arse in her sexy mini dress. Or maybe she just wanted to go inside. Either way I'm going to slice me a piece of that lovely arse off at some stage later today. But I might wait until my embarrassment about Helen dies down first.

"Give me a few minutes, I need to find out what's going on at work," she says pulling out her computer.

I'm feeling drained. I feel like I've been out on a rave bender. My body feels spent from all my methadone. I'm probably still in shock. What I need is something to calm me down. Valium and plenty of it, something Jane won't know I've taken.

I pour myself a large vodka and down a handful of valium. Fucking hell look at me, covered in bruises, belly full of valium, glass of vodka... Christ! I've become a 1960's housewife.

Jane comes into the bar as I finish my first drink, she walks over to me to give me a hug but stops as she gets near me. "Oh babe, you don't half stink. I can't get near that. Now why don't you go take a nice long shower and then put on your biggest and best hard on for me to fuck?"

Now normally sex with a girl for me is reasonably straightforward. I do my best to cum and if all goes well and she gets to cum then 'jobs a good un' as they say. But with Jane, I don't know what's coming next, never mind who's cumming. I have a long shower washing the Cider Mission events off me. What I need to do is fuck Jane, have a smoke and then sleep, and maybe have a couple of drinks inbetween. I'll see how I go.

As I enter my bedroom dressed only in my towel, Jane follows me in. She's dressed in a pink and black leather leotard with shiny black ankle boots and sporting what looks like a German SS officers cap on her head. Where the fuck did she gets an SS officers cap from? Who the fuck sells Nazi shit like that? Don't you need to go to a specialist auction house with a permit for that sort of shit? How serious is this girl? It's very refreshing to know it's not just me that takes things up a level. She looks so fucking hot with her tits out like that. But still, where did she get a German SS officers cap from? Is she like a collector of Hitler & Co shit? I've never been to Jane's house... Am I going to find Nazi flags and swords adorning her walls?

Now any other time I would thank the gods for a girl like Jane, but I'm not quite sure who's fucking who here? There's always some unspoken rules in sex that's what makes it safe. With our Jane it feels more like who can take the most pain. And then when that bloody great dildo of hers appeared I become slightly more verbal with my fears. But she just laughs it off. "Come on!! Surely you can take as well as you can give!"

If I'm being totally honest with myself reader, I would have to say no, I probably can't take as well as I can give, but I'm not telling her that, am I? Maybe I should have been a little bit more upfront with my sexual limitations. I should have done that from the very start, especially as we enter the latest round of 'give Keith a good hard bum slapping.' I don't want to be that guy who ends up in an A&E department after a sex experiment goes wrong. I'm trying my hardest to convey a tough guy image here, but some of it really hurts. That's never been my thing, being whipped. I thought when Jane brought it up it would be a bit of kinky fun, I thought she meant me whip her, which she did. But I didn't realise she wanted to also give me a good slapping. Don't get me wrong, I do like a good sex game. Just not one where I get battered.

I didn't go out to hurt her, I had it in mind it was all going to be a bit of slap and tickle kind of thing.

The first time she did it to me I was bending over butt naked thinking 'Aren't we having a right giggle here?' And then fucking THWACK! Right across my bare arse! I shot up like a fucking pigeon, it was that painful. I wanted to scream, but I thought 'Hold it together Keith, you can take it, old son.'

And then she just went fucking nuts on me. I really felt I was on the ropes. At one stage she had two whips on me, one in each hand going for it. How dedicated is that?! At that point I tried climbing into an old empty wardrobe for a bit of protection. That was my worst sex idea yet, she just opened up the door, lent in and started whacking me. And the more that I said "Ouch! That fucking hurts!" the more she kept whacking. I'm not feeling sexy when I'm getting whacked. She basically chases me round the bedroom – looking damn sexy I might add – while hitting me with a bloody whip. Why would that make me feel sexy? I'm doing my level best to protect myself from the whacks and the cracks that are coming from all angles. I'm not quite sure if she's aiming for my balls, but when one of her whips finds its mark, it fucking hurts big time.

I never would have thought to ask her if she's into whips and Nazi SS hats. It's way too late to have a safe word now. I would look like a proper big Emily if I asked her for a safe word. You can't ask for a safe word this late in the game. Especially when it gets proper hard – and I'm not talking about my dick – I just end up running for a corner to try and shield myself best I can. Then she just stands over me raining blow after blow on me with her whips, sounding like she's a tennis player in mid-service. Her face looks playful enough, but she has the strength of a Victorian blacksmith. And if one of her blows does hit my balls, then I'm partially paralysed and then I can't even run for cover.

As I said, the sex is great but the lead up can be a bit fucking brutal. Now tonight we had plenty of sex but the whipping again left me somewhat battered and beaten. And each time the whip cracked against my arse, she's now making me thank her after each stroke. I'm getting slightly worried where she plans on taking these beatings to. She doesn't seem to mind when it's my turn. She just lays there and takes it but I can't be as rough with her. It's not really in me to be violent in sex, yet with Jane it doesn't seem to bother her.

After we finish, there's more welts and whip marks across my body than ever before, except now she's drawing blood from me. Even my bottom lip has a lump on it. It's not a loving kind of sex we're having, it's more of a punch in the face type of sex.

The way things are going, I'm going to have to go and see my dentist to have a filling looked at. And the strangling, I don't get that either. Why does she want to be choked when she comes? What happens if I choke her out while I'm making her cum? Am I supposed to then perform CPR on her? I suppose as I was the one strangling her, it's down to me to bring her back to life, that's a lot of responsibility, that is. This sort of sex is probably more suited to your A&E doctor type guy. Someone who's had some practice in the art of reviving dead girls, whereas I'm more your pilled, stoned and pissed guy who might pass out as soon as he cums.

Who's going to believe me when I tell them that she wanted me to strangle her until she passed out? Also I've never done CPR, so she's taking a bit of a chance on me there. Then the police are going to see all the whip marks on her and they're going to assume that I'm a serial killer, which as it turns out, I might be. It looks like we have gone at each other hammer and tongs, and yet when she kisses me, she does it so tenderly – and then from nowhere, she can suddenly bite me as quick as a bat. I can't help feeling I'm in so far over my head here and yet Jane seems to be so calm and focused. When she returns to the bedroom, she's dressed in a cute little matching set of pink lacy underwear with cute little love hearts and teddy bears printed on them. If only those little teddy bears could talk.

She looks so sexy and beautiful with her toned body as she rubs moisturiser over her long, tanned legs.

It's not until she turns around and I can see my handiwork that I clock what I've done to her arse and back. Jane doesn't seem that fazed about it. She tells me don't worry about it; the marks will be gone tomorrow. She's even managed to leave marks on my wrists. I look like I might be self-harming now.

"Right then! I'm off to get some supplies. Fancy a trip to the supermarket?" I ask.

"No, I best stay here near my computer. I want to know if anything changes."

"Fine," I said, "I will wander alone on the forest floor foraging then."

"Wait; what you were planning on getting?" she asks.

"A bottle of gin," I said.

"And the food supplies?"

"Lemons."

And with that answer Jane quickly reevaluates her poor decision and says, "Wait, I'm coming with you."

She then proceeds to get dressed like a demon while telling me that she needs salad and fruit to survive.

We hadn't been shopping before so it felt a bit like we were being a proper couple and you could tell we were new at it. I went for the ready meals; Jane went for the raw foods and fish, even though I know through experience that Jane can't boil water. Need I say there were no frozen joints of lamb going in the trolley. She went about the shopping aisles as if she were a trained chef reading the packet ingredients from cover to cover, while I stood behind her pretending to know what I was doing. It was the first time I noticed other men in the supermarket. None of them seemed to know what to do. They all seemed to be following their wives about in a bored fashion wondering what to put in their trollies. Unless it was beer, wine or cereal, they had no idea. And when they did put something in their trolley that the wife didn't like, they got told off like a little bitch and told to take it out and put it back on the shelf.

Of course, it was me who found the important stuff like the gin and tonic.

And the lemons weren't too hard to find. Turns out they are kept in the vegetable section, so I had everything I needed. It felt nice as we went about as a couple. It was probably the only normal thing we've done so far in our brief relationship. We've done things to each other that you could probably be arrested for, and yet this was the first time we held hands.

With the car loaded, we headed back to Grangemore.

"We could do with a night out," said Jane as we drove home. "It's been an intense few days."

"Yes," I agreed, "We don't seem to do anything these days apart from robbing, and murdering. I miss the old days, don't you?"

If I'm being honest with myself reader, living with Jane is starting to feel like living in a full-time action movie, except in this movie I don't have any body doubles.

"We have an address," said Jane, "On one of the Greeks who can identify you."

"Really? That was fast," I said.

"And the good news is he lives alone."

"Why is that good news?" I ask.

"Because then there's no witnesses."

I fucking knew what was coming next. I said, "Jane please don't ask me to go murdering again. Can't we have a night off? Christ, even Fred and Rose West took a night off."

"Sorry babe, we haven't got the luxury of time. We have to act quickly before they have time to form ranks."

"So where does this guy live, then I ask?"

"Sheen, London, no. 261 Sampson Street, Apartment 1b. I'll go on our database and have look around when I get home so you know what the house looks like and its basic layout."

"What do you mean the layout? I'm not going round to his bloody house Jane. The man's in the fucking mafia." I'm thinking 'Fucking hell girl, how hard do you think I am? You don't just rock up to some mafia blokes house giving it some. Them lot have guns they do, then what happens is I get shot as an intruder. I'll have no defence.'

"We have to do him now Keith, otherwise the more time that they have, the more chance they have of finding you."

Again, with the 'we'. "What am I supposed to do if I come face to face with him? He looked quite tasty when he was chasing me. I think I might be punching just a bit above my weight with this one."

"You can do it Keith," said Jane. "We will be properly stuffed if you can't. It won't be long before they find you."

"Well, tonight it is then. I hope it's a full moon. Any suggestions of how I should take him out?"

"I've got one thing that may help," said Jane, "I've got a can of pepper spray."

"Great! I can bust into his house and spray him with a can of spicy vegetable juice that should do the trick."

"It's the same stuff as the police use babe, it's proper strong. It blinds you. That's why police use it."

If anyone is keeping score of how many arguments I've lost to Jane, do me a solid and please keep the score to yourself, will yah?

We get back home to Grangemore around four o'clock, just in time for the Gin & Tonic Hour. I make a couple of decent doubles while Jane puts the food away.

"I'll make us nice pasta for dinner," she threatens.

Fuck, that's all I need. I'm about to put my life on the line by attempting to kill some mafia hood and now Jane wants to poison me with her bloody cooking.

"Yeah, that would be great," I yell over my shoulder as I head back down the hallway to my bar for a line of blow. Now, I don't normally do blow this early in the day, but I thought it's about time that I was good to myself. I chop myself out two lines of blow. I snort the biggest one up first and save the smaller line for Jane. Christ she's already finished her Gin & Tonic by the time she joins me and she's asking for another one.

"Would you like a line?" I ask.

"Yeah, go on then," she says, as she snorts it like a bison. I put on some music and let the coke do its work.

"I'll be back in a minute," said Jane. So I go out to the kitchen to get a couple of lemons. Jane's put everything away, I've never seen the fridge with so much food in it. I can hardly see the vodka for the vegetables.

Jane tells me, "We have some good news on one of the Greeks. One of the two that can identify you is probably going to be home alone in

Sheen tonight for a couple of hours, if our intelligence is accurate. His full name –"

"Wait!" I said, "I don't want to know the man's name or anything about him, he lives in Sheen, so let's just call him Mr. Sheen. It's much easier for me that way."

"Okay," said Jane, "Mr. Sheen plays squash tonight as he has done for the past few months. He leaves his house about 10.00PM and, as I said, if our intelligence is right, he should be alone and he doesn't get back to his house until around 12.00PM."

"12.00PM! Who the fuck plays squash at that time of night?" I ask.

"Apparently our Mr. Sheen likes his late-night squash," said Jane, "So let's hope he will be tired out."

"Tired out? The man should be fucking exhausted playing bloody squash at that hour of the night. I've never heard of anyone playing squash at that time of night besides Elvis. How do we know he's going to be alone?"

"We don't," said Jane, "The only information I can get on him is a couple of months old. We know he hasn't got a wife and the last time we did check on him he didn't have a girlfriend. But that was a couple of months ago, so you need to be careful. We don't need any more witnesses cropping up. At least it gives you a good couple of hours to prepare for it. Do you mind if I go and have a quick nap?" she said.

"Yeah, go for it. I'm going to rest up myself until it's time." But instead of resting I did a couple more lines of blow.

Chapter 18

When Jane returns, we spend the evening sitting at my bar not drinking. Well, I had a couple of shots when she wasn't looking, which is almost like not drinking.

We were calm and gentle which was nice and then as time was marching on, Jane asked me if I had any sort of plan of how I was going to do it. I just said I'll come up with a plan closer to the time.

The problem was, I didn't have a plan. You try dreaming up ways to kill someone and then imagine yourself actually doing it. I was thinking maybe use a hammer but that just feels so brutal. Then I thought of smashing an iron on him. That would do some damage, but what if he hasn't got an iron? I can't do a knife, that's just too full on. All that stabbing and cutting – not to mention the ripping. Then I thought, why don't I take a plate of Jane's roast lamb over? That would do the job. Then I kinda ran out of ideas. All the ones that had any humanitarian threads to them were a bit thin on the ground. What a crap hitman I'm turning out to be. I'm not good with fights to the death. Maybe I could borrow Jeff and send him in with his ball-busting hands. Give him five minutes with Sheen, then wait until the high-pitched screams die down. Then I know it's safe to go on in and check for any signs of human life.

Again, I kiss my beautiful Jane goodbye and again I travel into the murder capital to add one more name to its tally.

I still have no idea what I'm going to encounter, or how I'm going to kill him when I get there. I've got Jane's can of Spicy Juice which might irritate his eyes for a minute. All that's going to do is piss him off and probably make him really angry with me. I've really got get myself a gun. I turn off onto Sheen Road and locate the apartment building where he lives. It's dark but being in a nice area, there's good street lighting about which could give me away. I park up and sit watching to see who's about. After about twenty minutes, I get up the courage to see if I can break my way into Apartment 1b. The building, which is only three floors high, has a small alleyway to one side where the residents keep their wheelie bins and there's a gate at the end. And it's got barbed wire tangled around the top of it to stop little bastards like me climbing over.

Now, to anyone with any sense, barbed wire might be a big turn off from breaking into. But that's my only way into 1b. I have no choice. I quietly climb up on top of the bins and look over the gate. There's no one about and to my right I can see three small gardens which each downstairs apartment has. They in turn, back onto the neighbour's fences and from where I'm standing, I'm looking right into their kitchens where I can see a family sitting at a table eating. I know I can see them but hopefully in this small alley there's enough darkness to cover me.

Now climbing over barbed wire at the best of times is probably best left to your more highly trained military SAS-type person. So I drag some old cardboard out of one of the dirty stinking bins and drape it over the wire. This is all the shit they left out of the book: *How To Be A Brilliant Hit Man*. The chapter on breaking into houses didn't mention anything about going through people's bins and crawling over barbed wire.

Within one minute of my assault, the barbs had my crotch and both legs as well as an arm firmly snared in their evil metal grips. As far as Mr. Barb & Mr. Wires' invention goes, they got their burglar deterrent just right. Every time I moved, the barbs either dug themselves in to my trousers or deepened their vicious scratches. As I'm stuck draped over the gate, I'm looking directly into someone's kitchen and there's a baby in its highchair at the table pointing at me while the rest of the family eat on.

The fucking pain is unbearable. My crotch is being cut in two. I had no choice but to unbuckle my trousers and try to get myself down. I was hanging quite high up on my crown of thorns and looking down I could see the path was made of bone-shattering concrete.

So as I undid my belt – which wasn't that easy to do – I managed to slowly unzip my fly and raise myself up to free myself.

Then, as I can feel myself becoming free, the cardboard rips through the barbs. I wince in pain as my hand gets stabbed. Then as I free my stabbed hand from this one nasty-arse barb, I slip halfway out of my trousers and find myself hanging upside down over the alleyway gate with my trousers firmly hooked onto the barbs. My arm is now free and I've ripped my shirt off on the way down. This is not good, especially for a seasoned unpaid hit man. I can't get my shoes through my trousers and because I'm upside down, I can't raise myself up to untangle them so now I'm just hanging there with my trousers tangled up around my ankles. My underpants seem to have now wedged themselves firmly up my butt crack like I'm wearing a G-string.

What a fucking mess this is. I try wriggling about trying to free myself, but my trousers have firmly attached themselves to the many metal barbs. I've got blood running down my hand and it's dripping onto the ground.

Talk about not leaving any clues about. You could rebuild a complete me with the amount of DNA I'm leaving about. And then as I'm flailing about, my trouser rip off me and I fall to the hard ground in a crumpled splatted heap. Christ it hurt! So much for quietly sneaking in. Now I'm lying there in my underpants and ripped shirt with my shredded trousers tangled up in the barbed wire. So first off, I have to wrestle my ripped trousers down from the top of the gate. No point in putting them on because they're shredded. Then I find an outside tap and wash all the blood away from where I was hanging upside down. That took ages going back and forwards to the bloody tap dressed in only my underpants.

What a bloody debacle. If I get caught by the police I'm going down as a dribbling pervert, not as a hitman.

I need to gain entry before my underpants burst into flames. Also I really need to go and get some sun. My lily-white legs are reflecting light here. There's two flats on each floor and 1b is first on my right. I can see there's people home in the other two flats. So I quietly creep up to the back door like a proper trained commando (in his underpants) and try the door which is locked, but luckily there's a small window that looks unlocked. It's quite high up and it looks a bit small but it's my only option. So I quietly carry a deck chair over and climb up to take a look, and yes the window is unlocked. But there's not much of a gap to crawl into. So I manage to hoist myself up under the window and lever my head in to have a look around.

I'm now looking straight into Mr. Sheen's kitchen and it might be a bit of a squeeze to get through but if I can get my head in, I figure I must be able to get the rest of me in.

So, I hoist myself up off the chair and begin to attempt the worst house break in the whole history of badly thought-out break-ins.

I get my waist through the pea-sized window. Talk about a struggle. I should get the Houdini Award for this. I'm grazed and I'm in a lot of pain, but I'm almost through. The problem now is where I'm about to drop doesn't have a kitchen bench to land on. It's just a straight drop down to the hard floor. If I put my arms and hands out, I might be lucky and not snap my wrists, as it's a good seven-foot drop.

If my Greek guy walks in now, I'm fucked. I'm hanging upside down. I can't defend myself if he comes at me. And then all of a sudden as I'm hanging there with my shoes stuck in the window, one of my shoes comes off and I go sailing headfirst down the wall and land on my head on the hard concrete floor and then everything went black and very quiet.

I don't know how long I was out for, but when I came to, one of my legs was still caught up on the window and my other leg was bent over my neck. I couldn't pull that move off if I was asked so I'm not sure how I've managed to pull it off now. If you were to walk in and you were a practicing proctologist, you would probably name this new position after me. You wouldn't need to rummage round with your fancy rubber gloves, you could just peer straight on in. Once I untangled myself out of my famous Baxter-bum opening position, I just sat there for a couple of minutes trying to recover. I was feeling bruised, battered and sore, and at the same time, very naked as I had lost my underpants along with my shoe.

Now my shoe and underpants are locked outside on the back porch. I need my underpants – not only for my dignity and self-respect, but also because that's also the last thing I want to leave behind. I start looking around his apartment for some clothes to put on. I head up the stairs to his bedroom and start going through his drawers looking for something that fits. I find some underpants but they all seem to be thongs. I decide to give up on the underpants and settle on a pair of long black pants and attempt to put them on.

Now I say attempt, because I'm a waist-size thirty-four and this guy's waist size is a tiny twenty-eight so his pants are all way too small. My stomach is spilling out over the top of them and I'm having trouble breathing, let alone walking. So I remove them and put on one of his G strings, which is fucking small. Then I find a shirt which is just as small. I can only manage to do up a couple of buttons on it. And again my stomach is spilling out between the gaps. So I continue on with my search and settle on the biggest shirt he has to offer which just so happens to be in shocking pink. And again, it's way too small so I end up tying the shirt tails together. So now I'm looking more like Daisy Duke in drag than a scary hitman. I still have no idea what time it is but what I do know is that I've been here for quite some time now so he must be on his way back soon. I decide to go back downstairs and see if I can retrieve my shoe and underpants before he returns.

I try getting the back door open but it won't budge. I'll have to wait and steal the back-door key off him when he gets in. So now I revert to looking for a weapon to do the evil deed of killing my victim with, and even *that's* not as easy as it sounds. I can't use a knife – that's just too grim – and so all that's left really in this sparse house is a lemon squeezer and a large metal whisk. So if he's got any fresh eggs in his fridge maybe I could whisk him into a large fluffy pavlova and bake him slowly to death. I have to take short steps in my tight G string. If I try and take regular steps, my ball bag keeps popping out and starts rubbing along the seam which really hurts. There's fuck all stuff in this apartment. The living room consists of a black leather couch and a matching chair. There's not even any artwork. I need something on my feet and the only thing I can squeeze into of Mr. Sheen's are his sky-blue ski boots.

I check out the contents of his fridge. There's only one egg in the egg shelf so that idea of baking him into a pavlova is out. There's some butter and a small bag of carrots. Less is more seems to be the theme around this man's pad. There's no photos about, no unpaid bills, not even an unwashed teacup. But I do find an unopened bottle of vodka. So there I am standing in the mans' kitchen drinking his vodka in his G string that's way too tight while wearing his ski boots which do nothing to complement my shocking pink shirt. And still I haven't come up with a plan on how to kill him yet, apart from strangling him with the kettle cord which might not be too bad a way to go. It's certainly way more effective than my pavlova idea.

I then have a good old nosy around his apartment and the only odd thing I find out of the ordinary is a large dildo in its opened box called 'The Pleasure Driller.' It was hidden under a t-shirt in his bedroom drawer. Apart from that, he seems very ordinary. And then in a moment of clarity I suddenly remember *rubber gloves.* The First Rule of doing a break in is: You Don't Leave Fingerprints About.

Fuck! What was I thinking? So I go and find some old some yellow washing up gloves that are in an old plastic container stashed under the sink. I can't believe I'm sitting here drinking the man's vodka with my fucking fingerprints all over the place. Now I have to go and retrace all my steps and wipe every little thing down that I touched with a feather duster. What sort of hit man have I turned into? First I play dress ups in my intended victim's G string and then when I've nailed down the most inappropriate look I can possibly come up with, I then put on his yellow love-gloves and go around giving his entire apartment a bloody good spring clean.

Not once have I ever read an advert anywhere which reads:

Wanted: Hitman

Must be a competent with kettle cords and be a whizz with a feather duster.

Must have some experience (nonsmoker preferred) and have an outrageous dress sense.

Good gate climbing skills an advantage.

What a bloody debacle this has turned out to be, and I haven't even killed him yet. I'll get old and see his face in my dreams, then I'll confess all on my death bed, and then get better. Then get arrested and banged up. It's always the way.

The house is quite dark now. I can't have any of the lights on in case I'm seen. I have the dim kitchen light over the oven on, otherwise I'm in darkness. Hopefully my victim will just think he's left the light on and not bother to give it another thought. Time is really dragging here. I can't put the TV on to check the time because he could be home at any minute so to keep myself busy, I've been through all his drawers and found nothing of interest. There's not even an old computer lying about. This guy lives like a monk, perfect for a mobster. I would have thought that being a hitman would mean that things would be on my terms when really, it's all on his terms. It's all about when he shows up, or maybe he won't show up. It's all up to him really.

He's the one who decides what time death with be and how much effort he will put in to fighting back. And when it's time to finally surrender, all I have to do is pick out the location. It's me that has to do all the mental prep for it. As far as he's concerned, he's having a lovely old time playing squash. It's not him who has to come up with creative ways of knocking someone off. So let's just remember here it's all me that's doing his very best to make it as painless as it can be for the victim.

I take a look through his front window. There's a half moon hanging in the sky so it must be getting late. He can't be too far off. How long can a game of squash go on for? I've decided it's going to be the kettle cord that kills him. I'm going to wait behind the door and as soon as he enters, I'll whip the cord around his neck and do the deed. That, my friend, should be quick and easy. He won't even see my face or hear my voice. And being that he's a mafia type guy he will probably really appreciate my professional and diligent work ethic. It should all be over in a few seconds, as long as he doesn't struggle too much. I'll leave him in a very modest position – maybe have his hands clasped over his chest with his eyes shut, just in case a family member is the first to discover him. And now that his apartment is all clean and dusted that should also help with the family's bereavement.

It's getting darker so maybe if I turn on a couple of the gas rings on the hob it might be enough light to help me see in the dark better. So I turn two of them on to light and then all of a sudden a car pulls up in the car space at the front of the house. I can't go to the window and have a look because whoever it is will see me standing in their head lights. What a way to announce myself with me standing there with my stomach oozing out of my tight pink shirt holding a kettle cord. I know it's got to be him. I can feel my heart speeding up here, I'm sure it's him. Christ! I hope I don't have to see his face.

I quickly grab my kettle cord and get into my strangling position behind the door. I'm going to get one chance at this, so I better make it count. I can hear his car door shutting – "Last time he'll be doing that,' I tell myself. Then I hear another car door shut and then two voices talking. SHIT!! He's brought a friend back with him and they're heading for the front door. 'ABORT ABORT!' That scared voice in my head starts screaming.

There's nowhere to hide in this little apartment so I run for the kitchen, put the cord back on the kettle then – for whatever reason – I picked up a medium sized frying pan and then legged it up the stairs as quick as I could. And then I hid in the bedroom behind the door. Now the problem with that little Olympic run up the stairs was my seam of my G string has acted like a cheese grater on my ball bag. I can almost smell the burning skin as the hot pain screams in me. I bet you somewhere in the National Hitman's Association there has to be a medal given out for this sort of thing. Something like a Purple Heart, but this one should be just a bit bigger than your average medal with a bit more purple in it.

My legs are shaking as I hear them walking in together. The first voice I heard said, "Oh I must have left the oven light on." And then they lock my only way out. Now the little voice in my head is screaming out, 'FUCK! FUCK! FUCK! What the fuck are you going to do now? He's going to have to come up stairs at some point, and then I'm proper fucked because his mate is going to then come to his rescue when he finds me trying to kill his friend and then he'll start attacking me. I'm in this stupid G string which I can hardly move in; I've got to take this off if I'm going to any chance of fighting. I step out from behind the bedroom door to try and hear where they are. It sounds like they're making tea in the kitchen so now's my chance.

I quickly size up the bedroom and then try and slide myself under the bed but my bloody great ski boots won't fit under unless I turn them sideways and I'm not double jointed, so that's not happening. Plus the bed is so low if anyone sat on it with me under it would cave my chest in. I don't have any choice here I'm going to have to hide in his wardrobe which faces the double bed. I wince my way back out from under the bed and then try and climb into his small wardrobe. I manage to hide myself of sorts in amongst the hanging garments. Now when I say hide, if he opens his wardrobe, all he's going to see is the back of his frying pan as it slams into his face.

I wished now I had Jane's pepper spray, but that's sitting on the passenger's seat in my car. If I did have it, I think I'd spray myself in the eyes with it so I wouldn't have to see what's coming.

So, my entire hitman weaponry now consists of an old metal frypan and a couple of unused metal coat hangers. Fucking great help that's going to be. And to make matters worse, the bloody wardrobe doors won't shut properly and there's at least a five-inch gap in the opening. I can't believe this is the way it ends for me dressed up as an escaped mental patient hiding out in mobster's wardrobe holding his frying pan, trouserless.

Then I hear footsteps coming up the stairs. The person then goes into the bathroom and starts running a bath. I can hear him humming a tune as he walks into the bedroom. Christ, it's him who was chasing me, I can see him through the crack in the wardrobe doors. He's about my height but quite lean as I watch him take his shirt off. I'm going to have to make the first hit really count. If I miss, I might as well hand him back his frying pan and say, "Here! Your turn."

Now he's taking of his trousers, and he's wearing one of his thongs. I wouldn't have thought the Greek mafia would be thong wearers. I would have thought the only blokes that were walking around in thongs today were the Chippendales. And yet here I am naked, watching a man do a show for me in his thong while I perv at him from his wardrobe.

Then as he's standing with his back to me, he bends over and whips his thong down. Fuck me! I did not need to see that. Jesus Christ why did he take his thong down like that for? I wasn't ready. The last open arse I thought I would see was Jane's, not some man's I'm about to hit in the face with a frying pan. And now he's naked walking in and out of the room to the bathroom. What did he take his thong off now for? I can hear the bath being turned off and there're no more comings and goings in the bedroom anymore. So that means one's in the bathtub and one's downstairs blocking my exit. As soon as I make a break for it, he'll see me coming down the stairs dressed as some deranged drag queen and most likely shoot me. I try again to shut the wardrobe but there's something wrong with the bloody doors and it's facing the front of the bed. I try pushing myself back into the wardrobe so hopefully they won't see me but it's no use. There's only so far I can go back.

Then I hear the second pair of feet coming up the stairs and some guy that I've never seen before comes into the bedroom and sits on the end of Mr. Sheen's bed. I'm thinking that's a very casual thing for a friend to do. He sitting there looking at something on his mobile phone while I sit no more than a metre away, hidden in this flimsy wardrobe. I've got my frying pan at the ready (if there is such a thing) and as I'm listening to his mobile, it's then I suddenly realise he's watching porn.

Why is he watching porn in his mate's bedroom? Isn't he afraid of getting caught? I mean there's always a time and place to watch a bit of porn but in your mate's bedroom while he's having a soak in the tub! Yeah, I'm sorry, but I gotta draw the line with that one; I don't want my male friends sitting on my bed watching people go at it. It's fine if it's a girl but that's something a mate doesn't do. And he's got the volume turned up real loud. For fucks sake. There are four basic rules of watching porn.

First rule. You don't let your mates catch you watching it in their bedrooms on their bed.

Second rule. Turn the fucking volume down.

Third rule. Wait until you get home, and you're alone.

Fourth rule. Always practice the above three rules.

Our man here seems very confident that he's not going to get caught. Every now and then he looks at the gap in the wardrobe doors. He mustn't be able to see me hiding in amongst the clothes looking straight back at him. I'm thinking I could maybe burst out, clobber him with the fry pan and make a break for it down the stairs. But if Mr. Sheen comes out of the bathroom at the same time, I'm going to run straight into him and then it's all on. Then the damnedest thing happened. The guy on the bed took off his t-shirt and then lay back on the bed and while he's watching porn he starts rubbing his crotch.

I can't believe this guy is so laid back about the whole thing. Then he takes his cock out!! Fucking hell; he's huge. I'm not sure if that's a prosthetic, it looks way too big to be real. Can you get a prosthetic penis nowadays? From where I'm hiding it's looks a good job if it is a prosthetic. I wouldn't say no to a consultation with his doctor if that's the end result. If his mate walks in now, he's going to go mental. No doubt they will come smashing into the wardrobe and then I'm going to come spilling out in my new party outfit. Poor Mr. Sheen when he sees the both of us, he'll think he's been suddenly magically (I say magically) transported to a wank fest in his bedroom. This guy is lying directly in front of me with the biggest erection I've ever seen and he's in no hurry. It's got to be a good ten inches. How the fuck does a girl take that bad boy? The more he strokes it the more it looks like it's growing. I'm amazed that a human is capable of keeping something so big and so hard up for this length of time. If it was me, I think I'd pass out.

Shit! I can hear the bath being emptied. That means Mr. Sheen's out of his bath and still this idiot is just laying back here watching porn having a lovely old time with himself, not having any idea that our Mr. Sheen is about to walk in on him jerking off.

And then of course it happens. Sheen walks in, and there's just silence. You could hear a pin drop. He's standing in front of the bed in his towel. I can imagine the rage building in him as he looks down on his own bed seeing his friend doing the disgusting to himself. Yes, there will be some initial shock to deal with once you've seen the size of his dick swaying away like a unicorn's horn. But any second now the shock is going to turn into blind battering rage.

But then something really odd happened. Mr. Sheen, as cool as a cucumber, dropped his towel and just stood there. Didn't say a word, he was dead silent. Then Mr. Sheen calmly crawled up on the bed over the guy who was also saying nothing. Then he did the strangest thing; he reached around the back of himself and he took that huge dick with both hands and he stuck it up his arse. ARRRGH! Jesus fucking Christ! Well, it's anyone's fight now.

Then of course it became very apparent that this was not a fight to the death unfolding but two gay men having a bit of sexy time. It's like our Mr. Sheen is performing CPR on the man except he's using his arse. Christ, the way he's riding that massive dick, Holy Mother of Mary. And now Sheen's taken out his pleasure driller and is pushing it down his friend's throat.

I really want to go home now. This is really not working for me, this hitman thing. This went on in front of me for a long time, and I'm only a metre away. I now have that look on my face, like someone who's had way too much Botox. And before anyone jumps on their box and starts yelling at me; "Homophobe!" I have nothing against gay people but being a straight male, I'm just not used to seeing this sort of thing. I'm not saying I'm totally unaware of it; I'm just saying I've never felt the need to watch any of it. Especially front row from a closet.

And just as they're getting into the 69 position, his dumb arse friend in a moment of pleasure kicks out his foot and hits the wardrobe and then both the wardrobe doors slowly swing open. Now both doors are fully open with me standing there clutching my frying pan with them both only a metre away from me munching on each other's privates.

I'm standing there in full view with my hot pink Daisy Duke shirt slowly unravelling which makes me look like I'm open for all sorts of mucky business. I couldn't reach out and shut the doors and just as I'm thinking I'm proper fucked here. Mr Sheen's special friend decides to come up for air and clocks me standing there in all my finery. Meanwhile, Mr. Sheens got his head down gobbling for Britain when his friend's eye look up in stunned disbelief. Sheen's oblivious to all of this as he's too busy playing the role of the cock-munching monster. Then Mr. Sheen's friend lets out a high-pitched yell of red alert but Mr. Sheen's not looking up because he thinks his friend's just loving what he's doing to his cock. So I have no choice now but to come out of the closet.

As Mr. Sheen's friends face goes from pleasure to fear I decide that this is my moment to bail. I'm not killing anyone tonight, not dressed like this.

Chapter 19

My mission now is to get the hell out of here with my life so I jump out of the wardrobe and as soon as my ski boots hit the floor I launch into hitman mode. For some unknown reason instead of yelling like I'm a warring Viking with his shield and axe thrust in the air, I stood there with my frying pan and then I started yelling that Arabic cry that woman use at wedding celebrations called the zaghrouta. Now, I didn't even know I could make that lalalalalala, sound. I have no idea where that came from. If Barry Gibb had heard me doing it I could have become Keith Gibb, the fourth Bee Gee. And at the same time while belting out my Arabic Celebration cry, I cracked Mr. Sheen hard over the back of his head with the back of his frying pan while he had his friends extra-large John Thomas still wedged firmly in his mouth.

His friend who also just so happened to have the Pleasure Driller in his mouth then let out this ARGGGGGG!! sound through his gritted teeth then he sat up like a bolt of lightning. So in my panic I slammed him in the face with my frying pan and then his eyes did this thing where they went this weird pool ball shape. And in between my absolute terror and me screaming my, "Lalalalalala," at them, I belted Mr. Sheen again with his frying pan and I think he was out cold. So then I bolted for the bedroom door and because I'm in boots more suited for the high-altitude ski slopes in Austria I tripped on the landing and then I go tumbling down the stairs taking out every spindle on the staircase with my massive blue-sky boots.

Now I'm fumbling around with the front door lock and the bloody thing won't open. I'm fiddling and twisting it and then finally it releases and opens. Now I can smell freedom and probably some fear along with it as I run through the front door slamming it behind me and then I bolted for my car. But as I start running there's an almighty BANG!! And then a massive flash of bright light from behind me. I go flying up in the air and land on the grass verge just outside the building. I've got bits of grass in my teeth and my body has grazes all over it. There's car alarms going off, including mine. I can see lights being turned on in the houses across the street, I pick myself up and limp towards my car as fast as I can. I wasn't sure what really happened; I was just limping away as fast as I could.

Why the explosion? Yes, well... I may have had something to do with that.

I may have forgotten it at the time, but remember just before they rocked up in their car? And it was getting a bit dark? And I couldn't turn on any lights? Well, I may have turned on two of the gas rings but just as I was about to light them, they arrived home. So in my haste I may have forgotten to turn them off. And while the three of us were all upstairs rehearsing for our new play: 'The Pervert in the Wardrobe,' the apartment was slowly filling up with gas. And when I slammed the front door on the way out the draught blew back the gas which was then ignited by the pilot light which caused this massive explosion. And that, dear reader is how the entire back of Mr. Sheen's apartment ended up in his neighbour's back garden.

The only good thing about the explosion was it blew my shoe and underpants like a fireball onto one of his neighbour's roofs which meant the police had no DNA evidence from me. Remember I'm outside at the front of the house and I couldn't see any of the damage. So I hadn't even figured out yet that the explosion was down to me. So I leg it running naked down the street in my ski boots, and if you've ever tried sprinting in ski boots you end up looking like you're a spaceman running in zero gravity.

It might even have been funny, if it wasn't me doing it.

But what I didn't know was that Mr. Sheen and his friend Horse had both gone up in the explosion as well. And that both men's heads had been blown clean off and landed neatly together in the neighbour's back garden along with Mr. Sheen's kitchen. Except in Mr. Sheen's mouth was his friend's large penis and in his friend's mouth was the Pleasure Driller. Again, I didn't know any of this at the time. When I hit Mr.

Sheen on the back of his head, that's when his friend's penis must have got bitten off and choked him out and when I hit his friend Horse in the face, he must have had the Pleasure Driller in his mouth which I may have helped knock down his throat which choked him out.

I've really managed to take this hitman thing up a gear. I'm choking my victims out on cocks and Pleasure Drillers. I must be coming across to the boys in the crime lab as one very creative hitman.

So anyways, I've legged it back to my car. I've hidden my keys behind one of the front wheels in case I lost them. I get in, still wearing my ski boots. The leather seat is freezing cold in my butt and then I try and drive away – not easy in big, clumpy ski boots. My foot was hitting the accelerator and brake both at the same time so I'm not really moving. There're a car alarms still going off around me. I need to get out of here before my car gets spotted by some nosy bastard neighbour. I'm trying to drive away but with my foot just as hard on the break as it is on the accelerator I couldn't possibly drive any slower past the apartment building. I know I have to get these bloody great boots off if I'm to succeed in getting past ten miles per-hour. And I know I have to get out of Sheen before the place is swarming with cops.

Now my bloody car has just gone into fucking limp mode because of my erratic use of the breaks and accelerator. My new top speed will now be a blistering thirty-five miles-per-hour so I should make Grangemore in the next couple of days if there's not too many traction engines clogging up the roads. These fucking ski boots are ridiculous to drive in. I can hear police sirens coming, as I turn into a side road to take me as far away from here as I can possibly go. It's no bloody use. I'm going to have to take these stupid boots off. I can't drive so I pull over where there's no one about and take the stupid bloody things off. I put them back in the car and as I'm just about to get back in the car I notice an old lady watching me from a window. To the right of her window there's a sign advertising it as a care home. For a second we stare at each other. Is this what my life's come down to? Standing in front of little old ladies naked while they're sitting in their retirement homes? I get back into my car and try to make myself feel better by telling myself that I probably just made her day.

I can't believe what I saw tonight.

It all happened only a metre away from me. The cum explosion was the bit that I know will stay with me for the rest of my life. Our Mr. Sheen the gobbler king made a right old meal out of that scene. As I said, I have nothing against being gay. It's just being a straight male and given the choice, next time I would probably choose a couple of grinding hot lesbians' wardrobe to hang out in.

Chapter 20

It was a bloody slow drive back home in limp mode. Everything was passing me, even a milk float.

I'm so lucky the Old Bill weren't out on the road. If I was dressed, I would've pulled over to the nearest services and grabbed a cab home and then got a tow truck to pick up the car in the morning and take it to the garage. Imagine me walking up to a cab like this. I wouldn't stand a chance of getting a ride.

So I had no choice but to drive in the slow lane with my hazards on. By the time I turn into my road, it's the middle of the night and then when I was about a mile from my house, the bloody car lost all power and I was broken down on the side of the road.

So here I am not wanting to bring my London life down here (remember both worlds can't collide) yet here I am ramming the two of them together by parking my bloody London car outside my house. I manage to limp the broken-down beast into a paddock entrance so it's at least its off the road and somewhat hidden from the road.

Great! Now I have to walk the mile home, naked. This night just keeps getting better and better. I'm going to have to put on my ski boots otherwise I'm going to cut my feet to ribbons on the stony road. It's also getting bloody cold as the clock strikes three. I tie up my pink Daisy Duke shirt best I can to keep warm and then start my walk home.

Just as I start to find my stride, there's a set of car headlights coming up behind me. Quickly I run for the cover of the side of the road. I lay face down in the grass until they pass by. Last thing people need is to come across a man naked wearing ski boots on a quiet country road at three in the morning.

I lay there waiting but instead of the car driving past it starts to slow down. 'Please don't stop; just keep on going.' But what does it do?! It fucking stops, but not only does it stop, I then hear car doors opening. I lay as still as I can, hoping they just get back in their car and fuck off. Christ, now they're walking down to where I'm hiding. I start to shimmy my way along the side of the verge as if I'm trying out for an officer's post at Sandhurst.

There's bloody prickles everywhere. And as I'm dragging myself along I slide right through a freshly laid pile of fox shit. I can smell the shit all over my chest. I've even managed to get it all over my face. I can hear people walking down the road with the gravel crunching under their shoes. All I have to do is lay perfectly still and I should be fine. Of course, as soon as I thought that, there was someone standing over me shining a torch down on me as I lay there covered in shit.

"Hello Keith! I thought it was you. Are you okay?" the foreign voice asks. As I slowly look up, wondering how the fuck to talk my way out of this. I then realise it's my two German Gardeners Eagle and Wolf standing there.

"Hey guys," I said looking up at them, "Whatcha up to?" Now, looking at it from their perspective, it probably looks like their landlord likes to get naked at three in the morning and then go outside and have a good old roll about in some freshly laid shit.

"Are you finished? We can give you a ride home if you are." Holy mother of Mary! Did you hear that? Their asking me 'Am I finished?' They think this is what I do when I'm not fucking monkeys. They now have it in their heads that I like rolling in fox shit. I slowly stand up while Wolf shines his touch up and down me.

"What are you doing out here?" asked Eagle.

"Well – funny you should ask that! Just as you guys pulled up, I suddenly realised that I've lost my pants. And I was just having a little look around for them."

"You have something smeared all over you," said Wolf.

"Yes, that's um some shit," I said feeling hopelessly embarrassed. "As I was looking for my pants I slipped over and accidentally rolled in some fox poo. But hey! What about you two? Have you guys had a nice night out then?"

They both just stared at me with worried looks.

It may have been the longest drive down to my home I've ever under-taken: stinking I was.

Then Wolf asked, "How is your friend the monkey? Are you guys still together?"

"No," I said quietly, "We're not together. He's gone back to live in his house in London."

"Oh I see. That's a shame," he said.

"Yes," I said, "It was for the best."

It's now four in the morning. Jane's in bed asleep so I go and shower all the stinking fox shit off me. I can even taste it. I then knock back a double single malt. I'm trying to make sense of the day but it's too late in the morning to get my head around it all, so I go upstairs, slide into bed and crash into a deep sleep.

When I do awake, it's gone nine-thirty. Jane's already up and sitting downstairs having coffee and probably eating my Pop-Tarts. I get dressed and go downstairs to deliver the good news that I failed as a hit-man and maybe ask for a less dangerous mission next time. A mission without man-on-man porn might be top of my list. Jane looks up from her computer as I walk into the kitchen.

"Hello babe," she says with smile. I'm thinking if she's smiling it can't be too bad. "Word has it you had a bit of a to-do last night."

"Just a slight drama," I said. "Our man Sheen decided to bring some company home with him so there wasn't a lot I could do apart from watch."

"Why didn't you just leave if he had company?"

"Believe you me, I wanted to! I ended up hiding in his bloody wardrobe for most of the evening watching their live show."

"What show?" asked Jane.

"Never mind," I said, "I'll have another crack at it as soon as things calm down. Any news?"

"Any news?" asks Jane. "You're asking me if there's *any news*. Christ, Keith wherever you go you seem to make the bloody news."

"What the fuck do you mean by that?" I said.'

"Keith, why blow them up?! It was all supposed to be low key! Why did you have to do that?"

"Jane will you calm *down*. NO one got blown up. The only damage that was done was I probably wrote off a frying pan and some stair spindles. A quick trip down to their local hardware shop should remedy that one. I thought the Greeks were good at building and doing repairs. What about their temples still standing after a thousand years? And no one got hurt apart from a couple of tarts I smacked over the head with a frying pan."

"So what you're telling me is your weapon of choice for a hit on a mobster is the good old dependable frying pan."

"Yes it was," I said, "And let me tell you something else – they certainly weren't expecting it."

"Babe, you blew two people up in his apartment. Why?"

"No I didn't!" I said, "Look, they both got a little tap on the head and that was it."

"Tap on the head?" said Jane, "What did you tap them on the head with, a stick of dynamite?"

"What the fuck are you talking about?" I asked.

Then Jane turns around her computer screen to show me some bombed out house in some foreign country.

"What's that got to do with me? Why are you even showing me that?" I said, getting a little miffed.

"Why? Because babe, *you* did this."

Now I'm starting to think we're having two different conversations here.

"Why did you do that shit to their heads? That means war when you do something as serious as that!"

"Serious as what?" I said, "I hit them with a fucking frying pan and that means war? Fuck these guys can take things to heart, can't they?"

I think it was then that Jane started to realise something was amiss too.

"Keith – did you stuff their cocks into their mouths?"

"WHAT!! What the fuck do you mean by that? All I did was watch, hand on heart! I just watched. I most certainly did *not* join in."

"This photo is the back of their apartment after you left. They're saying you did it with the gas. Was that your plan from the go: blow the building up? Are you enjoying what you're doing?"

"No, I'm not enjoying what I'm doing," I said while putting a delicious Pop-Tart in the toaster.

"The reports are saying in one of the victim's mouth was the other victim's severed penis and the other victim had a dildo rammed down his throat."

"Their heads were found in the next-door neighbour's garden," said Jane, while eyeing up my Pop-Tart. "But the mafia doesn't know about the gas thing yet. All they know is that someone's lopped of their guy's heads and then stuffed their cocks into their mouths. And when a mafia guy cuts off a head and stuffs the victim's cock in its mouth that means a declaration of war on the family."

"So the Greek mafia now thinks you're a real hitman working for another cartel that wants to take over. Hence the beginning of World War Three. MI6 are going into bloody warp drive over this. They're saying the Greeks have closed ranks. They're saying that the removing of the victim's heads is your calling card."

"I can assure you Jane, I have never – on purpose – ever taken another person's head off."

"Then how the fuck did their cocks end up in their mouths if you didn't do it?"

"Right!" I said. "They did that bit to themselves." Of course, Jane's just looking at me like I'm a bit thick so I spend the next few minutes explaining my wild out there story to her.

"Gay?" she said, "And they did all this in front of you while you stood watched them while you were holding a frying pan?" Then Jane notices the ski boots in the corner of the kitchen.

"First time I've noticed them. I didn't know you skied?"

"Yeah! Love me skiing me," I said.

"What were you trying to do then? Make it look like a suicide? Was that your plan?"

"My plan went down the shitter," I said, "All I was trying to do was get myself out of there, but I was naked."

"You were naked? Why were you naked? Did you join in?"

Oh for fucks sake, I thought, why would I want to join in? Just because I'm naked apart from my shocking pink shirt, watching two naked men have their sexy time doesn't mean I have to join in. Now she thinks I'm in the closet. Why the fuck would I take a frying pan to a gay love-in? She's also got this little vein that pops out on her neck when she's frustrated. I'll remember that one for next time. I'll remind her just as the steam starts coming out her ears.

"No, I didn't bloody well join in. I lost my pants on the gate and then my underpants slipped off me in his kitchen."

"Please God tell me you didn't take that bloody monkey with you?"

"No!" I replied, "Jeff had other plans."

"Ok listen," said Jane, "We might have a slightly bigger problem on our hands and you might want sit down for this."

"Go on then," cause I'm thinking it can't get any worse than this.

"The information we're getting is saying the Greeks think it's a war, both cartels of the victims' families met late last night. These two families are well-connected and they go way back. Last night they decided you're the first on their to-do list."

"Jesus Fucking Christ!! Are you fucking kidding me? The mafia have me on their to-do list? There must be way more evil people around than me that should be on their to-do list."

"Our information is saying they've sent for a hitman to find you."

"A fucking hitman has been sent to find me?! Are you fucking kidding me? Are you sure the hitman is looking for me and not some other guy called Keith or – maybe it's a Kevin he's looking for? Christ! How's it come to this? Is he any good?"

"He's their best man," says Jane. "We know very little about him. He's been the mafia's man of choice for a number of years. No one seems to know anything about him. He pops up in very odd places and is gone almost before the hit has gone down. We don't have a photo or a fingerprint. All we have is a name that the mafia use for him."

"Go on then," I said. "What's this guy's handle then?"

"He's called Mr. Deacon," said Jane.

"All we know is he's somewhere in his fifties, he's white, and he keeps a shaved head because of the many wigs he wears."

"How many years will it take before he finds me?" I ask.

"He's good at finding people Keith. It won't be a matter of years: it will be a matter of days?"

What the fuck have I got myself into? I'm looking at Jane's mouth moving but I'm not understanding anything coming out of it. When do you ever hear the sentence 'a hitman is out looking for you'? It's not my fault they blew themselves up, how was I to know their kitchen would go up with a bang? For all we know they may have always wanted to go out like that, arm in arm, cocks in mouth.

"There are still two people who can ID you, including Royce and that is what this Mr. Deacon will be relying on. Oh – and one other thing we do know about him, he likes crisps."

"He likes crisps? Who doesn't like crisps?" I replied. "I'm now looking out for a bald crisp eater who might be wearing a wig. That's got to narrow it down to at least half the male bald population in England."

I'm still in disbelief that I've got a contract out on me, I need a drink. Its 10.00AM and here I am knocking back doubles again. I look at my phone. There's one or two messages for some blow but first it's ring a local garage and get my London car fixed and off the roadside. I've got some deals from my last buy, weighted and ready to shift. As soon as the car's ready, I'm off to London to offload this gear.

As Keith gets busy planning his day, Jane starts having some thoughts. "I can't believe he's managed to lop of two people's heads. He's single-handily set in motion a mafia war which took tens of years to broker a peace agreement between. A war that governments around the world will be dreading, yet he managed to start it all off in three days. If I find out he's been bullshitting me and he did take that monkey with him, I'm going to lose my rag. All he had to do was kill him and now he's cutting off their heads. And why stick cocks down their throats? How fucking angry is he? You have to go to some effort to do something like that. I know he says he didn't do it and I want to believe him. It's just so weird the whole story about him hiding in wardrobe naked with a frying pan. Why would you hide in wardrobe when you could just call it off and leave? And why a frying pan? What is he doing – slapstick murdering? Why would two hardened mafia hoods want to put on a sex show for Keith to watch? I tell you one thing for sure: you don't want to use the phrase "heads will roll" around Keith Baxter. The money is so close. It's in our bank accounts. What the fuck is he planning next? He's driven over a London hood, twice. Then blew up two Greek gangsters, along with their house. What's he got planned next, crash a hot air balloon packed with dynamite into their HQ? How dark is he prepared to go...?

Well, the car was easy to sort, rung the local village garage and they came out and reset something. That took all of two minutes then he drove off and charged me a hundred and sixty quid for it. But at least I can get my London life out of here and back to where it belongs. While Jane had a shower, I loaded up the car with some deals. I roll a nice big joint and peg out with that until Jane comes back downstairs looking damn sexy. Jane tells me she's on her period, but not to worry; there's other things we can do. I'm hoping she means anal. Problem with that is, if I do Jane, she wants to do me. *That* part I don't like.

My first drop is to Darren and Barry's. I'm bit embarrassed about going back there really. I hope they let me live my dance routine down that I performed in their ballroom and promise to keep as our little secret. Saying that, Darren and Barry haven't kept a secret since the mid-eighties and I'm pretty sure that everyone in the gay fetish scene has been shown the video of me and my naked bear out on the dance floor giving it our all. I always like seeing Darren and Barry's house during the day. They've got a pool; there's something about a pool. I just like looking at it, they give you that feeling of 'Haven't I done well?!' I should get a pool installed at Grangemore. I'd like a swimming pool, me.

"Hello Keith darling!" says Barry, "Come on in dear." Both of them have pink Espresso cups in hand.

During the day they both dress as if they're on holiday in Tuscany. Barry's wearing a fez. He's looking very similar to the shop keeper in that old TV show Mr. Bean. Then Darren enters the room wearing a turban.

"It's Hat Day today!" they both tell me in excited voices, "You have to indulge us Keith darling, pick out a hat. There's some behind the sofa there." I look behind the sofa and there's three hats to choose from. One's a large 10-gallon white cowboy hat with an arrow through it, there's a really tall top hat to make someone short look a bit taller and a big black Mickey Mouse hat with extra big oversized ears. I thought the cowboy hat suited me. We sit there the three of us drinking coffee out of our pink espresso cups while wearing our wonderful head attire and then they bring up my naked bear. I knew the topic was going to be brought up sooner or later. They were skirting about with the regular 'normal-person-chat' for all of two minutes so I could sense it was coming.

I know I provided hours of entertainment that night with Mr. Naked Bear, along with some prime video footage of us that I'm sure has been circulated about. In Darren and Barry's world it's all about blow and cocks and of course anything else you want. I like how they both have passion in their lives. They have such a great laugh about it all. Me – I don't really have a lot of passion for cocks and naked bears. They both sit there firing off questions at me both at the same time while talking loudly over each other.

And when they can't be heard over each other they then use their big old drag queen faces to catch any last drops of my attention I have left. The big question was how did I come to meet Splash? And I'm like "Who's Splash?"

And both Darren and Barry scream with delight! "Who's Splash? Why your big naked bear is Splash!"

"What, is he a lifeguard?" I suppose buoyancy wouldn't be a problem if he was.

"No one knows what he is darling, he just seems to turn up at events barking with his handler."

"We see him around at certain venues, but we had no idea you were so into him."

"I'm not so into him," I protest, "We got cuffed together and we hung out for a while."

"A little birdie told me they saw the two of you sneaking off to the downstairs toilet together."

"He needed a wee," I said.

"You're quite the cheeky pony," said Barry. "What you do with your spare time Keith darling is your business."

"Why is he called Splash?" I ask.

Both Darren and Barry just look at each other as if to say, "OMG Stella."

"Splash; you're kidding darling? You mean he hasn't asked you?"

"Asked me? Asked me what?" I ask.

"Asked you to wee on him of course?" said an excited Barry.

"Christ, no fucking way! Why would he ask me to wee on him?" I said in a startled voice.

"That's what Splash does" said Darren, "People think he's sweating but he's not; he's just drenched in piss."

"Well, that's just plain weird," said Barry, "He asks everyone to wee on him."

"Did he wee on you?" asks Darren, "That could be something new for him."

"God no," I tell them, "He just barked at me and swung his big cock ring around."

"Don't you find it a little bit odd he didn't ask you?" said Barry.

"No, I fucking don't," I said.

Then Darren said, "It is a bit strange Keith; he asks everyone."

Fucking great I thought as I sipped my coffee, now my clients think I'm into pissing on big fat naked men called Splash for entertainment. And I think I'd remember if he asked me to wee on him... maybe he thinks there's something wrong with my wee?

Right! Next drop off is Belle's. It's still weird knowing I've got a hitman out there looking for me. Everywhere I look there's a bald man. I'm discounting the big fat bald men of course, just in case there's a chase involving running and jumping over fences. And the shorter ones I'm also discounting due to the fact height is probably quite important if he's into using strangulation. It's not like a short hitman can drag a kitchen chair around with him to climb up on in case the right moment presents itself. Each time I get into my car I now find myself checking the back seat to make sure my hitman's not hiding under a blanket waiting for me. That would be the perfect place to attack me. The only way around that is to drive a two-seater, but then I'll end up looking like a hairdresser selling drugs.

The traffic is slow getting to Belles. I park up and again I'm looking out for bald men eating crisps. Vampire Brad answers the door and asks me to follow him into the kitchen. Of course, I'm on the lookout for Jeff and his wandering ball crunching hands. So far so good! I'm carefully watching all the doors as I walk through knowing at any second a hairy hand could come shooting out from nowhere and drop me to my knees.

"Miss Belle will be with you in a few minutes sir, please have a seat," says Brad, in a dead kinda way.

I sit in the seat facing the door. If that fucking monkey's about, I want to see the bastard coming.

I sit there quietly at the table waiting for Belle. Then, all of a sudden, I feel this rush of intense pain shoot through my body... AAAAAGH! My fucking balls! That fucking bastard ball-crunching monkey was hiding under the kitchen table the whole time. He was waiting for me, the sick demented little prick. He knew damn well I would be checking the doorways, the hairy bastard. I can't move. I can't even wipe my eyes, the pain is so intense. He's got me at my most relaxed. My legs are squeezed tightly together. I want to throw up as I watch his evil self slink out the kitchen door smiling and looking well pleased with his handiwork. Just at that moment Belle enters the kitchen.

"Hello Keith," she said, "How's your week been?" I can hardly lift my head as the pain is still hanging on.

"Hello Belle," I manage to squeeze out in a girly high voice.

"You don't sound well Keith. Have you been having a few late nights?"

I want to say NO! It's your evil demented monkey, who just shook hands with my balls again. Please get me a bucket before I throw up. But I'm in too much pain to get the words out, so I just say, "Yeah."

Belle starts racking a line out while I try and breathe deeply to ease the pain. And I tell myself that one day I'm going to hire my very own hitman to take that fucking monkey's nut sack clean off, with a blunt bread knife. I know all the monkey lovers out there are condemning me for thinking bad thoughts about Jeff. But I'm telling you there's something sinister about him.

I take my leave by following Vampire Brad out while I carefully check each doorway, looking for a stealth monkey's hand that could shoot out at any given moment. I've tried walking out with my hand covering my balls, but he can come at you from behind. Jeff would make a great hitman. I even check under the coffee table as we walked past it. I can almost feel my balls shrivelling up as they try desperately to protect themselves from the crushing hand of Jeffery.

Meanwhile, at London Victoria, unbeknownst to me, a hired hitman by the name of Mr. Deacon is met by two little known mobsters on Platform 2. He's dressed in a smart dark suit with polished black shoes and black socks. Both men who have been sent to collect him are a little surprised in how little their guest has to say. In fact, the cold dead stare from Mr. Deacon makes both men feel quite nervous as he makes no effort at conversation whatsoever as they walk him to where their car is. He has only one small suitcase with him. He doesn't plan on staying long. Both of his greeting party try to make small talk with him but with each question comes a simple but firm "Yes," or "No". Both men are relieved it's not them he's come looking for. The trip to the hotel where Mr. Deacon will be staying is close by, but in the car with the cold-blooded killer sitting in the back, the journey is anything but quick. It's slow and very quiet, as Mr. Deacon sits motionless in the back seat looking out the window showing no emotion.

****

Now our Mr. Deacon would probably say different to all of that. So, to keep things on a level playing field I'll let the fabulous Mr. Deacon speak for himself.

Thanks for that Randall. First off: Great book – bound to win a prize. Secondly, What do you mean by 'showing no emotion?' What the bloody hell is that about? I'm a hitman, what sort of emotion do you want? I'm murdering people for a living and thirdly I'm being hired by people that kill for a living. Why should I offer one ounce of emotion to those two mobster thugs? When I take out someone they don't even know I'm coming. It's over in seconds. These two slabs of beef in the front seat here do it because they enjoy it. They take hours of pleasure in doing it. Sometimes, yes, I do take my time but that's because I don't want to get caught. I'm not doing fifteen years in a nick for one of these guys. That's way too much life to sacrifice. These two guys in front here would just carry on doing the same old racket if they ended up in prison because they don't know any better. I'm not some monster who has to kill, I don't need to fill some empty void because my dad fucked off when I was a toddler. I don't do what I do because I'm angry with my mother. She did her best.

I've never killed any of my family, except maybe my mum's sister, but to be fair she had that coming. Her name was Auntie Joy and she was anything but joy. She was this big old fat angry woman always bitching and moaning about shit. I happened to drive past her once on a country lane where I grew up and I knew she knew my car, so I had no choice but to stop and give her massive fat arse a ride into town. And then she demands I drive her miles out of my way to collect some package she wanted. I'm like eighteen years old, I've got no money and she wouldn't chip in for gas. She would say she would, but you never saw a cent from her.

Anyhow, she started on one and her big mouth just went on and on, with her big old saggy bingo wings flapping about with all her gesturing. And I had this hammer sitting under my seat which I never really intended to use as a weapon; it was more to intimidate with. But she just wouldn't shut up. Then she started eating a banana that was all black and rotten. There were bits of chewed up banana falling out of her mouth because she continued talking shit. And this time I just had enough. I didn't say anything. I just reached under the seat, grabbed the hammer and swung it as hard as I could at her oversized head. The ball of the hammer just went right through the side of her skull and stuck there. I remember she just went quiet and then fell backwards dead.

She looked so stupid with the hammer sticking out of her big ugly head but at least it made the noise stop. Luckily I knew of a pig farm close by so I drove there and fed her to the pigs. The only downside was I had to drag her massive arse across this field then undress her so the pigs could get at her. She was fucking enormous she was. The pigs thought it was Christmas. It only took a couple of days for them to devour her. Then I went back, gathered up her bones which had been gnawed clean and then threw them off a cliff into the sea. And her big head I kicked that out like a football and as it flew out into the air her false teeth came flying out of her mouth. Funny because I didn't know she even wore false teeth.

And finally, thank you very much Randall for sharing that deeply personal information with everyone about my addiction to crisps. *Yes,* I like crisps. Maybe a little more than most; I think it's the salt really. I open a bag and I just have to finish them. No matter what size bag it is, I finish it. And before you go and open your big fucking mouth again giving away my life history, I happen to like porridge also. I have it everyday; I have done for years. I never need a breakfast menu. It's always the same; porridge please. There you are! It's all out in the open now Ran-

THE MONKEY AND THE DEALER

dall, you big blabber mouth. And since you're so happy to talk about my addictions, why don't we discuss some of your addictions? Maybe we could have an open discussion with your readers about your wearing of ladies' undergarments. Or as you like to sheepishly refer to them as your gentlemen's support pants? Would you like me to carry on, Strange Boy? No!! Didn't think you would.

****

Meanwhile, one street over from London Victoria, I'm about to get into my car to make my next delivery. I quickly check the back seat for any hitmen. And then I remember a film where the killer hid in the car boot and crawled in through the back seat and killed his victim; so that's two places I need to check from now on. I check my phone for any messages. There's a couple from a client and there's also a message from Butterfield. Christ, that's worrying. Is he on to me about Royce? He doesn't need to try and find me. He just messages me, he knows I'll turn up. He's sent me the code for how much he wants in blow. Ten grand's worth. Is that how he's going to kill me? Setting up a fake drug deal and then stealing my blow? I can't *not* go. No one refuses to go and see Arthur Butterfield. When the man sends for you, you go. There's no excuses or arguments about it; you turn up.

I do my last drop off and head back home. The thought of Butterfield really worries me. Royce isn't dead yet? Has he come round in the hospital and managed to speak to Butterfield and give him my name? I'm right worried that I'm walking into a trap here. I stop off at a services. I sometimes call in here for a meal so I don't need to eat my way through a box of Pop-Tarts at home. I order the roast pork and veg. As a general rule, I normally order the roast every time I come here. You always know where you are with a roast; unless it's been cooked by Jane that is.

I arrive home and Jane's out, but there's note on the table telling me she's gone into work. I make ten grand's worth up for Butterfield and at the same time I go out into the grounds and hide my day's cash takings. I have various plots around Grangemore where I've buried my cash.

I hear Jane's car returning home. I know it's Jane because she drives so bloody fast the car slides in the gravel as she pulls up. I clear away my coke scales and greet Jane at the kitchen door. She looks as sexy as ever and she gives me a deep hello kiss. She tells me she's been at her work trying to find out if anyone has any info on our Mr. Deacon. "He's in London; that much we know. When he came in, we're not so sure. And we don't know who he's met with yet. But remember London's a big place with ten million people in it, so we have time on our side for the moment."

I tell Jane that I've had a call from Butterfield and that he wants to see me.

"Did he say why he wants to see you?" she asks.

"No, he said just come round for drinks and nibbles. Are your people watching his home?"

"No, not yet that's going to take a couple of days before the paperwork comes through and only then do we get the green light, but CID might have eyes on him. Too early to say yet."

"What's happening with Royce?" I ask.

"Well, his brother has been tracked down and he's now at the hospital. Hopefully he's going to pull the plug; as far as we know Royce hasn't shown any signs of improvement."

"Do you think Butterfield has worked things out yet?"

"I don't think so," said Jane, "The word through our contacts is he's laying very low. If he knew anything, he should be making some kind of move by now, even if just to save face."

Chapter 21

I head to Butterfield's thinking is this my last journey? There're no other clients I'm seeing so if anything goes wrong, at least Jane knows where I've been. It's nice having someone watching your back. I've never had anyone watch my back, not in this job.

In case Butterfield's house is being watched, there's a little back alleyway via another street which Royce showed me in case I ever thought I was being followed. I park up and sit in the car for a few minutes just to make sure things are safe. If there's anyone watching they won't be in a car, not at night. When neighbours see strangers sitting in a car outside their house all night they start ringing the police to complain.

I make my way through the alleyway. These bloody alleyways are all the same: full of weeds, low hanging tree branches, and every bit of fence has been tagged by somebody so important he had to leave his name by way of a spray can. I used to do house burgs through alleyways like this when I was a kid.

I find Butterfield's large silver back gate after a couple of minutes. There's no tagging on Butterfield's door.

He keeps a key under an old brick by the door. Again, who's going to break into Butterfield's house? I unlock it and go on through. The garden itself is quite large and very nicely laid out. Tracy likes to spend when it comes to her garden. I knock on the back door and this big angry geezer in a black suit opens the door. He doesn't say anything except, "Yea."

I tell him who I am and that I've got a delivery for Mr. Butterfield.

"What fucking delivery is that then?" he asks.

Just then Tracy Butterfield appears. "Oh hello Keith. It's alright love," she says to the gorilla in the suit, "Come on in Keith love and follow me. Let's go through to Arthur's office."

We go through to the hallway and it's rammed with big giant men in black suits. In fact, the whole house is full of people.

"Now I don't mean to be picky Keith," said Tracy "But are you planning to wear that outfit? It's just that Arthur likes the more traditional dress for a funeral."

"Who's fucking funeral are we having?" was my first thought. I didn't know anything about no funeral. Now I'm starting to panic a little; is this how it ends? They throw me my own funeral?

"Harry!" yells Tracy. Then some big bald giant the size of the door appears in the hallway.

"Yes Miss's B." All of Arthur's staff call Tracy - Miss's B. "Can you get Keith here a jacket and tie for me before Arthur sees him? You'll have to excuse my Arthur, Keith. It's a very upsetting time for him. He doesn't cope well with funerals at all. Have you got the package love?" she asks. I put the packet of blow on the desk knowing they now have all my blow for free.

I'm quietly thinking what a fucking sap I am for walking right into this with my eyes open. And why are all these people I don't even know bothering to attend my funeral? Is this to make an example of me? Then there's a knock at the office door and the ugly giant Harry returns with a black jacket and long black tie for me. He doesn't say anything to me. He just hands me the clothes and asks Tracy, "Will there be anything else Miss's B?"

"No, we're good," she says, "You best get yourself ready with the rest of the lads."

"Okay," said the angry giant and he quietly closes the office door.

"Put your jacket and tie on Keith," said Tracy, "You don't want Arthur catching you half undressed, now do you love?"

I put the tie on. It's just luck I'm wearing black jeans and a white shirt. I slip the black suit jacket on. It's about four sizes too big so now I look like I'm about five and I'm wearing Dad's suit jacket.

Then another big man in a black suit knocks on the office door and advises Tracy that it's twenty minutes to curtain call. Then Tracy hands me a package. "It's all their Keith love, put that somewhere safe," she says. Now I am fucking confused. She's given me my ten grand and told me to put it somewhere safe. Like where? I know Butterfield's going to ask for it back just before they kill me, is it just to humiliate me some more?

Tracy smiles at me and says, "Well, at least this should take the edge off," pointing to the bag of blow on the desk.

Now the wicked bitch is telling me there's going to be a celebration after they've killed me. I couldn't help myself I could feel tears welling up in me. I had it all me: the big house, the flat in the London, the hot girlfriend and now it's all gone. I can't help it. I feel myself starting to cry. I'm thinking I don't give a fuck who sees me in this state. I hope the bastards remember my distraught face forever. Then one of Tracy's daughters comes into the office to see her mum.

"Hello Keith," she said. She could clearly see I'm in a state about my own impending death. She gives me a look of pity and tells me it will all be over soon. Tracy stands up and gets ready to leave the room while giving me a little smile. "We all have to be strong Keith," she says while holding her daughters' hand who's also started to well up.

"Does it have to be done this way?" I ask. "There must be a way out."

"I'm afraid so," Tracy said, while giving her daughter a little hug. I'm a little surprised the daughter is even upset considering I hardly know her. If she's knows it's so wrong, then maybe there's others here that think the same way.

Another large man in a suit knocks on the office door. "It's time," and just looks blankly at me.

"Righto," Tracy says, "Let's get this over with then Keith."

I can't believe they get themselves so upset about this and yet they're still prepared to go through with it. The three of us walk out into the lounge room which is full of people who have come to see me being murdered. Their wives and girlfriends are all dressed up for my funeral and they're all standing around looking at me in my big stupid over-sized coat. The three of us walk to where Arthur and his henchmen are standing. I look at Arthur and I can't help myself. I burst out into tears. I've never done this before at a funeral but I feel I have full right to at my own funeral. Arthur puts his shovel like hands on my shoulders and says.

"It's done son, it will all be over soon." I nod accepting my fate and tell him I'm really sorry and that I wished I could turn back the clock.

"We all do Keith," he said while giving my shoulder a hard squeeze with one of his hand shovels. "But it's the way it has to be."

"One-minute Arthur," I hear one of his henchmen say to him. Christ the horrible bastard likes to do everything by the clock, they would love him in Japan. Arthur raises his huge arm above his head. The room falls silent except for me. I'm the only one blubbing.

The room's filled with large bald men and their horrid little gold digger girlfriends who will be sucking up my free blow in less than a minute. Then one of the bald heads says, "It's time Arthur." By now, I've become almost hysterical. I can't control my crying anymore. I'm now sobbing like a little bitch. I look at Arthur and plead with him. "Please Arthur, no! It doesn't have to be like this."

"I'm sorry Keith lad," he said, "It's out of my hands now. I can't stop it even if wanted to."

And I'm standing there crying and looking around at all the people, pleading with them saying, "Nooo! Please no!"

Then one of Arthurs henchmen hands him this long samurai sword. I'm now bawling my eyes out. I can't believe they're going to cut my head off, this is really going to hurt.

And then Arthur, the big ugly bastard, the man that could have stopped this murder from being committed, raises his sword up into the air and in a big loud voice he says, "Terry Royce!"

And then everyone in the room yells out "TERRY ROYCE."

Now they're shouting his name out so the last words I ever hear is the person that Jeff murdered. And where's our Jeff the bastard during all of this? He's at home isn't he, watching TV while eating a bag of salted peanuts.

Of course, what I didn't know was that it was a funeral; it just wasn't my fucking funeral. It was Terry Royce's funeral and at that moment when Arthur Butterfield toasted him to the crowd in his lounge room is the exact moment when Royce's brother turned off his life support. And then Butterfield's daughter looked at me and said, "Ooh, you really loved him didn't you Kevin?" and I didn't know what she meant or why she was calling me Kevin because I'm still sobbing my eyes out so I just said, "What?"

And she said, "I didn't know you were so close, you and Uncle Terry."

And all I could say through my crying was, "I don't understand." And then she gave me a little look of pity and walked off to join her mother.

Then I noticed the large, framed photo of Royce on the grand piano with the condolence book open. Then the penny dropped, all these people were here for Royce, not me. So that's why Tracy gave me my ten grand. They were never intending to kill me, this is all for Terry Royce. I'm just here providing the blow.

Now that I've realised I'm not being killed, I start to feel a lot better in myself, and I don't mind saying having a good old cry can clear a lot of shit out. Especially when you know you're not the one that's going to die. In fact, I'm starting to feel really good about myself now. I've got ten grand on me and that fucking horrid animal Terry Royce is finally dead, so that's one less thing to worry about. Now I'm going from a sobbing Mary to a chuffed little pony. The fucking relief I felt was overwhelming as I slammed back a glass of Butterfield's free scotch.

****

Meanwhile, in a clean and rather unassuming three-star hotel in Central London, Mr. Deacon sits at a table in the restaurant alone, eating tomato soup with a fresh crusted roll. He's wearing his pressed dark suit, polished black shoes and a clean crisp white shirt. The waiter comes over and asks would he like another glass of red wine with his meal. He says, "No thank you," and looks straight ahead, making it clear he doesn't wish to engage in small talk. Deacon is single, has no children, lives alone in his three-bedroom house in a quiet street. He drives a very average silver car and has two cats called Cat and Hat, which he leaves with a cattery when he's away on business. If he listens to the radio, it's Radio 4. He drinks three cups of tea a day, all with a dash of milk and three sugars. One tea in the morning, one at 3 o'clock and one before bed. His routine never changes. Today he's going to visit the burnt-out van me and Jeff used for the heist. Mr. Deacon has two hobbies. One of them being he likes growing flowers in his well-equipped glasshouse at his home. But the hobby he gets the most joy from is forensics and anything unsolvable. Where the police forensics teams fail, Mr. Deacon excels. He wipes his mouth with his folded napkin and leaves the restaurant. He has a driver provided by his employers. A young man of twenty-two years named Arron. Arron wants to be a hard man one day and he's decided he wants an easy life and he feels that crime might just provide the perfect platform for that. He's not the most intelligent of lads - they never are in crime. But he's obedient and if you want to join an organisation that uses fear as it's calling card then you need to be obedient, just in case you upset any one of your handlers.

Arron will take Mr. Deacon everywhere and anywhere he wants to go. And when Arron comes to the end of his useful service, he will be strangled by Mr. Deacon and then his twenty-two year old body will be dumped in the water somewhere. Mr. Deacon knows water washes away any important forensic evidence that could connect the body to him. He doesn't see killing as enjoyment or a sport, he just knows he's very good at it. Strangling someone to death is an art form, an art form that gets faster and smoother each time you practice it. Luckily for Arron, Mr. Deacon is well practiced and it shouldn't take too long.

****

I finally leave the funeral in full swing with my blow being snorted all over Butterfield's house and bottles of whiskey on the go. I wasn't killed but I have been appointed a coffin carrier by Royce's mum of all people.

After seeing me sobbing all over the house she feels it's only right I should be a pallbearer. I've got no more drops to do, so it's off home. Of course, I'm still looking out for bald hitmen. I start telling myself I'm making this far too easy for him. What I need is another drink and another line of blow to sharpen me up a bit.

Chapter 22

Of course, once home, Jane greets me with the good news of Royce's death and the fact I'm still alive means he can't have told Butterfield. I pretended I didn't know and that I'm relieved he's gone. What am I going to tell her; "I just blubbered all through his eulogy at his wake." We decide to go out on the lash to have a bit of fun for once. Jane knows some door bitch on some door of some club that does a fetish night. I would rather just have a normal night out. Mind you, I'm starting to think there's no such thing as normal in my life anymore. But it's Jane who's calling the shots here. We're heading off into Brighton to a club night called Heaven On A Stick.

Before we leave Grangemore, I put together a few pills and some blow to keep us going for the evening. I know I'm going to be flying tonight so I also book a Bentley and a driver to take us there and back. When I'm pilled, I like my style me, and that's what selling drugs affords me: style. My dad and mum couldn't afford style or choice. They both worked their arses off and for what? A rainy holiday in Blackpool, home of the knackered beach donkey baying out, kill me now.

Jane finally comes downstairs dressed in white knee length boots with gold buckles all the way up the sides and a short white PVC jacket held together with a black belt.

"You look lovely," I tell her.

She tells me she doesn't really have that much of her stuff here to wear. I reassure her that the other clubbers will love her outfit.

"I'm not wearing this *in* the club," she said laughing, "I'm only wearing this in*to* the club."

Then she undoes her coat and all she's wearing is pink fishnets, stockings and a white PVC thong with a bit of glitter thrown over her tits.

"That's my favourite outfit so far," I tell her, "And I bet it's easy to dry clean."

"I'll drive down babe, you drive back," she said.

"No need; I've got a car and driver sorted," I tell her while racking up a couple more lines of blow.

Our driver George and his blue Bentley arrive on time at 11.00PM. We arrive in Brighton feeling good and as we pull up to the club we can see a long queue that's formed outside. We hop out and join on the back of the it. Well, I do. Jane walks straight up to the front of the queue and starts having a word with the doorman. One minute later she comes to the back of the queue and says, "Come on then!" Jane knows the door bitch, who's called Jody, through some friend and she lets us go in for free, which was nice.

I clock her at the bar later in the evening and I give her a pill and buy her a glass of champagne to say thank you. A couple of hours after that, she passed me coming out of the toilets and this time she snogged me.

By this time, it's 2.00AM and that's heads down time on the dance floor for me with a well-mixed house track. My head is full of pills and blow. I have my hot, half-naked honey in front of me on a packed dance floor. I mean who the fuck wouldn't want to be in my shoes? By 4.00AM, it's only the hardcore who are left on the dance floor and the horny people are now hitting the couple's rooms.

There's two couple rooms in the club, each one holding about fifty people all having free ranging sex. You kinda find a limited space for you and your partner or partners and crack on. Anything goes really. You can always just sit and watch if you want to. The only rule is you don't touch anyone unless they invite you to. The couple's rooms have everyone in them, all different shapes and sizes. There's the very beautiful and the very average. Something for everybody. Me and Jane have a steady rhythm going by now. It starts with a glass of champagne, then on the hour it's a large line of blow and a pill and in-between that it's blowjobs and fucking and then hit the dance floor again. I've never seen Jane dance before – she's right sexy the way she moves on the floor.

It's now 5.30AM. The club still feels busy and there's a lot more people hooking up with each other as all their drugs have kicked in now.

Me and Jane are on the double vodkas by now followed by large lines of blow and then we hit the dance floor with the hardcore. It's fucking brilliant it is. The people on the floor look amazing as I swim around them in haze of blow and MDMA, while the loud bass thumps through me. We exit the floor at about 6.30AM covered in sweat and find a quiet corner where Jane gives me head for a while. It feels fucking amazing even though my cock has shrunk somewhat from all the drugs burning off in my body. After that we hit the couples room again where I go down on Jane this time. There's one long bench in this couples room and its full of people eating either cock or pussy. As soon one couple vacates, it's replaced by another stiff cock and a wet pussy.

We leave the couples room as it's getting quite full now, and we head to the bar for a quick pick me up. We both decide on a double Cointreau over ice, being that it's now seven in the morning. The double shot of orange-flavoured spirt will not only be refreshing but at the same time it should be body nourishing. Jane goes off to the toilet and I discreetly cut out two lines at a darkened table. But because Jane got talking to someone in the ladies toilets for what seemed like ages, I ended up doing both lines myself. Then Jane finally comes out of the toilets so I cut us up another two lines and pretended I had waited on her to come back.

Then, as I look to my right, I spot him and at that exact moment he spots me, and then we just stare at each other. I'm frozen in a slight panic; he looked exactly the same as I remembered. He's even wearing his ring.

That's right folks. Who else would you expect to see at a nightclub in Brighton called Heaven On A Stick but fucking Naked Bear? I would know the owner of that cock ring a bloody mile away. He then starts walking towards me and because he's so massive, sweaty and naked everyone just moves out of his way.

I'm now saying to myself, "Please don't come over here, please don't come over here." But he does! He walks straight up to me at the bar and just stands there looking at me with this vacant look on. I looked at Jane and her face said it all. Then he grins at me and puts his arms around me and gives me a big long sweaty hug. Not just sweaty, but wet because he's covered in clubbers stale piss. I've got no shirt on and I can feel all his thick mattered wet body hair drying itself off on me, while his big cock ring is pressed hard against me.

His hug was one of those hugs that just went on way too long. Jane had taken a step aside at this point and was just as surprised as me. I could feel all his wet piss rubbing off on me as he squeezed me even tighter. I just stood there waiting for him to release his grip. It was a truly a horrible experience and he hadn't shaved again so his face was all flabby and stubbly as he rubbed it all over my face. He then released his grip on me and held my face in his big sweaty hands and then rested his piss-stained forehead onto my forehead as if we were communicating through some special powers that only the two of us could understand.

What if he just picked me up and ran? I couldn't do anything; he's so massive. He has the biggest man boobs I've ever seen. I don't know if they're pierced or not. You can't see his nipples for all the blubber. And then he turned around and waddled his way back into the crowd without saying a fucking word.

Christ, I could do with a towel. And I now seemed to have acquired more body hair than what I arrived with. As I turn around I meet the barman's eyes. Even he's looking at me with that look of "*Wow.*"

I don't why but I said to the barman "Well, that was weird..."

Then I looked at Jane and she was just looking at me with her look of "*Wow...*" and then she said, "You're friends with the Splash Man."

"You know him?" I said.

"I know of him," said Jane, "But not in the way you guys know each other."

Then Jane leans in and whispers in my ear, "He likes to lay down in the urinal and let strange men wee all over him. That's why he's so wet; you're ok with all of that?"

I was still in shock. But just as I'm about to explain things the door bitch who let us in arrives and grabbed Jane by the arm and said, "One last dance." And then they both fucked off onto the dance floor leaving me holding the drinks. And now Jane thinks I like pissing on fat naked men. I finish my drink and decide to have a look around the club at the beautiful naked people. I didn't see Naked Bear's handler Princess anywhere. Must be her night off. Either way, if anyone handcuffs me to Naked Bear again, I'll gnaw the bloody cuffs off with my teeth. Speaking of teeth, I'm grinding mine for Britain here. One of the drawbacks of taking E is you tend to grind your teeth rather hard on the comedown.

The club seems to be pumping even though it's turning 7.30AM. My body is full of drugs and I'm starting to come down which is always the way. The bar's now shut and when the bar shuts then it's time to go home. I call George, who's on double time now, to meet us outside the club with his car.

Chapter 23

We get home and we are both so fucked, it's straight to bed and that's where I stay until about 4.00PM. When I awake there's one or two messages from clients wanting, and then there's a message from Butterfield telling me Royce's burial is tomorrow 11.00AM. This is so fucked, now I'm carrying Terry Royce to his bloody grave.

Jane and me hung out together for the evening, slowly coming down. We talked about shit and ordered a takeaway and drank some nice red wine. We then moved onto my other Greek friend who can identify me. Jane's found out our man lives in Kingston so we both agree that's what his new name will be: Mr. Kingston. Our Mr. Kingston lives by himself on the ground floor and does no sport and seems to stay in most evenings. So Jane tells me, as if she's addressing an SAS group before they go in on a mission. He's thirty-eight years old, born in Greece and has over forty criminal convictions to boast about. But interestedly he's had a stern warning from his masters about doing drug deals outside the organisation. So, if we can make this one look like drug deal gone bad, then that could throw the mafia and the police off our scent and make them think it's gang related.

Jane has some excellent ideas when it comes to covering your tracks. Given a few more minutes though I'm sure I would have thought of the same idea. She continues on saying, "Throw a bit of cash about. Make it look like you tried robbing him of his drugs. Don't be too obvious but make it look like some sort of fight has gone down. But this time try leaving his head on."

"So then, tomorrow it is," as she toasts Mr. Kingston.

"No," I inform her, "Tomorrow is booked out for my dear friend Terry Royce."

"I still don't understand why they picked you to be a pallbearer," said Jane, "It's just really weird they want you at his burial?"

"I guess when Butterfield looks at me, he probably thinks of me as a bit of a hard man, I suppose."

"No, it's definitely not that," said Jane.

It's a busy day, as I catch the morning train from my station to East London where Royce is to be buried. I make sure I arrive early and look the way Butterfield wants me to look. Black suit that fits this time, black shoes and black tie.

"Alright Keith," he said as he greets me, looking even more menacing with all his hardened storm troopers around him. He introduces me to some of the other pallbearers.

Now the thing about Royce's pallbearers is they're all tall, very large with tattoos and shaved heads. They all look exactly the same as each other. So they must be wondering who the fuck I am, and why am I carrying their lieutenants coffin.

Anyone that was remotely close to Royce is at the burial. Of course they're all looking at me and wondering who the skinny pallbearer is and why isn't his head shaved. Then one of the pallbearers gathers the rest of us up and takes us through what we will be doing. Now I just assumed we carry the coffin from the church to the hearse, and then when the hearse gets to the gravesite, we back it up to the hole and slide him in. I've only ever been to two funerals and they were mum and dads which were both cremations. But no, Butterfield wants us to walk the coffin behind the hearse as it's only a short walk from the church to the gravesite. And he also wants us to stop outside some pub on the way so the thugs inside can raise a glass to the dead animal in the box. And then there's a few choice words to be read out by some priest that's never met Royce, because if he had met him, he wouldn't bother saying any kind things about him.

So me and the other pallbearers file up to the coffin with me looking like I'm at the wrong funeral. My position has been given as right front pallbearer. As I said I've never been a pallbearer before, so it's all a bit new to me, this lugging boxes about. There are six of us, standing at the ready to lift and walk. Now I fully intend to let them carry most of the coffin, I'll just pretend I'm mucking in. Then we're given the order to lift and carry the dead corpse of Terry Royce out. Well fuck me, I wasn't ready for the weight of the coffin when I lifted it. Christ, it weighs a ton.

For some strange reason Butterfield has had Royce's coffin lead lined. Why? I have no fucking idea.

The only coffins I know that have ever been lead lined are for the royals. So the weight of the coffin was way heavier than I was expecting. Looking over at the other pallbearers, I can see only a slight strain in their faces as we stand at the ready to march out of the church. The six of us start shuffling past the mourners as we slowly walk out. By the time we get to the church doors, my arm is already starting to feel the strain. The box weighs a fucking ton. I hope his bloody grave is just on the other side of those church doors.

We turn left and start marching down the road in silence with the mourners all following us on foot. I look over to the three pallbearers who are on my opposite side and they don't even look like they're struggling with the weight. We've only marched about twenty meters and I'm starting to really feel the strain. This coffin feels like it's been carved out from a solid oak tree. I try relaxing my arm so the other five can take up the slack, but then the coffin starts to list and become unbalanced, so I have to pick up the weight again. It's a lovely hot sunny day. I'm in a black three-piece wool suit which is cooking me from the inside out. We're nowhere near this fucking pub which we're supposed to be stopping outside of. I can't even see the bloody building yet. Christ, my arm is really starting to hurt now, and my legs are even feeling the strain. If we could pick up the pace a bit, I might make it. I can't swap arms, can I? Then as we're walking (I say 'walking') some fucker comes up off the street with a bloody great wreath and lays it on top of the coffin making it even more heavy. Fucking hell! I'm really struggling here as it is, and now this prick goes and dumps enough flowers on it to fill a church. I still can't see the pub let alone the gravesite. And now more people are walking out with more wreaths to put on the coffin.

I try and tell one woman, "There's just too many flowers love," as she steps out dragging this wreath which I think she has made using whatever grew in her own garden, God bless her. And if I'm being honest it looked a bit shit next to all the other wreaths, plus it looked really heavy and she had some runner beans and a butternut squash woven into it for some reason. Is that what Royce's favourite veggies were? Beans and squash? Anyways this old bat is having none of it and still lugs it on top of the coffin. My arm has no feeling anymore. I can see the pub now but it still looks a long way away, and for some unknown reason, maybe it was because of all the pain I was in, I thought we would be stopping to have a couple of beers while we're at the pub to toast fuck knuckle here in his lead box.

I'm bloody cooking in this suit. I'm starting to stagger now. Why wasn't this dead giant cremated first and then his ashes put in the coffin? Oh thank Christ! I can see a bunch of well-dressed people standing outside on the street. This must be the pub. If I don't put this box down, I'm going to throw up. Is this what Butterfield had in mind for me all along? Sending me on a death march carrying the person I helped murder? I can't go on! I can't feel my arm anymore, even my legs are starting to shake. Was this the game plan... march me to Royce's gravesite and then ask me to hop on in with him? They wouldn't get any argument from me. Not at this point, I would agree to anything as long as I could put the jolly green giant's box down.

Finally we get to the pub and as I said, in my mind I thought we were going to have some drinks and a well-earned rest. So we turn and face the pub with all of the people standing outside. So I start lowering my side of the coffin down and then the other five voices carrying the box all go, "WHOA! What you doing? You can't put it down here!" And one of them called me a dumb arse. It was then I realised we weren't getting a break. Then some women step forward with this huge wreath that takes two of them to carry over to the coffin. I'm thinking, "No bloody way! What's coming next, a life-sized crucifix?" It then takes the two of them to lay this bloody great wreath which may have been made out of solid granite for all I know onto the coffin. And then some half-pissed muppet walked out with a litre bottle of JD and put that on top of the coffin to lighten the load.

I look at the other pallbearers. They all looked much fitter than I am. They just keep looking straight ahead. And then it happened. The heat just got to me, and I start to feel that sickly feeling of wanting to throw up. First my mouth fills up, and I try keeping my mouth closed so it would go back down, but that didn't help and I end up spraying it about like an angry blender. It is horrible, it's all over my face and chin, and when I try to hold it in some long strands come out my nose! Now there's big bits of dangling snot hanging out of each of my nostrils. I'm trying to wipe it off but my sleeve just drags the snot across my face and I can also taste that burnt sick taste in the back of my throat. I've got bits of spent food all over me, while all these bastards standing in front of me are holding lovely cool pints of beer.

Now the people behind us can't see it, but for the people outside the pub, they have the perfect view.

And then it happened: the big blow came. This time all my sick came up, every little bit of fluid and undigested Pop-Tart blew out of me. And when I mean blew, I mean it was on my shoes and on my trousers. I even managed to get it on the coffin and the wreaths. Everyone outside the pub is in shock that this is happening right in front of them. Small children turn away and cuddle their mothers. Some of my sick landed on the pallbearer next to me. He looks really pissed off so I mouth 'sorry' to him but that just seems to make him even more angry. There is now a big pile of sick on the ground, and I'm the centre of attention, not Royce.

So then we start to move off in the direction of the cemetery and the mourners who are following us are now walking through my pile of sick. And even though I feel better after chucking up, I'm still staggering which probably doesn't see me at my best.

After staggering for about two hundred yards, the cemetery gates finally loomed into sight. Now the mourners go one way and we go in another way, and for some perverted reason the hearse is in front of us. Why are we following the bloody hearse? Why can't we ride in the hearse? There's no bastard about watching. My body is about to shut down. These animals I'm working with here, they carry bodies for a living. They could probably dig a grave out of solid marble. This is a normal day's work for them. Then we go over a little rise and there the mourners are, a right happy bunch they looked. We walk to the grave with me gasping for water and air and then we place the heaviest man ever born on the ground.

I had pain everywhere. I could even feel an old sports injury I haven't felt since I was eleven. Then I just collapsed to my knees with my arms over Royce's coffin, because I didn't want to make a complete spectacle of myself. My body felt like I was an elderly man; I've never worked so bloody hard in all my life. When I looked up at the people at the grave, I must have looked like I was crying, because I was in so much pain. I've probably aged my body a good ten years today. I think I can feel one of my lungs working as long as I just take little short breaths. Having that joint first thing this morning was not one of my best ideas. I try and stand up but my legs have gone, so I just lay there with my dead blue arm draped over Royce's coffin.

There's so much pain in my chest now. Then somebody steps forward and it's Royce's mum, and instead of helping me up, she gets down on her knees and starts howling along beside me. Then we look at each other: she the grieving mother, and me probably having my first heart attack. The state she's in she can't tell the difference from a face that's having a heart attack or a good cry. Then the pallbearer crew tells me to pick up the coffin again, except this time there's these long belts under the coffin which I'm told we lower it down with. So we lifted it up and I'm needing brute strength to do this. Then we slowly start lowering the evil monster into the freshly dug earth. As it gets to the bottom, I know I can't drop it, so I start doing this weird panting sound so I can stagger my air release.

And then it's finally over: the big bastard's down. I look around for a pat on the back but that's not happening.

Christ, I can see why hitmen get so well paid if this is what you have to go through, just so you can sign the job off. And then everyone just walks off, including Mrs. Royce who only two minutes ago was holding my forehead. And now there's just me there with some worker guy waiting eagerly with his little digger to fill in the hole.

Chapter 24

I arrive back to Grangemore where a slightly worried Jane is waiting for me.

"How did it all go?" She asks, as I walk through the door, happy to be alive.

"It went well. I made a couple of new friends and helped put one of London's most notorious hardened criminals in a deep hole never to harm anyone again. And how was your day?" I ask while walking my drained body through to my bar to pour us both a large ice-cold vodka. We both take a sip of our drinks and raise our glass, "To Royce!" We both say at the same time.

"Any new news?" I ask.

"Our man Mr. Kingston seems to be going about his business as normal. I've worked out that he's brought a ticket to tonight's event at the Royal Albert Hall which happens to be an opera."

"What, you think I should take Kingston out at the opera? Isn't that a bit dramatic?" I ask.

"Well his house might be a little bit more difficult to access than I first thought. His apartment's on the fourth floor. So unless you have perfected the art of Spiderman climbing, there's not much chance of getting in unnoticed."

"Christ Jane, I've never been so busy. Can't I have the night off? Why can't I go murdering tomorrow; I've always been told Thursdays are an excellent day to go murdering on."

"I don't know where Kingston will be tomorrow or the next day," she tells me while finishing the remains of her drink.

Meanwhile in a cafe near a wrecker's yard in London, Mr. Deacon eats a large bag of plain salted crisps. The reason he's near a wrecker's yard is because there's a certain burnt-out van that he wants to look at. It's the same white transit van that me and Jeff burnt out that he's come to see.

The police haven't bothered with it; to them it's just another stolen builder's van. They don't know there was once twenty million pounds sitting in the back of it. And inside the van's burnt-out cab, they have no idea that was where one of London's hardest men met monkey boy Jeffery, the ball-crushing champion of Chiswick.

The fire brigade had soaked everything when they put the van out so the chances of finding any clues in it are slim if not impossible. There's no sign of any cash in the back, or the wooden pallets it once sat on. All that's left is the burnt and melted tarpaulin which covered the cash which has now melted to the van floor. There's nothing in here. It's clean, I took everything with me, I made sure I did. All except for one tiny little scrap of a clue. The burnt-out tag off my Elvis wig which was sitting in the coffee holder. It still has a small piece of writing on it which gives part of the name of the shop I brought it at. Mr. Deacon has no idea if it's to do with the heist or not, but for the moment it's all he has. He finishes the remains of his crisp packet and throws the spent crisp bag in the back of the van. His ever-so-obedient driver Arron is waiting for his master in the car by the gates of the wrecker's.

"Any luck?" He asks, as his master climbs into the passages seat.

Mr. Deacon looks straight ahead. "Take me back to my hotel and then wait for me." Arron starts the car and heads in the direction of the hotel.

"It's the first time I've been out here, didn't even know there was a car wrecker's here," said Arron, hoping to make some sort of human contact with his master. But Mr. Deacon says nothing and continues looking straight ahead. Arron's slow to learn that Mr. Deacon doesn't make small talk or friends; it's a fatal error that will cost Arron his young life in the coming days.

I arrive at the Royal Albert Hall at 9.45PM being told the show ends at 10.15PM, so I hide myself behind a tree and wait for our Mr. Kingston to come out. There are loads of cabs waiting about so I keep an eye on them just in case I have to follow him in one. And then as the crowd start emptying out, I clock him by the entrance of the building and it looks like he's alone. Instead of taking a cab he starts walking along the street with all the other concert goers. Now I'm a proper hitman stalking my victim as I carefully stay well enough back as not to alert him. Then I have this weird thought... what happens if my hitman Mr. Deacon is following me?

I kill Mr. Kingston, Mr. Deacon kills me, and what happens if there's a hitman following Mr. Deacon? I bet you I'm the only hitman here who hasn't got a gun and silencer. Bloody typical that. We head down a side street and by now the crowd of walkers is starting to thin some, so I'm having to stay well back.

So far I've not been spotted. I have no idea where he's going or even if he's meeting people. There's a whole bunch of restaurants up ahead and Mr. Kingston turns into one so I quickly cross the road and hide in the doorway of the restaurant opposite. So far so good. He then takes a seat right in the front of the window by himself. Is he waiting for someone? I'll just have to sit and wait and find out, then the door I'm hiding in front of opens and there's some waiter guy holding the door open for me.

"It's okay," I tell him, "I'm just waiting for a friend."

"I'm sorry Sir," he said, "You can't stand there. You either come in or stand out on the street."

"I won't be long," I tell him, but no, Mr Very Important Waiter here has suddenly got himself some power over someone and wants to use it to make himself feel a whole lot better about himself. I don't want to go inside his bloody restaurant, but because he's making such fuss I'm going to have to now. So in I go to this really busy restaurant and where does he sit me? Right in front of the window, looking straight into the restaurant where bloody Kingston is sitting. As soon as I sit down, I realise that we're only a dozen or so meters apart and when he looks up he's going to see me sitting there.

I can even see he's checking his phone, we're that close. Then the waiter comes over and asks me what I would like to order. I said, "Just a beer will be fine thanks."

He informs me that I have to order food if I'm drinking in the restaurant. "Fine then, just a cup of black coffee will do, thank you." But then he tells me I still have to order food, if I want to sit in the restaurant.

"Fine," I tell him and so I look at the menu and I order No. 7.

"Are you sure Sir?" The waiter asks.

"Yes I'm sure," I tell him, "I have ordered off a menu before thank you."

I don't really give a fuck what I've ordered, as long as I can sit here quietly for a few minutes and watch Kingston, without him clocking me.

I carefully look up and see Kingston is reading a book and having what looks like a coffee. Then, next thing I know, there's a waiter beside my table wheeling a trolley with a set of burners flaming away on it. And then he's got a pan that he's flaming up with hot oil and then he starts cooking all these chunks of meat in it. There's all this flame shooting up in the air, you couldn't miss the show from across the road. And why was he cooking so much meat in front of me?

Well, I had unwittingly walked into his restaurant called 'Platters', which was an Argentinian restaurant famed for their large servings of beef cooked at the table. And what was super special about my order was that the No. 7 was a dish made for four, but if one person can eat it all, it's free and it wasn't that uncommon for someone to have a stab at the free meal deal. And because I was a bit hesitant at coming into the restaurant and not really being engaging with anybody the waiter took me for what's known as a 'No. 7 cow bender.' The staff at Platters simply referred to a bender as a person who can eat a platter of cow for four, and thus bending the shape of the cow to fit in their stomach. Remember I'm trying to keep a low profile here, as seven-foot-high flames keep leaping from the large fry pan into the air at the front of the glass restaurant.

Of course, everyone's watching this waiter toss the joints of meat around in the flames with shards of hot oil spiting into the air. Christ, I can't even lift my head now as there's so much drama going on around my table. Kingston must be alerted by now and of course the waiting staff think I'm in training here with my head down getting mentally prepared to eat my bodyweight in medium-rare Argentinian beef. I'm still none the wiser. I'm thinking this annoying bastard waiter here, has decided to cook the entire week's meat for everyone at my table. Then to put the spotlight on me some more, this giant walked out of the kitchen dressed in a chef uniform and then came and stood in front of my table while single handily blocking out the moon and stars.

"These are the rules," he said in a loud voice. "You cannot leave the table, not even for a toilet break until you're finished."

Then as I sit there with my head down wondering what the hell is going on, I start to read over the menu and it's then that I quickly realise what the fuck I've just gone and ordered. Christ I have to stop all this attention raining down on me before Kingston pops over to join me for a slice of my Argentinian beef feast. Then two of the staff come dancing out of the kitchen playing acoustic guitars and singing some shepherd's song from way back when. And they come right up to my table, while the beef merchant adds even more cow to the hot pans causing more fire to come shooting up in the air. And I still can't look up because Kingston is bound to be watching the talent show being performed across the street from him. And now the staff are beginning to get really excited as they watch this young bull sitting at the table meditating with his head down. It's not often you get such a serious bender like me. The average bender they get in here weighs in at a good twenty stone plus.

How many songs do these two guitar players know? Talk about roll out the shepherd's 'Best Of.' Everyone's standing around me in a half-moon shape so as to make sure the restaurant opposite still has a clear view of me. So now my table of one has swelled to two guitar players with their seemingly endless shepherd's song sheet, a waiter and his assistant making fire leap to the roof, along with the manager who has also decided to join the Argentine carnival to make my table stand out even more by reciting a prayer over my pan of cooked cow. I still can't look up as I know Kingston's eyes must be on me now, so I just have to wait it out. And then thud!! One of the pans of cooked meat has landed in front of me, the staff and even the diners around me cheered along with big hand claps.

I lift my head just enough so that I can see the pan of meat. Holy fuck! That's a lot of meat. There's nothing else but meat. Everyone's looking at me as a silence falls over the restaurant. So I don't have any choice really, I can't leave until Kingston leaves so still with head down I picked up my fork and stabbed at one of the joints and then lifted it to my mouth. And as soon as I bit into it all the staff and even some of the other diners broke into a spontaneous cheer chanting, "Bender! Bender!" I start tucking in and if I'm being honest here, it did taste very nice. It's a shame Jane can't work a couple of shifts here to learn how meat is cooked. So while my man Kingston waits for his bill, I decide to start eating like a demon, just to put on a bit of a show for the staff. And as soon as Kingston stands up, I'm out of here. After all, the staff here have pulled out all the stops for me with all their shepherd songs and the likes. It's the least I can do by way of saying thank you. There's so much meat in the pan as I pick my way through it... how the hell does one person eat all this?

I slightly raise my head up just in time to see Kingston's waiter returning not with the bill, but a plate of food and a glass of wine. Ohh crap! Now I'm expected to eat my way through this dead animal. The waiter tells me I still have an hour remaining. Christ, I can't sit here for an hour eating chunks of bloody meat. I really want to look up as it's not easy knocking back slabs of cow with your head in a lowered position.

What the bloody hell is wrong with this man Kingston, doesn't he have a home to go to? Okay! I'm nearly done on the platter. I've eaten more meat than I've ever eaten and my stomach feels stuffed full to the point of being stretched. I make a deal with myself as soon as this giant platter of cow is done, I'm bailing out.

Then, as I eat the last chunk of Argentine beef from the pan, the bloody guitar players return with more uplifting shepherd tunes attracting even more attention to my table. "I can't go on," I tell the excited waiter, "I'm done. I'll pay you anything to make it stop."

Now any waiter who's worked at Platters has seen their fair share of benders come and go. And they know if a bender can get one giant platter of dead cow down them, then there's a good chance of getting a second one down them. They just need a little bit of encouragement that's all.

The encouragement came at me by way of another platter of cooked cow arriving to more "Bender!" chanting and yet more Argentine shepherd songs. But this is just too much as I raise my head up to see Kingston is still sitting there taking his time with his food. Meanwhile, I've eaten my way through half a bloody steer. I can sense my hearing is starting to shut down as my body starts amassing the damage that I'm doing by eating Daisy the Cow. I had no idea that eating so much cow could affect your hearing and now my breathing even feels laboured.

'Please Kingston, get up out of your lazy arse chair before I overdose on protein.' I stab my fork at a freshly cooked chunk of meat from my new pan.

"Big hand for the Bender!" My waiter yells as the staff and guests start applauding me. I have to force the fork into my mouth as I've all but lost the will to chew. Even my teeth feel sore. I'm sweating all over now, especially my hands and feet and my ears are popping as if I'm coming in for a landing.

"Twenty five minutes to go," the waiter yells, as he slaps me on the back with: "You can do it Bender!"

I raise my head up a little and see Kingston is readying himself to leave. About fucking time too. If I have to lift another piece of meat to my lips, I'm going to pass out. My plan is simple. As soon as he exits the restaurant, I will stand up, throw a couple of hundred cash on the table and quietly walk out and follow him. If I do it quickly then I can make it to the door before any of the staff tackle me. So as he leaves the restaurant, I get ready to exit and then I stand up. Christ, standing isn't that easy with an entire cow digesting inside you. Suddenly the waiting staff are on me encouraging me to take up my seat again, I look at the waiter who was doing most of the talking and then he looked at me with that look of, "Are you ok Sir?" I hadn't realised how shit I looked because I hadn't seen myself in a mirror yet. I certainly felt like shit I can promise you that. I dropped two-hundred quid on the table and staggered out.

There was no cheering as I left, there was no voices chanting, "Well done Bender, you did your best!" No one was patting me on the back and telling me I was a real trooper as me and my really sore neck headed for the door before I lost sight of my target.

He's about fifty yards in front of me as I begin to follow him. Of course I'm not too far into my journey before I realise at this pace, this is going to be quite brutal. Already I can feel my stomach cramping in pain and I've only just gone a few yards. I still don't know how I'm going to kill the bastard yet. We're well off the high street now, and the streets are getting darker and much quieter. My stomach is really cramping up, and I'm starting to stagger more than I'm walking. I have to clutch my belly as Kingston sets the pace. And it's the sort of pace you don't want to attempt with a side of beef in you. Then I feel a big fart coming on.

At least I hope it's a fart… Yep it was a fart. I could feel my underpants flapping with the gust of wind. I'd like to think the fart helped but all it really did was set me up for an even bigger fart.

Then Kingston stops and starts checking his phone. He's seen me as he looks back so now I'm going to have to walk past him because if I stop and start doing my shoelaces up it's going to look a bit weird. Plus I'm wearing slip-ons. I have no choice but to walk right past him which is a bit pointless because then I'm in front of him and I don't know where he's supposed to be going. I can't stop farting as I approach him. It wasn't the distraction I was going for. And then just as I pass him we look at each other. I should have just looked down as I kept walking but I just had to take a look at him close up.

And then he kinda clocked me but he wasn't sure where he knew me from, and I just panicked because I can't fight with a whole moo cow in my stomach so I lunged out and went to push him. And at the same time this enormous loud fart ripped out of me. I nearly lost my balance as my arse cheeks blew wide open and at the same time Kingston's face said it all really. I could see behind him there was one of those London basement flats with the stairs going down off the sidewalk. I just hoped he would end up falling. But when I lunged he got such a fright from my fart that he stepped back over the edge of the wall and crashed to the bottom. I hadn't seen the metal gate at the bottom of the stairs. It was one of those old Victorian style gates with large spears adorning the top of it, and that's what Kingston landed on. I stopped to look down at the carnage and at the same time release another long wet fart.

He had several spears through him, and they had gone right through his back and were sticking out his chest. He was looking up at me while coughing up blood as his life quickly drained out of him. I quickly looked around. There was no one about so I staggered out of there. I didn't even have to touch him. He did it all for me. Is that how hitmen do it? Just by farting?

I know I can't get a cab because every cab driver in a mile radius is going to be pulled in and interviewed and asked if they had picked up any farting hitmen that evening. I'm still having to limp as my stomach is in one big beef knot, and there's way too much beef in me to throw up without taking out my intestines with it.

I'm trying to walk away as fast as I possibly can but with all the cow sitting in me it's humanly impossible and the faster I go the louder my farts are becoming. I now sound like I'm walking on a street built of creaky old floorboards.

I finally limp far enough away and find a station where I can catch a train to Grangemore. I have to sit in this strange set of positions on the way home as my stretched stomach takes on the mammoth task of breaking down a cow. I get a cab home from my station but by now my stomach is really bad, and I really need to take a dump so I ask the driver to drop me off outside my gates because I don't think I can wait another second before I shit myself. I throw some notes at the driver and head for my driveway clutching my bum cheeks until I can make it behind one of the big oaks.

Now we've all had a few decent shits in our lives. I'm sure there must be one or two dumps when you've looked down at the great mass and thought, 'Damn!! Did all of that come out of me?' Well, this shit was one of those.

It was so long and thick and there was just so much of it. I was leaning out with my arms holding myself up against the tree and when the turd finally snapped off and hit the ground it made a thud. I know this dump wasn't containing any of the cow I just ate, it was probably leftover Pop-Tart residue which scratched up my arse on the way out. And just as I'm feeling the relief, there's suddenly a fucking torch light on me.

"Hello Keith," says Wolf, while shining his powerful LED torch on me and my huge dump. "Me and Eagle wanted to wait for you to finish. We are out counting bats. We have seen seven so far and one wandering badger."

I can tell by their faces they think of me as disgusting, then Eagle says something in German to Wolf and they both have a wee snigger at me. My arse feels like it's on fire being all stretched out with Pop-Tart. Wolf keeps shinning his bloody torch on my turd as I pull my pants up.

Of all the times they need to go searching for a bats, and a wandering badger, just as I've eaten a bloody cow. Fuck, I need to go again. Now I have to ask my gardeners if they wouldn't mind leaving me because I'm about to go again. How embarrassing does this have to get? I must look mad learning up against a tree with my pants down trying to curl one out. I've got to start drinking more water. This one feels like it's the remains of more Pop-Tart coming out. It feels very deep and very dry, like there's a lot of crushed up biscuit in it. My stomach is so extended from my digesting cow that anything old left in me is being asked to evacuate. Oh Christ it's another big one! I want to crap in a different place but Eagle and Wolf are standing on the other side of the tree waiting for me to finish. I can feel it coming out and it's as dry and stale like a loaf of old bread.

I have to make some kind of noise to alleviate the pain and discomfort. So my stuck poo sound came in the form of an "Eeeeeeee" noise, finished off with some deep breaths. It's hanging well out now, but I can feel there's more to come. I look between my legs and I can see it hanging there all ready to snap off. So I give it one more heave ho and grit my teeth for the big push.

And then it drops out with a thud right beside turd one. Jesus my eyes are watering. I'll have to dry them first so I can at least focus. I look down and fuck me that's a lot of shit. Then Wolf and Eagle suddenly appear with their torches at the ready and I can see on their faces even in the dark that they're both thinking, 'Has he eaten the monkey after he fucked it?' I then buckle my pants up and walk down to the house. (I say 'walk'). I'm limping and I'm way too drained to explain myself to two bat-counting Germans. As I look back over my shoulder I can see Wolf and Eagle discussing my massive shit under their torch light. Of course, I'm going to have to take a shovel and go and bury it in the morning. I did try and cover it up by kicking some sticks and leaves over it but it was just too big.

My gardeners must think I am so disgusting, but at the same time you would have to be just a little impressed with the sheer volume of cookie dough that had just come out of me.

Jane's sitting at her laptop in the kitchen as I walk in.

"Oh my god!!" she says as I limp in, "Are you hurt babe? What happened?!"

"Kingston's dead," I said, walking past her into the bar. I so wanted a drink but there was no room left in my stomach for one.

"My God, what's happened to your stomach? It's huge," said Jane.

I tell her thanks to Kingston I had a run in with a large cow. I just need time to recuperate and I'll be all right.

"How did you do Kingston in?" Jane asked.

"Well!" I said, "We ended up fighting it out, didn't we? Hand-to-hand combat. He had me pinned down. He was knocking seven bells of shit out of me. I couldn't get near him. I don't know how many black belts the man had."

"Whoa!!" said Jane.

"I ended up fighting back with a couple of street moves I knew. Never underestimate what a house key can do to a man's face. We must have fought for thirty minutes, neither one of us backing down. Then, I don't know where it came from, but I had this incredible burst of strength almost superhuman like. I managed to get him off me then I picked him up – and let me tell you he's a heavy fucker! – I then raised him above my head like a weightlifter and threw him onto a metal gate one floor below. Except this gate had those old metal spears on the top which went right through his heart."

"You killed him by throwing him onto a metal gate? Christ Keith," says an amazed Jane. "Is your stomach okay? It looks really bloated babe."

"As I said, our man Kingston knew some ancient form of martial arts. He managed to get a few hard kicks in."

"You sure you don't want to go to A&E? It looks really swollen."

"No I'll be okay. I just didn't figure on Kingston been such a well-trained fighter."

"So you're positive he's dead," said Jane.

"He's dead. I went downstairs and pushed one of the gate spears right through his throat. It was the only way I could be sure," I said while trying to sit in a position where my stomach could eat its cow.

"Ugh it sounds awful. Can I get you a drink?" asks a worried and shocked Jane.

"Not now. I just need to sit still for a while."

"So Kingston's definitely still got his head on?" Asks Jane.

"Yeah, I made sure I left it on," I said.

What a day. My new girlfriend/blackmailer thinks I can fight like a demon, my gardeners think I like shitting behind large trees in the dark and I killed a person with a fart. I'm one of those people that should have a film made about them. I don't think it would get a PG rating.

We watched some telly as my cow settled in and then we both turned in for the evening.

****

Dear Diary.
We didn't have sex tonight on account of my massive swollen cow filled tummy.
I'm looking forward to my next shit though but I'm also a little worried about the volume again.
Yours sincerely,
Keith.

****

Chapter 25

I woke at about nine thirty. Jane was still asleep, but my stomach had been busy through the night digesting its cow. I just lay there thinking I really need a good fart, and I hope there's enough loo roll in the bathroom.

At the same time in London, hitman Mr. Deacon has just entered the costume shop where I bought my Elvis wig and Jesus beard for the robbery. The staff member that Mr. Deacon talks to couldn't give a shit about an old burnt scrap of receipt.

That is until the very generous Mr. Deacon offers up two hundred pounds for the info. Now that gets the shop assistant's attention. Mr. Deacon is now asked to come back after closing time. He knows money gets people talking. Clean, crisp fifty-pound notes get him all the info he wants. All that's needed is for him to count the bills out, and that skinny arse shop assistant will be singing like a bird. During the day the shop assistant will troll through the camera footage that matches the date on the bottom of the burnt receipt. And around that timeframe will narrow it down to three possible suspects. A women and two men; one of them being me. By five forty-five this evening Mr. Deacon will have some grainy footage of the three of us downloaded to his phone; it's now just simple elimination.

By six fifteen, Mr. Deacon has handed over the money to the thankful assistant. He smiles at her. He's not smiling because he likes her, he does it because he's watched other people do it. That's the way Mr. Deacon has learnt, watching and then imitating. His brain is just wired slightly different from ours. His parents would have seen it first, the lack of empathy, watching him with other children, especially at that child's 10th birthday party his mother took him to. He doesn't feel empathy, but he's learnt to show it, which gives him the freedom to walk about with us defenceless humans.

Then the phone rings. *"Hello Buckland J Randall speaking. Can I help you?"*

"Yes hello, this is Mr. Deacon. If I could again, just clear up a couple of small points you have made in your book of shit there Randall."

"First off why is my brain wired differently? Maybe it's your brain that's wired differently. Did you ever think about that? Remember it's Keith's stupidity that got him into this situation. I mean, who takes a fucking monkey to a robbery? What did he think would happen?"

"And that children's birthday party you referred to with my mother? The birthday boy was called Tarquin. And he was an annoying little shit, and because he wouldn't stop singing Happy Birthday to himself I kicked him as hard as I could in the nuts. I didn't think he would miss them. No one saw me do it and he couldn't tell anyone because he was in so much pain with all his wailing and puking. No one liked him anyways. I was only there because my mother dragged me there promising me cake if I was nice to him. I didn't realise they were just about to cut the cake when I did it, so then we all had to stop so Tarquin's mummy could rush her little prince to A&E to have his nuts pulled out of his fat little stomach."

"It's not about empathy. He was a spoilt little shit who needed putting back in his place. You know what happened to Tarquin? When he turned thirty, he went under the knife and had his balls removed. There! Told you the arsehole wouldn't miss them. And now Tarquin goes out under the name Tammy and I've heard she's still just as annoying. All I'm saying Randall is don't listen to everything you hear. And another thing; I have empathy. But in my line of work that's not something you need in bucketloads, is it? And you're a fine one to talk about empathy Randall. What about all those affairs you had during your first two marriages? Would you say you had no empathy, or would you simply say you acted like a prize prick?"

****

Christ my arse is sore. I've managed to shit more in the last twenty-four hours that I have in the last six weeks. It's oozing out of me like a sausage Pop-Tart machine. I should have enough protein stored in me to see me through the long hard winter of discontent. I would really like to have sex but my gut looks like I've swallowed a football, and Jane doesn't like football. So instead we congratulate ourselves with a couple of lines of blow.

Jane tells me that the Ear is hearing things about Butterfield, the Ear is 'Command Central,' so Jane tells me. She also receives confirmation that Kingston is indeed dead. They're saying it could've been an accident, he may have just fallen.

"Well, I try and be as professional as I can," I said, "You have to be if you're doing a hit."

"If the police are accepting that Kingston's death was an accident," said Jane. "You may have pulled the perfect murder off, not a lot of people can do that."

"It's all in the planning," I tell her.

"Yeah, it's all in the planning. That's what it is," said a sarcastic Jane.

Funny, as Jane left the kitchen I suddenly saw a small crack in the veil. That very thin veil that sits over your eyes when you're lovestruck. A crack can be in anything, be it a wall, or a mirror, even in the sky. The more you try and pretend it's not there, the bigger it gets. Of course, I didn't want to know any of this at the time, so I just went about my day. But like it or not, a crack is still a crack.

For the next two days I sat in a haze of good booze and my best blow. When I say my best blow all that means is I haven't cut it with anything yet. I've told myself that Kingston killed himself, and that I really had very little to do with it. However, I don't think the mafia would see it that way, even if I did kill him with a fart.

I also get a message from Lee from the Two-Four Sixty. The band have two days off from a tour they're on and he's boarding a jet from Holland in an hour and would I like to take tea at three at The Ritz where he will be staying? Now what that really means is bring a ton of drugs with you and let's fucking party. The cool thing about meeting up with Lee is we can do loads of drugs which we both have a healthy moorish appetite for, and we both have the money to do whatever we want. But this time Lee had plans for us. He signed off with, "Bring passport." I arrived at The Ritz and had a lovely afternoon tea in a private room.

He had a jet lined up ready to take us to a party in Venice. So after tea and scones we left the hotel and went to the plane with Lee's driver.

When we get to the airport, Lee's jet is waiting for him on the runway. Fucking James Bond this shit is, I love it.

I need to go for another shit, but I can hang on, then I can go in the plane's luxury toilet. We get dropped off at the plane's steps and as we walk onto the plane there's four hookers sitting waiting for us. These jets are smaller on the inside than you think, so I take my seat and we start the take off. An hour ago I'm at The Ritz and now I'm off to Venice with four stunners, a rockstar and a big bag of drugs. I excuse myself to the bathroom as more devoured cow is wanting to come out of me. But as I looked for the bathroom at the back of the plane I couldn't find one. Then a slight panic set in.

"Where's the bathroom Lee?" I asked, "I really need it."

"Bathroom?" said Lee, "It's a jet. They don't have bathrooms; just piss into a bottle."

Now my panic hits an all-time high. "It's not a piss I need." All four girls heard me say it and all four looked at each other as if they've never taken a shit before.

"You have to wait until we land," Lee tells me, "Or it's the emergency toilet."

"I don't give a fuck what sort of toilet it is, I need to go now," I tell him. Then Lee points to the seat by the door which looks the same as all the other seats except under this seat there is a makeshift toilet, quite basic really with one major design fault: it's a toilet with no screening. I have no choice here, I have to take a shit in front of everyone. I'm on a private jet and I'm shitting into a plastic potty with a plastic bag in it that you tie up with a drawstring when you're done. Of course, Lee thinks this the funniest thing of all time watching me unbuckle my trousers and sit fully exposed. The four girls are all looking at the floor as if they're bracing themselves for impact.

Lee the laughing bastard hands me some vodka cocktail he's just made called a Shitting Cowboy. Then he looks at the girls and addresses them. "Right then girls. Who's up for giving Keith a right royal rim job tonight then?"

Of course, there's dead silence from all four girls. Fuck, this is embarrassing sitting here in front of everyone.

And this shit wasn't like the last few shits this one was the runny one, backed up with all the windy noises.

The four girls look like they're about to throw up. Then it comes time to wipe, and that means crouching in a tight space with a packet of wet wipes that are tucked in beside the seat. I try and position myself with my exposed arse facing the pilot's door. I have a quick wipe and sadly the news is not good, it's a messy one and I'm going to need a lot of wet wipes for the job. It's all sticky and treacle-like and the more I wipe the more mess there is. I'm hunched over with my pants around my ankles and my schlong is swinging away in full view of everyone. Then the jet hit some turbulence and I then fell onto one of the girls as I was in mid wipe.

Unlike Lee none of the girls are finding any of this funny; in fact the one I fell onto looks like she might pass out. Then as I wipe the remaining cow out of my arse the smell starts to fill the cabin.

"Oh fuck me Keith, that's fucking wrong," says Lee. "You need to see a specialist about that." All four girls have their hands over their mouths trying their best to gulp clean air. And then fucking Lee sensing my total embarrassment pushes a button in the roof which then released the oxygen masks which fall from the roof. Then the girls put their masks on, Lee didn't because he was laughing so much he couldn't. Then I try and close the poo bag up and some of the poo covered wet wipes have fallen out and have now stuck to the side of the seat. There was even one stuck on the bottom of my shoe; I must have gone through an entire packet of bloody wet wipes trying to mop up my shit.

The flight didn't take too long, thank Christ. We had a car meet us at the airport which drove us to our posh residence. Some super-rich bloke's daughter fancies Lee and in return he gets their place for the weekend.

The first thing I do when I hit my room is shower and change my underpants, much to the relief of my two hookers that Lee' has given me. And no reader I won't be asking them for a rim job. Mind you, if I turn the lights out I might.

It's 7.00PM in London and Mr. Deacon has just arrived outside my London flat. His detective type brain has tracked me down to my street. He hasn't worked out which house yet; they all look the same in London. He knows there won't be any mess outside my flat because he thinks the robbery was done by a proper professional, and not some mad old hoarder like that bloke Sid who lives across the road from me. The neighbours call him Sid to his face but behind his back we all call him BagPuss on account of all the shit he brings home. So you can strike all the messy properties on my street off the list. Also my street is kinda small; there are only about thirty homes on each side. He slowly walks both sides of the street having a right good butchers while wearing a simply understated blond coloured wig. He looks just like your postman on his way home from work albeit a well-dressed one. Then he takes up residence in his car, only this time he's alone. Mr. Deacon knows that if he has to spend any length of time on a stakeout with his young driver listening to his rambling bollocks, then he would have to kill him earlier than he wants to. He opens a large bag of crisps. There were only two other people in the shop footage he needed to identify. One of the people is way too old, walks with a stick and should really be in a care home. And the other person is a woman who's some pissed-up housewife with six out-of-control kids married to a pissed-up husband who likes knocking her about.

By the time I had cracked open my first beer in Venice, Mr. Deacon had finally narrowed it down to just one person, me. He takes his empty crisp packet and carefully folds it into a small square and puts it in his inside jacket pocket. He drives himself back to his hotel thinking, "Good day's work." He knows it's not long to go before I show up.

There's a real buzz about Venice, and this time I'm staying in some big grand house with expensive shit everywhere. Lee has gone to great trouble by carving out the word, 'Party,' in blow on an antique silver tray. We start off with a pill which turned out to be a strong pill that whippet-thin escorts probably shouldn't be taking. And as the night wore on that started to become more and more apparent. By the time we left the house, two of the girls were blowing bubbles as we sailed out to a boat called the *Serina* where the party was being held. Lee called it a boat: I would have called it a ship.

The ship was moored out in the water getting bigger and bigger the closer we got. Of course, by now me and Lee had already snorted enough pills and blow to drop a horse. I was just amazed how big this ship was. They had lowered a long set of stairs down to our little boat which was bobbing about as our hookers were helped onboard by the boat's crew.

The party was pretty cool; they had some famous DJ from Denmark I'd never heard of spinning tunes.

I got the phone numbers of two hot models by telling them I was Lee's stepbrother. I've really got to stop doing that. I'm starting to sound really sad. And I managed to consume a lot more of Lee's drugs and still managed to kick back a bottle of expensive brandy. Sounds like a perfect day out for me. When we got back to the house I could tell even in my pissed state that my hookers didn't want to know me after my jet shit. And the last thing I needed was a pity fuck from some pay-and-display that looked like she had lost a bet. So the three of us went to our respective rooms where I'm sure they breathed a collective sigh of relief. The rest of the stay I can't remember because Lee's drugs just seem to get stronger and stronger.

Chapter 26

I ring Religious Brian, my ever-present, ever-vigilant neighbour as I'm getting a cab back to Grangemore.

"Keith, how's your mother?" he asks.

"She's fine Brian," I say as I slump into my seat ready to be bored with Brian's conversation.

"Make sure your mum gets all her flu jabs," he continues.

I know he's about to start on one, and when Brian starts on one he can be a bloody nightmare to stop. So as soon as there's a break in the rant and he needs to draw breath, I jump in before his lungs can fill back up.

"Just quickly Brian, there hasn't been anyone round to the flat looking for me has there?"

"No one!" says Brian, "Only that nice man from last night."

I could suddenly feel my pulse speed up a little when Brian said that.

"Which nice chap would that be Brian?" I asked.

"He said he had recently moved into the street just down from us and you were going to help him with a shed."

"What did he look like Brian?" I asked, while trying to sound calm.

"Oh, he was a nice man," says Brian, "Very polite he sounded, from up North. I didn't get his name, smartly dressed he was too. It's nice to see a person taking a bit of pride in themselves these days, you don't often see that. And the funny thing was, and you know I'm not one to gossip Keith, but I think he was wearing a wig."

By now I'm not listening to Brian and his waffle. I know who my visitor is. No one ever visits me at my London address. It has to be my hitman – Mr. Deacon. Christ!! If he can find me there that quick, he's bound to find me at Grangemore. I've gotta get back home fast.

I get to Grangemore about midday, instead of 6.00PM due to the fact I came in on Lee's private jet, except this time the road out to the house was closed due to some roadworks going on so I get my taxi to drop me off on the road at the back of the house, thinking at the time it would be easier walking across the paddocks with my bag, not knowing while I was in Venice it had rained severely making the ground muddy. So I start the muddy descent down through the forest in my sixteen-hundred-pound shoes that are more equipped to strutting around in nightclubs than quagmires. I end up carrying my suitcase above my head because the wheels got bogged down in the mud.

Great. I'm in mud up to my ankles, plus I quite liked these shoes which are now going to have to go in the bin. As I clear the forest, I notice a black car parked around the back of the house but just dismiss as someone visiting Wolf and Eagle. But then as I got closer, I suddenly remembered that Wolf and Eagle were in Brighton for the night. So, whose car was it then? Has Mr. Deacon found me already? The black car looks brand new, left-hand drive with Greek number plates. Now I'm starting to feel a little panic set in as I hid behind a wood stack trying to figure out who the car belongs to. I'm thinking if that's Mr. Deacon then Jane's inside probably dead and Mr. Deacon is waiting for me to walk through the front door so he can kill me.

Now, with Grangemore being a really old property there's an old cellar with a trapdoor which is at the side of the house, locked and now covered over by a large bush. There's only one spare key to it and that's in one of my garages, just in case I ever lost the original. So, I creep around to the side door of the garage, sneak in and retrieve the key from an old jar sitting on a shelf. The cellar door itself I've never opened and crawling through the bush was made more difficult not knowing where exactly the door was. Now I'm not only muddy and wet, I'm all scratched up as well from crawling through the spikey bush. I manage to locate and open the door and climb down into the cellar. Then I start trying to figure out what am I going to do once I confront him. I don't have a weapon; all that's down here are a few bottles of wine and some old garden chairs.

I make my way through the maze of cellar corridors until I'm standing right under the lounge, and I can hear voices. But they're laughing. One of the voices is a male, which I have a feeling I've heard before but where, I can't remember. The female voice sounds like Jane and they're discussing shit but I can't quite make out what. Then I'm thinking, what the hell am I doing? Why am I hiding in my own cellar?

And then suddenly the male voice boomed out laughing. As soon as I heard that laugh I thought fucking hell! I'd know that laugh anywhere, that laugh belongs to Rupert, my old lawyer mate who I brought Grangemore from. What the fuck is going on here? Why would Rupert be here? Rupert – if it is Rupert – and Jane seem to be laughing a lot. Right, I had enough of this for a game of soldiers, I'm going upstairs to sort this shit out.

I go up the stairs leading up to the kitchen and at the same time Rupert and Jane unbeknownst to me have gone upstairs to one of the bedrooms. So, as I burst into the lounge with my "Ah Ha!" face on, ready to say the magic words, "Caught you!" But of course, there's no one in there because they were on the floor above me. But there on the coffee table was Jane's computer and she hadn't shut it down like she always does. So I decided to take a quick gander before I confront them.

As I scrolled down her personal email I noticed there were emails from the Greek embassy. She seems to know some important people around the world. As I started reading through one, that's when I noticed it was signed by our Rupert.

Fucking hell! Rupert's been talking to Jane for the past year. And as I read on I soon realise the bastards had set me up. They're planning to rob me of all my money and Grangemore. To think that I saved that ungrateful bastard's life by meeting up with Butterfield on that fateful day and here he is in my manor trying to rip me off. And there's this other bank account on one of his emails that's linked into my bank account. They're about to unload all of my hard-earned (stolen!) ten million into his bank account. Now I'm proper pissed, and it's about time those two smart arses got what was coming to them. But before I dish out the world's best hiding to Rupert I just have one or two small changes to make on Jane's computer. First off I unload Jane's entire bank account that's holding her ten million into my bank account. Then I delete anything belonging to me so there's no trace including all the bank details. They must think I'm a right fucking dimwit. I then check my account and see that it now has some twenty million plus sitting in it.

The bastards!! I can hear them upstairs having sex in my bed, I can hear Rupert's big loud booming laugh. Buggered if I know why he finds sex so funny. How could I have been so bloody stupid? I pour myself a double vodka and contemplate them coming back downstairs to find me here. I'm going to have to kill them. It's either them or me. If they're planning to steal my house and money, then they've already planned on how to get rid of me.

Then suddenly out of the side of my eye I clock a shadow walk past the outside window of the lounge.

Shit!! I've got company. I take a sneaky peek through a small window that looks down the side of the house towards the garden. And there's some guy peering through one of my windows into my cinema room. And then as he leans back, I see his head looking up and it's bald. Now my heart is banging, I know who that is. No one sneaks around a building peering into windows unless they're up to something. If he was doing my house over he would have rung the bell to make sure no one's in. I have the feeling he's hoping someone is in and that someone is most likely me. Jane said he would find me. Just as I had got things back under my control, a bloody hitman is outside my house. Why the fuck didn't I just stay in the building trade? I don't remember dad ever coming home after a day's grafting complaining about hitmen waiting for him outside the window. Not once did I hear about a bald hitman trying to sneak a bomb into his nail bag or lunch container.

I'm shitting myself here, I'm far too young to die. Is this what God has had in store for me all this time? What an absolute bastard of a god he has turned out to be. What have I ever done to deserve this? I'm one of the good guys. Yes, I'm a drug dealer, but only because of product demand. If anything I should be the one here being bloody knighted for keeping half of London's nutters too stoned to get up to anything too evil. Then I hear Mr. Deacon break a window into the cinema room. Of course Rupert the Humper and Sexy Arse Jane don't hear anything, because they're still too busy going for it hammer and tongs up in my bedroom. Christ, now Mr. Deacon is in my house. I can feel my throat go dry and my body tense up. This man is a proper pro. All I can spot for a weapon is either a bottle of single malt whiskey or a wooden duck that I keep as a door stop. Fuck knows why, but I went with the duck. Panic manifests itself in many different forms especially when a hitman has broken into your house.

And then it suddenly struck me. Hang on! I'm a bloody hitman too.

Why am I hiding from this bastard for? I know the layout of the house far better than him, I squeeze the neck of my wooden duck and quietly open the lounge door, and with one eye I peered down the hall-way.

And then he loomed into view. Mr. Deacon was standing in my hall-way holding what looks like a gun, walking down towards the lounge room. It's the first time I've clocked his face. He looks so cold and ice like, and then suddenly he stops at the bottom of the stairs.

He stands still as a statue. He can hear Rupert's stupid big loud laugh coming from my upstairs bedroom. Like a lioness on a hunt, Mr. Deacon slinks up the stairs, his pistol aimed at the ready. Now anyone in their right mind would probably take this moment to run for their lives, especially if all you have to hand for self-defence is a small wooden duck that I'd now named Lester. But I am too shit scared to make any noise as he quietly climbs to the top of the long staircase. I am about to find out what this man of evil had in store for my two lovely back-stabbing houseguests. I hope he takes his time with the big stupid goofy one who finds sex so hilarious.

Suddenly I heard Jane scream, "NOOOOOOOO!"

And then came the noise of two pistol shots followed by two loud heavy thuds on the bedroom floor.

Then there were another two shots fired, he's committed to his work, I'll give him that. And then there's nothing but deathly silence.

Then as Lester the Duck and I stood watching the hallway, I could see Mr. Deacon coming back down the stairs towards the lounge. The only place I could think to hide was on the floor under a shelf which I could just squeeze into. I could hear him walk into the room and walk around the sofa. He was making sure there were no witnesses. Then I heard him walk around into the bar where I was hiding, still clenching Lester like a frightened teddy bear. I suddenly came face to face with his shoes, which were black and shiny. I lay there still as a dead person knowing that's what I will be if I make a sound. I'm just waiting for him to bend down and blow my brains out.

He stood there for what seemed liked ages. Both of us remained in dead silence. Then he and his polished shoes walked out of the bar and back out into the hallway. Still, I didn't move. Was he waiting by the door? Was the old pro waiting for my escape? My breathing was slow and heavy as I lay there clutching Lester.

Then I heard footsteps on the floor above me so realising that it must be Mr. Deacon, I very quietly squeezed out of my hiding place and peered through the crack in the door just in time to watch Mr. Deacon dragging Rupert's body down the stairs tied up in the same bed sheet that he was fucking Jane on only ten minutes ago. The blood stained sheet was tied at each end with black cable ties holding Rupert's lifeless body in.

You've got to admire a pro when you see one at work. I must get me some black cable ties like that. He then carried Jane's small frame down with ease all tucked up tidy like in the duvet. It doesn't seem so real when their bodies are all covered up and you can't see anything. Mr. Deacon carried both bodies out to Rupert's car and then stuffed them into the boot. I'm watching all this as I slink from window to window trying to keep as low as possible so as not to be seen. The only good thing out of this is Mr. Deacon probably thinks Rupert's me, and if I'm dead then I'm home free.

Then it dawned on me, the money!! He's going to want the money. I bet you that's part of his job, recovering the bloody money. That means he's going to tear my house apart looking for clues, and, along with a few old coins down the back of the couch, there's a pretty good chance he's going to stumble upon me.

I head for the front door but it's locked, and of course I don't have my keys, do I, because they're in my bag in the basement. So I'm trapped in here with the very scary Mr. Deacon who has a gun. And all I've got to fight back with is Lester. I'm not a hundred percent sure I can take out a professional hitman with just Lester. I really need to get myself a gun. I sneak off to have look for a better type of weapon in one of the hallway closets and to my delight among Rupert's old tennis rackets which I've never used or even bothered to take out is his old bow and arrow and next to that was small tin of pale blue shoe polish. I don't know why but I smeared the blue polish all over my face thinking it would camouflage me. I just ended up looking like a Smurf. I put Lester carefully down beside me and quickly load my bow up with a sharp pointed arrow. Then I sneak back down to the bar picking up an old pith helmet I had once worn to a fancy-dress party. The brilliance of the pith helmet is it's really strong. I know this from accidentally smacking my head on a door frame while once wearing it and I didn't suffer any pain. The not so brilliant part was I now looked like a big game hunting Smurf. Then I remembered my homemade bullet proof vest I kept hidden in the bar that I kept my puff rolled up in. I put it on. It's got some random hook hanging off it which I tied Lester to, just in case I needed back up.

Mr. Deacon is still moving the bodies about outside so I take up position with my bow and arrow in the hallway facing the door that he will soon walk through. I crouched down behind a small coffee table that I had quietly dragged out into the hallway and with bow at the ready I sat there waiting. And then at that moment Mr. Deacon suddenly walked into the hallway and straight away clocked me and just froze in front of me. He didn't have his gun in his hand and I knew that he knew he was fucked.

I slowly stood up with bow at the ready.

"Well," I said, "It looks like the chase has come to its end."

I could see he was clearly shocked. He didn't say a word; he just looked at me with this blank expression.

"They forgot to tell you," I yelled down the hallway, "That the man you were hunting was an expert hunter just like yourself. Except this time my friend, you forgot that to catch a hunter; you have to think like a hunter." I knew I had him right where I wanted him. Then suddenly the desperate fool reached for his gun.

"Freeze!!" I yelled, "I'm an expert with this. You don't think me and Lester here are just going to let you walk out of here, do you?"

I could see his face trying to work me out. It was all happening on my terms. He was like a startled deer caught in the bright headlights.

I took careful aim. This was one shot I wasn't going to fuck up. "What's it like to face off another hunter?!" I yelled down the hallway. Lost for words, he just stood there knowing he was trapped.

Chapter 27

What the fuck is going on here?

Now due to the 1977 act of fairness and trading standards Randall has been asked to let Mr. Deacon speak.

Thank you Randall for giving me the chance to speak even though you had little choice in the matter.

As you can plainly see readers, someone in my game gets given the task of getting rid of some right nutters. I'm not complaining; I get well paid for it. But some of my victims like this chap Baxter may have some very serious mental health issues going on. Now the way I remember it going down is quite a bit different to Mr. Baxter's version. I mean come on... would you take the word of a common drug dealer? I know I wouldn't. The way I remember it was, I was walking back into the house which lead me into a long hallway. I'm minding my own business, and there he was, this nut job, crouching down behind a table dressed up as Papa Smurf, and he was wearing some sort of fancy-dress Edwardian hunting helmet, the sort of hat you would wear to hunt tigers while you were perched on top of an elephant. So, I'm thinking "Who the hell is this clown?" And secondly, "What's with the Smurf outfit?"

Then he slowly stands up and he's dressed in this horrible bright orange waistcoat with what looks like a wooden duck hanging off it. Then he introduces me to the invisible man whom I believed he referred to as Lester. I'm now thinking maybe this manor house is all part of some small niche mental hospital and him and his invisible buddy Lester are both here for the public's safety. Now, normally I wouldn't bother with a Smurf after all he probably can't help himself. But the way he started yelling at me I thought, "To hell with this; he's just way too annoying."

But get this, the idiot then stands up ranting about being some great hunter, whatever that means, and it's then that I see he's pointing some old antique longbow at me. So, I'm thinking he's not going to actually try and shoot that thing at me, is he? And if he does fire one off at me and it ac-

tually gets anywhere near me then I can assure you, I'm going to rip that bow out of his stupid little Smurf hands and go to work on him with it.

And then he starts yelling at me something about him and his invisible friend Lester not wanting me to leave. Now it's not very often I make a kill where society should actually be thanking me for getting rid of such a defective one. I mean how much of our hard-earned tax money is it costing us to keep this fool in a special psychiatric hospital like this? The NHS is crumbling and yet here we are having to look after a crazies like that. And believe me Randall, I'm using the term crazy here with the greatest of respect. But are we really doing him and society any real favours by keeping people like him and their invisible friends locked up in such grand opulence? One thing's sure as mustard, he's probably going to have his eye out with that old bow and arrow the way he was waving it about.

Anyways, I'd had about enough of this angry little Smurf yelling at me, so I reached for my gun. And then next thing I know he's fired an arrow off at me, the dangerous little shit. Now when I say he fired an arrow at me, I mean he shot the ceiling with it. No wonder he's locked up in here with a temper on him like that. The staff in this place are going to be dead chuffed coming to work tomorrow morning knowing that their Smurf from hell and his invisible friend Lester won't be bothering them anymore with his crazy ranting and carrying on.

Then, he just stood there looking at me, and I thought for a second maybe he might calm down and say something clever. But no, there was little to no chance of that happening.

So then what does this crazy fool decide to do? He starts doing this strange high-pitched animal noise which sounded something like a distressed baby howler monkey calling for its mother, and then he bolted for the stairs. And I'm thinking "Do I just let him go? No one's going to believe anything he says, as he looks so medicated up. I'd be surprised if he could remember anything from two hours ago." But then I thought "No! Bugger him. I've had enough of this little Smurf prick and his invisible friend Lester. I'm sure the nurses and doctors here don't get paid near enough to have to put up with this kinda of shit." As I said I'm probably doing every-

one a huge favour here. And I'm doing it for free which I thought was nice of me.

****

Christ, I'm fucked now I thought! I've just gone and hit the bloody ceiling with it, and that was my only arrow. Then we both just stood there looking at each other. What was going through Deacon's mind, what was he thinking? Was he asking himself have I got any more arrows left? Maybe he's thinking he's finally met his match. Having a deadly arrow shot at ones-self can unnerve a man, even if it did miss him and hit the ceiling. Then suddenly he reached for his gun and as he did, I let out this primal roar like a male lion. I have no idea where that came from. And then me and Lester bolted for the stairs. But Mr. Deacon was probably more worried what I might have upstairs in the way of a panic room – or worse, a bevy of guns.

So as I was climbing the stairs two at a time, I could hear Deacon's feet climbing the long twisting staircase behind me and then he fired a shot off which I heard go whizzing past my ear. And then for whatever reason as soon as I got to the top, I flew off the staircase into the first bedroom to my right.

But just as I flung myself off the staircase, unbeknownst to me, brave wee Lester had decided to dislodge himself from my 'bulletproof' jacket (I say 'bulletproof') and had landed beak first facing the top of the staircase. And as Mr. Deacon went to place his outstretched foot on the landing, it instead landed on poor Lester's little fragile wooden beak. And that's when his foot slipped, sending Mr. Deacon into the air. And as Lester launched Mr. Deacon upwards, the only place left for him to go was all the way back down the stairs again.

Mr. Deacon fell tumbling backwards down all thirty-six stairs, gun still in hand cocked and loaded and by the time he was halfway down the stairs he had already broken his left leg and ankle, along with his collarbone and both wrists. I'm standing behind the bedroom door listening to all this unnatural noise. Then just as the thumping and tumbling hit its crescendo, there was sudden silence. I knew he must have slipped, but I thought this is probably just a trick to get me out of the room. I thought about it for a quick minute and then decided the best and only way out of here was the way I came in.

I quietly open the door and peered out with one eye, I couldn't see or hear anyone. My hands were shaking with fear. I then slowly ventured out onto the landing and looked gingerly over the staircase, and there he was. The unstoppable Mr. Deacon laying on his back with his head facing the other way buried into the bottom stair. I looked at his still body, just waiting for him to spin around and start shooting bullets up at me.

But he didn't move, so I made the decision to venture down and see how hurt he really was.

I slowly crept down to him thinking any minute he's going to spin around and shoot me.

But nothing!! He didn't flinch; he appeared to be out cold. I snuck down to the bottom stair picking up a glass vase from a small alcove on the way down. Any minute now I was expecting him to roll himself over but still he just lay there. Then as I stepped over him, I could see that his left eye was open. I quickly swung around and smashed the vase over the back of his head and rolled him over. But he was already dead. The fall down the stairs backwards had snapped his neck clean off his spine. His face looked so blank and his blue eyes that were wide open stared back at me. The inside of his jacket was tossed open and there were lots of neatly folded crisp packets spilling out of the inside pocket.

Now I have to get my shit together and fast. I've got cash buried all over my property along with enough blow to fill a chest. And now I've got two dead bodies in a car that doesn't belong to me parked on my driveway and a dead hitman at the bottom of my stairs. I dragged his lifeless body out to Rupert's car.

Carrying a dead body is not as easy as Mr. Deacon made it look. I ended up dragging him out by his feet and managed to get him onto the back seat of the car, all floppy like. I really must get myself a gun and some cable ties. Now where do I drive my party of the dead to? And it was then I had the most brilliant idea ever; it may be my greatest idea yet.

I spotted the digger out in the field. The digger was on loan to me from the farm next door to help Eagle and Wolf sort the drainage out in the lower field. The same lower field that wrecked my lovely nightclubbing shoes in only an hour ago. And since I had learnt to drive a digger when I worked for my dad, I figured it was probably about time that I found out if I still possessed those practical skills.

The digger fired into life and being an older model, I remembered how to work it and then slowly, I drove the lumbering beast over to my lawn. And there I started scooping out large buckets of freshly dug earth, conscious of the fact that Wolf and Eagle would be back soon. Within a short time, my digger had dug a very large and very deep hole in my lawn. Then I retrieved the keys from Rupert's coat pocket and drove his car out onto my lawn and drove it up close to the hole which was way bigger and deeper than I had realised. I put the car into drive and watched it flop into the large hole, and then I listened as the engine stalled itself silent. As I looked down the hole, Mr. Deacons body had rolled itself over and his face was pressed up against the back window, his cold dead blue eyes still wide open looking back at me.

It took only an hour to fill the hole back in with the massive bucket, I even managed to lay the grass back over it. Then I drove the digger back out onto the field with no one the wiser.

I then headed back inside and upstairs to the bathroom. I then showered, which took ages as I had to rub all this blue shit off my face, and it made my face ache. I thought of my three friends in my back garden buried four meters down in their nice roomy coffin. Jane would've liked that. She liked nice cars. And Rupert got to come back and live at his beloved Grangemore once again. And Mr. Deacon? Well, he did like a nicely laid out lawn. And the Greek mafia would later think he found the thief, killed him and then stole their twenty million and went on the run with it, so that tied up that loose end.

And me? Well, after my long shower, I got dressed, went down to the bar, cut myself out two lovely big lines of blow and rolled myself a decent sized joint. I made a promise to myself to retire from being hitman and take some time out to see what twenty million can do for a young geezer like my good self who already has everything. And with that I snorted up my two lines, poured myself another whiskey and drank a toast to the fallen and the buried. And then as I sat sipping my single malt looking out of the windows onto the lawn that I had just a few hours ago dug up and buried a car in. I thought to myself I've done a pretty good job with that digger; I think dad would be quite proud of me knowing that at least one of his life lessons he taught me I actually managed to retain.

And secondly, maybe I should go out tonight. I could do with a good laugh, me.

After all, it's about time I was good to myself.

THE END

Acknowledgements:

....

Liam Gallagher (editor)

The man who made a long story short.

You must have really needed the money, Liam! No matter what any-one says, you're not to take all the blame.

Ross Harper-Stanford (artist) cover design.

Great at drawing monkeys and dressing me up dolls.

What's not to like? It's Jeffery Bojangles captured by the moonlit shadows.

To Pete my dealer, you brought me through it, you big lug you.

To my wife Honey who said she had read the book when we all know she hasn't.

....

Randall would like to take this opportunity to thank Jeff's handler and trainer Jackie Damonte for keeping Jeffery calm.

And Teddy Robins, founder of the Holsom Monkey Boy Treats company.

No Chimps or other primates were hurt or harmed in the making of Monkey & The Dealer.

....

.

Stuntpersons - UK & Amsterdam.

Stuntpersons -Venice

Michael Peek
Lisa Holman
Harry Pims
Hans Goulder

Barry Mayfield
Stan (cannonball) Warrens
Jock Holiday
Eric (Ernie) Smarts
Jimmy Boo Chong
Steve Cooper
Frank Martin
Alan Jones
Richie (The Shark) Bruce
Lyn Baker
Mohamad Acmed
Enzo Fiora
Alec Smit
Peter Wong
Winny (Vodka Mary) Hoch
Ace Becklin
Mia Chin
Eddie Songbird
Stunt Monkeys
Holly Weatherfield
Josh Camron Mayfair
Katie Woo
Mr Tangles
Gavin Padwell
Micky Massison
Larmar Alfonza
Coco

Chapters of this book were filmed in front of a live studio audience.

Kenwood & Bruster - Giving the Dog A Bone productions OBD.CBD.LBW.

George and Brad would like to thank the following:

Shane, Bruce, Haner, Emily, Sarah, Carl and not forgetting Larna and Tina two of the hardest working interns ever.

All the staff at Elmwood Film Studios along with the production staff at Big Noise Sound Studios.

Gastronomic Voyage Catering for their mobile units that got into places catering trucks aren't supposed to get into.

Crew Prostitutes:

Deseray, Chanele and Molly (sore bones) Wendleen.

Head Cameraman: Duncan (one take) Sutherland.

Horse wrangler and cattle whisperer: Bucky Boy Owens.

Major Fruity Windlerlove OBE.MDNA. & Captain Leslie Frogmore Spats ESP.USB

Restorers of Wasp helicopters & WW2 fighter planes.

Ellery & Steel - classic V8 Car & Speed Boatbuilders.

Dr Nick Ferrari MD.CD.DVD.

Dr David Deathman.MD.CD.GTI

And all the night staff at the Red-Eye Pharmacie.

MacDonald & Scott - Boat Ramp Builders.

Vets on set Carlos Sandiego & Storm Bridgemen.

Big Carol's Doughnut Factory, especially the skinny twins and delivery drivers Mike (the barrel) Werner, and Massive Big Len.

Arron Morley ESQ suit maker to the apes.

Randy's - mobile 24hour – Beer & Roasted Nuts service.

Billy Ray Buttermen - Cowboy Hat Maker to the ** Stars**

Mac and Scooter from Scooter&MacNeil customs chopper shop.

Tracy and Rafels She Cuts-He Blows - mobile hairdressing.

Dr Dean Hollyman MG.BGT.- the bleach king for that Hollywood Smile!

Getty's Downtown Bar & Grill

Lisa j   Dallas   Doormen
Management
Foxy   Lisa B.   Vince Hains.
Tony T
Spooky   Angel   Clay (big nose) McCloy.
Fingers Mallery.
Brandy   Big Lips Amber
London Met Police for the use of their staff & patrol cars.

Thank you to Major Col Robert Pottersbee DMC.OMG*MI6 for giving us permission to film in MI5's classified areas.

Take A Chance Airlines - The no-frills airline for all your budget freight.

Thanks to our pilots, Emma, Dassy, Paul and Biggles, along with all the ground crew and drinks staff, especially Buffy (mind the gap) Leghorn.

Special thanks to Dutyfree Sally and her people carrier for all those midnight runs.

Marvins Menswear for Men * London * LA * Frome * Rome
Katie Jane Starr ladieswear & Hats since *1955*
The Rude Rubberwear shop
Wish Those Wrinkles Away Ltd - The Botox Fairies.
The Big Shoe Shop - for the larger foot.
Rays Wigs & Kilts for the gentlemen about town.
Rabbit In A Hat- joke emporium.
Dapper & Large Glove makers for the more unusual hand.
Rick's Mobile Gin bar.
JR Lazyboy Cycling - sales & repairs.
bucklandjrandall@outlook.com

Lightning Source UK Ltd.
Milton Keynes UK
UKHW021442020922
408195UK00004B/366